BEFORE THE FALL

What we found by the alley mouth stopped me like a brick wall. A body, twisted and broken. Blood dripped through the metal grille of the walkway with a steady plop. Dench crouched by the body and turned it over. Someone had taken a knife to the body's throat so viciously that the spine gleamed wetly in the fitful light.

"Goddess, saints and martyrs," Dench muttered. "The shit's really going to fly now."

The face, covered in blood, was of a boy, no more than twelve or thirteen. A Downsider, no question. Poor bastard: survived the horrors of the 'Pit to freedom and then gets himself murdered.

Guards tried to keep people back but the temple was emptying fast now the sermon was finished, and the pub over the walkway spat out as many people, most of them drunk and spoiling for a fight. It was like trying to hold back the wind.

"The guards." A boy's voice, shrill with fear and hate. A Downside accent. "The guards, they killed him. They've been killing all those Downside boys."

Dench whipped round, but it was already too late. The crowd surged, other voices called out, Upsiders and Downsiders both. Two guards fell under a sudden swamp of people.

BY FRANCIS KNIGHT

Fade to Black
Before the Fall

FRANCIS KNIGHT
BEFORE THE FALL

orbit

www.orbitbooks.net

ORBIT

First published in Great Britain in 2013 by Orbit

Copyright © 2013 by Francis Knight

Excerpt from *Bitter Seeds* by Ian Tregillis
Copyright © 2010 by Ian Tregillis

The moral right of the author has been asserted.

A CIP catalogue record for this book
is available from the British Library.

ISBN 978-0-356-50167-3

Typeset in Garamond by M Rules
Printed and bound by CPI Group (UK) Ltd, Croydon, CR0 4YY

Papers used by Orbit are from well-managed forests
and other responsible sources.

Orbit
An imprint of
Little, Brown Book Group
100 Victoria Embankment
London EC4Y 0DY

An Hachette UK Company
www.hachette.co.uk

www.orbitbooks.net

To Aran – the answer is four foot six,
except when it's turnip. True story.

Chapter One

No-Hope-Shitty: the name says it all really. This particular part of the city, so far down it was almost the even-worse Boundary, was one of the crappier shit-pits. The smell of hopelessness, fear and the sweat of too many people seemed ground into the dank buildings that crammed every available space.

I made my way along a swaying walkway that was only nominally attached to the clutch of gently mouldering boxes they called houses down here and tried not to think how far down the gap underneath went. To keep my mind off the drop, I swore at Dendal in my head. Some damn-fool notion he'd had was why I was here in the arse end of the city. Trying to find someone I wasn't even sure existed in a maze of synth-ridden houses and rotting walkways that looked as though they'd turn on me at any time and dump me down twenty, thirty, floors to the bottom of Boundary, or even further to the newly opened 'Pit – to Downside.

Heights, or, rather, depths, make me nervous and nervous makes me cranky, so I kept on swearing at Dendal in my head. Downsider music, all wailing voices and thumping drums, rattled crumbling walls unused to anything more raucous than the occasional bland hymn. Wary eyes peered out at me from cracked windows. Here was somewhere I really didn't want to be, not an Upsider like me. The whole area was crammed with recent Downsider refugees, fearful, and not without cause.

I'd ditched my usual outfit: the leather allover and the flapping jacket that made me look like a Special. It was handy for scaring the crap out of people, but Downsiders had a particular hatred for the elite guards and that hatred was just as likely to overcome the fear that was radiating through the thin walls. I am many things but suicidal isn't one of them, so I'd dressed to blend in with an old-fashioned button-up shirt and a pair of tatty trousers I'd found that didn't quite fit. Just another guy feeling his way in this new and strange part of a city most of the Downsiders hadn't even seen before a couple of months ago. To them, the Upside of Mahala was the mythical come true, the alien place where things and people were weird. I kept having to remind myself of that. I'd even tried my best with my face, tried to give myself that Downsider blue-white undertone to my skin, rearranged things so I didn't look as threatening.

That disguise had its drawbacks, though. I'd been scowled at, sniffed at, spat on and sworn at on my way here. The

sudden influx of refugees into Upside – only into the less salu-
brious areas such as No-Hope, but still – on top of the demise
of our major power source and the resulting loss of trade, jobs,
food and everything else, had made everyone, Upsider and
Down, tense. There had been incidents all over just lately,
from both sides, events that made parts of No-Hope a dangerous place for someone like me, for anyone not a Downsider.
They'd also made other places just as dangerous for the
refugees. If I showed my real face here, if they knew it was me
who had caused all those things, I'd have been pitched over
the side of the walkway before I'd taken half a dozen steps
from the office.

I stopped on a corner between a boarded-up apothecary and
a little grocery store that had run out of even really crappy
food, wishing I'd brought a light of some kind, but candles
were scarcer than food then, and I don't like to use rend-nut
oil. The mingled smell of rotting fish and day-old farts wasn't
a nice kind of aftershave and doesn't pull in the chicks. Sadly,
it was that or nothing, so I went with nothing.

Since the Glow had been destroyed by yours truly, power
was at a premium. Down this far in the city sun was a rumour.
It wasn't much past noon up in the rarefied air of Over Trade.
In Heights and Clouds and Top of the World, Ministry lived
in the sun, shielding it, stealing it from us dregs. That much
hadn't changed – yet. It might never. Down here in Under,
beneath the factories and warehouses of Trade that were eerily
silent now, it might as well have been midnight. Even the

cunning network of mirrors and twisted light wells that gave my office a shred of real, actual sunlight for about three minutes around noon and an almost constant dusk for the rest of the day, failed this far down.

I told myself that I didn't need light for what I was here for. True, I didn't. Rather, what I needed was pain, my pain. Which was a bitch, but I'd tried everything else, and everything else hadn't worked. Dendal was waiting and I didn't like to disappoint, and not just because he's my landlord and boss. He's my boss because if he concentrated he could spread me over a large portion of the city. He could do it accidentally too, which was more likely, but I always found it best not to make him wait. He gets all insistent about his little obsessions and it's easiest just to go along. Besides, I owe him a couple of legs, in that without his help I probably would have blown mine off long since while I learnt my magic. So, here I was.

The boy Dendal was after was a Downsider refugee; no records, no known address, not even a name to go on. All I had was a scrap of cloth and a hunch of Dendal's. It was magic, or nothing.

Left to my own devices, I'd have said screw the little sod and abandoned him to fend for himself, no better or worse off than thousands of others quietly starving to death in the dark down here. Responsible isn't high on my list of qualities. In fact, I usually try to make sure it doesn't even appear on the list. But Dendal's persuasive, and also really good at guilt-tripping me even if he doesn't mean to. I hoped he would appreciate it, because this was going to hurt, and I don't like to hurt.

With my good hand, I rummaged in my pocket for the scrap of cloth Dendal had given me. There wasn't anywhere to sit that didn't involve what was probably synth-tainted water. The damn stuff still lingered, still made people sick from the inside out even now, so I crouched down and leant back against a rickety wall that I hoped would take my weight. I was getting better at this, but still had a tendency to end up on my knees when I tried because it usually felt as though I was about to pop an eyeball, or perhaps a bollock.

I laid the scrap of cloth on my lap and stroked it with my good hand. My anchor, that cloth, the little bit of someone that would help me find them, in this case a boy. If I didn't know someone well then I needed a prop to help me find them – something of theirs usually, something intimate to them.

On the plus side, I didn't need to dislocate my thumb to power up my magic today. On the minus side, that was because I'd fucked up my whole left hand in the incident that had led to all the Glow disappearing. The hand was still healing and all I needed to do was try to make a tight fist to have white spots run in front of my eyes and power run through my veins. There has to be a better way to cast a find spell – any kind of spell – but I haven't figured out what it is yet. When I do, they'll hear the halle-fucking-lujah from Top of the World all the way down to the bottom of the 'Pit.

I made a fist and pain spiked through me along with magic, sweet and alluring, and oh so dangerous. It spun around me, through me, calling, always calling. In and out, quick as I could, that was the best way. Before it tempted me, before the black rushed up to claim me. I'd beaten the black before, once, but I wasn't so sure I could do it again. It was always there, waiting to trap the unwary, seductive and tempting. The price of my magic wasn't pain, it was the threat of falling into the black and never coming out, of losing my fragile sanity to it.

It came quickly, flowing up my arm from the scrap of cloth – the sure and certain knowledge that the boy was to the east, a hundred yards away and two levels down. The pungent smell of a rend-nut oil lamp overlaying the more insidious chemical tang of synth, an ominous flicker of shadows. Even more ominous-looking men. Four Upsiders in a half-circle around a boy on the ground. Upsiders who looked seriously pissed off. One of them made a grab for the boy and a knife gleamed in his other hand. In that gleam I thought I saw the rumour that was spreading everywhere but officially. Someone was killing Downsiders, and not just in fights either. Three dead boys already, and this looked like another in the making. No wandering along the walkways to find this particular boy; not now, not if I wanted to find him alive.

See, now this is why I don't like responsibility. Not only does my magic hurt like fuck, now it seemed I was going to have to risk a stabbing and I really liked that shirt. It would certainly look better without my blood on it. I could have left the boy, I could have turned away. It certainly would have been better for my health. But, despite what my exes will tell you, at length and in gruesome detail, I am not completely heartless. Only mostly. Besides, we needed this boy if what Dendal suspected was true.

Muttering under my breath about fucking Dendal and his fancy fucking notions of fucking charity, I clenched my fist tighter. The black sidled up behind me like a thief, waiting for its chance to drag me into its madness, its joy. *Come on, Rojan, you know you want me, you need me.*

"I'm not afraid of you," I lied. "So fuck off."

Pain was everything, magic was everything, every part of me. Universes were born, spun across my vision and died. I knew I was going to regret this but I shut my eyes, let the *where* of the boy seep in. The rend-nut stench grew stronger, surrounded me and made me gag. The air grew danker, colder. One final squeeze of my hand that had me groaning and then I opened my eyes and tried not to throw up.

A ring of very surprised faces in the flickering dark. Not very happy faces. I had, of course, announced that I was a mage about as subtly as having a big flashing arrow pointing at my throat saying "Please rip here", which, all things considered, could be said to be a Very Bad Idea. Way to go, Rojan, always leaping before you look.

The man with the knife recovered from his surprise the

quickest and loomed over me with a menace that seemed to come naturally.

I always come prepared.

I didn't fancy any more pain so I pulled my gun, pressed the end of the barrel against his nose and made a show of cocking it. Everyone stopped. Guns were still new enough, still expensive and rare enough, that I was pretty confident I had the only one for half a mile in any direction. "Hello. Anyone want to tell me what the fuck they think they're doing?"

Knife-man took two slow, careful steps backwards, but he didn't lower the blade. A quick glance round and I realised why. In my rush towards responsibility I had failed to see the other men outside the circle. The crowd of them behind me. Looking big and mean and very ugly. I'd heard of this in whispers, of Upsiders going around mob-handed into the refugee areas when it was quiet, finding some poor Downsider on his own and stomping him before getting the hell out. Of them boasting about it afterwards in Upsider bars. Is it any wonder I'm such a cynic?

Three of the men stepped forward. I'm a fairly big guy, broad enough with it, and I can look threatening when I need to, but these guys had it down to an art. A mean look to them, like they probably kicked their way out of their mothers' wombs, head-butted the midwife and then got stuck into mugging their parents and strangling the cat.

I was beginning to wish I hadn't bothered getting out of

bed that morning, or that I'd never met Dendal, or even that I'd stayed dead when I'd had the chance.

The boy crouched by my feet, dripping sweat and fear.

"In my pocket," I said. "Left-hand side."

He didn't hesitate, but delved into the pocket and pulled out my pulse pistol. A very specialised and until recently ever so slightly illegal piece of kit. The kid stared at it for a moment as if it were a live snake before he seemed to get a grip of himself, and the pistol.

The Upsiders were moving in, wary, careful, but closer every second. I risked a glance behind: a shabby door that looked half eaten by synth and damp. I backed towards it and the boy came with me. He was shaking fit to bust and what happened next was probably inevitable.

He pulled the trigger. Now, a pulse pistol is, as I said, a specialised piece of kit. It doesn't fire bullets, it fires magic, at least provided it's a mage pulling the trigger.

Dendal had been right about the boy. He fired, the razor flipped out and sliced his thumb and the whirring mechanism took the pain, the magic, magnified it and blasted it out of the end.

I imagine the Upsiders were ever so grateful that it was non-lethal. Eventually grateful, at least. The pulse leapt out and jumped from one to another, far more power there than anything I'd ever been able to coax out of it. The zapping pulse dropped everyone it touched, shorting out their brains and sending them slumping to the dilapidated floor to wallow in shallow synth-tainted pools.

The boy had let out a yelp when the razor cut his thumb, but now he stood as though his own brain was shorted out, staring dumbly at the pile of limp bodies.

We didn't have time for that. The pistol knocks them out but they soon wake up again, and I only had one set of cuffs on me.

I made a mental note to congratulate Dwarf on the improvements he'd made to the pulse pistol, grabbed the boy and made a run for it. Courageous to the end, that's me.

Chapter Two

It took some persuading to get the boy to come with me – I'd saved him from a good kicking, or worse, but he knew from my voice I was an Upsider and from his point of view that meant I was a bastard. I can't say he was wrong, but I can be persuasive when I want to be, not to mention he was half starved and I had come prepared with food. Not much, and it was a crap not much, but it was all we could find, all there was. He shovelled it in like he'd not eaten in a week, which he probably hadn't, and followed me with a suspicious scowl that said he'd be off at the first hint of trouble.

Mesh walkways crisscrossed above us, leaving no shadow in the gloom. They sagged away from walls, dripped who knows what down our necks. The further we got away from the 'Pit that Downsiders had once called home, the more jittery the boy became. At least once we got to the level of the office, the walkways were firmer – but the drop was longer. Further up

11

the buildings get less squashed looking, but down here the weight of the city above, below, all around, was a pressure you could feel in your bones.

By the time I got the boy back to our new offices it had begun to rain, a slow cold seeping through all the levels above us, a steady drip that always seemed to find the crevices in your jacket or around your neck to sidle into. We'd had to move office because being associated with the old me was now a dangerous thing. I have this way with people – I'm great at really pissing them off, and this time I'd outdone myself. Whole battalions of Upsiders were pissed with me, or would be if they found out I was still alive. The Down-siders weren't far behind and, to top it off, most of the ruling Ministry, while unofficially ignoring the fact I was still alive, would be pleased if I ended up in lots of small, messy bits. So currently I was not me, Rojan, bounty hunter, pain-mage, shirker of responsibility, pathological womaniser and phys-ical coward. I was Makisig, Maki for short. I was still all the other things, though I was trying to be subtle about them. Especially the mage bit. We'd only been legal a few weeks but there was still a hell of a lot of hate about, and legal isn't the same as safe.

Dendal had a knack for picking sodding awful offices, too. This one had previously been a front for a Rapture dealer and off-their-faces lowlives had a habit of wandering in and asking if they could score. Some of them got quite unhappy when all they got was a lecture from Dendal about the evils of drugs, beer, sex and anything else he could think of before he sent them on to the other huge drawback of the offices.

The temple next door.

I could hear them now, chanting and praying their sanitised, Ministry-approved prayers. People playing with their imaginary friend. Not that I would ever say that to Dendal. He gets very focused when the Goddess is involved. I suppose a bit of faith gave people hope, which was about all that could be said for it. They needed hope now more than ever.

At least we were far up enough that some of the little power there was ran a light at the end of the street, so even if we didn't see more than a minute or two of the sun at noon, and a hazy fourth-hand light after that, bounced down through the mirrors, we could see where we were going. Sometimes I wished we didn't have the light; all it illuminated was grubby, damp and depressing.

I aimed the boy at the office door. He would come in handy as a shield against Lastri – secretary, harridan and person who made sure Dendal ate occasionally and didn't bump into anything too hard while he was away with the fairies. Also one of the *very* few women over eighteen and under about forty-five I've ever met who, despite her severe and primly attractive features, I have never tried to talk into bed. I'd never make it out alive.

She smiled at the boy as we came in, put a motherly hand around his shoulder and steered him to the small kitchen

13

at the back while flinging me a look that said it hoped I strangled myself in my sleep.

Dendal was at his desk in the corner; he always was. His grey hair puffed round him like an errant cloud and his thin, monk-like face was pinched in what looked like concentration but might just as likely have been a daydream. *More* likely even. Paperwork surrounded him, as did an array of candles that put the temple next door to shame. I said a quick hello and got a vague, dreamy look in return. Not quite with it, our Dendal. Oh, he's a genius all right, smartest mage I ever met. When he's anywhere approaching reality that is, which is about once a week if I'm lucky.

"Hello, Perak," he murmured. At least he'd got the gender right, if not the sibling. Then something on one of his pieces of paper caught his eye and he burrowed into his little fairy-land again. He only really concentrated on his messages. To him it was his Goddess-given duty whether he used his magic or not, to help people communicate. It looked like today he was up to the more mundane pastime of writing letters for the majority of people around here who couldn't. No magic, no dislocated fingers, just Dendal's vague tuneless hum and the scritch-scratch of pen on paper that had been part of my life for so long I only noticed it when it stopped.

So far, so normal.

I chucked my jacket on to the sofa squashed in the corner, patted Griswald, the stuffed tiger, on the head and aimed for my desk. At least the boy hadn't generated any paperwork, for which I was thankful. I checked the desk carefully, making sure it hadn't laid any ambushes for me, and sat down, ready to do something about my hand. At this rate it was never going to heal, what with finding people and my little sideline at Dwarf's lab.

One of Lastri's pointed notes sat on the desktop, a superior sneer in the slope of the handwriting. Another boy to find but at least I had a name to go on, so maybe I could get away with just searching some records rather than buggering up my hand any more than I already had. It would have been even better if someone was actually paying me for all this searching, but all I'd got so far was Dendal's assurance that I was doing the Goddess's work. All very well, but she wasn't paying my rent. Luckily the landlord – Dendal – tended to forget what I owed, though Lastri was distressingly accurate, not to mention insistent.

The other reason for the change of offices, an extra partner in our motley little crew, sat at his desk. Pasha still had a face like a sulky monkey nesting in a rumple of dark hair, but since the Glow had gone, and with it the ill-gotten pain that powered it, he'd seemed to grow. Less jumpy now, but still plenty angry.

He looked up from the news-sheet he'd been scowling over. "What happened to you? You look like shit."

He was still a git. I braved the vagaries of my desk drawer. The trick was to open it up, grab what you wanted and get your hand out quick, before it realised what you were doing and slammed shut. It was unreasonably possessive of its contents, I felt, and I only had one good hand left anyway.

I managed to get out the mirror without incurring any broken bones and studied my reflection. Pasha was right: I did look like shit. I would like to point out that the mirror was a new thing and not lurking in my drawer because I'm incredibly vain. Well, I am quite vain, but that's not why it was there. No, it was there because of the new direction my magic had taken, and because a lot of people thought I was dead and I wanted it to stay that way, or I would be.

I still had a bit of juice left from my earlier hand-mangling so I did the best I could to tidy myself up, rearranging my face back to my more usual disguise. It's weird seeing someone else's face in the mirror every day, but better than being dead. I only let the disguise drop when I slept, or when I shaved. Shaving the wrong-shaped face is hard and, I'd discovered, usually ends in blood and swearing.

I couldn't do anything about the rather spectacular shiner, though. My new skills weren't up to that yet, in the same way that I couldn't rearrange my voice, though I was working on it.

Pasha wandered over, sat on the edge of the desk and grinned his monkey grin. I couldn't help but like him, no matter how hard I tried not to.

"So, who gave you that and why did you let them?"

"She caught me by surprise. I've decided to give up women."

16

His snorted in disbelief before he closed his eyes and twisted his hands in his lap.

"You can stop that as well. I told you: you don't read my mind, I won't permanently rearrange your face." It came out sharper than I'd intended, mainly because I didn't want him figuring out just why the lady in question had belted me one. And the lady before that and, come to think of it, the lady before that as well. Let's just say, saying the wrong name at a delicate moment isn't a good move and leave it at that. I was definitely swearing off women. Definitely, for *sure* this time.

The Kiss of Death, Lastri calls me. I never mean to, but I kill any budding relationship stone dead. Usually it was for more varied reasons, granted. Being unable to resist temptation tops the list. Like responsibility, willpower rarely makes it on to my list of good points. Why deny all those women their chance? So many, and all so lovely . . .

My wandering eyes had stilled for a while, but were back to their old tricks in something like self-defence for my heart, which, if I'm brutally honest, was as mangled as my hand. Playing my old games took my mind off that, meant I didn't need to think about it, what I'd lost and Pasha had gained.

Pasha took the hint and changed the subject. "So, the boy, you found him? Any joy?"

"Found him, and, yes, he's a pain-mage all right. Lastri's feeding him up, I expect. Built like a stick, and he was about to get the crap kicked out of him by a load of Upsiders. Makes me wonder what the little sod's done."

Pasha gave me a cryptic look, but the words were pure viciousness. "Was born, perhaps. Had the audacity to come up here when we stopped the Glow and opened the 'Pit. Got the wrong skin tone, the wrong accent, worships the wrong way. Take your pick."

His tone took me aback – Pasha looked like a monkey that's lost its nut, but he could be a lion when he wanted to be, and he would always roar in the defence of Downsiders.

I hadn't meant it that way; it had just come out as part of my sparkling and charming personality because I was pissed at having to use my magic, but I was still getting used to Pasha's way of looking at things. "I don't think—"

"No, I've noticed."

I did think then, though. All the insults when I'd worn a Downsider face, the snarls and spits. The rumours of the Upsider gangs stomping lone Downsiders. Pasha still had it, that blue-white tone lurking under dusky skin. Brought up in the 'Pit with no sun, not even the few minutes a day some-one Upside managed. You could usually tell a Downsider at a glance, and the accent was what really gave them away. Given that the Ministry would rather they weren't here, the embarrassment of them even existing when they'd been denied for decades, the chances of them getting a look at the real sun from up in Heights or above was slim. It might take years for that unearthly pallor to go. It might never go.

"You seen this?" Pasha slapped down the news-sheet he'd been reading on my desk. I caught sight of the headline:

DOWNSIDERS SPREAD NEW DISEASE. Near the bottom was another article about Downsiders scattering malicious rumours of what had gone on in the 'Pit, and how it wasn't true, followed by a frankly laughable account of what had "really" happened. Which, naturally, given that this was a shadow – not officially sanctioned, but a mouthpiece for some of their more vocal ministers – Ministry news-sheet, was a load of old bollocks. As was the bit about mages and our unholy ways and it was all our fault. Well, it was mostly untrue. I am fairly unholy. And I had screwed everyone pretty hard when I'd destroyed the Glow.

Plenty of people would believe it, though, about the Downsiders, and that was the problem. Why is it that a lie is always so much more persuasive to a mass of people than the truth? In this case, it was so they didn't have to think about what had been going on under their feet all those years, so they didn't have to feel guilty about it. People will do anything to avoid guilt.

No wonder Pasha was looking pissed off – he was a Downsider *and* a mage, so he was screwed both ways. I grabbed the sheet off him, scrunched it up and lobbed it into the bin, or tried to. It bounced off the rim and ended up teetering on the pile of other papery missiles that had failed to reach their target in what I like to call my filing system.

"No one believes what they read in there," I lied. "It's not even official."

"You don't. Plenty of others do. And it's official enough. So are most of the other news-sheets. They're all printing the same. Some Downsiders tried starting their own press up, but that lasted about a week before it got fired."

"You had any trouble?" I asked.

His bitter shrug said it all, a lot more than his words did. "No more than anyone else. A lot less than some. Being able to read their minds helps me avoid it, and news like Jake gets around. Look, are you ready to go? Because we'll be late."

I bit back some smart comment that would only inflame things and nodded. "Go get the boy. I'm not sure I can face Lastri again today."

The monkey grin came back. It went without saying that he and Lastri got on famously. I was pretty sure she was only nice to him to really grind it into my face how much she hated me, but Pasha seemed to like her. I have no idea why.

The boy was noticeably rounder in the stomach when Pasha brought him through. There was a smear of sauce by his mouth, and he snickered when he looked at me. I wondered what Lastri had told him and decided I didn't want to know. I could sense one of her vendettas coming on.

Chapter Three

I hurried the boy and Pasha out before Lastri could launch whatever evil plan she had in mind, and shut the door on her. The sign in the window was fresh-painted:

LICENSED MAGES, ALL MAGICAL THINGS ATTEMPTED. SPECIALITIES INCLUDE INSTANT COMMUNICATION, MIND-READING, PEOPLE FOUND AND THINGS REARRANGED. DISCRETION GUARANTEED. FEES AVAILABLE ON REQUEST.

Licensed mages: that was very new and I liked that part. It meant I didn't have to hide from the guards any more. Sadly, the general population wasn't as quick to give up years of Ministry-induced prejudice. Neither was the Ministry if truth be told, but we had them by the bollocks and they knew it. They needed us if they wanted this city to live, if they wanted any of the little power they were getting, if they wanted Trade up and running, and they did. If only they'd tell everyone else that – we'd had two arson attempts in the few weeks since mages had become legal again.

Of course, Ministry being the pucker-arsed and slow-moving behemoth it was, and also being in control of everything from the flow of food to what news was allowed out, I wasn't holding my breath. Even with a new archdeacon, it was taking far too long to change. Wouldn't have surprised me to discover they weren't telling people on purpose – not many people knew about my and Pasha's little sideline in the lab, all that was keeping the few lights on the walkways lit, the little heat going. Then again, given the current feelings about mages, I wasn't sure I wanted them to.

Maybe that was why there were so many guards on the walkway outside. It was wide and solid here, and my nerves were grateful for it, but it gave them more room. They'd been patrolling a lot more lately as food and heat and light grew scarcer, and, with few left with any jobs to keep them occupied now the factories were shut, tempers had begun to fray. Two of the guards lounged on a now-useless carriage, all its brass icons of saints and martyrs dull in the dim light, its Glow tube black and dead. I hurried past – my ever so slightly illegal past was still too fresh in my mind.

The doors of the temple were open, shedding soft candle-light on to the street, making it look almost, but not quite, habitable. The prayers reached even out here and the boy seemed to perk up. Downsiders – so raw and visceral about their beliefs. So different from the sort of insipid piety the Ministry insisted upon.

Pasha shot me a sly look over his shoulder as he went in with the boy – he always went to temple before we went to the lab. "You should come in. You never know, you might see something you like. We've got a guest preacher. Besides, I said I'd meet Jake."

That was just cruel.

I stood outside for what seemed an hour but was probably only a minute. To go in, or not? Me and the Goddess have an arrangement; I don't believe in her, she doesn't dick about with my life. Of course, what with the Ministry being what it is and all that piety sloshing around, whatever form it took, it's not a view I admit to just anyone. I like my limbs where they are.

In the end, it was the thought of Jake that made me go in. As soon as I got past the vestibule, I could see how things had changed. The saints and martyrs stood where they should, all blank-eyed statues with the faithful doing their duty at their feet in turn. There was Namrat, the tiger, the stalker, with a black cloth over his face, as was proper. The lights were bright but somehow dim at the same time, covering everything in a subtle glow. Behind the chanted prayers, silence seemed to flow from the walls, from the shush of feet on the carpet runner up the aisle. I may not be a believer, but I've always appreciated the serenity in temples, the reverent hush, yet there was something else here today, something extra.

The blandness that Ministry had insisted upon for so long had been encroached upon by vivacity. Behind the altar there were two murals instead of the old single one. On the right, the Ministry-approved version of the Goddess, all smiles and twinkles and flowers. She looked benign and welcoming, if a tad constipated. Namrat the tiger was more of a pussycat cosying up to her feet than a threat. Death, in Ministry-approved scripture, wasn't to be feared because you'd get everything you wanted the other side if you were a good boy and kept your mouth shut and your head down. A little something to help the poor plebs endure the utter shit that they had to put up with in life. Made them more . . . biddable. Made me want to puke.

On the left was the change, maybe what brought a fresh air to the temple, a heart thump of new life. A hastily erected painting of the Downside Goddess in all her vicious, splendid glory. Primal and raw, maybe as she had originally been before the Ministry sucked all the life out of her and left only blandness. No pastel colours as on the right, no pretty birds and flowers, this was livid colour and passion, blood and sacrifice and death. Namrat was no pussycat here; he was all tiger. Rippling, graceful muscles under a glowing orange and black coat, big eyes, bigger teeth. This picture depicted the Goddess sacrificing her hand to Namrat, to appease his hunger, to stop him stalking us. A stupid, useless sacrifice as far as I'm concerned because he stalks us now, his hunger never sated, and we call him Death. Well, *I* don't, but you see what I mean.

For Downsiders, Namrat is something to fight against, and that's when you get your reward after he inevitably wins – the reward is for the fight, for the sacrifice. I can at least respect that, even if I don't believe it.

I turned away from the murals and looked about for Pasha. He walked off to one side, the boy trailing his steps as he reached Jake, with the man-square that was Dog hovering behind her as always. He's a big lad, is Dog, with muscles on his muscles, glossy black hair to die for and all the mental capacity and ability to see everything as wonderful as a five-year-old. A five-year-old with a big fuckoff sword he knew how to use. A dangerous combination, and one reason why I'd taken to keeping a couple of lollipops in my pocket.

Jake looked up from her prayer, and the smile she gave Pasha . . .

I should have "I am a sucker for unobtainable women, especially her" tattooed on my forehead. Maybe something snappier, my forehead isn't that big. "I am an idiot" perhaps.

She'd changed, too, since she'd come up from the 'Pit. Still all the grace of ten dancers, still with that you-can't-ever-know-me look, the ice queen who was waiting to melt, but less brittle now, less sharp. She'd let the bright red dye – her defiance, her shield – fade from her hair and now it was a soft black, no longer bound tightly but left to curl around her face and across her shoulders. A softness in her eyes, too, and especially, and I so wished this was not true, when she looked at Pasha. Tied together with invisible string, glued with all they'd seen and done, experienced together, and short of murdering Pasha I'd not a chance in hell. I'd settle for all I could get, though.

Dear Goddess, I will start believing you exist the same day she smiles at me like that. Deal? What the fuck was I saying? *Dear Rojan, it's about time you got over it. Amen.*

I tore myself away from the cause of my black eye – hers being the wrong name I had inserted into the delicate moment – and on to who else she'd brought with her.

Erlat smiled up at Dog, who looked like he'd been hit with a fifty-pound gladhammer. No surprise, because Erlat was polished to a gleam like jade, as easy on the eye and as hard to see through. Everything about her was elegant, from the smooth coil of dark hair at the nape of her neck to the slinky cut of her dress and the way she moved, as though she slid through the world without leaving a ripple. It looked like Dog had forgotten how to talk because he just nodded dumbly when she spoke to him and grinned like the big kid he was.

Yet even Erlat's graceful poise looked strained today. She kept fiddling with the coil of hair and darting quick, furtive looks at the Upsiders that crowded the temple. I went to stand with her and was about to ask her what she was so worried about when the prayers stopped and a deep, soothing voice boomed out from the altar. Erlat forgot about me, her focus riveted on the preacher.

I didn't really pay attention to the words at first, figuring they'd be the usual "Isn't the Goddess lovely, do as you're told now and you get a nice afterlife" brainwashing Ministry bull-shit. Instead, I watched the congregation. The two Goddesses should have given it away, but perhaps I was feeling a bit dense that day.

Most of the Ministry temples refused entry to Downsiders, thought their ways of worship disgusting and heretical. The way so many priests had got the vapours when the 'Pit had opened up had kept me amused for weeks. The Downsiders, predictably, had said "screw you then" and opened their own, smaller temples, most of them one-room affairs that turned back into bedrooms when the prayers were done. Just another way of everyone showing how much they hated "the others". Stupid, of course, but that's people for you. Why like anyone when hating them is so much more fun?

Only Pasha, Jake, Dog, Erlat and the boy were all Down-siders, obviously so, and they weren't the only ones in here, not today. Yet they got no funny looks, no sneers, and that was odd. They were, it seemed, welcomed. I could even see the sign of their devotional on Erlat's hand, a black circle on her palm and a spot of blood in the centre, a practice that had most Ministry men fit to split.

Then what the guest preacher was saying seemed to register.

"And so all of us are people first," he said. "Upsider or Down, Ministry or not, we are all believers. This man," he pointed to an Upsider who started at being pointed out, "this man wants what is best for his family, what it is only right

27

they should have. Food, warmth, safety. This man," his pointing finger picked out a Downsider flanked by two children, all
shadowy skeletons in clothes, "wants the same. Do you hate
either of them for wanting what you want?"

I let the simple words, the even simpler message, wash over
me without taking them in. The congregation hung on his
every word, and I could see why, *hear* why. The words almost
didn't matter; it was the depth of his voice, the rolling
smoothness of it, the utter conviction that rattled in every syl-
lable. It was hard to stop yourself getting pulled along by it,
no matter the simplicity of the sermon, but I managed it
when he started saying we should praise the Goddess for
giving us this test, this chance to show her how faithful we
really were. Grateful for slowly starving to death? Bollocks to
that, was all I could think.

Yet who was in the congregation was telling. A man who
was a leading advocate for Downsiders, who spoke often and
eloquently and was mostly ignored by everyone. Another, who
was his equivalent among the Upsiders. Spokespeople, perhaps, for their factions. Both steady, reasonable men from
what I knew of them, and maybe that was why they were so
ineffective. Want something doing? Get someone with a
burning passion, get an extremist who thinks he's doing the
Right Thing, who can make everyone burn as he does. People
will follow that. They don't often follow anyone whose main
message is "I think we should be nice to everyone".

This preacher was different, though, because that was his

message but his burning need for it came through. An extremist of a different nature perhaps, but if you burn, people will warm to your flame no matter how crazily it leaps and devours the curtains, the house, the city, the world.

It showed in the eyes of the people up by the altar with him. Two altar boys, watching him with rapt attention, and a woman, not much more than a girl, really, maybe twenty though there was something childlike about her. More to keep my mind off Jake than for any other reason, I watched her as she gazed first at the priest and then at the Goddess, the more vivid one. A Downsider without a doubt but that didn't bother me, not with the way she stood with her eyes demure, a pose belied by the intensity of her gaze.

She caught me watching and it seemed to startle her, but I smiled the old faithful, never-fails smile and got one in return. Pretty, she was, in an ethereal kind of way, with short, black hair that floated in the air, a blue-white undertone to her dusky skin making her look otherworldly and such a burn behind her eyes.

The priest shot me an isn't-that-inappropriate-during-a-sermon look. I left him to it, and left her with a wink that made her giggle behind one hand and the priest frown and stumble over his words. I turned back to the congregation before he could call anyone to throw me out.

The biggest shock of all was the huddle of people right at the back of the temple. You could tell they were Ministry and something high up by the fat, sleek smugness of them, by the bland masks of piety that stank of fakery, to me anyway. All except one, and his was a face I knew. My brother Perak. The new Archdeacon.

Frankly, it's embarrassing. I might have been the only person in the city who didn't believe in the Goddess – or at least the only one I know – and my brother "ran" the Ministry, was the mouth of the Goddess. But maybe, just maybe, the city of Mahala had a chance, if the rest of the Ministry would actually let him *do* anything without having a group apoplexy.

Yet at least Perak was an improvement on the old Archdeacon. Less of a torturing bastard, which was nice. More visible, too – the old Archdeacon had kept himself under wraps and secret, but Perak's openness, his willingness to see and be seen, was starting to endear him to Under even as it was pissing off the cardinals he insisted followed his lead. Hence his appearance here.

Perak watched the new preacher keenly while his entourage tried not to get too close to any of the oiks from this far down. One of them watched, aghast, as Dog carefully made his ash and blood devotional, his tongue poking out of his mouth in frowning concentration. It was tempting to wander up to the Ministry man and make the devotional myself, just to see how quickly he moved, but I restrained myself.

Perak muttered something and it was interesting to watch the responses, from a quick, earnest nod from one, a hatchet-faced woman in her forties decked out in a cardinal's robes, to outright glares at Perak's back from others. One particularly fat and smug-looking cardinal looked like he'd swallowed a cat. Or perhaps that he would happily throttle Perak on the spot. I took it that Perak's reign as Archdeacon wasn't going smoothly.

I let my gaze wander over his little company. Bishops and cardinals by the lush robes, and none of them looked happy to be here. Ministry had never given a steaming crap about anything or anyone under Trade before now, never ventured down here where the sun feared to shine. All they cared about was, was there enough power for the factories, enough people to work there, to grind down and make a slave to their wealth?

Maybe Perak was giving them a nudge in the right direction but from the news I'd managed to find, overhear or bribe out of someone, it looked increasingly as though they might answer that nudge with something else, like a stab in the back.

The sermon finished and the alms box came round. Perak put in enough to feed a dozen families for a week, if they could find any food to buy, that is. The others put in, too, some more, some less grudgingly. Fat Cardinal looked as though he was contemplating stealing the box back.

I looked around the temple with a jaundiced eye. They were all fools, every one. For thinking the Goddess could help, would help, or that praying was a useful thing to do. Nobody was going to help us but us. I wanted to shout it out, tell all of them how useless it was, but I caught sight of Perak's face, shiny with belief, Erlat's look of sudden hope, and I couldn't.

Instead I turned on my heel, hurried out into the rain that was a welcome relief from the piety, all the bile curdling in my stomach like a bad pint. At least I knew why there were so many guards tonight – they wouldn't be taking any chances down here with the Archdeacon in attendance.

"Hello, Rojan."

The voice was no more than a whisper, right in my ear, but the sound of my real name almost stopped my heart. Then a man stood in front of me, with a careworn face adorned by a drooping moustache and the frazzled manner of someone with too much on his mind. Dressed like a guard, but he wasn't one. Dench was in charge of the Specials, and the merest hint of them on the street could cause sweaty palms, guilty consciences and mass panic. The elite guard of the Ministry, who'd spent years sending convicted criminals to the 'Pit, and not realised what they'd really been a party to.

"You must have the wrong person." I tried to push past but he wasn't having any of it.

"Don't give me that shit, you weaselly bastard. Don't worry, no one else heard. Just wanted to see how you're doing, that's all."

Yes, and I'm a banana. "Fine. Busy. You know."

A smile twitched his moustache. "So I hear. You're doing a good job, with the magic and all, replacing the Glow. Three factories up and running now, is it?"

"Hoping for four next week. And more lights and some heat before the winter sets in."

The food we could eke out for a while, though we were all getting skinny and I spent the best part of every day with a grumbling stomach. But the heat, or lack of it, would be a major problem before long if we didn't get our fingers out. It often feels cold enough in the dead of winter to freeze your knackers off. "Still finding more mages. But it won't be enough, not to replace all we had."

Dench's sigh came right up from his boots. "That's what I was afraid of. I'm still clearing up the last mess you made. Don't make any more, all right? It's getting bad on the streets. Just to add to it all, I've got four dead Downside bodies with their throats cut and I haven't a clue who did it. And it's going to get worse unless we can—"

As if to make his point for him, a commotion echoed from an alley at the end of the street. Indistinct words shouted in a harsh voice, running feet, the subtle sound of knuckles hitting flesh. Dench was off in a flash, and I followed him, as much out of curiosity as anything. I kept my hand on the pulse pistol in my pocket, just in case.

What we found by the alley mouth stopped me like a brick wall. A body, twisted and broken. Blood dripped through the metal grille of the walkway with a steady plop. Dench crouched by the body and turned it over. Someone had taken a knife to the body's throat so viciously that the spine gleamed wetly in the fitful light.

"Goddess, saints and martyrs," Dench muttered. "The shit's really going to fly now."

Someone behind me threw up noisily, and I wasn't far off myself. The face, covered in blood, was of a boy, no more than twelve or thirteen. A Downsider, no question. Poor bastard: survived the horrors of the 'Pit to freedom and then gets himself murdered.

Guards tried to keep people back but the temple was emptying fast now the sermon was finished, and the pub over the walkway spat out as many people, most of them drunk on whatever paint-stripping hooch someone had managed to brew up in their bathtub and spoiling for a fight. It was like trying to hold back the wind.

"The guards." A boy's voice, shrill with fear and hate. A Downside accent. "The guards, they killed him. They've been killing all those Downside boys."

Dench whipped round, but it was already too late. The crowd surged, other voices called out, Upsiders and Downsiders both. Two guards fell under a sudden swamp of people.

Then it was a maelstrom of arms and half-glimpsed faces, of blood and shouting and a firing gun. Even that didn't stop the mob. The whole simmering mess boiled up and over, right there at the bottom of the temple steps. Guards against population, Upsiders against Down, everyone scared and hungry and cold, and had been for weeks. It had to come out somewhere.

I backed up into a boarded-up shop doorway, trapped by a baying mob. Two baying mobs, three if you counted the guards. Dench was in there somewhere, too, drowning in angry people – I couldn't see him but I could hear the swearing. He probably counted as a mob all on his own.

I looked around desperately and caught sight of Pasha and Jake at the top of the temple steps, beyond the mob that had taken this end of the walkway. Jake had her hand on her swords, the hard, brittle look about her again. I felt more than heard Pasha's voice in my head, and for once I needed no coaxing.

Come on, quick!

I needed no props, no scrap of cloth or picture, not to find Jake when she was branded on my heart and brain. I dropped to a crouch, just in time to avoid something smashing into the door and showering me with glass and booze. One quick squeeze of the bad hand, and a picture of her in my head. That part was all too easy; the eyes, the mouth that might smile at me if I was lucky, or good and noble, the hands that itched to use her swords.

A surge of pain, of magic, of true bliss, the lure of the black, more tempting even than her. A simple rearrangement of where I was, and then I was on my knees in front of her, trying my best not to throw up on her boots.

Pasha didn't give me any time to recover. There *was* no time, I saw, when my eyesight cleared. He yanked me to my feet and into the vestibule of the temple. Jake and her swords covered our backs – I had no doubt what would happen to anyone foolish to come within striking distance. A kick in the nuts and a sword through the face.

Erlat comforted the boy in the vestibule, both of them pale and shaky but unharmed. Dog patted the boy's hand awkwardly, while the other hand held a sword about as big as I was as nonchalantly as I might hold a dinner knife. He looked worried now, but managed to wave.

I didn't feel much better than the boy looked, and I was pretty sure my disguise had slipped, too, because he looked as though he had no idea who I was.

Part of the mob broke away, men from the pub; drunk, belligerent and looking for trouble in the temple. Jake slammed the door shut but there was no bar or lock – it was a temple, anyone could come in whenever they wanted, that was the point.

"Perak?" I asked.

"His guards got him out of the back door. Which is where I'm thinking we should be heading," Pasha said.

That was as far as we got before the door slammed open again. Three drunks swayed in the opening, and two of them had knives.

"Fucking Downsiders in our temple," the biggest one said and hefted his knife. "Stinking the place up, scattering ash and blood. Defiling the Goddess, that's what they're doing. Shouldn't be allowed."

"But I do allow it." The preacher stepped up beside me and faced the men head-on. "Would you tell priests how to run their temples?"

The drunk sneered and looked like he was about to say

something but a series of shots echoed along the walkway too close for comfort, followed by a chugging sound, one I'd not heard in long weeks.

A carriage rumbled round the corner, pulled to a grinding halt and spilled out Specials. In their close fitting allovers, the Goddess's own elite looked more like something from Namrat, come to eat us all. The allovers squeaked as they piled out of a carriage built to hold a dozen. Metal plates, inserted along the forearm and shin of the uniform to ward off knife or sword blows, clanked dully. The faint light of the temple's candles where it spilled into the street gleamed off the smooth surface of the uniforms. Smooth as water, all the better to slip someone's grip. Knife hilts showed in odd places, thrust into little pockets out of the way ready for just the right moment. These uniforms were built for attack and defence, designed long ago for the assassins who served the warlord who founded our city. Together with the set, stolid faces of the Specials and the reputation that preceded them, the uniforms worked well at intimidation, too.

Stillness rippled outward from where they stood in an implacable line, followed by everyone else moving back, and back again. No one messed with Specials, not ever. Not even the Archdeacon, as the last one had discovered, because while they might work for the Ministry, they swore to the Goddess, not any man. While in practice that usually meant they obeyed the orders of the Archdeacon – the mouth of the Goddess – it also meant that if an archdeacon were to be naughty in the sight of the Specials, he'd damn well know about it. Though not for long.

Each of them had a little pain magic, not much but enough to give them the edge in any fight, fair or otherwise. Enough to power that one carriage between them; two of them sat in the front seats and I could see the hint of blood and bandage from here.

One of the Specials stepped forward and inspected the suddenly silent crowd. His face looked as though it had been carved out of stone by someone practising while drunk, all slab-sided and with an odd angle to his jaw. Something very unprepossessing about a man whose glare could make you believe he could shoot bullets out of his eyes and was only waiting for the opportunity to do it. "Home," he said. "*Now*."

To emphasise his words, the rest of them raised guns and pointed them into the crowd.

Which miraculously wasn't there any more; people leaked away along alleys, down stairwells, into dark doorways. The drunks at the temple door slunk off with the rest, not so drunk they didn't know trouble when they saw it. Within minutes, all that was left were a few of the braver guards, a slightly dented and extremely pissed-off-looking Dench and the dead body. And us in the temple.

"The Goddess always provides," the preacher said smugly and I restrained myself with an effort.

Dench caught sight of us lurking in the doorway and after a consultation with the lead Special, he trotted up the steps.

"Father Guinto, glad to see you. You," he pointed at me, "come and take a look."

Confused, I went down to the walkway with him. The metal was slippery with blood and spilt booze, making my boots skid and me hold on to the handrail for dear life.

"That was a bit too close for comfort," Dench murmured and I noticed the blood on his knuckles. "We're right on the edge here, Rojan. Next time, it's going to take more than a few Specials to break it up. This is a big pile of black powder waiting for a spark. And that spark is going to be one more of these."

We looked down at the broken body. Some poor kid in the wrong place at the wrong time, and look what he'd got for his trouble. "Someone said they saw the guards do it."

Dench's moustache bristled at that – I often thought it showed more reaction than he did. "Not *my* guards, I'll tell you that. They know damn well I'd murder them myself if they stepped out of line. Besides, there weren't any guards down this end of the walkway. They were all up by the temple, keeping a look out because of Perak."

I cocked an eyebrow at the way he said it, a subtle warning.

"The old factions in Ministry are shifting now," he said. "Not to mention the Storad and Mishans circling the city like sharks. Tricky bastards, and they're bound to be up to something. Maybe even this."

Ah, yes, the city's ever-so-friendly neighbours. Or they *had* been, all the time they couldn't trade with each other except through us. Now, not so much friendly as waiting with salivating jaws. The sneaky-bastard warlord who founded this city in a handy pass between two nations knew what he was about. Basically, this city was founded on extortion – pay us, we'll let you trade for what you need. There was no other way for the Mishans and Storad to trade with each other, or nothing that didn't involve several hundred miles, or so I'd heard. I could be wrong – officially Outside didn't exist.

Over time we'd added to the captive market by being more sneaky and devious and very, very inventive. We grew, the city ran out of space and had to grow up rather than out because we filled the whole pass. We traded our inventions for food, because we had almost no land left to grow our own, but we got rich, and soft. Too soft, too reliant on our machines, on the power that ran them so that now, with no power, we were vulnerable.

"They're waiting to see if we die so they can pick over our bones," Dench said. "Maybe help along that dying a bit. They've parked an army on our doorstep, one either side, waiting, pushing. Got the ministers all in a twist and they're lashing out all over. If Perak doesn't get Mahala back up and running, and soon, I wouldn't give a rat's arse for his chances of making it to the New Year. Even if he does, he's always going to have enemies there." Dench smiled at that. "Not condescending enough to all the lowlives, your brother. Wants everything more equal, and of course if Down here gets more, Up there gets less. A viewpoint that is unique, and vastly unpopular, up in Top of the World, as I am sure you can imagine."

"He's on his own there. What are the chances of me getting up that far?"

"Slim to bugger all. I'll keep my eye on Perak, but if I do that I can't be down here too."

"So you want me to . . . ?"

"Keep your eyes and ears open, that's all. Let me know if anything strikes you, because if we don't catch whoever it is, the city is in big trouble. And keep up with the lab, most importantly. Getting the power back on would go a long way to solving our problems, even if Ministry is busy denying you exist or what you're doing. We're relying on you."

Four words to strike dread into my heart.

Two of the Specials came with a blanket and covered up the boy, more gently than might be expected. One murmured a prayer over him, picked him up and carried him to the carriage.

Father Guinto met him on the way and more prayers followed, a blessing. For a Downside child, from a member, however lowly, of the Ministry. I'd never thought I'd see the day.

"How did he get to be a priest?" I muttered.

"Because he's good at it. But mainly, I suspect, because he didn't tell anyone that actually he's a good man till after he got ordained."

For a man of the Goddess, sometimes Dench is as cynical as me.

Chapter Four

Dwarf had come up in the world since the 'Pit had gone, fairly literally. Instead of a crappy little lock-up under Trade where the thump of the factories used to rattle your bones to dust, he had a nice, clean lab to work in that was almost, but not quite, in Heights. Or it had been clean, until he'd moved in. Dwarf couldn't work unless he had chaos around him. He said it aided creativity. I was more of the opinion that he was just a messy bastard, but I couldn't fault his results.

We'd left Jake and Erlat helping Guinto at the temple with Dog playing bodyguard, like Jake needed one. Me, Pasha and the boy manoeuvred our way round piles of sulphuric-smelling crates, bottles of mineral oil, bits of cog, bundles of cobbled together wires hanging from the ceiling so I had to duck into Dwarf's home from home.

The Ministry, thanks to the fact that the new Archdeacon was the brother of the old, dead me, and the fact that Dwarf was the one person who could work out how to get the factories running and the lights on, had given him everything he could have asked for.

Except one thing: a power source. A long time ago, pain-mages ran Trade, the machines, the lights, everything. It was all power drained from their magic, their pain. But Ministry had decided pain-mages were messy, and dangerous, what with the number that went bananas when the black got them, generally taking a portion of the city as they went. A particularly nasty altercation between two magical rivals had almost toppled the whole place when an area under Trade was blasted into bits. The Ministry said enough was enough, banned mages and rebuilt some of the area, calling it Hope City. A name which had lasted all of about a day, when the more familiar No-Hope-Shitty had replaced it.

Instead of mages and their pain magic, the alchemists had come up with synth. Only synth had caused an epidemic which had decimated entire parts of the city. Even now, years later, people still died of the synthtox.

So, panic in the Ministry. They'd brought in Glow, a supposedly side-effect-free power source. It had worked pretty good, too. Right up until I destroyed it all. Every last drop. I told you I was good at pissing people off, didn't I? Well, Glow was that same pain magic. Only, to get the amount they needed it wasn't the mages who were supplying the pain.

I don't think I need spell it out any more plainly, and I'd rather not, because then I'd have to remember what that looked like. Anyway, so I screwed an entire city to stop it, to stop them, and get the 'Pit opened so the Downsiders could leave. Now we had bugger all power, not a lot of food and not much to trade to get food, because the factories had shut down without Glow. Long story short, we were fucked.

This is where Dwarf came in, and me and Pasha and, we hoped, our new little friend would, too. Dendal helped out, when we could get him in this reality. Thing was, pain-mages had been illegal till a few weeks before, on, well, pain of death. Now they needed us and our magic before everyone starved. Unofficially, of course. We might have been legal, technically, but Ministry hadn't yet seen fit to tell everyone what we were doing, because most of them didn't know this place existed and Perak was at pains to keep it that way. If the population – never mind most of Ministry – had known what we were up to, using that same old pain, the lab would have been so many little bits of metal. It didn't matter that it was our pain we were using, the Downsiders had nervous tics at the thought that someone might use someone else's pain, and the Upsiders had spent the last twenty years being told we were against the Goddess and should be handed over to the guards if found.

And the Ministry . . . the Ministry hated us and always had. We were a threat to their power, I think that was the problem. Even Perak couldn't do much about that – the Ministry is factions within factions against factions, but he was working on it. If we could come up with enough Glow to get Trade running properly, he reckoned he could get more than half the cardinals on his side. At least *nominally* on his side. Until we could do that, though, we were mostly secret, for the good of our health.

Frankly, given all this I thought Dendal was nuts to advertise we were mages, but then again he's pretty nuts all over.

Dwarf hunched under a precious Glow lamp, tinkering with something mechanical. Or electrical. I couldn't quite grasp the difference. Not my field of expertise. Dwarf's sausage fingers manoeuvred something with a precise delicacy and he sat back with a sigh.

He's well named, is Dwarf. Short and squat, with a mobile, rubbery sort of face that could give trolls nightmares. An absolute genius with anything mechanical and, lately, with newly discovered electricity, too.

"Rojan!" he said when he looked up, and then his face took on the shamed scrunch of a loved-to-death stuffed bear. "Er, welcome, Maki. Is he the one?"

Pasha nudged the boy forward. The look of Dwarf made him tense – I'd seen it do that to grown men, given the weird stamp of his face, but the boy held up well.

"One what?" The boy looked set to run, every muscle stretched and ready, his eyes darting to and fro, looking for escape.

Dwarf got down off his high stool with the help of a pair of crutches – his legs had been fairly well mangled about the time I fucked my hand – and was eye to eye with a twelve-year-old

45

boy. "You know you're special, don't you, boy? You can do things others can't."

The boy tried to back up, but Pasha caught him in gentle hands.

"It's all right," Dwarf said. This might have gone across better if he hadn't looked so much like a gargoyle anticipating its next meal. "Mages are legal now. You don't have to hide."

The boy tried to run then, and I caught a glimpse of tears on his cheeks. Pasha held him by one shoulder and, despite all the knee and elbow action, he went nowhere.

Dwarf climbed back onto his high stool. "A Downsider, yes? We haven't recruited any of them yet. Don't doubt they'd see it differently, what with what the mages did to them." He looked back at me. "Where'd you find him?"

"A hospital tipped us off." I neglected to mention that the nurse in question had been one of the ladies who'd whacked me one. "No family, or, if he has, he wouldn't tell the nurse."

"And about to get the crap kicked out of him when he was found." Pasha frowned, making him more monkey-like than ever. "Not the first. Or the last."

"Mages, or Downsiders?" Dwarf asked.

"Both."

"I'm not a mage, I'm not!" The boy stood, pink and indignant, to cover his fear.

"So how did you fire my pulse pistol then? Nice job, by the way, Dwarf. Took out every guy in front of him. Very handy, considering."

"It's a gun, anyone can use them. Some of the guards do. Why wouldn't I be able to fire it?" The words shot out of the boy like belligerent bullets.

I felt sorry for him then. He stood straight, his eyes too big for his scrawny, too-pale face, but he had a cocky way about him that made me grin. Made me think other things, too, such as how that cockiness was probably covering up a boatload of fear.

I pulled out the pulse pistol and handed it to Dwarf. "Shoot me."

His face rolled up into a grotesque grin. "My pleasure."

Dwarf made a show of holding it to my temple before he pulled the trigger with a theatrical swoosh while the boy's eyes and mouth competed to see which could be rounder. The razor swung out and sliced Dwarf's thumb, but instead of a jolt of juice that ended with me slumped on the floor all that happened was a dry click, and Dwarf swore and sucked his now bleeding thumb.

For a moment I thought the boy was going to piss himself, but he got under control quick enough and eyed the pistol eagerly. "Why couldn't he fire it? Why aren't you on the floor?"

I pulled out my more conventional gun – the one I prefer using because, although it's only got one shot and has a habit of misfiring at awkward moments, the person it hurts is not me.

"This is what you've seen the guards carrying. It uses black powder and a spark to fire a bullet out. This one," I swapped with Dwarf, "doesn't use black powder. What powers it is magic and if, like Dwarf, you don't have any magical power it won't do anything but cut your thumb. If you do, it takes the pain and magnifies it, concentrates it into one pulse. You didn't kill those men, but you did knock them out long enough for us to get out. And, incidentally, let me know I'd found the right boy. Like it or not, you're a pain-mage. How you use it, well, that's up to you. You don't have to be like *them*." Code for "you don't have to be a murderous torturing bastard".

He nodded thoughtfully and stared at the pulse pistol for a good while before he looked up at me. "So you're a mage? What about him?" He nodded at Pasha.

"Him too."

"Did either of you . . . you know. In the 'Pit?"

"I didn't even know the 'Pit had anyone in it until a couple of months ago. Ministry kept it all locked up tight. We thought it was infected with synth, so everyone stayed away."

The eyes grew wary again as he regarded Pasha. "He's from Downside, though. They took my sister."

Pasha could hardly bear to look at him, at any of us, as he pushed up one sleeve. There in the tender flesh under the thumb a mark had been burnt into his skin. A brand, to say which mage had once owned him. A mark that shamed him – the Ministry had set about powerful rumours Downside about the branded, so that any escapees would be brought right back, or killed. "Little Whores" the rest of the Downsiders had called them, not realising then, and many still didn't, no matter the truth of it.

So the brand was a mark that shamed him, made him a target even more than he already was, and one that made Pasha proud, too – that the mages had tried to get him to join them and he couldn't, *wouldn't*, do what they wanted: torture people for power, and the pleasure some of the mages got from it as well.

Luckily, the boy didn't land on the disgust and revulsion side of the fence, but on the pity.

"My sister," he said, awestruck. "Her name was Janny."

Pasha's smile twisted and he shook his head. "There were so many, and so many forgot their names. Were made to forget them."

A subject bitter to Pasha's heart – while Jake had never known any other name, Pasha had been older when they'd taken him, and the circumstances different. He had a family Upside, somewhere, and all he needed to do was remember his name, their names, to maybe win back something like a normal past. He'd spent a long time with Dendal trying to recall that name in the face of other memories that promised punishment should he manage it. "I'm sorry."

The boy nodded again, blinked back tears and took a deep breath. I was starting to like him, especially when he said, "All right. Why did you bring me here, then?"

Dwarf clapped his hands and grinned. "Excellent! You're

going to help feed the city, light the city – you're going to *save* the city. You'll be a hero and all the girls will love you, which is the only reason R—" He caught himself in time. "The only reason these two do it, for the women. It's probably best to show you. Come on, come on." Dwarf clattered off on his crutches.

Looking somewhat bemused, and I can't say I blamed him, the boy let us lead him through to another area, just as dimly lit. On the way, Pasha managed to get a name out of him – Allit.

Dwarf called it his experimental lab. Me and Pasha and the couple of other mages we'd managed to find called it the pain room. Stacks of Glow tubes ranged along one wall, making Allit flinch. I could well imagine why, but we weren't going to torture anyone to fill them. Anyone except ourselves.

We made our way past the bulk of what Dwarf and his assistant Lise assured me would be a fully working electricity generator/magic enhancer/thing any day now. He'd been saying that for weeks, and Lise glanced up from where she was tinkering with a load of cables right in the guts of the thing. A flash of a smile and she burrowed her way back in – like Dwarf she was only happy when tinkering. I really wished they'd stop the tinkering and get on with it.

Lise wasn't quite sixteen, but a genius alchemist and one of the few people in the city to have a handle on this new electricity. She was also my half-sister – a recent discovery, and I didn't know her at all, it felt like.

I stopped listening to Dwarf's little lecture-cum-tour of the lab and went to watch as Lise reached inside the machine with a screwdriver.

"Do you think you can get it working soon?" I asked.

She glanced up at me and away. "I hope so. It's getting pretty bad out there. A riot down by one of the temples, I heard. They brought the Specials in."

I didn't know what else to say; what *do* you say to a half-sister you only recently met? Especially when you killed your shared father. "Oops" doesn't really cover it. I kept trying, though, and it kept getting easier, week by week. I was starting to like having a family again, people to care about.

She tinkered around a bit more then stood back. "We could try it now. You game?"

"I – not right now." My whole body seemed to throb, starting at my hand and echoing out to the rest of me and I hadn't even given my juice for the day yet. "Maybe after the pain room. It's ready, then?"

She shoved her hands in her pockets and frowned at all the dials like they were trying to thwart her. Funny how pretty she looked like that, her dark hair flopping over her eyes and what my ma used to call a "donkey" line between her eyebrows. People say we look alike, me and Lise – we both take after our father – but I hope I'm never pretty.

"It's not quite right," she said. "The interface is out of whack. But I'll get it, don't you worry."

Stubborn determination was something of a family trait,

hence that "donkey" line. Makes us Goddess-awful to live with.

Lise pulled something out of her pocket and stared at it as if she couldn't remember putting it there, before her face cleared and she held it out for me to take. "Oh. Yes. I made this for you."

A glass tube with a stopper on one end. It looked suspiciously like it should have been attached to a syringe and for various reasons I have come to hate syringes with a single-minded passion some people reserve for their in-laws. I didn't take it, but, given Lise's expertise with alchemy, I was intrigued. As long as it didn't get jabbed into me.

"What is it?"

Green is what it was. A virulent green that seemed unnatural. Nothing that colour should ever be injected into a person, that's what I was thinking.

Lise flashed a grin, always most alive when talking about her work. She launched into a long and complicated explanation, but I only understood half the words. Something about a re-synthesis of an existing organic compound that might be valuable as an ... an ... nope, can't remember or pronounce what she said. There were other words, like valency and allotropy and something that sounded like it had too many Xs and Zs in it. Her voice trailed off at my blank stare.

"Pretend I'm utterly ignorant of all forms of alchemy," I said. "You won't have to pretend very hard."

A delicate frown probably revealed that she didn't think

anyone should be ignorant of alchemy, but she tried anyway. "The solution Doctor Whelar injected you with, that made you numb."

"You can keep it away from me." I still had nightmares about that, about being totally powerless, about being *normal*. Well, normal-ish, in that I couldn't work any magic when I couldn't feel any pain.

Lise sighed. "No, this isn't it. It's what I made from it. A very interesting compound, and it has lots of—" She gave me a despairing look and skipped the long words. "It has lots of different ways of being put together, and each one does something a little different."

I glared at the green. "All right. What does this one do?"

Her turn to glare at the green. "I don't know. I managed to test all the others, on myself. Nothing very spectacular though at least one might be helpful to the doctors at the hospital. But this one, I don't know. I tried it and it didn't do anything."

"You injected it into yourself?" I tried not to come over all big brother, because I've never been comfortable with the job, the prospects or pay. Or indignant younger siblings.

"I *did* manage to live to fifteen without you. Anyway, I tried it on Dwarf first, and I learnt from you how to bugger myself up."

What was wrong with them that they had to test things on themselves? It wasn't the first time I'd caught them out either. But as Lise had so artfully reminded me, she was technically almost an adult, and I wasn't any better myself either. I gave in with as much grace as I could muster. "So what's the problem?"

"Would looking at it under the microscope help you understand? It's a really good one, one of Dwarf's own. You can see *everything*."

I was perturbed by the way she blushed when she said Dwarf's name, but figured it had to be some weird crush thing. I mean, he looks like a doll that's been buried for ten years then dug up and had experiments run on it. With scalpels and clamps. Don't get me wrong, man's a genius. A twisted genius: give him anything mechanical and there's no better. Given Lise's own talents, that expertise had to be the source of the blush.

As all this flashed through my mind, Lise glared at me again. Although we didn't share the same mother, it was like being ten again and figuring out just when it was best to stop what you were thinking before you got a ding round the back of the head with a spoon. I figure that look is universal among women. I decided that discretion was the better part of not getting a ding round the back of the head, and said, "I don't think even one of Dwarf's microscopes would help."

She raised her eyes to heaven and waved her hands as though asking the Goddess for some damned help, please. There's something about Lise that always makes me feel unutterably dense. Maybe it's the scare factor of her brains, or possibly it's all that puberty going on. I tried a self-deprecating grin, but it didn't seem to help.

"Look, it's really easy," she said. "You know we've been running a few tests on you all? Trying to quantify magic? I mean, the possibilities are— All right, don't look at me like that. We need to know how to make the interface with the generator work properly. You, Pasha, Taban, Dendal, you've all given us some blood to test. And under the microscope, this," she waved the green tube, "shows changes when introduced to your mage blood, but not to mine or Dwarf's not-mage blood."

"Is this going to end in 'And so I want you to inject it into yourself'? Because the answer is 'Not on your fucking life'."

I'll give this to my sister – she has a really impressive pout.

"But we need to get the generator going, and soon. Yesterday would be good, you don't need me to tell you that. And this could be the answer to the interface problem."

I won't bore you with the details of the not-really-an-argument that followed. Suffice to say, it ended with Lise looking smug and me with a vial in my pocket along with a carefully wrapped syringe and a promise to try it, before I headed to the pain lab.

The problem was, Lise was right. The generator was like my pulse pistol only on a much grander scale. It would take magic, magnify it, and pulse it out to all the machines of Trade, power up Glow lights, you name it. With an added twist – Lise and Dwarf had worked out how to turn magic into electricity, and they reckoned electricity could do things even magic couldn't. Even if they were wrong, with that electricity we could power everything – Trade, carriages, lights, heat, with the minimum of magic, and pain, to power the generator/magnifier/transformer/whatever you want to call it. Less pain was the thing, though. An idea which I found very appealing.

Until that happy day came, we had this. Two chairs facing each other. A Glow tube attached to the back of each one on some sort of rig that looked like someone had had a lunatic dream about rivets and robot giraffes and then made the dream a reality. It might look weird but the rig made the Glow tubes easy to swap out when they got full. On one arm of each chair was a gruesome-looking mechanism, a version of the improved pulse pistol that would take our pain, magnify it and dump it into the Glow tubes. A first aid box for afterwards. My hand was never going to get any better till Dwarf and Lise got that generator working.

"All right, Allit, you sit here." Dwarf got him settled on a crate, and came to plug in me and Pasha. "It's not pretty, but you need to see how it's done. All right?"

I settled back in the chair, my stomach in all kinds of knots. Not pretty was putting it mildly. Painful, stupid, dangerous, sickening, the road to madness, that's what it was. One of us was going to fall into the black, sooner rather than later, because it was wearing us down, sloughing off parts of what held us together, grating off chips of sanity. Well, that's how it felt to me, though Pasha and the others seemed to be holding up okay. But I felt better if I imagined it wasn't just me, and I had to do it.

I'd taken away the power, and, until we could get Lise's generator working, I had to do something or a load of Downsiders would have come up out of the 'Pit just in time to starve with everyone else. Pasha did this because he knew it was the right thing to do, because he was that kind of guy. I was doing it because guilt and the consequences of being responsible for the first time in my life were eating a hole in me and it was this or drink myself stupid. Plus, there was this lady who I wanted to think I was good and noble.

Pasha and I settled into the chairs and shut our eyes – we'd learnt early on that watching someone else go through substantial amounts of pain only makes it worse. Dwarf clipped us in, one of his cables snaking from a holster round our arms to the Glow tube at our backs. I took a deep breath and squeezed my bad hand into a fist. Not-quite-healed breaks ground against each other, pinged and growled under my scarred skin. Magic was everywhere, all in my brain, singing across my skin, lighting up my nerves like fire. It was beautiful, terrifying, maddening and fucking glorious. A dim noise penetrated, and I recognised my own voice as I groaned the pain out of me. Recognised too the wet crack as Pasha dislocated another finger, the strangled grunt as he socketed it back home again.

The light of the Glow grew brighter, seared my eyes but I

barely saw it. The black was coming for me, had grown these last weeks.

Come on Rojan, it whispered. *Come on, fall in, let go, let yourself become me*. I wanted to, oh I did. *You want me, you need me*. The black was everything you feared or hated wiped out. The black was cool, was comfort, company for the alone, fearless for the fearful, was excruciating bliss. Mages had lost whole lives in there.

The dark edges of it flapped at the corner of my mind, always closer, every day, making me a little mad even when I wasn't using my magic. I had tried the black once, and liked it, so why not come again? Why not stay this time?

I launched myself out of the chair with a yell, dragged the mechanism off my arm, threw it on the floor and stamped on it. A cog, probably something vital, whizzed off into a corner and landed with a tinkle. It was only a pair of hands dragging me back and the look on Dwarf's face, as though I'd killed one of his children, that stopped me pounding it into dust.

My heart staggered back to something like a normal rhythm and Pasha let go of my arms. Allit sat in wide-eyed shock on the crate, a glass of something sweet and fizzy forgotten in one hand.

"It's good," Pasha said to him, when I couldn't speak. "And it's not so good. The pain is only the start, but it's not the pain that's the problem, not really. Our pain is all that's keeping Mahala running, all that's between us and starvation. It's all we've got, all anyone has got, and we can't even tell anyone.

You can imagine how that would go down. But all the same . . . it's like nothing else, ever. It's like standing on Top of the World and seeing everything spread below you, like basking in the glow of the Goddess's smile. But while it feels like her smile, it's on Namrat's face. It will take you if you let it, take you and keep you, and *that's* the worst. Because there are times you'll want it to. You think you're up to it?"

Allit watched the Glow globes, the pulse and power of them in a city with no power, no nothing. Except this. Glow to run some of the factories, to make things to trade, to get us all food to eat. Something rather than nothing. Grey mush to eat rather than starve. Do something that was an abomination, or so he'd have been taught by the priests, do the unholy to save the city.

That's how it always starts, isn't it? People doing what goes against the grain because they think they're doing the right thing. That's how my father started Downside, using others' pain to save the city. But I wasn't going to be like him. I wasn't, I couldn't. I might be, and that was the thought that was haunting me. That was what the black was hanging on to, using it to try to drag me in – not that we were doing the unholy, that we were abominations in the eyes of the Goddess. Hell no, because I don't care what she sees. No, it was the fear that I'd be like him. That I'd fuck it all up even worse than I already had, that I was responsible for this mess in the first place. I told myself to shut the fuck up, I wasn't helping. It worked. For a bit.

Allit nodded, a determined little thing, and held out his hand.

"Not yet." Pasha laughed. I envied him that sound, that feeling. "Not yet. First you have to see what you can do."

Pasha and Dwarf took Allit off to put him through the exercises Pasha had thought up. Didn't rate them myself, but you never knew. They left me, on purpose I felt, with the pain room.

I stared at the machine for a while, hating it, and hating more that I wanted to get back on it. Not because I had a city to get back up and running, but because I wanted to see the black again. I was losing my mind quite clearly, maybe had already lost it.

Yet people were relying on me, whether they knew it or not. Relying on the little power that we managed to pump out, the meagre trade goods that were being produced and bartered with our lurking neighbour countries for food. I had to pull myself together when all I really wanted to do was fall apart, fall into the black where no one relied on me and I was free of the fear.

All in all, I was glad when the door opened and Jake came in, trailing Dog, as always, to meet Pasha after the pain room because she couldn't bear to watch. Her in the room took my mind off my mind and on to other bodily parts.

I'm a sucker for women, all of them. Tall, short, skinny, plump, more than plump, I don't mind. It's not what they look like, as such, though I like a pretty face as much as the next guy. Unless the next guy is Dwarf, who takes what he can get. No, it's the way they move that gets me every time, and Jake had such a way of moving, all artless grace as if she oiled her muscles, wrapped up in snug and slippery leather topped today with a silk shirt that clung to all the best places that it dried up all the spittle in my mouth every time. I'd seen her fight like a tiger, like Namrat himself. She fought as though every moment was her last, that maybe she wanted it to be. Her eyes were the giveaway, haunted still by all she'd been through, but there was something strong in there, something that could never be broken, not truly, though some had tried and left their mark.

I would rather die than say that, which led me to the utterly banal, 'Hello.' All charm, that's me.

The door opening again saved me from making a total arse of myself, although when two Specials came through it was a toss-up which would be worse, making an arse of myself or having my arse handed to me. They weren't all pleased about mages being legal.

Dog looked a little bewildered, which wasn't unusual, but he followed Jake's lead as she backed up to a wall, wary on the instant, each hand dropping to a sword that she knew how to use all too well. Her gaze flicked to me and away again and I was acutely aware she was wishing I was Pasha, which did my ego no good whatsoever.

Perak's entrance calmed me – a bit. At least he didn't have his little entourage of cardinals this time but he had that faraway look in his eyes, the one that generally meant I was going to get dropped in the shit and have to take responsibility. I'd rather take the Specials.

He smiled at me, perhaps not even noticing how I looked, and wandered over to the generator. "Will it be long, do you think?"

I mustered up the spit to speak, which is hard when you've got a Special glaring at you as though he wants to arrest you for being alive with intent. "Dwarf says a few days, but he's been saying that for weeks."

Perak nodded as if that was what he expected and twiddled a knob. It came off in his hands. "Oh. Well." He blinked hard and looked round at his Specials. "It's all right, you can go."

I let out breath I wasn't aware I'd been holding as they shut the door behind them.

"Rojan, I – I'm in trouble," Perak said. He didn't look at me but kept fiddling with the generator. "No one – I mean, Ministry – is what I thought. Not at all."

I pinched at the bridge of my nose. Probably only Perak, and maybe Dendal, had ever been under any illusions about the Ministry. I wondered how he had taken it when he'd finally realised that Ministry wasn't about faith but control. Badly, I suspected.

"I don't suppose they are. Question is, what are you going to do about it?" Not a lot would have been my answer, except maybe raze the whole of Top of the World where Ministry reigned, let everyone from Under come up to Heights and

Clouds and look at the sun, share it, share everything. I was more likely to spontaneously turn into a woman than that happen any time soon.

Perak didn't see it that way. When we were growing up, I used to wonder if we had the same father, because, while I'm the ultimate cynic, Perak is the opposite. He *is* hope. It gave him a certain, and incredibly annoying, optimism that everything would turn out all right.

Now his eyebrows plaited together in thought and he took on a determined look, almost as though he was paying attention. Wonders will never cease. "I'm going to change it," he said. "Make it what it was always supposed to be. You know some of them even want to recreate the 'Pit, the, the . . . you know."

"The torture, Perak."

He grimaced at that word; his daughter had almost become a victim herself as the mages tried to force me to join them.

"They say it's the only way, that the ends justify the means. That people will die if we don't. What's worse is they're right, people *are* dying. Starvation, cold, fighting . . . Other cardinals are convinced that all this is a plot to undermine them, discredit the Ministry. They don't believe it is true, it's just some Downsider plan, misinformation, the start of a coup perhaps. All of them, almost every last cardinal, see the people from Under as nothing but a means to provide labour, and Downsiders as vermin who only know how to fight and kill each other. The Death Matches—" He cut off at that and glanced at Jake and Dog. "I'm sorry, but they use that as an excuse, to show what barbarians you are. I'm trying to put things right, to how they should be, but that only makes the cardinals hate me more because that way they'll end up with less than ultimate wealth. You know, I had three delegations yesterday. One of them outlined ways we could discreetly dispose of Downsiders, hell, anyone from Under who looks too uppity, so that the rest of us can survive, another quoted scripture to show that Downsiders are heretics, agents of Namrat and should all be burnt, and the third – I'm not even going to tell you that."

"What do *you* think, Perak?" Jake was wound up tighter than one of Dwarf's springs, but her voice was soft.

Perak tried a smile, but it came out wrong, frazzled. "I think I have too little support among my cardinals. I think most of the cardinals I have make me sick. I think I wish I had no faith, like Rojan, so it wouldn't be such a shock. I think what the mages down in the 'Pit did made the Goddess turn her back on us, and it's only priests such as Guinto, people who are willing to believe, who will bring her back. I think I'll be dead soon, that this city will tear itself apart, if you don't get the power back on."

The pleading look had me swearing in my head, because this was how it always started with Perak. It always ended with me in the shit.

It was like that time when I was twelve and he was ten and

he'd somehow managed to piss off every single bully within a half-mile radius of our crumbling house. He was small for his age, and they were hulking great brutes. They'd have killed him if they'd found him. So who took the kicking of a lifetime? Who spent a month pretending he didn't have broken ribs and accidentally firing off random spells every time he breathed too hard? Ma never did work out what had happened to her saucepans or why the bedroom suddenly turned blue.

Yet Perak wasn't telling me anything I didn't already know, couldn't see on the street. We needed power and we needed it right now. We needed more mages, and I was the one who had to find them because that's how my magic runs. When I looked back at him, I realised that there was more he wanted to load on to big brother's shoulders.

"Go on, out with it."

"The Storad, the Mishans . . . you know they're outside the gates?"

"Perak, even Dendal knows they're outside the gates."

Perak's smile was most peculiar – almost world-weary, cynical. Not what I'd associate with my dreamer of a little brother. "I don't suppose he knows how many there are. Not very many people do, but I can see them from up in Top of the World. Not just a few. An army each. The Mishans perhaps we could manage, *if* we got some power back soon. Note the perhaps and the if. Not a straightforward people, though, all backwards and forwards and no telling what they'll take as an insult. Sneezing at the wrong time might be enough to set them against us in earnest. And the Storad . . . the Storad are hard men. Their ambassador in particular, and a man with a secret, I think. They're *all* men with secrets. But, of the two, I fear them the most."

"Hard fighters," Jake said suddenly, and Perak shot her an enquiring look. "Some of them, the mountain tribes. It's, I don't know, like a religious thing with them."

I thought back to a Death Match I'd watched, one where I'd been certain she was outclassed against a Storad who was slick with his sword; obviously not quite slick enough. I noticed she neglected to say that fighting was a religious thing for her, too.

Perak inclined his head. "So I hear. On the one hand, we have a temperamental lot of loosely joined tribes that out-number us ten to one, but are hot-headed, volatile perhaps, prone to fighting among themselves. I can arrange that they do just that. On the other . . . the Storad. I'm doing my best to stall them, placate them, deal with them, both the Mishans and Storad. But they know we're weak. I think they're wait-ing for something, but I don't know what. I do know we haven't got long. The ambassadors have both said as much in roundabout, diplomatic terms. Five days. At best. That's how long we've got."

I opened my mouth to say something really smart and cutting, about how he didn't want much, did he? He didn't give me the chance. The utter defeat in his voice caught me off balance, and made me notice the new lines on his forehead, the first touch of grey in his hair.

"And just to top it all off, we've got someone murdering Downsiders, we've got Downsiders up in arms and Upsiders hating them just for being here. We've got anarchy just waiting for one more spark to make it explode. And I don't think that's coincidence, do you? If that happens, this city is lost, whether you get the power back on or not."

He didn't say it – "please find whoever's killing those boys" – but he didn't have to. It was in the defeat in his voice, something I'd rarely heard in a brother who thought everything was an opportunity. He had his hands full of ambassadors to placate and disgruntled cardinals who didn't want change, any sort of change, and especially the sort Perak would bring. Dench had already hinted that he didn't have the time for this, not if he wanted to keep Perak safe, and his Specials and the guards were hard pressed enough with keeping a lid on the explosion.

Which left me.

I *was* going to say: "Goddess's tits, Perak, I'm having enough trouble keeping my shit together just keeping the Glow at this level, never mind getting everything up and running in five days and, oh, finding a killer while I'm at it."

Then I caught sight of Jake. The way she was looking at me, hoping.

Like I said, the reason I do most things is so the lady will think I'm good and noble. Not because I *am* good and noble, but it's a hell of a way to get them interested. This was going to be a fuck of a lot of being good, too much for my liking, but it might have its advantages. Besides, it was Perak asking.

"All right, I'll try. I can't promise anything, though."

"I knew I could rely on you. I'll send Dench with what we've got on the murders, though it won't be till tonight probably. It isn't much, but maybe it will help. And thank you."

It surprised me, then, that his smile was almost worth it all on its own, the way the worried creases smoothed away, how his shoulders stopped hunching somewhere up around his jaw. Helping my little brother. It felt kind of good, in fact. Until I started thinking about what it actually meant, and the work – and magic, pain – it involved.

Perak left and I sank into the chair, trying to ignore the contraption on the arm, the way it seemed to call to me. I had other things calling, and the reason was smiling at me in a way that made me feel quite odd.

She perched on Pasha's chair opposite me. "You know I'll help, we both will, however we can. There's been more killings than they've let on, you know that?"

No, I hadn't known that. "How many?"

She shrugged, and the ice cracked a little. Downsiders being murdered, people like her and Pasha. Little Whores, both of them, tainted by the mages, branded. Collaborators is what those brands and rumour said, even when they were anything but, had spent their lives fighting against what had gone on. They were walking targets, hated by everyone who knew their secret, knew the mark on their wrists, something I hadn't really realised in my own quest to avoid getting lynched.

"I'm not sure exactly," she said. "Maybe a dozen? Any Downsider could tell you that. Upsiders don't care. Ministry don't care, except Perak. He sees, but the rest – we're only Downsiders. We don't matter. If it was Upsiders getting murdered, or Ministry, they'd have the killer caught by now." That last with a pained twitch of her lips. A devout follower of the Goddess, she was, with a faith that somehow shamed me. Made me wish I did believe. I would, if I could believe as hard as she did.

"I care," I said, and the smile . . . good job I hadn't finalised that deal with the Goddess, or I'd have to have started believing right then.

Pasha came back in at that point, shattered the moment when she turned her smile on him and racked it up a notch.

It only took a couple of minutes to tell him what Perak had said.

"All right. What first?"

And that was the question. I could spend my time trying to find one person in thousands upon thousands, and all the time we weren't getting the power back on, helping people live, we were helping people die. A dozen Downsiders were dead, and that was bad, but not as bad as a hundred a day dying, a thousand a day, and it was heading in that direction.

More if the Storad and Mishans made good on their threat. Yet one more murder and perhaps it wouldn't matter, because there'd be no city left.

What we really needed was more mages. *Lots* more mages. Then, with more power about, I could concentrate on finding the killer.

It was up to me, and I hate it when it's up to me. "Until Dench brings us what he's got, I can't do a damned thing about finding the killer. When he brings me that, I'll start. Until then, the power is the thing."

I fumbled around in my pocket for the name that Lastri had given me, possibly another mage. Possibly. I had a name to go on, so maybe I could just go to the records hall and ... I wasn't kidding anyone but myself. A record search would take days and we didn't have days.

Lastri hadn't only left a name, but something else, too. A lock of hair. The note said he'd gone missing a couple of days before after some sort of incident. Not unusual when the magic grips you the first time, often by accident. Sometime about puberty, you get a knock, or hurt in some way, and it kind of leaks out, raw and untamed. Often scaring the crap out of the proto-mage and anyone or anything nearby, such as Ma's saucepans.

He was a Downside boy, so his feelings regarding mages would be complicated at best. Like Allit, he'd probably deny that he had any magic, anything to distance himself from what had gone on in the 'Pit. He'd run away and finding runaways, that was my speciality.

"I can stay, do another session," Pasha was saying. I hated it when he was so, so, so damn fucking *nice*. Not to mention good and noble. It seemed to come naturally to him. Bastard.

I glanced up, and caught the grey tinge around his eyes, the slight tremor in his hand.

"No, it's all right. Get some rest, come back then. I'll see what Dench has got for us."

Before they left, Jake crouched in front of where I sat. She'd always had a phobia about touching – hardly surprising when you consider – but she brushed my hand with hers, a tentative thing, and I felt oddly blessed, almost as though the Goddess was trying to tell me something. Which only goes to show how knackered and fucked up in the head I was feeling.

"You get some rest, too."

"Yeah, sure." I couldn't trust myself to say anything else, in case everything spilled out.

When they'd gone, I sagged back into the chair and looked at the Glow contraption. Darkness lurked in the corners of my vision, waiting for me. I told it to sod off.

Mages, power, that was what I could do right now. Until I'd spoken to Dench, or I managed to get hold of a prop to help me find whatever weirdo was killing all these Downsiders.

I was fully aware that all this was an excuse. To find the boy Dendal thought might be an emerging mage I had to use magic. Well, I didn't *have* to but that would take minutes rather than days we didn't have. Funny, isn't it? That I was so scared to use my magic once upon a time, because I was scared of the black.

I was right to be, but in those dark days I had no choice, not really. I could have not done it, I suppose, but the thought of Jake looking at me afterwards was almost as much of a spur as the thought of how pissed Dendal would be. He'd start banging on about not living up to my potential, disappointing the Goddess and so on and so forth. That was enough to give anyone the heebie-jeebies.

So I lay back in the chair and put my hand on the contraption. I shouldn't, I knew that. I'd done my stint for the day, enough, more than enough, more than I could handle. Any more was a risk, a big one. So was not doing it. That's what I told myself, but I knew that for the lie it was. Fuck, I wished I was the man I'd been, who could shrug off guilt and responsibility, who could pretend he was a cynic, make people believe it, too.

I held the lock of hair in my good hand and squeezed the pain out.

The whirl of it took me for long, long breaths. I was everywhere, nowhere, I was bliss and I was blessed. No fear here, not in the black, no fear of people knowing me, expecting things of me that I couldn't deliver, expecting me to be a better person because they thought I was. No fear of fucking it all up. No skimming it, not now, not after so much in one day. I was deep in the black, swimming in it, wanting it. Shaking from a need that no one who wasn't a mage could ever know.

The hair, I had to concentrate on the hair but it was hard when that seductive voice kept on calling me.

Come on, Rojan, sink in, swim in fearless freedom. Come on, you know you want to.

The old me would have given in, wouldn't have given a crap about anything but losing the ever-present fear. I wasn't that different, but I did have one thing I hadn't before. People weren't just relying on me, they were believing in me, too. They believed in me, so I had to.

The hair, concentrate on the hair. Even with my eyes shut, I was a blinding brightness in the black, searing my eyelids with it. A moment of vertigo, of the sensation of tumbling end over end in a void, and then the knowledge came, thundering up my arm from the hand that held the hair.

A mile to the west, a hundred yards up from where I was. Somewhere cold and airless. I pushed harder, so that I was half there and yet still half in the pain room. Achingly cold and with a smell I recognised, a lingering hint of decay over and above the familiar smell of the city. Too dark to see, so I pulled myself back some. Still dark, but not black now. A small rendnut lamp meant I could see outlines, vague humps in the shadows.

The glint of light on metal; instruments laid out with cool precision. Scalpels, knives, weird clamp things that I didn't even want to know what they were for. A stone slab, well scrubbed but still with dark marks engrained into it.

I knew where I was, and my stomach shrivelled. A mortuary,

73

one I was intimately acquainted with, having seen my own dead body there or what looked like it anyway.

I turned to look down at the boy. Dead. Not just dead, but with a slash across his throat so that the spine was a hint of white showing through a now bloodless cut. The murdered boy from outside the temple, whose death had nearly caused a riot.

Chapter Five

By the time Dench found me, I'd discovered a bit myself from the mortician's records, or the few he'd allowed me to see without proper authorisation. A dozen murders: Jake had been right, and the details I'd got made my stomach wish it had never been born. All young boys on the cusp of puberty, except one lad in his twenties. All Downsiders, all with their throats cut back to the spine. I'd seen a few other things to make me shudder, too – mostly a certain doctor, previously in my father's employ. The good Dr Whelar, now performer of postmortems on murder victims, once inventor of a nasty little potion that shut off magic by making everything numb. I still dreamed about the time I'd been without my magic, the way he kept poking me with that syringe. The good doctor's motives were, at best, self-serving and the thought of him being involved, however vaguely, with these murders gave me a pain. Or maybe it was indigestion.

Dench didn't have much more for me. We sat in a dingy bar up at the top of No-Hope and he laid out what little he had. Only two bodies had been identified and that was scant help because they'd both been missing from home when they died, one for a week, one for a month. Their families hadn't been able to shed even a drop of light on where they might have been, or who with. Dench had some pictures but I wasn't that keen on looking at them, because they were all done after the kids had died. He shoved them under my nose anyway.

"We all have to do things we don't want to, Rojan." His careworn face had an extra edge of frustration to it under the faint glow of rend-nut lamps and his usually impressive moustache looked limp.

"You're head of the Specials. You can do what you want, to whom you want. Must be nice."

His smile was as cynical as my own, but there was a twist of something different about him today, of some regret. He'd always cared too much for a guard of any sort. It was what made him one of the good guys in a world of bastards.

"If only that were true," he said. "But none of us is free to do what we want. Not even Perak. He's trying, mind, and he's got everyone all in a twist. The older cardinals want everything to stay the same. The new ones want change, but not the sort where they lose anything, which is the sort Perak is trying to accomplish – and they don't like that. So Perak's going to have to work damned fucking hard if he wants to actually see any change rather than everything staying the same just with him at the helm. And then there's all the business with the ambassadors."

I suppressed a grin at the thought of the ructions Perak was making. Dench didn't usually talk much and especially not about what he did, or what went on up in Top of the World, so I made the most of it. "Ministry could do with a big stir. And what business with the ambassadors?"

Dench's moustache drooped even further and his shoulders slumped. I gathered Perak wasn't making his life an easy one, even if Dench did agree with the sentiment of what he was trying to accomplish. "I'll give you this; him and you have about the same level of tact and diplomacy. That is, fuck all. The Mishans are, well, frankly they're a bunch of idiots. But there's a lot of them, and they could overrun us if they get in. The Storad . . . they're even trying to be reasonable. They've come up with deal after deal, and all we need to do is agree to a partnership. They've got coal."

"Coal?"

"Some power source they mine, and they're making some of their own machines now. Offered us a deal: sell us the coal so we can use that instead of you and your pain. Have to give up a few other things, though, and Perak won't listen to reason on that, he won't even *try* to negotiate and that's one thing he's got the cardinals on his side for, though not for the same reasons. *They* don't want to lose their precious status, to be able to lord it over Outsiders and hold them in our pocket by holding all their trade. *He* thinks you're going to get him his power back on so we won't need to trade away any of our advantages just to stay alive." He gave me a sideways glare. "You and that fucking generator. I pray to the Goddess it works, I really do, and in time, but I don't think she's listening. Perak's put all his hopes on it. On you, for fuck's sake! Sometimes I think he's completely insane. Come on, tell me. Do you think it will work? Because I don't."

Dench never got this worked up, or not that I'd seen before, and I'd certainly never heard him say fuck half as much. The moustache bristled with a life of its own and his eyes looked like they might pop out of his head. It was quite an education.

"You'd be better off asking Dwarf, or Lise. I've got no idea how the thing's supposed to work. But they tell me it will, and I believe them. In time? I don't know. That's why I'm trying to scare up as many mages as I can, so at least we can have more power than we have now. But even if it does work, if we get the power back on, or I find enough mages that we don't need the generator, then we've still got these murders and they could be enough to topple this city if we don't stop it. It was close enough last time. Next time you might not be so lucky, and nor will anyone else.'

We looked back down at the pictures and the faces of boys who would never get any older.

Dench's shoulders slumped again and the sharp tone left his voice. "There's a plan behind this. Don't know what or why, not yet, but I can feel it in my bones. Spent enough time in the Specials to know it when I see it."

"Is this really all you could find?"

Apart from the pictures, all he had were the reports from the mortician detailing approximate age and so on, date, time and place of death and not a damned thing else.

Dench spread the pictures out across the table again, and tapped at one now bloodless throat. "This isn't random. I'm sure of it, sure as shit stinks. Somebody targeted these boys. Don't know why, but someone really hated the poor bastards, or hated what they represent perhaps. Downsiders, hmm?" He paused, as though an idea had just struck him. "Find the link, and you'll find your killer. Perhaps."

Without another word, he left to go back to Top of the World, back to keeping his sharp eye on Perak and juggling pissed-off cardinals and ambassadors. I didn't envy him.

I looked back down at the pictures. I didn't envy myself much either. I spent a fruitless couple of hours checking out where the boys had died, but apart from the fact they were all murdered close together, which could mean anything, all I got was rain down my neck.

In the end, I went where I'd lately taken to going when I needed to think and a sharp mind to ask all the right questions and tell me not to be such an arse. My one refuge from the world. Right then, I needed that something fierce because my head was spinning so fast I thought it might fall off.

Erlat kept a house in the Buzz, a discreet place for the wealthy gentleman, those from Over Trade who had money to spare but wanted to taste the underbelly, as it were, when they wanted some kicks but weren't brave enough for Under proper. The Buzz provided those kicks in small, hygienic doses. It was a byword for clean whores and drugs that wouldn't make you go blind, probably. A place more like a ghost town lately.

Erlat's place didn't look like much from the outside – a house like a thousand others just here. Walls dark with grime and synth, mean windows that shed a patchy light on to the walkways which were at least fairly solid. The splashes of paint were new, grouped around the door. Someone had tried, unsuccessfully, to scrub them off.

She hadn't been here long, only a couple of months since the 'Pit had opened up, but she ran a good house and word had spread. The Buzz patrons always loved to see a few new faces – as well as parts further down.

Kersan opened the door for me and let me in with a deferential smile. The waiting room was as plush as any I've seen, with rich velvets draping the walls, artful drawings, mostly of nudes with modestly placed hands and a few less modest that hinted at the business Erlat ran. Scented candles worked their magic on me and my shoulders stopped their habitual hunch against the world. Erlat's house was calm, was order, was an oasis in the shit.

"Madame is with a client," Kersan murmured. He was one of the few who knew who this face was hiding, but he was as discreet as they come. He had to be, in his job. He probably knew the grubby secrets of half of Clouds. "I'll inform her you're here as soon as she's free."

I'd like to point out at this juncture that I am not, and never have been, a client of Erlat's, not in the usual sense. Along with Lastri, she's one of the few attractive – in Erlat's case *very* attractive – women I've never tried to talk into bed. In this case, I try not to think about why Erlat is here, running a brothel.

It's not my business to judge, and I try not to. I've nothing against ladies who work this profession. But Erlat's from the 'Pit, and not just that: she was brought up in the pain factories. Erlat did this because it was better than all she'd previously known, because she was trained for it, and she's happy that now she gets a choice of her clients; that, in her words, they cherish her. She once told me she knew nothing else, no other way to be. There's something rather tragic about it, about her, that she expects so little from life and even I can't just ignore that. Added to that I liked her and if I tried talking her into bed I'd screw it up at some point and she'd want to strangle me and, so, well, I haven't tried.

It wasn't long before Kersan ushered me into her room. She'd managed to salvage a fair bit of stuff from her old place: the lounger, the bed that looked like it was made for six. The bath. Ah, the bath – until I went to the 'Pit I'd never experienced the luxury. Now I was becoming addicted, especially as my own living arrangements currently meant I was sleeping on the sofa behind my desk. The best I managed there was a quick sluice in the sink, but Erlat's bath was a thing of beauty. Shaped like a large barrel, it came up to my chest, deep enough to sink right in.

The deal, unspoken but real in my mind, was this: I got a bath and Erlat to help me untangle my thoughts, tell me what an arse I was. Afterwards, we talked and she could be herself. No pretence of seduction except when she teased, no smooth talk and practised wiggles. Instead, I did my best to make her laugh, though it always seemed to end up being at my expense. I didn't mind – I liked to hear her laugh, to know that for a few moments she'd forgotten why she was here, why she felt she knew nothing else. Besides, she helped keep my rampant ego in check and my sanity on this side of lost. I never heard the black in Erlat's house.

Erlat was a sight to make a grown man believe. I'm not sure in what, but she made me believe in all sorts of things. I'm not certain how old she was – come to think of it, neither was she – but she had a serene poise that came from seeing the very darkest of what life had to offer, straightening her shoulders and bearing it with grace.

The face of a young woman, maybe eighteen or twenty, with smooth skin and a mouth that seemed built to laugh, especially at me, and most especially when she was making me blush. And eyes that had seen far more than a girl her age should. There was something about Erlat that always twisted my gut a little, put me off balance. Not that she was a Downsider, or that she'd once worn brands. Not that she ran a brothel either – hell, brothels are some of my favourite places. I couldn't be sure what it was, only that it happened.

She was dressed today in a green robe that skimmed the floor, but was split up the side to give enticing glimpses of a smooth thigh that I tried not to notice. Her dark hair was in its usual elegant coil at the nape of her neck, showing off the angles of her face to perfection. We'd gone past the stage when she thought she needed to be someone else, smooth like a precious stone, polished and impenetrable – her professional persona – with me, and I could be myself with her, too. Perhaps that was what I didn't want to screw up by jumping her.

"Starting to smell, are we?" she asked with a raised eyebrow.

"Stink like anything."

Her nose wrinkled in a delicate show of faux-disgust. "I can tell. Off you go then."

She didn't turn away when I started to undress, but stared at me with a frankness that made me blush. Again. Erlat's the only person alive who can make me blush.

She laughed at me, and made a show of turning her back. "You're such a prude, Rojan. Are you sure you don't want company in your bath?"

I got out of my clothes quick before she turned back again – a trick she tried every time, a game she liked to play with me. I slid into the water just in time. "Quite sure, thanks."

83

As usual, the water felt hot enough actually to peel off skin. I dangled my bad hand over the side and shut my eyes. Or tried to. I kept seeing dead bodies, dead boys.

Erlat's hands on my shoulders jerked me out of my thoughts. Her fingers kneaded the muscles there, forced them to loosen. She didn't usually stay – she normally left me to my bath and we talked after. This time, though, her hands were welcome.

"What is it?" she asked. "Still mooning over a woman you hardly know, like a teenage boy? I told you, I could make you forget her. On the house, too. Oh, the things I could show you. I could ruin you for other women."

She laughed at the way my shoulders tensed up again under her hands. She loved to tease me about the fact that I wouldn't take her up on her offer. At least it stopped me brooding, which was, of course, exactly why she said it.

"So what is it then?"

I often wondered if Erlat didn't have a little magic of her own. She always knew when something was on my mind, and always seemed to know the best thing to do, or say, how to tease me till I spilled it out. It was easy just to let it all out, tell her all the thoughts that were plaguing me while she soothed and kneaded. Damn, but she was good.

"So what are you going to do about it?"

"I don't know yet. I need to concentrate on getting the power back on, but five days isn't going to be anywhere near long enough to get the generator going, and I'm not sure I'm going to last that long. And these boys dying – we need to catch whoever's doing it, or there won't be a city left to save, not once everything kicks off. But I came here first because I wanted to tell you to be careful. All of you here."

There: I had admitted it. That was why I'd come, a confession that didn't come easily, wouldn't have come at all if it had been anyone else. Erlat's house wasn't just full of working girls; it was a refuge for all sorts of waifs and strays, mostly Little Whores who didn't have anywhere else safe to be. I thought back to the new splodges of paint around her door. "More careful. Maybe shut up shop for a while. That riot outside the temple was just the start."

A thumb pressed right on a nerve. It didn't hurt but it did make my arm spasm so that my good hand splashed about in the water to no command of mine. "I don't need you to tell me how to run my business, mister playboy fancy pants mage. I've weathered worse than a bit of paint and I don't need you to play the dashing hero."

I sat up in the bath and turned to face her, splashing water over her best rug. "I know that. Just be careful, all right? Please?"

Her look was brittle, sharp, as if she was about to say something caustic, a look I'd never seen on her before. I had no idea why what I'd said had upset her. Whatever was on her mind, she didn't say it. She didn't say anything else at all, not even to tease, which bothered me all the way to the office.

I kept to the edge of the buildings as I hurried along the

rickety walkway towards the office, my coat collar flipped up against the drizzle that dripped from every eave for fifty or more levels above me. It was heading towards dusk somewhere up there, but the only way to tell down here was a chill in the air as the sun left. A hint of the winter that was fast approaching.

Dendal was still in his corner, scratching away with a pen by the light of his candles. A comforting sight, familiar, so that I could almost imagine that the last weeks hadn't happened. I patted Griswald's moth-eaten head and fell into my chair.

I shook my head and tried to shake the weariness from me and the growing fear that I was going to lose my shit, any day now. Fall right in and never come back. Maybe take out some part of the city when I went – Top of the World, perhaps, or Clouds. Then Under could see the sun again with the added bonus that up there was where all the Ministry men lived. I could make them have to live in No-Hope. It sounded very tempting.

"You can do this, Rojan." Dendal's soft, papery voice right by my ear.

I fell out of the chair and my heart near enough hammered through my ribs. "Namrat's fucking balls, Dendal, stop doing that!"

He stood looking down at me as I picked myself up, his hair a wispy cloud around his head. Back from the fairies for once, I could tell by the sharpness of his gaze. And the fact he'd got my name right.

He sat in the wonky chair on the other side of the desk. "Well, you can. We'll find enough mages, power up the city. That's what the Goddess wants us to do, and she's given us what we need to do it. That's why she sent you to me all that time ago, for all this."

His mouth set in a determined line and his watery eyes were certain.

Again, I wished that I could believe like that, that I could be so sure. "I hope so, Dendal, I really do." But hope was hard to come by.

"Told you before, you need a little faith, a bit of belief."

"And I told you—" I didn't repeat myself, because I didn't think I believed in all those things any more. Except the part about not crossing the Ministry, and I can talk *almost* any woman alive into bed if I put my mind to it. The *almost* is the real kicker.

Anyway, we had more pressing problems such as piss all power and not much time to find it in. A pain-mage who could have really helped, the same fucked-up sort of boy I'd once been, was dead with no chance of unfucking himself, and this pain-mage, me, was too strung out to be much good despite Erlat's massage. Oh, yes, and I needed to stop a serial killer before the city exploded in righteous indignation. "The boy was murdered."

Dendal muttered a prayer, the usual bullshit about how the boy would have a nice time now he was dead. I resisted the urge to say if the Goddess was so nice, how come we all lived in a shithole having shit lives? Couldn't we have a bit of heaven before we died? Maybe some nice food rather than the reconstituted grey mush that seemed to be all we ever got. I'd have sold my soul, yes even worshipped the Goddess, for another taste of the bacon I'd only ever seen in the 'Pit and which had disappeared like smoke once we'd opened that 'Pit up. Disappeared straight into the guts of the Ministry men up in Clouds and Top of the World, I had no doubt.

But Dendal believed, and I owed him a lot, so I kept my mouth shut on the bitter bile that threatened.

"It's all part of the same thing," Dendal said after a moment. "The murders, the power. But you can do it. I know you can."

He frowned in deep thought, and I had to wonder if he *knew* this. Part of his magic, his Minor, was just . . . knowing things sometimes. Not very useful things usually, like what colour socks someone was wearing. Did he know it, or was he just guessing like I was? Asking him wasn't much use, because he'd just shrug and change the subject.

"Can I do it in time?"

He smiled, all beatific and angelic so it made me sick. "If the Goddess wills it. I know it burns you, I know. I've always known that about you, that you aren't who you pretend to be." He held up a hand to stop my sharp retort and I found myself wishing the fairies would come and take him away to play again. He's not here in mind and spirit very often, our Dendal, but when he is, it's uncomfortable for everyone else.

He sees too much truth. Maybe that's why he's away so much – there's only so much truth one brain can handle.

He opened his mouth to say something else, and I steeled myself for a small sermon on self-belief or the Goddess or possibly something about controlling myself, my magic – he's very big on that, is our Dendal – when it came.

It started off small, a whooshing noise that crept up on us as we talked. What stopped Dendal mid-sermon was the sound of glass shattering, the muted roar of a thousand pissed-off people that, with that smash, grew to a scream, a howl.

While Dendal twisted a finger, drew on his magic, I ran to the window and pressed my face against the glass. Light greeted me, in a street that had rarely known it. The light of fire, of half the buildings in the street ablaze or just now catching, sending whirls of embers and smoke upwards, a prayer to the Ministry.

"Another murder," Dendal said behind me. "And a guard murdered in return. There's—"

I turned from the window and made a grab for him. His eyes were shut so he didn't see what I'd seen. "There's no time for that, because there's a mob out there baying for blood too."

Something shattered against the door and I wished, not for the first time, that Dendal hadn't won the argument about the sign. The baying mob were Downsiders mostly, with a powerful hatred of mages more than likely. Upsiders wouldn't have been much better. Guards and fear and confusion had mostly kept them from us up till now, but this had tipped them over into not giving a crap about any of that.

Another thud on the door, a whoomph of flames and a senseless, formless screaming outside. This was past just a murder, or even a dozen murders. This was all their fears spilling out into hate, one that might ignite the whole city – Upsiders had plenty of hate to let loose, too, and I didn't fancy any Ministry man's chances down here today.

I didn't fancy our chances much either, unless we got out, right now. The word mage was all over the front door and that would be enough for many of those people out there to try to murder these people in here. I kept a tight hold of Dendal and bunched my bad hand.

"Rojan, no—"

I didn't reply, I couldn't. Words were beyond me. I'm pretty sure I fell, and that Dendal held me up. I held an image in my head, the safest place I could think of. The pain room. Hardly anyone even knew it was there, and it was buried beyond locked doors and some out-of-uniform Specials who lurked in the street outside. Besides, anyone would have to get through Dwarf and his lab. I wouldn't have tried it, even with a mob at my back. Dwarf's contraptions were his babies, and he'd defend them as viciously as any mother.

I landed on my knees and threw up all over the floor. Dendal helped me up and on to a chair. I looked down at my hand, my poor hand. I was going to lose it if I kept this up, but that wouldn't be a problem because I was pretty sure my sanity would be way ahead of it.

"Rojan, is the generator supposed to look like that?"

With the sound of rioting echoing outside – screams, shouts, calls to "murder the bastards!", though they were vague on which particular bastards they wanted murdering – I ground the heel of my good hand into an eye, tried to grind a bit of reality back into my head and looked over at the generator, our hope.

Our hope, the city's hope for power, for warmth and light and food and not getting fucked over by our neighbourly Storad and Mishans, lay black and smoking, surrounded by a thousand little cogs and other bits of metal I had no name for. I blinked hard, hoping it was just my eyes, but it was still the same when I looked again. That's when I noticed the rest of it – the dented door off its hinges, the smashed glass all over the floor mingled with tiny cogs. The pool of blood the other side of the doorway.

I made myself get up and look though my heart was telling me to run, far away, this wasn't my problem, not really, and if I looked I'd be lost. I didn't want to look, to know, but I had to. The first thing I saw was a pair of feet, Dwarf's boots sticky with blood. Then his body, the throat slashed back to the spine, his face more a mess now than it had ever been. I couldn't seem to move for what felt like for ever, until my brain managed to garble out a single coherent thought.

I stared around his lab wildly, taken by panic. Lise, she should be in here somewhere – she was hardly ever anywhere else. Bloody footprints led away from Dwarf's body and I followed them, calling for her with a voice I didn't recognise.

The surgical precision of the damage didn't register then – that only came later. It was eerie nonetheless. Many of Dwarf's contraptions were intact or merely removed in one piece but everything, *everything* that we'd been working on for power, all the gizmos that he'd used to try to magnify the magic, to integrate into the generator, was either gone or lay in bits. Smashed, twisted, ruined bits. Right then, I didn't care.

"Lise!"

She was here, I knew it. I had a bit of juice left, and I used it. There, that big cabinet in the corner. I tried not to see the bloody handprint on the handle and wrenched it open.

Once again, I was on my knees, and wishing, wishing hard that I believed in a goddess, a god, anything, so that I could pray. Instead I swore at Namrat, told him to stay the fuck away from my sister. Even I have to believe in Death, but that didn't mean I had to let him in.

Her dark hair was matted with blood, her skin pale and clammy, but she was breathing. Just.

Her and Dwarf had been the hope, not the generator. Their brains, their way with contraptions, Lise's alchemical genius, the way she instinctively knew how to harness electricity, *that* had been our hope.

I picked her up as gently as I could, laid her on my lap and checked her over. A sodding great lump on the side of her head with accompanying cut and blood. Blood leaking out of her nose and ears, too, and even I knew that for a bad sign. Another cut on her throat, a slash gone awry it looked like to me. Someone had aimed to do to her what they'd done to Dwarf, but hadn't quite managed it, disturbed by me and Dendal turning up perhaps. Still, it was bad enough. Lise was losing more blood by the second.

Dendal shuffled his feet behind me. "Here, I brought this."

The first aid kit from the pain room. Bandaging someone when only one of your hands works is tough, believe me, but Dendal helped more than he hindered for once and at least we managed to stop the throat wound bleeding. Lise never stirred, never made a sound, and I kept checking she was breathing, roughly every thirty heartbeats or so.

"We need to get her to the hospital." Yeah, obvious, but I wasn't thinking straight at that point. Someone trying to murder your sister will do that to you.

I went to bunch my hand again, wondered if this would be the time I lost it, when I let go of the faint thread keeping me here and let myself fall into the black. If Lise ... I hesitated to think the word "died". If Lise went, I didn't have much left to hold me here.

That's when Dendal came into his own. He'd certainly picked the right few hours to be in reality. His grip on my wrist was surprisingly firm.

"No, Rojan."

I tried to shake him off, but the old fart was stronger than he looked. "Yes, Dendal. Look, she has to get to the hospital. There's a riot going on outside in case you hadn't noticed, and this is the only way to get her there safely."

His smile was infuriatingly benign, as though I was some little kid he was indulging. "Look out of the window."

"What?" For a moment, I thought he'd gone back to playing with his fairies, but I glanced up at the window and saw instantly what he meant.

Dwarf's lab was pretty high up and it had a reasonably unimpeded view of parts of Trade and Heights and the underside of Clouds. It even got some sun, an hour or so a day, which was luxury.

No sun came through the windows now, no moon or stars. The hulking warehouses and factories of Trade were limned in firelight as No-Hope-Shitty burnt. People ran along swaying walkways, dark figures against orange flames. A phalanx of what I could only assume were guards tried their best to douse the buildings, under a steady stream of projectiles from above. A gang of rioters were working their way along the street below us, methodically breaking every window. A slim figure, hooded and indistinct, ran out of this building and headed for the stairwell that led straight down. All I could make out was the swirl of a dark cape.

But the part that made me see Dendal was right stood straight ahead, over the backs of a row of factories. The Sacred Goddess Hospital, a bright new beacon of Ministry benevolence, was ablaze. Not smouldering; the fire was gutting it, ripping through it like a knife through a throat. If I'd not listened, if Dendal hadn't stopped me, I'd have appeared right in the middle of it.

Sacred Goddess was the only hospital that I'd trust enough with my sister. All the ones further down were for those with little hope and less money, run by scammers, madmen or plain quacks. All the ones further up – I needed to know where, precisely, and I didn't. Not that they'd have let us stay. We'd be thrown out for being from Under faster than Dendal could say fairy.

Any doctoring that needed doing, we were going to have to do it. Only I'm fairly crap at even basic first aid past what I needed to know for repairing after a spell and Dendal – yeah, well, Dendal isn't someone I'd trust with a pair of scissors.

"If I go to get someone, will you promise me you'll look after her?" I asked. "No wandering off in your own head?"

He huffed, affronted. "Of course!"

It would have to do. I couldn't risk my magic to get me there – for all I knew where I needed to go was on fire too – so I used the rather more mundane door.

I took a look back as I shut it. Our hope, the city's hope. My sister. My sister in the care of Dendal. We were all depending on a man who spent ninety-nine days out of a hundred singing happy songs and playing with sparkly fairies in his head.

We were so screwed it was almost funny.

Chapter Six

It wasn't far, almost straight down twenty levels, but that trip is one I try not to remember. Flames and heat, smoke and embers, screaming men full of hate, screaming children full of fear. Wondering whether the superstructure would hold up. They'd built for times such as these, long ago, before Ministry had taken over. A solid backbone of the city that was supposed to hold up against fire, against mages going batshit crazy, against alchemists playing with black powder and blowing up parts of the city and themselves on a regular basis. It'd worked, mostly. When it didn't, it failed spectacularly, as it had over in the Slump.

That had been a better part of the city once, where the demi-rich used to live and stare up at Clouds and wish they were rich enough – or magic enough – to live there. Alchemists, doctors, those sorts of people. A quiet and reasonably non-shitty part of the city. Until a mage had, almost inevitably, gone totally off his tree in the incident that led to us being banned.

Now the Slump was a mess of girders and stone, great fat splinters as big as trees, mingled with dust and ghosts. It was downmarket even for rats. I tried very hard not to think about the Slump as I hurried.

Not thinking about that meant I thought about other things, like the riot around me. After the first flush of hatred, things seemed to have settled down into a more subdued grudge match and the further down I got, the quieter it got. If you were poor enough to live this far down, energy was for other people and the unrest above hadn't reached here. Yet. It would.

I hurried as best I could, keeping to the shadows out of anyone's way, and it wasn't long before I stopped outside the door to my old rooms. The passageway still smelled of old socks and cabbage. This was home, or had been. I had no home now, except the sofa behind the desk at the office. I'd given these rooms away.

Pasha answered on the third knock, still buttoning his shirt, his hair awry and his face sheened with sweat. His monkey face screwed into a scowl. "It's a hell of a time for a social call."

The door to the bedroom was ajar and I caught a glimpse of Jake's naked back as she lay on the bed, of the scars that marked her, inside and out. Pasha moved to block the view, and I wondered whether she was still phobic about being touched or whether Pasha was working on that. Whether perhaps I'd interrupted him working on that.

"Well?"

I pulled myself together and gave myself a mental cold bucket of water to the groin. "Haven't you been listening?"

"What? We were – I was listening to what I wanted to."

He opened the door wider, and shut the door to the bedroom with his foot. The main room was bigger than I remembered, maybe because they had bugger all to fill it with. At least they'd managed to clear off the globs of paint that a couple of vengeful exes had decorated it with.

The remains of a meal lay on the table with a guttering candle in between the plates and I caught a hint of perfume and the glimpse of a shirt dropped carelessly on the floor by the bedroom door. Ah. Well, Pasha was going to have to wait a while longer to work on it, a fact which gave me a perverse and guilty satisfaction. Really, I should grow the fuck up.

I shut the door behind me. "Listen," was all I said.

He stared at me for a moment, frowning, then he shrugged and twisted a finger out of its socket. It didn't take him longer than about three seconds.

"Shit – what the hell happened?"

"Another murder. Then someone murdered a guard back. They got into the lab and . . ."

I couldn't bring myself to say it, but I didn't need to with Pasha – he lifted the words right out of my head. Probably lifted a few I'd rather he hadn't, too, but I put on a brazen front about that. "Lise – the only decent hospital I could get her into is on fire and she needs help. You're the only person I could think of." Not strictly true; I knew a few nurses, very well indeed. Sadly they also knew me well enough that they'd all cheerfully strangle me.

Pasha was already rummaging in a cupboard and he came up with a familiar box. He'd spent a lot of time stitching Jake back up after the Death Matches and, if nothing else, he was damned good at looking after people. There were a few other bits and bobs in the box that might come in handy, too, painkillers for starters. I was quite tempted to ask for some myself, just to make it all go away, the black tatters on the edge of my vision, the creeping voice telling me how wonderful it would be . . .

Jake appeared in the doorway, fully dressed and all business, buckling on her swords. A look passed between them, that old feeling of unsaid words being spoken, of the invisible string that bound them together.

"We're walking," Pasha said to me before I could suggest a quick spell. I think he'd seen a lot more than I'd thought in my head. "And bad news like Jake soon gets around."

Good, because maybe that would help us through quicker. I couldn't help jiggling, wanting to run, but it would be useless – and dangerous. A running man in a riot is a target for everyone, but especially guards. We wouldn't do Lise any good if we were arrested, or mobbed.

By the time we'd gone up two levels, I was glad Jake was

with us for more than something nice to look at. The gangs had moved down now. There was a lot of furtive running in and out of doorways and more and more came to swell the angry numbers clotting in lumps on the walkways. A lot of Downsiders in this area. Some of them had crude torches made from whatever wood they'd been able to find and the flickering orange glow made faces demented in the dark.

Jake stalked towards them like a tiger and they fell back, muttering, to let us past. A legend she'd been in the 'Pit, a Death Matcher like no other, and while they didn't know it'd mostly been faked, it didn't matter because, when cornered, Jake fought like Namrat himself and her swords were for more than show. Especially now, when anger radiated off her like a cloud and her hands were twitching on the hilts of those swords. Angry at the world and everything in it – in other circumstances, she'd have been one of the mob, would have been leading them, no doubt.

My back prickled when the mob turned and followed us, and I imagined the stab of a knife, the thud of something big and heavy on the back of my head. Felt the built-up hate with a focus now. It seemed to charge the air like Lise's electricity.

At the end of a walkway so blackened by fire I kept imagining it was turned to ash and would drop us, screaming, into the yawning drop underneath, stood another group. Upsiders this time, yet with the same look of hate, the same charge of it in the air around them.

We were dead, I was sure of it, due to be stomped flat

between two snorting, charging opponents. I was already curling my hand with a groan, and trying to pretend I didn't hear the voice, didn't want what it offered, when the priest appeared.

Guinto simply stepped forward from out of a darkened, smouldering doorway, for all the world as though he was taking a stroll. His gentle smile seemed to radiate goodwill, to reach inside and make you want to be good to your fellow man. I resisted the urge – I've been a cynic too long to suddenly start thinking everyone is nice and the world is a fluffy, lovely place when patently this part at least is a shithole. Cynicism is harder to give up than drugs and women put together. Instead I wondered how in hell he was doing it and realised it didn't matter, because he was and I might live to the end of the day, which is always a bonus.

The effect on the mobs was dramatic – they lowered torches and clubs and a few even shuffled their feet like naughty schoolchildren.

Jake hesitated and I could see it play out across her face, in the clench of her jaw and the way her eyes held Guinto's. Anger fighting with piety, with wanting the Goddess to look on her kindly, to love her as the mages had always told her the Goddess wouldn't because of what she was. To lay about with her swords at every injustice aimed at Downsiders, or to take what Guinto was offering? Piety, a need for the Goddess's acceptance, won, but only just and her swords were still ready because the Downside Goddess was all about fighting.

Jake was the first to go forward and ask for Guinto's bless-ing, and then the mobs became not mobs, but people again. Clubs were surreptitiously dropped, and the torches lost their menace.

"That's one hell of a trick," I said and Pasha shot me a vicious look.

"No trick. It's just that we believe something you can't see, won't see."

'Pity rolled off him in waves and made me want to smack him a good one round the chops. 'Pity from Pasha, some screwed-up Downsider who had everything I wanted, and who I liked anyway, despite myself. Hating him would be like kicking a puppy. So instead I snapped out, "We don't have time to play with imaginary friends. *Lise* doesn't have time."

He looked like he was about to snap something back, but he bit down on it and glanced at Jake. The Downsiders were following her lead, following something real and sub-stantial from their old lives. The 'Pit had been full of misery and pain, but at least that was what they knew and they found comfort in the familiar. Guinto leant over and whis-pered in her ear and she nodded before she began talking quietly to the Downsiders. She flicked a meaningful glance at Pasha.

My feet were getting jittery and I kept seeing flashes of Lise, bloodied and barely breathing. All we had left, all Mahala had left. Pretty much all I had, too. "Pasha—"

He held up a hand, as though he was trying to hear

something, then nodded. When he spoke, I realised what Jake had done, what she'd shoved down her constant anger for. "I'm going. I'll be quick, I promise. Guinto's told her we can take Lise to his temple – he's got rooms there, and a couple of his parishioners are nurses. You stay and look after Jake."

Look after Jake? It almost made me laugh; she could kill me as soon as blink. Yet the look on Pasha's face was serious, and I knew that wasn't what he'd meant. "But Lise—"

"I've already spoken to Dendal. She's pale, but breathing steadily. He's got the bleeding stopped. We'll get her to the temple, it's not far from the lab. I've sent Dog to check on Erlat, but I don't think the fires got that far from what I can hear. Please, stay. It's all Downsiders between here and the lab, all as full of hate as these were a few minutes ago, I can hear them." He paused to lick at lips stiff with anger, and I wondered how much he could hear, and whether he agreed with them. "Look, an Upsider, in that lot . . . you'd be more danger than safety to her, and you're in no state to be trying any more magic and changing how you look. You know I'm right about that. Keep an eye on Jake for me."

He didn't say it, in his voice or in my head, but I was pretty sure I knew what he was thinking – that I was too strung out, would only get in the way, that I might say or do something in a mob that would make it all worse. I was a liability. He was right, which didn't make it any easier to swallow. For once, though, I did swallow it, because I trusted Pasha. These last few weeks, it had been mostly me and him powering up the tubes, and sharing pain makes you share other things, even if it's never said.

"Look after Lise. I—"

I didn't need to say it. He nodded tersely and disappeared into the smoky gloom, leaving me to endure an impromptu sermon. Bastard – he'd done that on purpose, I was sure.

If I listened too hard I was going to puke and thinking about whether Pasha had got to Lise yet, whether she was going to be all right, made me come over all jittery so I took a deep breath, let it wash over me and watched Jake. Among strangers she was still brittle, the ice queen, but as a Death Matcher the Downsiders knew her, looked to her perhaps. Some of the Upsiders knew her, too, that was plain, though that was more caution concerning her swords, her anger and what drove her.

Guinto moved between the groups and something came in his wake, ripples of feel-good that had Upsider and Down looking warily, but, importantly, not angrily, at each other. After a word from Guinto, one Downsider even offered a hand to an Upsider, and it was accepted. Animosity seemed to drain from the air. Yet there was something about Guinto that made the hairs stand up on the back of my neck, something just that touch creepy. He was smooth, too damned smooth, and I never have been able to trust a man who smiles that much. Perhaps that says more about me than it does about Guinto, but I kept expecting to find out that his benevolence was a trick, a veneer to fool us all before he had everyone at each other's throats even worse than before. The old bait and switch that Ministry have used so well. I hoped not, but it wouldn't have surprised me.

"Amazing how he does it, isn't it?" The soft voice startled me from my thoughts. The girl from the temple, looking even more angelic and ethereal today in a soft white dress that flowed and clung and made some very naughty thoughts pop into my head. I know I'd sworn off women only the day before but, hell, promises are made to be broken, especially given that my chances with Jake were less than bugger all.

A guy's got to take his fun when he can, right?

Besides, I seriously needed some distraction from thinking about Lise. There's nothing like a pretty woman to distract me from something, anything, so I cranked up the smile. "Nowhere near as astonishing as you look in that dress." Cheesy, yes, but that kind of stuff really works if you sound like you mean it, and I always do mean it. That's my trouble.

It worked this time, too, because she blushed prettily and tried to hide a smile behind her hand.

I took the other, kissed the back of her fingers the old-fashioned way, and her blush deepened. 'A pleasure, I'm sure. I'm—"

"Maki, yes, I know. I've heard a lot about you. None of it good. My father says you're a terror with women, but he hopes to lure you to the way of the Goddess."

Good luck to him with that. At least she was helping take my mind off Pasha, whether he'd got there yet, whether Lise was still alive . . . I wanted to grab Jake and run after Pasha, but I'd be worse than useless in the mobs above, no real help to Lise, and the girl's hand on my arm felt good. It kept me there, for now, that and a sense of something wrong down here, somewhere. Something subtle, but there.

I might not be able to rummage in people's heads like Pasha, but there are some fringe perks to being a mage. My perk was telling me I needed to stay, find out what was lurking underneath here, that it would help later. Help find whoever had done that to Lise and Dwarf. Dendal had said, and I believed him, that all of this was linked. Getting the power back on, the boys being murdered. A riot had kicked off over the last of those, and now here was Guinto soothing it all like he had magic of his own.

Or maybe that was just my excuse for a quick flirt. Guinto repelled and fascinated me in equal measure, and anything I could find out about him would perhaps help stop the creeping up my back every time I looked at him.

"Your father?"

"Guinto. Adopted, of course," she said, probably because I looked sceptical. He was an Upsider through and through and there was no doubting she'd come from the 'Pit. "I'm one of his good deeds. Abeya."

"Charmed, I'm sure." See, I can be nice, too, when I want. Usually only when I've got a chance with a pretty woman smiling at me, true, but it's better than nothing and it kept my mind off everything else.

I would have followed up with something better – resolutions be damned – but Guinto came and put rather a crimp on the moment. A disapproving priest will do that to flirting.

He eyed me somewhat suspiciously but with a hint of challenge, as though I was a dare, something for him to overcome. There was something else, too, something that I'd tried to pretend I hadn't seen in his temple, in these mobsters-turned-people by his smile. Something that I couldn't share, that seemed fake to me, and anyway was certainly crushed by these riots. Hope. As far as I'm concerned hope is a rude word.

Guinto inclined his head in a paternal fashion that irked me no end and held an arm out to indicate the walkway and stairwell. I glanced round to Jake, and she was by my elbow. Close enough to touch and worlds away, but when she nodded I grudgingly followed Guinto.

He smoothed the way through crowds of angry Downsiders in a manner that had me almost admiring him. It certainly saved my backside, if some of the looks were anything to go by. I got away with a couple of spits and a few snarled not very complimentary names that made me wonder what Pasha had to put up with every day from Upsiders. With Guinto leading, passing out blessings and feel-good like crumbs for birds and Jake watching my back, it didn't take us long to get to his temple a few levels under the pain lab.

He led us through the main temple, though he had to stop every few paces as someone else clasped his hand, asked for a blessing, thanked him. Upsiders and Downsiders both. He glad-handed them, blessed them, smiled over them, and finally we were through to the rooms at the back.

A woman ran up to him and whispered in his ear. He thanked her before she darted off again. Blood stained the cuffs of her crisp shirt, making my heart stutter.

"Lise? Is she . . ."

A kindly smile that I didn't believe for a heartbeat, and then Guinto said, "She's steady. You can't see her just yet, they're still working on her, but she's out of immediate danger. Please, let me be the gracious host."

I'll give him this: his room was spartan in a way Ministry's never were. No luxurious carpets, no expensive wines in crystal decanters, no candles scented with herbs instead of the fish-guts smell of a rend-nut lamp, no grinding wealth and status into the faces of the poor bastards who lived down here. Whitewashed walls, a wooden floor polished to gleaming, a simple dark wood desk. I bet *he* didn't argue with his desk. Not Guinto the tranquil, who looked like nothing short of the end of the world would faze him, and maybe not even that.

There's a lot I could say about Guinto, but while I don't believe and never will, his faith was . . . reassuring. The solidity of his belief was like one of the safety nets under the walkways for the fallers and jumpers; I'd never had need of it, or wanted to, but it was nice to know it was there for those that did. Of course, those nets failed pretty often. So did the priests the Ministry sent down here.

He sat behind the desk and smoothed his hands over the worn wood. "A lot of priests have sat here before me, and will after me. The Goddess is our link to each other."

I refrained from mentioning that his predecessor in this particular temple had been so depressed at the state of things Under that he'd become a Rapture addict and thrown himself off a walkway. One of the better ones, he'd been, the ones who hadn't a clue how bad it really was till they got here. The priest before that used to steal all the alms and spend it on working girls, and he was a better one, too, at least compared to the one before him. Didn't seem polite to bring it up somehow. Especially given the way Abeya was looking at me.

Time for rule five. I have my own carefully honed set of rules that keep me in one piece. Rule one states mine is not to do and die, mine is to do the job and take the cash. Rule two is don't mess with Ministry unless you like being dead. Among others, rule five states always look respectable in front of their relatives.

Given that, what Guinto actually said threw me: "I believe we may have got you here under false pretences."

"What? Lise—"

"Is, as I said, steady and being looked after perfectly well by Pasha and one of my worshippers who is also a nurse. But this, you turning up, is a message from the Goddess, I think. You find things out, so I hear. So do I, as a priest. People tell me things, and, besides, Lise is a frequent visitor so naturally I was concerned when Jake told me what had happened. That isn't quite what I meant, though it was a convenient excuse to talk to you without any suspicion falling on me. Dendal tells me you find people, and Jake here seems to believe in you, despite rather . . . contrary reports."

"Contrary?" Actually, I kind of liked that.

Guinto's smile set to work again, but it was lost on me. "Yesterday was the first time I've seen you in a temple."

"Are you going to turn me in?"

"No, no. I believe faith should be willing, not forced. Well, we have faith aplenty," his mouth said, though I'm pretty sure I saw a "we'll convert you yet" in his eyes. "What we don't have is an answer."

"To what?" Though I had one of those sinking feelings I knew, and that it would involve me being responsible and shit. And also that I'd do it, purely because of how Jake had recommended me, how she was looking at me. Time to get that tattoo artist on standby for my forehead. Maybe it should just read "Sucker".

"You know what started tonight's unpleasantness? What started the unrest that led ultimately to your sister's injuries?"

I had my own suspicions about what had happened to Lise, and it wasn't rioters, but I let that slide for now. "The murders."

"Indeed. I want you to find the murderer."

"Listen, Father—"

"Please, call me Guinto. I'm Father only to those who believe."

I wasn't going down that road. There are limits. "Father, don't you think that if I had any idea how to track them, I would have by now?"

The laugh was genuine, I was sure. A full-throated guffaw that made Jake frown and fiddle with her swords.

"No, I don't," Guinto said when his laughter subsided. "But maybe you'll be more inclined when you hear everything."

"Inclination isn't the problem." It wasn't either – I was already trying to find out who this killer was, though I'd be damned if I'd tell Guinto that. I had other pressing things to contemplate, too, like Perak pleading with me to get the power going, quick, and the two people who could help the best were now dead or injured. Which left me with some nasty, nasty choices. Carry on as we were, which meant the Storad and the Mishans walking right on in, which didn't appeal. Screwing as much magic out of as many mages as we could find, which might get the power going but would probably mean several lunatic mages, me included. Not much better. Or the third option, which wasn't even an option – carry on where my father had left off and start torturing people. I felt grubby even thinking it.

Jake nudged me with the hilt of a sword and I realised Guinto had said something.

"These aren't random murders," he said again. "I don't think it's only someone taking things out on Downsiders. Someone is purposefully trying to stir up trouble. I'm sure of it."

Which had been along the line of my own, and Dench's, thoughts. The only question was: "Why?"

Guinto shrugged elegantly. "I'm not certain, but think on it. With each murder, even the 'unofficial' ones that not many Upsiders know about, with each one, unrest grows, until this one. This explosion of hatred – it was waiting to happen, and so someone *made* it happen. On purpose. Yet what does it gain anyone? Who knows? Maybe . . . " He shut his eyes with a pained look, and when he opened them it seemed as though he was making a confession that ate his soul. "Maybe even the Ministry, may the Goddess forgive me. I can – well, I can get into Ministry in a way you can't, find out what people are saying that even Perak – *especially* Perak – wouldn't know."

Even I, with my ingrained hatred of everything Ministry, couldn't quite see how they'd benefit from wholesale riot, and I said so. "Maybe you're right, though I don't know why. Besides, you're forgetting something. I can't find one person in a city just like that. I need something to focus on. Dench couldn't find me anything, and without that . . . " I can find people I know well without a prop, but a random somebody? I need something of theirs to focus on, something to link me to them.

"We thought, well, Dendal thought—" What was it with Dendal being coherent all of a sudden? And landing me right in it, too? Just when you want him to be playing fairy hide and seek, he turns up lucid as you please. "Dendal thought maybe the bodies would give you something. I can arrange for the mortuary to let you have access. I often go to make a final blessing on those that have died untimely. I can get you in, and not many can give you that."

Bodies. Some of them a couple of weeks old. Oh, yeah, great. Thanks, Dendal.

"I tried it," I said. "Boy I was tracking was the one that died outside the temple."

That was when Jake sealed my fate for me. "If you'd give us a moment?" she said.

Guinto stood with a benign smile and left.

"Lise?" was all Jake had to say. "Dwarf?"

"I don't know, I really don't. It could have been rioters."

"You don't really think that," Jake said, and her voice made me jump, the force of it, the hate that had shone through every rioter we'd seen. She wasn't like me, had seen and experienced more than I'll ever want to and that means I'll never know her, not truly. Never really understand what it is that drives her. All I can do is imagine, and sympathise. It's not enough.

Her stance changed, became a challenge, a threat almost. Anger bubbled just underneath the ice of her tone. "Do you?"

What was it about her that made me want to tell the truth when my whole life had been lies?

"No, I don't." And I didn't even think it was anyone in Ministry either, or at least officially — most of them knew nothing about the lab. Someone did, though. I blinked against the recollection of Dwarf's face, of his throat cut back to the spine. Just like the others. Dendal was right, this was all linked together. The destruction of the generator put a whole new spin on that idea. Perhaps the earlier murders had been nothing but a smokescreen to cover this particular attack, and the destruction of the generator. Or, as Guinto said, to stir up unrest. Or, perhaps, both. Either way, I had to find out who was doing it and stop them, quick.

"He's offering to *help*, Rojan."

Help, from a priest. It made me shudder just to think about it, and there was something so oily about the man I couldn't quite bring myself to trust any offer of his.

"I'll try the bodies," I said. And I would, try my damn-edest. Because it was Lise, and she was all I had except a brother whose every waking moment was taken up with his office and trying to stay alive long enough to make a differ-ence, and a niece I'd spilled blood for and had never even met. Because, no matter how I try to fake it, no matter the black gloss I spin on everything, Jake's always seen through that.

I hate it when people do that.

Chapter Seven

So that was how I found myself back in the mortuary at two o'clock in the morning, freezing all my vitals bits off. I'd satisfied myself that Lise was stable – no more bleeding and she was breathing better, had a bit of colour, and Dendal had promised to sit with her. Erlat was a worry at the back of my mind, but, as Pasha had said, the flames hadn't got as far as the Buzz. Pasha had got Dog on checking anyway and, while he's mostly just a big kid in a grown-up body, I'd trust him to look after anything I valued. Especially Erlat, because he'd been hit with the same sort of arrow of infatuation that I had with Jake. If anyone would look after Erlat, would bust a gut to find her and make her safe, it was Dog. I hoped that he wouldn't need to bust a gut.

Pasha joined me on my little trip because he'd said maybe he could help, though it was more like he wanted to keep an eye on me. When they thought I wasn't looking, he and Dendal kept exchanging knowing looks.

We'd walked to the mortuary through streets that had become suddenly, eerily, silent. No lights but rend-nut oil lamps with their fetid stench wafting over us, and the occasional building that still smouldered. It hadn't only been Guinto who had quelled it; the streets were silent, but, if you looked hard, not empty. A few limp and bloodied bodies lay in doorways and across walkways. I couldn't tell if they were dead or not, or who'd made them that way. Some guards mopping up the last of the embers, and here and there, in the shadows, Specials. Every one of them with guns and a weird look to them, as though they'd been pushed too far and weren't beyond pushing back. Maybe that would be enough to keep things quiet, for now.

I halted by a notice, hastily tacked to a still-standing wall. Two notices, when I looked closer in the gloom. The first was a proclamation that Perak had – according to Dendal – issued under duress. Ministry through and through, it read:

CURFEW ENSUES. ALL PERSONS FOUND ABROAD WITHOUT GOOD REASON TO BE ARRESTED. SPECIALS GIVEN EXTRA POWERS DURING THIS STATE OF EMERGENCY.

Short, and maybe it doesn't really capture the horror, because everyone Under knew what arrested meant. It had meant a trip to the 'Pit, though that wasn't an option now. The options left weren't much better. Pissing off Ministry generally meant you got to spend a while looking for your head, in their "behave or else" form of law and order. Things had been slack of late, since Perak had taken over, but it was still there, the fear of it, in the back of people's minds. They'd lashed out under pressure, and were now regretting it under the stern boot of the Specials, who answered only to the Goddess.

The second notice was Perak's personal message, I was sure of it. It talked of calm, of tolerance, of peace. And of a reward for information leading to the murderer's arrest. It might have been more impressive if someone hadn't scrawled "Bollocks" over it in a thick black pen. We'd lived under Ministry for too long to believe it could change, except for the worse. Even I couldn't, and I knew our new Archdeacon was a good man, though beset on all sides, and maybe he wouldn't survive the experience. Few good men survived in the Ministry for long.

When we got to the mortuary, someone was waiting for us. I recognised her vaguely – I thought perhaps she'd been the nurse who'd overseen me identifying my own body. Well, it had already been identified as me. I'd just wanted to make sure the bastard was good and dead.

The mortuary itself was one of the older buildings here in Trade. Seems a funny place to put it, if you ask me, but Heights and Clouds didn't want it – they had their crypts and mausoleums and such, all nice ways to pretty up the fact that you were dead. Yet too far down would be unseemly.

Ministry's version of the Goddess said death was a good thing, to be looked forward to. Earn enough gold stars in this crappy life, you get a perfect afterlife for free! We didn't get mausoleums. We were lucky if we got cremated and sprinkled somewhere not too smelly. Mostly bodies got dumped in the Slump. Once the mortuary had finished with you.

So the mortuary sat precariously balanced between a raft of silent factories that would usually have made the floor shake, and the once glaring but now dark shops, boutiques and arcades that made up the other side of Trade.

Outside it was an ugly square block of a building, squashed between "Alchemy Pros" and "Gizmos and Gadgets" and a series of small shops above, select little boutiques selling everything the man of wealth and leisure could want or imagine, but they hadn't had much to sell lately.

Inside the mortuary wasn't much better, all blocky lines, grey walls and carpets the colour of rotting moss. Maybe mortuaries are built to be depressing. It wouldn't surprise me.

The nurse was brightly efficient in her starched white robe, her face scrubbed and shiny, her dark hair tucked into a cap as starched as the rest of her. I have, it has to be said, a weakness for nurses. Maybe a reaction to all that starch. This one looked me up and down and raised an eyebrow and a corner of her lips. As good as a flashing sign, or it would have been, to the old me. Maybe I was getting old or something, but I returned a smile that was nothing more than polite and didn't pursue it. It had only been hours since I'd sworn off women, and you have to make a bit of an effort. I'd already fallen off the wagon by flirting with Abeya.

Pasha showed our credentials, including a letter from Guinto which seemed to do the trick. The nurse looked the papers over and turned her interested gaze on Pasha. This job must have been really boring. I supposed she didn't get to meet many guys who were actually alive. Pasha disappointed her even more than I had – he didn't notice the smile beyond a quick hello and a request to see the bodies.

She huffed off down the corridor like the world's most scorned woman, leaving Pasha and me to follow, he with a confused frown as to what he'd done to offend her.

The inside of the mortuary was colder than Namrat's heart, so that our breath formed clouds in front of us and I began to worry for those more important parts of me, that shrunk, scaredy cat, into my trousers.

The nurse opened a door and led us into one of the rooms they used for "scientific study". Basically that means chopping people up to find out how or why they died. Sometimes, it's rumoured, the cause of death is being chopped up on the slab, especially if the Ministry feel you've been a naughty boy. Once they're done, and for the cases of unnatural death made their report, the bodies end up being shunted out into the Slump where any rat unlucky enough to call it his home at least has some food.

A marble slab dominated the room with a stand next to it covered in all sorts of instruments of torture, or possibly morticing, mortuarying or whatever they called it. I looked them over with some trepidation. At least one appeared to be some sort of device to twist off your bollocks. I wasn't sure I'd fancy that even after I'm dead. If the rumours were true about chopping up live naughty people, that made what I was seeing even worse. And eye-watering.

Some marble-faced drawers were set into the wall.

"Here's one," the nurse said, her voice as chilly as the slab itself. "I'll get the rest sent down, those that are left anyway. I'm pretty sure some have been Slumped."

She said it the same way I might say "I ate dinner", with a cool detachment that shivered my shoulders, and left us with the body. A boy, again, about twelve or so. Throat slashed back to his spine, obviously a Downsider. Not the boy I'd seen earlier, the one I'd been looking for as a mage, but similar enough. A boy, as I'd been once upon a time, too far away to recall with much clarity.

We both looked, but neither of us really wanted to touch him. We had to, though, if we wanted to find out anything, and these bodies were almost all we had to go on.

Pasha's face became a grimace as he twisted his finger. A gasp, a wet crack. I shut my eyes, wished I could leave this, go home, dammit. Home to women and warmth and booze and Glow lights and not knowing where they came from. I squeezed my poor fist, and fought off the voice, the siren call.

Tricky this. My two talents, my Major and Minor, were rearranging things and finding things, or more specifically people. My Major I was only just coming to grips with – rearranging my face for example, or rearranging where I was. It got Dendal quite excited, the possibilities, but I was restricted by the way it made me throw up a lot when I tried anything too ambitious. Also by the fact that the more I used it, the more that song sang in my head.

Finding people was both my Minor and a lot easier. It didn't take so much pain, I didn't throw up on my boots quite as often, and it was more useful in earning money. A city this size, with the Ministry in charge, people go missing every day. Sometimes it's not even the Ministry making them disappear – runaways, men with warrants for their arrest, or merely glad to be away from the missus, so glad they stayed away, that sort of thing. Nothing too strenuous, or dangerous. I like my arse where it is.

Of course things had got more complicated lately, not to mention risky, but finding people I could do. We'd decided our best bet on finding the murderer was to figure out who the victims had been – most of them were unidentified and Dench had made little progress on that. But we had an edge that he hadn't. We had magic, and once we knew who they were, maybe it would become clear why them instead of any number of other Downsiders. Why these ones might give us a who. There had to be a link between them and I could hazard a few guesses, but we needed to *know* because hazardous guesses don't get you very far in finding a murderer unless you're very lucky.

Yeah, this was a long shot, but it was better than the alternative, which was me trying to find the murderer using something intimately connected to him – the dead body itself – as a prop. Seeing how close and personal I need to be to my props, I really didn't fancy that, especially as I figured it had as much chance of working as me turning into a priest.

Pasha did his thing, but the frown gave away the fact that nothing much was happening. We hadn't really expected it would. Dead bodies aren't known for thinking many thoughts for Pasha to overhear.

By the boy's feet was a ragged bag, his personal effects, I assumed. I opened it up and had a rummage. The boy hadn't had much on him, or maybe he'd been rolled after he'd been killed. A tattered pair of trousers, much patched and stained. Same with the shirt, and a pair of shoes that had seen better days. Nothing in the pockets. The only item I thought might do was a chain, an old necklace with something green hanging off it. A cheapjack thing it was, probably worth less than my spit, but maybe I could use it.

The trouble was anything of his would only tell me where *he* was. Useless. I was hoping, which is usually as helpful as a piss into the wind, that someone had given him the necklace. A mother, brother, someone who would know who he'd been.

It took four bodies, I'd thrown up twice, had long since decided the floor was quite comfortable if you ignored the cold and, hey, who really *needs* two working hands, before I got anything useful. The sure and certain knowledge that the ring in my hand was connected somehow, some way, with a dank box of a room nine hundred yards down, half a mile south. Slap bang on the border of No-Hope and Boundary, which was even worse. I could hear a woman weeping, quietly, as though not to disturb anyone. Such a sad and lonely sound that whispered away from me as the black came calling.

I let the ring drop from my hand and opened my eyes, concentrating on not retching up what little was left in my stomach. *So* glad I hadn't bothered with dinner. I tried to get up, and Pasha had to help me. My hand was one big throbbing ache, a lure for the black, and even though I wasn't casting now, it still sang to me, called me through my bones.

Pasha slapped me across the brain with an internal *Hah!* and my eyes came back into focus. "Don't listen to it. Don't," he said aloud.

"No, no, all right." My voice sounded disjointed, as though I wasn't really speaking. As though I wasn't really present. I looked down at my hand, expecting to see I was half here and half there, in that room with the weeping woman, that I'd begun rearranging things without noticing, but I looked pretty solid. More than could be said for my brain. Just fall in, that's all, just fall in and it will all go away, all your fears, all this responsibility, all these people depending on you will disappear . . .

I staggered with the force of it, the desperate want.

"Stop it!" Pasha's voice whipped in my ears and in my head. When I looked at him, his monkey face was panicked. "Stop, please. You know it's not the answer. And if you fall in – I'm not sure I can get you out."

His hand shook on my shoulder and we stared at each other. He'd never mentioned it since, and neither had I, hadn't even wanted to think about it, how I'd followed him into his black, into his own personal heaven and hell. How I'd brought him back, for her. He'd tried to thank me once and I'd told him to shut up. I'd saved him, condemned a whole city for her, for Jake and for a small girl who I'd still not met, my own niece who like most everyone else thought I was dead. Perak said she prayed to the Goddess every night to keep me safe in heaven, laid flowers at the feet of the saints and martyrs for me, and that ate at me in ways I can't even begin to describe.

"Rojan—"

"Shut up, shut up, shut up!" I didn't want to hear it, any of it. He'd been rummaging in my thoughts, I knew that now, but I didn't want to talk about it. All the while it was in my own head I could shut it out, pretend it wasn't there. I'd killed us all as sure as if I'd put a gun to each and every head in the city, and a small girl prayed that I was safe in heaven.

"I know where to go," I said, hoping the change of subject would throw him. Fat chance. "I know where he came from, who misses him."

"And we'll go." His voice was soft with pity, more than I could bear. "In the morning. When was the last time you slept?"

"Keep out of my head," I snapped, but it was too late. He knew, I could tell by his face.

"You've been going to the pain room a lot more than you should, haven't you?"

"No." I wasn't about to admit it, even if he knew. I had to keep some shred of my old self intact, and the old Rojan would have died before admitting to anything of the sort. He would have laughed, probably, said something short and cynically pithy, but I wasn't laughing today and pithy was beyond me. "Pasha, we have to go now, all right? The sooner the better. These murders won't solve themselves, and if they don't get solved . . . then the Storad and Mishans will get to have the smoking remains of this city, for all the good it does them."

"And since when did Rojan care about that? About anything but women and booze and cash?"

I glared at him. "Why do you always have to be so fucking right?"

His smile was grim and strained as he steered me towards the door. "It's easy when you can see the answer in someone's head. You're doing no one any good like this. I'm under strict instruction from Dendal that you get some sleep before the black takes you. If it does when you're like this, I don't think even he could pull you out. *I* will go and find this place, find out about our boy. Me and Jake, any Downsider will at least listen to her. And, yes, I can see where it is in your head."

The nurse turfed us out on to the dark and dismal walkway with a sniff of rebuke. "Pasha, I—"

"No buts, Rojan. We need you alive, and not in the black."

And then it was too late. What I hadn't realised until then was it wasn't only reading minds, hearing thoughts, that Pasha could do. Oh no: when he wanted, he could sneak into your head and suggest to it that a good long sleep was just what you needed.

I remember the walkway rushing up to greet me, remember the black suddenly fading in its song, and an arm catching me. After that, the only black was sleep.

He really was a fucking bastard. It was his best quality, and I always liked him for it.

Chapter Eight

I woke up with my nose shoved into the shabby sofa behind my desk, my feet resting on Griswald's mangy head.

Something hard – whatever it was that had woken me – prodded my shoulder. I opened one eye and thought about feigning death, again, when Lastri's face glared back. She wielded the ruler like one of Jake's swords and prodded harder, as though she was enjoying it.

I fumbled myself to sitting, my eyes rheumy and gritty. How long *had* it been since I'd slept? Too long, and when you considered every sleep I had was littered with dreams of a dark, dead city, of Jake watching me with reproachful eyes, of my niece saying her prayers for me, who could blame me?

"What time is it?" I asked.

"Time you sorted yourself out," Lastri snapped. "Time you grew up and grew a pair of bollocks." She snorted in disgust and, thankfully, left me to it.

I patted Griswald on the head and managed to get up. Dendal was in his usual position in the corner surrounded by a hundred different candles and Pasha sat, jittery all over again, on the corner of his desk, talking to Erlat. They shared a sideways look, conspirators in something and not just getting me to sleep, I was pretty sure of that. Whatever it was, they were welcome to it – I had enough screwing with my head without anything else on top.

Erlat murmured something to Pasha but all I heard was Jake's name and that "it's going well. Slowly, but she'll get there." The shoulder that was facing me seemed to do so in a very pointed way and she made a show of not looking at me as she dropped a comforting hand on to Pasha's.

Pasha's smile was strained, but he got up and walked her to the door. "Don't risk it next time. Keep out of sight where you can. It's getting dangerous out there, and . . . they mean business, Erlat."

"They always do." She flicked a glance my way. Not a nice glance, but not an "I want to strangle you" Lastri special.

I tried. I did, although I still didn't know what I'd done to upset her. But I got as far as "Erlat—" before she shut the door on me and what was, to be fair, probably going to be something sincere but lame-arsed.

Pasha came and sat on the corner of my desk, his jitters worse even while he laughed at me. "For someone who spends as much time with women as you do, you have no understanding of them, have you?"

"I have no idea what the hell goes on in women's minds. It's all right for you, you can see what they're thinking. How come *you* can tell her to be careful, but when I try, she stops talking to me?"

Another laugh that couldn't quite cover up whatever was making him fidget like he had an infestation of insects in his underwear. "When you have the answer to that, maybe she'll talk to you. She doesn't hate you anyway. Not yet. You've still got time to really piss her off."

He pretended not to see how relieved I was, so I pretended that I wasn't and made a mental note to go and see her. Maybe, and this was pushing the bounds of my knowledge of social niceties, apologise. For whatever it was.

I sat opposite Pasha and tried not to wonder if my left hand was about to fall off. It felt like it and the juice that gave me fired me up, woke my brain and other things best left dormant.

"You found the woman?" I asked.

"Didn't get the chance." His voice worried me, jittery as he was. His glance flicked to Dendal and back again. "Do you want to go and see how Lise is?"

I took my own, thoughtful look at the oblivious Dendal as he bent over his papers, his scratching pen the only noise other than his faint, cheery hum.

"Of course I do."

By the look of the grey light that was bouncing down off all the cunningly concealed mirrors and through grubby light wells, I took it to be mid-morning which meant we could see

129

where we were going. The streets were empty, too silent, too still. Too dead. We found a stairwell and headed down.

"I got us special passes in case any guards ask us why we're out," Pasha said and handed one over. On Official Special Business, it said, and that sent a shiver down me.

"What was it you didn't want Dendal to know?"

"Inquisition. That's why it's so quiet, why I told Erlat to be careful."

He didn't have to say anything else; that was quite enough to put the fear of anything you care to name up me. "Perak—"

"Hasn't got complete control. He said as much. Plenty of factions within the Ministry, all wanting their own thing. All wanting to save their own arses, their own everything. Well, one of them has called an Inquisition."

Which probably meant everyone was in even bigger shit than before. No one had called an Inquisition since, well, since the last time a mage had gone batshit. It was the Inquisition that had decided we were unholy, agents against the will of the Goddess. Ministry had fallen on that with glee and dropped on us the edict that made us illegal. The Inquisition had rounded up all the mages they could find, and no one knew *exactly* what had happened to them. There were plenty of less than savoury rumours though, ones that I didn't care to contemplate. Of course, they'd probably regretted that later when the synthtox kicked in, but by then mages were secret which was helpful when they started rounding them up again, as they had with Pasha, to help with pain-farming for Glow.

Thing was, from all I'd read and heard about the Inquisition, they weren't bound to follow Ministry. Once they were let loose, anyone in contravention of their orders was fair game. Before, they'd been sent after mages, and it didn't matter what lofty position they held, how much money they had – the Inquisition didn't care. They'd taken mages, heretics, unbelievers, people who complained about the Inquisition, people who looked funny ... anyone they thought was an affront to the Goddess. Hence my keeping my feelings about religion to myself for the most part. The Inquisition were a law unto themselves and the Goddess.

So who would dare order one? Someone very sure indeed they wouldn't be rounded up in the general "Inquisition everyone first, ask questions of the widespread bodily parts afterwards" mood.

Alchemical Research was the biggest, and most powerful, department. Perak had a few friends there, from his time working with them. But the new head was an ambitious man, and wasn't above a bit of backstabbing. An Inquisition didn't sound his sort of thing, though. I knew the rest of the departments – Theology, Law and so on – but not much about the individuals who led them, and even that little was more than most people knew. Ministry liked to hide who they were, which person did what, the details of those whats. Liked to keep everyone Under in their place through ignorance. It had worked pretty well, right up till the Downsiders started telling everyone a few truths, but Ministry were past masters at misinformation and starting the wrong rumour to counter the right one, so maybe only the Downsiders really believed it, and not all of them.

So who would dare order the Inquisition out?

"They started last night," Pasha said. "Down in Boundary. Picked up a load of people, all Downsiders of course, in the name of finding the murderer. And any heretics while they're about it, naturally."

"But the guards—"

"The Downsiders don't trust them. A guard was killed the other night – most Downsiders reckon it's the guards that are doing the murdering. A fair few Upsiders feel the same, from what Guinto tells me. That's just an excuse though."

The muscles in his jaw worked as he tried not to spit it out, tried to keep his tone level. "I couldn't get down to where that woman was, not unless I wanted to be picked up too, and I almost was." Shame radiated off him, perhaps because he hadn't stayed to get rounded up like the rest. Had an odd sort of honour like that, Pasha. "It's not really the murderer they're after, though that seems part of their orders. Heresy, that's what they're looking for. Us Downsiders are all heretics, because of the devotional."

Blood and ashes, the old way, as it had been Upside before Ministry sanitised worship, made it "better", "less violent", and, incidentally, stripped it of anything remotely majestic.

No music except on holy days, and then all you got were vacuous hymns waffling on about how lovely and nice the Goddess was. No stained glass to wash you with coloured light. No hellfire and damnation in the sermons. No blood in the devotional, just a nice little promise to be a good boy, thank you, Goddess. The Ministry had no romance in its soul, and it had sucked the soul from the city, too, made it a bland and tasteless thing.

Now here were the Downsiders with their raucous music, their vibrant belief, their blood and ashes and anger. Their knowledge of the truth. Too many for the Ministry to delete from their precious city. Someone had been waiting their chance, though, that was plain. An Inquisition to find the murderer and, while they were at it, quietly denounce any Downsiders they picked up as heretics, and a few more bodies made it to the Slump.

What could I say to Pasha? Nothing. Nothing that wouldn't have sounded trite, insincere or worse, because I wasn't a Downsider. I didn't have to put up with the spits and insults and the fear of being picked up because of how I looked and sounded. I could never really know what it was like for him, same as no one can ever really know what it's like for anyone but themselves and that's a blessing and a curse, I've always thought.

Usually I'd have said the insincerity anyway because I'm all charm that way, but not to Pasha. Not today. A sudden attack of tact, perhaps, but I was sure I'd get over it.

We reached a stretch of walkway that passed under the lab. The stench of wet smoke curled around us and made me cough as I wondered if any of the machinery we needed had survived. It was almost time for our daily session, and we needed Glow now more than ever, but it wouldn't do much without Dwarf's magnifying gizmo.

Pasha stopped suddenly, startled, his eyes wide, mouth open. Then he ran along the swaying walkway, not towards the temple where we'd left Lise but towards the stairwell that led to the lab. When he got his gun out, I ran after him.

I'd thought he was running for the lab, but we hadn't got there before he suddenly stopped. A dim landing where clanking walkways twisted off into darkness. A dim landing and, oh shit, a body I recognised. Taban from the lab, fellow pain-mage, with his throat cut back to his spine. So much blood. It robbed me of my voice, as though I was the one with his throat cut.

"Did you hear?" I managed to ask Pasha as we stared down, and wondered how I'd managed to go all these weeks working with Taban, passing the time while waiting for Dwarf to hook us up, taking our minds off what was to come by sharing a morbid joke on the nature of what we were doing, and I knew nothing about him other than he was a pain-mage and knew some seriously filthy jokes. Had been a pain-mage.

"The killer?" Pasha said. "No. No, just Taban. I – he was thinking of his wife, how he wouldn't get to see her again."

I'd never even known he was married, never asked, too

134

damned obsessed with magic, with pain and the lab, with righting my mistakes. I blinked hard and stared up, and up, past labyrinths of walkways that staggered drunkenly between houses, a never-ending net that had me caught. Up past looming buildings that stole the sun, past the vast seem-to-float estates of Clouds. Top of the World was up there somewhere in the gloom, full of ministers, cardinals, priests, arseholes and maybe a good man or two. Maybe.

I didn't really see any of that – I was listening to a voice, not any voice but a Voice, my father and his hypnotic magic, explaining to me how he was doing it for good reasons, that it was right, it was in praise of the Goddess. How I'd hated him for treating people like fucking cows, milking their pain, and now I knew for certain I wasn't much different. That had always been my fear, that I'd be like him. Only I was – it had snuck up on me without detection, a small decision here, an overlooked detail there, an unnoticed person, only wanted for their pain...

Fuck that. I'd climb Top of the World and face the height, or, rather, depth, from its lip, stare at it full on and scream in defiance as I dropped into the Slump before I became another him.

I looked down at Taban, a smudge of extinct life surrounded by greyness, a sucking blandness that seemed to eat at your soul if you looked too long. Bizarrely, I wished I was back in the hellhole of the 'Pit. It had been a shitty place in a world of shitty places, dark and violent and so grim it made me want to fork my eyes out, but it had been noise and colour and a vibrant, fervent grasp at life, at wrenching every last drop out of it and feeling it drip into your mouth. The 'Pit had been *alive*. And I'd destroyed it as surely as I had the Glow, and let the Downsiders out of slavery into this – into a long slow sucking of the soul, and probably a grisly death at the end. Go me.

It took a while to get everything done – call the guards, tell them the fuck all we knew, have the body taken to the mortuary. When we were finally free to go – the passes worked wonders – and I turned towards Guinto's temple and Lise, something else stopped me in my tracks. Or, rather, a few someones.

As I said, there hadn't been an Inquisition in years but I knew trouble when I saw it. Perhaps that uniform was seared into the group consciousness or something, because all of a sudden my bollocks seemed to be making a bid to hide under my shirt.

Specials induced a kind of sweating dread whenever they appeared anywhere, the mere sight of the uniform making guilty thoughts appear in the heads of even the most blameless. They were pussycats next to these guys.

Ministry set a lot of store by uniforms, and it made sense. A guard's uniform wasn't much different from anyone's normal clothes, but they were all the same colour, and had a tabard over that that designated them as guards. The uniform said, to the law abiding at least, "Just your regular guy, who'll help you out if you need it. I'm an *officially* regular guy, you're safe with me." Wasn't strictly true, of course, but the uniform gave that impression to your man on the street.

A Specials' uniform was made for stealthy combat – a hand-me-down from the assassins of the old warlord who'd founded Mahala. A leather allover with subtle armour, inserted plates of metal that you couldn't see but could stop a blade dead, hidden knives that could whip out and take you in the eye or heart before you could say "shit". Understated, silent and scary with it. The uniform said: "Hey, I'm quiet and soft and could kill you in an eye blink, and no one will see, or care, so do as you're damn well told."

There was nothing understated about these guys. A breast-plate etched in whorls of red and black that seemed to, but didn't quite, depict a nasty fiery hell with what might be the twisted faces of damned souls screaming imposed over the top. A short helmet in the shape of Namrat's head, all teeth and snarls, with a visor that covered the eyes so they could see out but you couldn't see in, making them appear eyeless, soulless. Metal gauntlets the colour of blood – so it wouldn't show per-haps. All in all, the Inquisitor's uniform was balls-out "I don't give a fuck who you are, I'm judging you and if you come up wanting, I will crush you like the pathetic bug that you are and send you screaming into hell so that Namrat can rip your soul to shreds. I may piss on you afterwards."

Ministry set a lot of store by uniforms because, as a way of telegraphing just how fucked you are, they *work*. Well, they were working on me anyway. No matter the orders of an Inquisition, what made them dangerous was that when they were set in motion, they were *always* on the lookout for heretics and unbelievers, whoever they were. Part of their strength and part of the reason they're dangerous, even for whoever gives them their orders.

Given that I am a heretic, an unbeliever and a mage to boot, I was feeling fairly vulnerable.

They came along the walkway as though they owned it and, frankly, if they'd asked, I'd have handed over the deeds without a squeak. Pasha didn't seem to have noticed them, rubbing his forehead as though trying to rub out what he could hear. He stared down with sick fascination as the guards covered Taban and muttered a few snatches of sentences under his breath that I didn't quite catch but that sounded like a prayer.

Luckily the Inquisitors didn't seem to have noticed us yet either – they were busy breaking down the door of a house at the other end of the walkway, though one, a captain perhaps by the extra ornamentation on his helmet and a specially tormented-looking soul on his breastplate, looked our way. The eyeless visor gave him a detached quality, a predator eyeing up his prey.

Under his gaze the guards started to swear and rush to get Taban's body on to a stretcher and hoisted up to a block and tackle that would take it to the level of the mortuary. If even the guards were left sweaty and panicked, me and Pasha were screwed. The guards were done with us so I grabbed Pasha's arm and dragged him into a dark doorway. He started to say something, loudly, but shut up quick when he saw my face. He flicked a glance back towards the walkway, flinched and then set his mouth in a grim line. Pasha the mouse was about to go all lion on me, I could tell. If he did that, we were probably both dead.

"Just keep quiet, act calm and we'll get away, all right?" He made to say something, but I cut him off. "You open that mouth, they hear your accent, you might as well be dead already. Look, down in the 'Pit you looked after me, right? You showed me how it worked, made sure I didn't do anything stupid that'd get me killed. This is me returning the favour. You've seen what they're doing, what you say they've done down in Boundary. You want me to have to go find Jake and tell her you aren't coming back because of some fool notion of yours? We shut the fuck up, get the fuck out, live to fight another day. Got it?"

He settled down a bit, looked less as though he was going to explode with indignation and I thought we might actually get out of this with our arses intact.

Then the screams started. Behind us, from where the Inquisitors had finished breaking down the door and were busy pulling people out of their home. Pasha leapt out of my grasp like he'd been struck with some of Lise's electricity and was halfway there before I could catch him again.

Luckily I was a fair bit bigger than him, because trying to hang on to a man who's writhing more than any snake is hard with only one working hand. I got to him before he made the corner of the next stairwell between us and them, before the Inquisitors could see him and decide they had room for one more. Pasha smacked me a good one and almost sent me flying. In the end, I had to sit on him to stop him.

He shut up, luckily – me sitting on his ribs didn't leave him much breath for talking. I leant forward and took a peek around the corner of the stairwell. No one seemed to have noticed us brawling.

The Inquisitors were doing a very thorough job. Not content with dragging out a Downsider family – father, mother, two boys and a baby – they'd started on the furnishings as well. Chairs flew out on to the street, followed by a table, a couple of filthy mattresses, ragged clothes that might pass for the family's best temple-going dress. Then the damning evidence, what the Inquisition had come for. A picture of the Goddess, all blood and violence and Namrat looking mean. Not a fluffy kitten or sunbeam in sight. Two pots with brushes – one black with ash, one to hold the blood.

The father's face, pale already in the giveaway that this was a Downsider family, grew paler still. His wife began to sob, quietly, desperately.

"Heresy," the lead Inquisitor said in a voice like the clanking shut of a cell door.

"No, I—" was as far as the father got. A gauntlet slammed into his face, brought blood from him and tears and screams from his family.

I couldn't look as they took the family away, couldn't bring myself to watch, and some small part of me was ashamed of that, ashamed of the fear that left me weak and wobbly. The bigger part of me was concentrating on not letting Pasha get up, because if I did, I knew, *knew*, he'd be out there roaring like a lion and it would do nothing at all except get him killed with them. Apart from anything else I didn't want to have to say to Jake, "Well, I could have stopped him, but I let him go and now he's dead, for nothing."

When the cries had faded, when the street no longer smelled of threat and Inquisitors, I got up off Pasha. Warily, it had to be said, but he didn't leap up to lump me one. I wouldn't have blamed him if he had – I was feeling pretty much like lumping myself at that point – but Pasha always surprised me.

He walked around the corner, slowly, as though he was dreaming. A soft hand on a wrecked chair, on what was left of the door. What was left of a home and family.

"We could have done something," he said. "We could have helped."

"Got arrested with them? Got taken up to Top of the World, found guilty, because, let's face it, we both are in their eyes, and chucked off into the Slump? Who would that have helped?" True enough, as far as it went. Not far enough, no matter how practical, and I knew that because there was a slosh of bile chewing at my stomach and a wish that I could scrub myself clean and douse myself with disinfectant. As if that would make my soul sparkly fresh again. If only it were that simple.

"We could have done *something*."

That was Pasha all over, why I liked the little bastard and sometimes hated him, too. He made me look past myself, made me look outside, and inside, too. I didn't like it very much, because what's inside is festering like a month-old corpse.

He picked up one of the pots, or, rather, what was left of it, and dipped a finger in. It came away black with ash and he slowly, deliberately, smeared it in a circle on his palm.

We should have been getting the fuck out of there, in case there were more Inquisitors, in case they decided to do a sweep of the whole area, but I stood and watched, transfixed despite myself, as Pasha brushed off the ripped picture of the Goddess and set it on a little ledge. He didn't seem aware of anything else as he pulled a knife out of his pocket. Small, bone-handled, with Namrat and the Goddess carved into the hilt, locked in their epic battle. Life versus death. To Pasha, to the Downsiders, it's the battle that's important, not promises of a golden afterlife though that's nice, too. No, it's the fight, the never-ending struggle that's the thing, even if you knew Namrat would always win in the end.

When he came to use the knife, to make the dot of blood in the centre of the devotional, I looked away. Too personal a thing to watch, even for me. The soft murmurs of his prayer were enough to give me goose bumps, especially when I heard my name in there.

It wasn't long before he came to stand next to me and we surveyed the damage, to the house, to the blood-soaked walkway where Taban had died, and for what? *Why?* Why him, why any of them? Why was my sister lying in a bed unconscious and lucky to be alive?

As usual, I covered up all my thoughts and feelings. "I hope you weren't praying for me to see the light and get converted."

That brought half a smile from Pasha. "No, I know when I'm asking too much." The smile turned into a sly grin. "I did ask that you not sit on me again, dickhead."

Arsehole. "Sure, and next time I'll let them take you, too, if it makes you feel better."

"I'm not ashamed to be a Downsider, and I'm not a heretic. Fuck anyone who says different."

I was glad to be away from that corner and we hurried toward Guinto's temple in silence for a while, until Pasha broke in thoughtfully: "They weren't looking for a murderer, did you notice that? A victim right there, and they didn't even glance at him."

Oh, I'd noticed all right. But then, what else could you expect from the Ministry but to use the murders of a few people they find inconvenient in order to make sure their boot of authority was firmly in place? It didn't even need Perak's approval – any minister could order an Inquisition. It did make me wonder who it had been, though, who felt safe enough to order it, what they were really after.

"We can't do much against a whole Inquisition," I said. "Not if we want to live. But there are things we can do."

When we finally got to the temple, I checked on Lise – still unconscious but improving, the nurse said, so I favoured her with a wink – and then we made our careful way down to the border of Boundary and No-Hope, to a dank and dismal box that someone called home, and a woman quietly weeping. I wondered if Taban's wife would weep quietly, and what it meant that this time the victim was no Downsider. There had to be a link, and I thought I had an inkling of what it was, but I had no way to be sure. Maybe the weeping woman could tell us if I was right.

We passed along a cesspit of a walkway, and the Inquisition had been thorough down here, too, I had to give them that. Doors ripped off, bedding and mattresses strewn everywhere, shattered pictures of the Downside Goddess, toys looking sad and lonely with no one to play with them. A one-eyed stuffed pink rabbit with ratty ears that flopped in odd directions stared at me, as though willing me to take it home and love it.

On this one walkway almost no one was home in a city where everyone was supposed to be home, under curfew. At least the Inquisition had gone, moved on to other places, other families. It wasn't much of a consolation. When it started to rain, a thin drizzle that sliced down through walkways and fall-nets, it seemed fitting.

We ducked under a stairwell ravaged by synth and time and there was the house I'd seen, scrunched between its neighbours like it was ashamed to exist, the top listing drunkenly as the house above squeezed it. The door was black with grime and mould, and damp ran down the wall. I took a deep breath and knocked on the door. It took a while for it to open a crack, and a bleary, wary eye poked round the edge. She took one look at me and tried to jam the door shut. "I don't know nothing, I don't! I'm no heretic either. Please, don't."

I looked down. Maybe the allover and the flapping black jacket that made me look like a Special had been a mistake, but my head had been too muzzed up to think about changing.

"We're not the Inquisition, or Specials, or even guards," I said to the shut door. "We need to know about the boy."

Pasha moved behind me, and I knew he'd be talking in her head, soothing words in an accent she knew and trusted. The crunch of his finger dislocating made me feel ill, but it seemed to work, between that and me assuring her we hadn't come to take her away.

Eventually the door opened again, the eye more wary than before. I held out my hand palm up and showed her the ring, the one I'd used to find her. Her hand flew to cover her mouth before she reached for it, and I let her take it in shaking fingers.

"I gave that to Jabol," she said. "It was his father's. Have you found Jabol? Is he all right?"

"I think perhaps we ought to come in," Pasha said. I was glad to let him take the lead; he had a natural sympathy, honed by years of working with the kids he'd rescued from the pain-mages in the 'Pit. He knew what it was to hurt and it showed in the soft tones of his voice, his gentle hand on her arm as he led her inside and sat her on the one rickety chair. That sympathy was something that always amazed me about him, something I wished I could do. When I try it, it always ends up coming out as sarcasm. Not helpful, so I kept my mouth shut for now and looked around.

The house was your basic one-room hovel with two sodden mattresses, a thin blanket apiece, the chair and a table made out of an old crate. A portrait of the Downside Goddess, with a stub of candle in front of it. A crappy little stove stood in one corner to heat the place and cook on, but it ran on Glow and seeing as the only places that got any of that these days were some factories and Ministry, it was good for nothing. The windowless space was lit by a guttering rend-nut oil lamp, wafting its sickening scent into every corner. Even supplies of that were running low.

The walls ran with damp from the almost incessant rain that filtered through all the cracks and crevices above, and down again through the floor to some poor soul even worse off than she was. The water held a faint tinge of synth and I made sure not to touch it. She didn't have much choice – she'd be drinking synth-tainted water same as everyone else down here.

The woman seemed to fit the room. Unfair, perhaps, but true. Her face was thin and pinched, all softness knocked from her by life, leaving only harsh angles. Her dark, sodden hair lay in tangled clumps around her neck, and the rag that might be called a dress couldn't hide the frailness of her, like a bag of sticks. No food, not for weeks probably. There wasn't much to go round and what there was, was vile. Everyone was getting thinner down here, but, by the looks of it, she'd been thin to start with and was now more than halfway to skeleton.

Pasha held the woman's hands and she stared at the scars that ringed his fingers, ran over his hands like vines. "You're mages." Her voice was full of horror and she yanked her hands away as though Pasha was infectious. "You're mages, them that took all them girls, all them kids."

"Not like them, no." Pasha held on to it well, but I could sense the frustration, the furious hurt. Wherever he was, someone hated him. Upsiders hated him for being a Downsider, Downsiders hated him for being a mage.

"The opposite, in fact," I said.

She didn't believe us, that was plain, but I couldn't say I blamed her.

"Where's Jabol? What have you done to him? What? Tell me!"

Her voice took on a hysterical pitch, rising higher and higher so that even Pasha's soft words didn't help.

When she slapped him and spat on him, I snapped and grabbed her by one shoulder. What sympathy I had for her was cold and hard now. "He's dead, that's where he is. And we didn't take him, or kill him. We want to find out who did so we can stop them killing anyone else, and for that we need your help. I know you're scared, I know that pain-mages did some terrible things, but we aren't them and if you touch Pasha like that again you'll never find out what happened to Jabol. Pasha suffered more at mages' hands than you can possibly know, so you leave him be and look at him like the man he is, not what your mind tells you he is."

She stood quiet in my hand, aghast at my words. Pasha looked just as shocked.

"What?" I said it more to myself than anything. Where had that come from? Not my cynical soul, surely. "And if you ever tell anyone I said that, I will pull your ears off, roll them up and stick them up your nostrils."

Pasha grinned his monkey grin, but my glare stopped whatever he was about to say.

The woman sat down abruptly. "Dead, he's dead, then. I thought he must be, to not come home for so long, but I always hoped, always. All we ever had in the 'Pit. Hope and faith." She started crying again, not quietly now but great heaving sobs that seemed they might pull her inside out.

I crouched down in front of her, waited till the sobs tailed off into a more desperate kind of blank grief, and at least attempted some tact. It was quite hard. "I know that, I do. But whoever killed Jabol, he's killed at least twelve others, Downsiders mostly. We need to stop him. I need you to help us." I thought it went quite well. Pasha certainly looked at me as though I'd had a personality transplant.

The woman looked down at the ring, stroked it with one forefinger, before she looked at Pasha from under shame-filled lashes. Her voice was thick with the tears she was going to shed, later and perhaps for months to come. "You brought me this back. I suppose . . . He left for temple, six days ago. He'd been a bit withdrawn, but boys are that way at his age, aren't they? Lucky to get two words out of him some days."

"Anything else? Anything happen earlier? Anything, well, odd?" Because I had a suspicion of our link and I needed her to confirm it.

She looked between the two of us, confused. "I don't think so."

Pasha clearly had the same suspicion as me, because he asked, "Did he have any kind of accident?"

"Accident? Oh, you mean when he slipped on the stairwell? A fortnight or so ago. Had a bruise the size of a dinner plate on his back, but other than that he was fine."

"And nothing odd happened after that?"

"Odd? Well, someone stole my best dress and at the same time left a lot of frogs on my bed. The lady next door ran naked down the street screaming, but we're not sure why. That's all. Not really *odd*, any more than everything is odd up here."

Me and Pasha shared a look. We had our link, and all that was left was one last question. "What temple did he go to?"

"Father Guinto's. Where else? None of the others let us in."

Chapter Nine

"But *why* would Guinto want to kill pain-mages? It doesn't make sense, especially when he offered to help. He got us into the mortuary, got us to the bodies, remember? Without that we'd never have found Jabol's mother."

Pasha was upset, pacing across the threadbare rug of the office. I sat at the desk, mindful of the drawers, and tried to talk to him but it was hard with Dendal butting in every few seconds. It would have been easier if the comments were relevant.

"Why would anyone want to kill us?" I asked. "Because the reminder is an embarrassment to Ministry, even if we are the only power source they have. Some of them don't care about that. Most of them don't even know we're making the Glow — Perak's keeping that as quiet as he can. I suspect most that do know, don't care except we're still around. Because a lot of mages have been right bastards to a lot of people. Because we're unholy. Because, because, I don't know!"

Because Guinto made my shoulder blades itch something fierce would be my answer, but I probably wasn't the best person to ask. Priests have this tendency to bring me out in a rash. "Look, I'm not even saying it is him." Though he was my first choice. One boy dies outside the temple he's preaching at, one boy after going to his temple, Taban not more than ten minutes' walk from him ... And Lise was in his care, a fact that made this all the more urgent for me. "We should talk to him, see what he has to say. You can take a peek, see what you find."

Pasha stopped pacing and stared at me, horrified. "Look inside a priest's mind? I – I couldn't. No, I couldn't."

"If you can't be good, be careful," Dendal said.

I ignored him. "Even after everything? You know, better than anyone, what people are capable of. Even those who say they serve the Goddess."

"But Guinto's not like them. He – he's the only one, only priest in the whole damned city, who doesn't spit on Downsiders, call us heretics. He's a good priest, a good man. It doesn't make *sense*."

"Hide in plain sight," Dendal said, and that was almost relevant.

"Yes, but if it's him ..."

I didn't need to be able to see into Pasha's head to guess what he was thinking. Jake and Guinto – she was fierce in her belief, and she believed in him. All the Downsiders did. Pasha, I think, depended on the fact that at least one person who wasn't a mage or Jake didn't think he was an abomination, treated him as though he was a person, not a thing to be despised. If it turned out Guinto was killing these boys ... I didn't want to be the one to tell Jake. I didn't want to see what that would do to Pasha, or think about the riot Guinto's arrest would cause. But people were dying, *mages* were dying. Without them we were sunk, every last one of us, and Pasha knew that as well as I did.

"We'll just talk to him for now, all right? You could take a look in some of the others' heads, couldn't you?"

Pasha stared at the ceiling, as though praying for guidance. I don't think he got any, but he nodded in the end, tight-lipped and furious.

"Picnic time!" Dendal said, and we left him to his own head.

Pasha was jittery all the way, tense and fidgety. He kept glancing up at the windows we passed, his hands twisting in front of him. Smudged faces looked down at us through the gloom, wary eyes following our progress. I wondered what they were thinking, but I couldn't quite pluck up the nerve to ask Pasha. He looked as though he'd burst if I said one word.

The temple was quiet when we entered; the curfew was still in effect, and not many were risking breaking it, not with an Inquisition around. A few brave souls had come, or maybe they'd been caught here when the curfew came in. They sat on the pews, heads down, and the murmur of useless prayers washed over me. The plaster saints and martyrs lined the aisle. Pasha stopped by each one to make the proper devotion but I headed straight for the altar, and the door behind it that led to where Lise was being nursed. Where Guinto should be.

Abeya slipped out of the door before I reached it and when she saw me, she dimpled nicely and ducked her head. Shame I'd sworn off women. But, screw it, I needed something to take my mind off what I couldn't have, and if I was going to do that I should do it properly.

I cranked up my best smile and took her hand to kiss it. When I made to let go, she kept hold of my hand and her smile was brighter than Glow. Made me feel all tingly, and pushed thoughts of Jake into a deep dark corner where I hoped they'd stay.

Pasha caught up, muttering darkly under his breath. Abeya ignored him and pulled me through the door. "I suppose you're here to see Lise?"

"Not only Lise, no."

She gave me an amused, sideways glance and blushed, but didn't stop until we got to Lise's bedside. "She's much better, but we don't know when she'll wake up. Or even if. It's always hard to tell with head injuries, the nurse says."

The room was filled with makeshift beds and patients and nurses – with the Sacred Goddess Hospital gone, and no one really trusting the quacks from Under if they had any brains, the temples had become temporary hospitals. At least doctors and nurses were spared the curfew, a small mercy and one in which I detected Perak's hand. The crowd made me feel at least a little better about Lise being here – if it really was Guinto murdering people, then he'd have to kill a dozen other witnesses too before he could get to Lise. Even so, I made a mental note to ask Dench to send a Special down here, just in case.

Lise did look much better. The lump on her head had gone down, the cuts were healing nicely and she had some colour in her cheeks. I extricated my hand from Abeya's and sat down beside my sister. "Hey, Lise, come on, time to wake up."

I sat and talked to her for a time, while Pasha paced like a tiger and Abeya watched me with an approving smile, but Lise never stirred. I left her with a kiss on her forehead, and a fervent wish she'd wake up, and soon.

Before I could ask Abeya if Guinto was there, he appeared in the doorway, looking soft-eyed and benign and a bit creepy to my mind. No one is that nice, not all the time, not even part of the time if experience was anything to go by, and it made me suspicious.

I nodded a brief greeting. "Just the man we wanted to see."

"Perhaps you've been persuaded to see the light of the Goddess?" The corner of his mouth curled and maybe he was making a joke, but it seemed pretty poor to me.

"When people stop starving, or trying to kill each other, or arresting people for being different, when we get the promise of a nicer time in this life rather than in some hypothetical next one, I might be persuaded. Until then, think of me as a challenge. A really *big* one."

The smile seemed utterly genuine, but I've always suspected the art of the fake smile was something they taught in the seminary. Priests *always* look genuine, even when they're creaming the alms and spending it all in whorehouses. Looking genuine is part of the job description.

Guinto motioned for Abeya to go and she did, not without a regretful glance in my direction. Definitely a promise there, and one I might have to follow up, even if only to get some more information on Guinto.

When she'd gone, Guinto's demeanour changed. Not so benign now, I thought. More guarded perhaps, making me ever surer he was hiding something. What, that was the question. If he was as good a man as Pasha and Jake seemed to think, maybe all he had on his guilty conscience was overindulging on sherry.

Guinto led us to his office, sat at his desk and arranged his robes, neat and precise. "Well then, if not for salvation, what do you want to see me for? Have you any news on the murders?"

Pasha beat me to it by half a heartbeat and that was probably just as well, as I'd likely have dropped out something savage. The bodies were haunting me. Just boys, who were discovering they were pain-mages, which was a difficult enough thing at the best of times.

"We thought you might be able to shed some light on a few things." Pasha shot me a meaningful glance, a "shut the fuck up and let me do the talking" look.

"For you, Pasha, of course." Guinto favoured me with a wry

look before he turned back to Pasha. "For my flock, my most devout parishioners, anything. How is Jake?"

"Well, thank you, Father. If—"

"And how goes things between you? After everything you've been through, the fire of the Goddess, the road is slow and tough, I know. But a union of two souls, in every way, is a blessing, a prayer to the Goddess."

Pasha blushed brick-red. "We're . . . working on it. Do you—"

"Good. You know I pray for you both daily, that you find what solace you can with each other."

Pasha looked utterly stricken, like a boy singled out by an overly harsh teacher in front of the class. "Yes, Father."

This had gone far enough. You may have gathered I'm not overly enamoured of the priestly profession. I have my reasons; years of experience of less than faithful priests, of those more corrupt than the worst pimp, of seeing the Ministry turn Mahala into a soulless place full of greed and the very worst that man could do to man. Of seeing my mother die from the synthtox, a disease both caused and denied by the Ministry, a long slow agony and not a breath of kindness or mercy from any of them, or from the Goddess. This was almost worse, worse than ignorance of what was going on, this was purposeful, and it made me want to slap the good and virtuous Guinto round the side of the head. Besides, it was reminding me that Pasha had everything I wanted, and yet I wouldn't have traded places with him for a second.

"Do you pray for all the boys killed, too, Father? For the people taken by the Inquisition for the crime of worshipping like a Downsider?"

There, that scrubbed the smile off his face. "Of course. I pray the Goddess embraces them, that their next life will be better than this."

"Well, it could hardly be worse, could it?"

He merely inclined his head and that infuriated me more, that he accepted it. That he seemed to have no burning need, no flame to put that right and only depended on the next life being better. I'd thought differently of him when he'd preached, but this was another side to him, one that left a sour taste and reminded me that, no matter what, he was part of Ministry with all that entailed.

"Did you know any of the boys?" I tried to keep the bile out of my voice, I really did, but some must have leaked through because he looked as though he'd been slapped. "Any of them come here to worship?"

"I don't know, how could I when no one seems to know, or care, who they were?"

"A boy called Jabol, did you know him?"

"I – yes, there was a boy by that name. He came to see me. He was worried that he was a pain-mage, that he'd be taken and made to do things he didn't want to. Made to torture people."

Pasha flinched at that, and Guinto spared him a sympathetic look. "I told him as I told you, Pasha. That he shouldn't use it, that it's an unholy thing, and has been used

157

to do unholy work. That he should strive to overcome it and never to use it, even if it seems for good. He should forbear to use it for the peace of his soul. To give in is to be damned. If you would do that, Pasha, would give it up, beg forgiveness, then your path would no longer be full of the obstacles you insist on putting between you and Jake."

By this point, I was hard pressed not to pick Guinto up and give him a good shake. The only way I managed not to was knowing that he'd say: see, this is what using pain magic does to you. I'd heard this all too often over the last years, while pain magic was banned. It's unholy, *mages* are unholy, unclean, not fit to join the rest of the city, and all the while Ministry had been saying that, they'd secretly been using it in ways more unholy than I liked to think of. That Guinto should say that to Pasha of all people, to a man who'd spent his life fighting that usage, who had such a fierce belief in the Goddess – it rendered me almost speechless with rage.

"Damned, my bollocks," I said when I could. "Was Jabol alive when you last saw him?"

Guinto put out a hand, as though to bless me against what I'd said, then seemed to think better of it. Probably very wise of him. I might have bitten his fingers off. "Well, yes. I had him go to each saint and martyr to beg forgiveness, and then before the Goddess. He promised to try to resist, to do as the Goddess wanted, as scripture demands. I last saw him before her mural, on his knees. A devout boy."

I made sure not to catch Pasha's eye. He stood, hunched and twisted against what Guinto had said, and I thought that you don't need to touch someone to inflict pain on them, to torture them. Soft words were enough, if they were the right words.

"Taban, he worshipped here, too? You gave him all this shit as well?"

Guinto's face hardened then and I saw some of the fire of his speech fill his eyes. He believed this, he really did. "He worships here, yes. And, yes, I talk to him about using his magic, about what it will do to his soul."

"Did he talk to you about how if he didn't, if we gave it up, we'd probably all have died of starvation by now?"

"As the Goddess wills. It's unholy. And so are you if you embrace it, if you can't see that it goes against all the Goddess is."

It was probably a good thing that Pasha grabbed my arm then, a good thing for Guinto at least, if not for my temper. Pasha got me out of the door before I said, or did, anything too rash.

I managed to hold it in until we made it out of the temple, and spilled my bile all over the street.

"Unctuous, snot-wiping, pig-fucking toad! Why do you go there if this is what you get? Temple is supposed to be about—"

"What do you know about temple?" Pasha's voice was quiet, crushed so that it made me want to shout all over again. "Nothing, that's what. He's right. The Goddess—"

159

"Fuck the Goddess!" Didn't look like it was our day for finishing sentences. "Pasha, you are, you and Jake – you're the reason I found anything to have faith in, made me have at least a little faith in myself, what I can do. That I should use it for more than earning cash and getting women into bed. You can't believe this, that you should deny what you are because *She* said so. And what was all that obstacles between you and Jake shit?"

"If I try hard enough, if I pray enough, I won't know, won't be able to hear . . . Me and her, it . . . I can't. She can't. We . . . I want to not hear, Rojan. I want not to know what's in other people's heads."

The old me would have internally given a little whoop of joy at this news. That things weren't all sunshine and kittens between them. The new me saw the way his face twisted, how he was being pulled in all directions and none of them good ones.

So instead I said, "It was always going to be hard. You're both fucked up by what my father did to you. Now you're Upside and things are different. Very different. It's going to take time, but if you want to, you can make it work. You will. I promise. But you are a pain-mage and there's fuck all anyone can do about that. You can't stop being what you are."

Then I wondered what the hell I was saying. A quick word here and Jake would have been a free agent, ready for me to swoop in. Yet somehow, this was more important. Pasha had, almost without my realising, become a friend, one of the first

I'd managed in long years. Realising that made my stomach twist, and also made me see that I'd changed. The old me would have said for the worse, too, and would have sneered. The new me saw that all my cynicism was still there, but now that I saw what the world did to people I cared about, now that I let myself care about them, all those thoughts hit home a thousand times harder. Made those cynical words choke me.

Pasha rubbed a scarred hand over his face. "I'm not sure what I disbelieve more, but I think you saying that comes out a clear winner."

"I'm not entirely sure I believe I said it myself. Look, you are what you are. You can't change it, and I can't change what I am."

"A prick?"

"Thank you, yes. There's not a man in five thousand that can do half what we do. Maybe no one else in the city who can do precisely what you do. And if you hadn't done what you did – all those kids down there, being told they had to atone, had to hurt if they wanted the Goddess to love them, where would they be? Still believing it, like Jake? Like *you*?"

He flinched as though I'd slapped him and I wished I could take that last part back. To make my own small atonement without anything as tacky as an apology, I said, "Without you using your magic, me using mine, they'd still all be there. Don't tell me that's unholy, because I will tell you you're full of shit."

That brought back a trace of his monkey grin, but it soon

turned wistful. "I don't want to be different any more. I want to be like them, all the other Downsiders, even if it means the Inquisition takes me." He waved a hand at the group of buildings ahead that looked as though they were only held up by their neighbours, with spit for mortar.

"I'm going to be, too. Just as soon as that generator is up and running and you don't need me any more. I – I think I found my parents. I had Dendal send them a message. My whole life has been anything but normal, and that's all I want. I want people to look at me like I'm a person, not a thing. Like this, I – I can't. Without my magic, at least Downsiders won't hate me any more. I'll have somewhere to be. Me and Jake might be able to . . . I believe in the Goddess more than I believe in my magic."

And I couldn't say a damned thing to that, because who was I to deny what he wanted? Poor bastard had lived a fucked-up life, which was putting it mildly. Hell, he was so screwed up he even liked me. He deserved a bit of normality. Still didn't stop me thinking dire swearwords at the Goddess, though. So I changed the subject.

"We need to be at the pain room soon, see if anyone's managed to salvage any of the equipment. Perak sent to Alchemical Research for one of their guys to come take a look."

Pasha looked sick at the thought of anyone Ministry in the lab, but it was all the chance we had, and a slim one. No one but Dwarf and Lise knew what miracles they could do with machines, or how they worked.

"Why don't you go and find Jake, have some dinner and I'll meet you there."

He nodded wearily, looking more careworn than I'd ever seen him, and I've seen him pretty fucked up. "What about you?"

"Couple of people to see. Maybe Dench, if I can find him. See if we can get someone to keep an eye on Guinto."

"And Abeya? You haven't changed that much."

I grinned at him and was pleased when he managed a monkey grin back. "Oh yes, and Abeya."

Chapter Ten

I didn't have to look far for Abeya once Pasha had gone. I stepped back into the temple and there she was, as though she'd been waiting for me. The way she looked at me, I was pretty sure she had been. Always a nice little stroke for the ego.

A rustle of lily-white robes, velvet that clung to her in ways that made some very distracting thoughts flash across my mind, and she was at my side, smelling like an angel.

"I hoped you'd come back."

The way she looked at me snagged more primal parts of my brain. Sort of naïve, but eager and knowing all at once. Hey, I was a free agent, why the hell not? Had to be better than mooning around after someone who would become available around about the end of the world. Besides which, I needed to find out more about Guinto, and if I could do that while enjoying myself . . . practical, that's me. "Who wouldn't come back, if you were the reward?"

Her smile was reward enough. She took my hand in hers and pulled me to a dark corner. Better and better, though I suspect even I would draw the line at doing that in a templ—

"I hoped you'd come. I wanted to ask you something."

Oh, *ask*. Right, sure. I gave strict instructions to the more rebellious parts of my anatomy, which, as usual, they completely ignored.

"Which is?"

One cheek dimpled as her lips twisted in a lush and very inviting smile. I wondered if she realised the effect she was having. My ego was positively rolling on to its back and waiting for a tummy rub.

"Dinner? Oh, no, don't worry," she said as my face fell at the thought of trying to make a small bowl of grey mush romantic or indeed anything other than disgusting. Then she said the words guaranteed to hook me. "I have bacon. Don't ask me where from."

Bacon! No meat to be had for love nor money anywhere and she had bacon! I could guess where from, too – the only people who'd have any of the meat that had been salvaged from the 'Pit were Ministry. My stomach rumbled painfully at the thought, and I tried not to drown in my own spit. There are times when it'd be handy to have a deity to believe in so you can say something along the lines of "Oh my Goddess", and actually have it sound sincere. I settled instead for, "You say when and where, and I'll be there."

I tried not to feel as though I was taking a bribe, but, fuck it, I'd have done anything just to *smell* bacon again. Sometimes I'm so shallow I disgust even myself, but food is food. Bacon doubly so.

"Right here," she said, sounding more like an angel with every passing minute. I didn't even care about that. "And right now."

The door was one of those secret recessed jobs that are impossible to spot until someone shows you they're there. As soon as she opened it, the waft of bacon hit me and pretty much removed all rational thought for a while. When I stopped salivating like a starving dog, I noticed where I was.

A small room, tastefully done, if rather austere. Plain whitewashed walls seemed more mellow under an oil lamp that didn't give off the stench of rend-nut. A bed with crisply turned corners, a couple of cupboards, a deep squishy sofa, and a low table, with a plate on it. With bacon. If I'd thought a bit straighter I'd have wondered who in hell precisely she got it from, but, shit, you don't ask questions like that when you're starving and someone offers you the food of the Goddess.

I tried to concentrate, to remember why I was here – information. Guinto, murders ... Hard, though. We were all slowly starving and I hadn't had a full meal of even grey slop in days. Might not manage to think again until the smell went. Best to eat the bacon first, stop it distracting me. Yes.

Abeya sat me down on the sofa and I all but sank in up to

my hips. She sat next to me and the softness of the sofa pushed
us together very pleasingly. I was beginning to wonder if I'd
been wrong all these years and had died and gone to heaven.
A corner of me actually began to believe it when Abeya leant
across, her softness a warm pressure against me, and kissed
me.

She tasted salty and yet sweet, and I was so surprised I
didn't move for long heartbeats. She broke away, and her hand
traced at my cheek. "Your father . . . " I managed.

She kissed me again, a kiss that matched how I'd seen her
in the temple – naïve, eager, touched with something else. It
was pretty hard to resist and I've always been crap at resisting
temptation anyway, at least where women are concerned, so I
thought "screw it", and kissed her back.

I'd figured she was new to this – that naïve look – so when
we fell back on to the sofa I made sure I was underneath, not
wanting her to feel blocked in. I'm a gentleman that way, plus
she was a Downside girl and maybe she had brands.

When we came up for air, it was the first thing she touched
on, all hesitant, as though I might turn her away. Not fucking likely.

"It doesn't bother you, that I'm Downside?"

It was a hell of a nice view from down there, but I swallowed hard and said, "Not in the slightest."

She bit her lip in what, it has to be said, was a very sexy
way, and let her dark hair fall over her face, as though she was
ashamed of the tone of her skin, the blue-white pallor under

the more usual dusty tones. "My father says you're a heretic – that you don't believe in the Goddess."

That brought a dash of cold water to my brain, and other parts. Her adoptive father, that's why I was here, to find out more about him. "That's true. I'm, er, an affront to his Goddess." Bad enough she knew that, so I thought it best to leave the whole unholy pain-mage thing unsaid. Why ruin the moment?

I didn't get any further because the door banged open making us both jump, and Guinto strode in. Abeya leapt off the sofa and I did my best to struggle from its squishy clutches. I needn't have bothered – Guinto grabbed the front of my allover and dragged me to my feet. He was pretty strong under those robes.

"Out." His voice was quieter than a temple at midnight and chill enough to make my shoulder blades itch. "I know what you're doing, but I won't have this. I won't have her hurt, not by someone who hasn't even the decency to pretend he believes. She suffered enough Downside. They were unholy and so are you. I'd rather starve than depend on you for food. So out, and don't come sniffing around my daughter again."

"Father—"

"Enough. I'll deal with you later, Abeya. But I will not have *this* in our house, in the Goddess's house. Not for this. Not for you."

It seemed I'd worked my usual trick of pissing everybody off and I wasn't going to get any more information now, so I inclined my head, extricated my allover from his grip and left with a practised – and hopefully infuriating to Guinto – smile at Abeya.

Guinto looked as though he was about to pop, all red and vein-pulsing in his forehead. Which at least meant he didn't see me pocket the bacon as I left. Waste not, want not, right?

Chapter Eleven

I'd not been as long as I expected at the temple, so I didn't go straight to the pain lab to meet Pasha. Thoughts kept scampering round my head and I needed to get them organised. Usually I'd have gone to see Erlat. I'd have had a bath, talked to her afterwards and she'd have made me look at things from a different angle, as she always did. I took a quick detour on my way up, east to the Buzz. Most of it seemed to have made it through the riots intact, though one or two buildings looked even worse for wear than usual.

Erlat's place looked much the same in the gathering gloom, though there were some new marks by the door. Scorch marks. The riots had made it here, it seemed, even if the bigger fires hadn't. A whole house full of Downsiders had to be a target. Someone had scrawled something so vile across one wall I didn't even want to look. I dithered for a bit, unsure of the welcome I'd get, but in the end screw it and do it seemed the best option. At the worst I'd get a new shiner as a pair for the one that was just starting to fade.

I was about to knock on the door when it opened under my hand, and I wasn't hugely shocked to have a cardinal shove me aside. The fat one from the temple. He looked disgustingly well fed compared to everyone Under, and way too smug for my liking. Behind him, Erlat stood, her face set in her practised look but her hands trembling.

"Are you—"

"If you ask me if I'm all right, Rojan, I will not be responsible for my actions." One deep breath, and then she was serene again, all elegance and poise. Not even a hint of tremble. "Was there something I could do for you?"

No warmth to it, none of the teasing banter we'd shared before. No one has ever been able to shove me off balance as well as Erlat. I preferred it when she was making me blush, rather than stammer like I was about to.

"I, er, wanted to say sorry." Goddess's *tits*, that was hard to say. It seemed to work though, partially, because she softened. A bit. A hint of the teasing smile.

"Do you know what you're saying sorry for?"

"I—" I started to come out with something glib, some lie to cover up the fact I was totally clueless, but something about the way she arched an elegant eyebrow stopped me. "No, not really."

Her laugh threw me even further off balance, and I blushed, *again*, when she said, "Oh, Rojan, you're the funniest thing that's happened all week. Come back when you know. Now excuse me, I have an appointment."

I blushed even harder when I turned to see Jake behind me, witness to my embarrassment.

"Come on in, Jake," Erlat said. "I'm ready for you."

I hurried away from the laughter that followed me out, and only later wondered why the hell Jake was going to see Erlat as a client.

Thankful that the darkness hid my flaming face, I shoved my memory of the episode to the back of my mind where I hoped it would die a lingering death and made my way straight to the pain lab to meet Pasha.

It wasn't far, but far enough for me to notice the atmosphere of caged resentment, of hate and fear. It would only take one more thing to set it all off again, and then maybe nothing could stop it. And when that happened, our circling neighbours, who sat waiting and watching as close as they dared, would fall on us. We'd kept the thumbscrews of trade on them for so long, they'd be fools not to.

The stairwell that led to the lab was fire-blackened but the damage seemed fairly superficial. I hoped so – I didn't fancy the whole place collapsing. I hesitated before I opened the door, remembering the way it had looked the last time I'd been here. Blood and bits of machines, Dwarf's body looking even more twisted in death than it had in life. I made a mental note to go to the mortuary, make sure he got a proper send-off rather than dumped into the Slump. I dreaded telling Lise that he was dead, and was surprised to find a Dwarf-shaped hole inside me.

It wasn't the remembrance of the blood that made me hesitate, but the knowledge that he wouldn't greet me like a long lost friend, wouldn't grab me and start showing me some new technical marvel he'd come up with, waggle his eyebrows over his abused-doll face in a way that always made me grin.

I sucked it up and opened the door. Given the choice, I'd have slunk off to the nearest bar and drunk hooch brewed from whatever scraps they'd found this week. I didn't have that choice, and, Namrat's arse, didn't I hate that.

The lab wasn't much better than when we'd found Dwarf and Lise, but someone had made an effort to tidy up, and the blood was mostly gone. No one was there just then, and I took my time going over what was missing, and what was still there. The spare pulse pistols were gone, leaving only the one in my pocket. The prototype portable magic enhancer, the one that Dwarf had hoped meant we could capture magic in Glow tubes at home, or wherever we were, that'd gone, too. All the little electrical gizmos, the practice sessions for what they wanted to incorporate into the generator and electrical magic enhancer, they were there but in more bits than there are stars. They'd even taken Dwarf's pride and joy – the detesticliser. Very useful for intimidation, Dwarf had always said, and I believed him. A serial killer in a pacifist's body, that's what he'd been, the gruff old bastard. I was going to miss him something chronic.

The door to the pain room opened as I stood looking at all

the gaps on the benches, the mangled bits of metal where there weren't gaps, trying to work out if we had anything helpful left.

Dench came in, his moustache drooping with worry. Perak followed, and behind them came a man I'd not yet met, a furtive looking ferret of a man in a lab coat who instinctively made me check that my wallet was still there. Right at the back, Allit stood with round wide eyes and a fearful look. At least he'd not been murdered yet.

Dench and I looked at each other without speaking for long moments, before he shook his head and said, "How screwed are we?"

"More than just screwed. The generator's had it, the machine in the pain room is a mess of wires and someone's offing pain-mages." It probably came out harsher than I'd intended, but all in all it'd been a crap day. I glanced at Perak. "The Inquisition isn't really helping either."

Perak looked guilty at that. "I wish that I could say I could stop it." He glanced sideways at the man in the lab coat, and I understood immediately that he couldn't say all he wanted. Where was Pasha when you needed him to rummage in someone's head? "They'll finish when their orders are complete. You're sure about the mages?"

"Two of the boys were just discovering their magic, like Allit here. A third was Taban. And this . . . " I gestured round the lab. "This wasn't rioters. This was deliberate. Someone really doesn't want us up and running."

Dench didn't look too surprised about the mages, I noted. No, not surprised at all. "Any ideas?"

"One or two. You?"

"One or two." His gaze was steady, but it gave nothing away. Guarded to the end, was Dench. Probably why he was in charge of the Specials. Speaking of which. "Your Specials, I know you don't have much magic, but could they help out? Until we get things back up and running?"

He chewed his moustache thoughtfully. "Don't see why not. You could do with a guard here, anyway, and I've got a few men making sure no one tries for Lise again. Discreetly, of course. I'll think on it. This is Bulahan. He's from Alchemical Research, here to see what he can do to help." The look of disgust that Dench tried and failed to hide indicated the Specials might be a good idea for more than we'd said aloud. Ferret-face was going to be a problem.

Bulahan stepped forwards, neat and precise. A pair of glasses kept slipping down his nose and he'd twitch it to push them back up, reinforcing the ferrety nature of his sharp face.

"I've done what I can with the collectors in the pain room. That seemed most sensible to start with. It's a bit of a rush job, so they won't be very efficient, but they will work for now. The generator, well, I don't even know where to start. The way it's wired – it shouldn't work. At all. It *won't* work, I can guarantee it. I'm surprised that anyone thought it would be good to go anytime soon. But given the . . . less experienced nature of the people you had working on it—"

"I'd be careful how you carry on that sentence," Perak said and the harshness of his voice surprised me. Perak didn't get angry, ever. He barely even got a bit miffed. "One of those people is my sister, and Dwarf – Dwarf was more a genius than you could ever comprehend."

Ferret-face blinked rapidly, but the recovery was masterful. "Well, yes, of course. I mean to come up with the concept of the generator is obviously superb, and, and . . . "

"And you will continue the work to the best of your ability. If necessary, I will assist."

The threat of the Archdeacon lowering himself to something so mundane as using a screwdriver shocked Ferret-face into silence. Perak winked at me. Who was this person, and what had he done with my head-in-the-clouds brother?

"Um, maybe we should get started for the day, um, Your Grace, if it pleases you?"

"Certainly." Perak raised an eyebrow at me. "Where's Pasha?"

"He'll be here soon enough. Let's get started," I said. Get it over with more like. It was simultaneously the best and worst part of my day.

Perak left, in the company of a phalanx of Specials. Dench hesitated at the doorway and gave me a grave look. "Usual place?"

"Good enough," I said. "You're paying."

He snorted in disgust at that and went, leaving me with Ferret-face and Allit. The boy looked utterly petrified, though

176

it could be for any number of reasons – the pain magic he was getting used to, the thought he might have to work in the pain room though it was far too soon for that. Maybe because Ferret-face was Ministry, and that made me itch, too. I wished Pasha would hurry up.

But the pain was waiting, so I got down to it. Ferret's rush job seemed to hold up well enough, though I couldn't get as much into the Glow tubes as usual and what I could seemed dim somehow. But painwise it was no better or worse than usual. Ferret-face didn't have Dwarf's sense of knowing when to make me stop and I almost tipped over the edge and into the black. What stopped me was the smallest of noises – a whimper from the other chair. Not Pasha, but someone else. Allit. When I forced my eyes open, Ferret-face had got him strapped into the chair opposite and he was trying to dislocate his fingers as he'd seen Pasha do.

I stood up and almost fell getting to him.

"What the fuck do you think you're doing?" I whispered to Ferrety. "He's not – he only found out he was a mage a couple of days ago."

I attempted to disconnect Allit, but he kept shaking his head and pulling away, all the while trying to dislocate that finger. Ferrety tried to stop me, too, muttering about "all the Glow we can get", but I snarled at him and he backed off.

I finally got the boy out and he fell into me, sobbing so hard his lungs must surely ache. "I wanted to help," he said at last. "Dwarf – he was kind to me and so was Lise, and you and Pasha, you're helping everyone. And I wanted to help as well, like you."

Someone wanted to be like me? That thumping sound was probably the Goddess fainting. "Too soon, Allit. You need to practise, start small before you get on the chair. Even if you practise, it's hard, devilish hard."

"But I wanted to *try*."

I was really starting to like this kid. The Ferret started to say something, but I cut him off with a "Your speciality is machines, not mages, right? Go and fix something." When he'd left, I got Allit sorted and told him to get ready to go out.

"Where are we going?"

I smiled, enjoying the secret. There was precious little else to enjoy that day. "To go and see a man who will teach you all you need to know about using magic. I'll help you, too, when I get the chance. *Then* you can help. You'll be no good if you kill yourself with magic. Can't tell you how many times I almost managed that."

Facing Lastri with a red-eyed boy in tow was much easier when I could casually toss her some bacon and say, "I brought you and Dendal something to eat, and this boy needs keeping away from the lab now Dwarf isn't there. I don't have time to teach him at the moment, so Dendal will have to."

For a second, I really thought she'd stab me in the eye with a pen, but the bacon made her mouth drop open and I left to meet Dench, thinking I'd scored at least a little victory. It would be the last one for a while.

Chapter Twelve

The Beggar's Roost had seen better days. A rathole of a pub, right down in the scabby heart of No-Hope with dripping walls and mouldy floors, and this was one of the upmarket places round here. Dench sat hunched over a pint of something that could loosely be called alcohol, if you were feeling generous. Citizens of Mahala could get used to crappy and almost non-existent food, but no beer was a serious matter and a few industrious souls were making a small fortune fermenting anything they could find.

I bought a pint for myself and peered into it, trying not to wonder what it was they'd fermented this week. Rats, by the smell. I put it down without drinking any.

Dench eyed me warily while pretending he was watching the Rapture addicts that passed for dancers on the stage. They moved with an odd, languorous sort of rhythm, an effect that was spoiled by the nothing behind their eyes.

"Mages," he said at last. "You're sure?"

"Not totally. But three of them were definitely, and a couple more we looked at were possibles. And how many people are mages? One in five, ten thousand men and boys? Less? What are the odds?"

He grunted in what could have been agreement, making his moustache flap. "Shit, this is the last thing I need right now. Half the fucking city hates mages. The other half merely loathes them. You said you had an idea or two."

"Remember where you found them all. One was outside the temple where Guinto was preaching, one was last seen *in* his temple and Taban was less than ten minutes away. The others weren't far either."

"Oh, you have got to be shitting me, Rojan. Look, I know you hate the Ministry, I'm not exactly overfond myself, not with how things have been lately, but you've got a real thing about priests. Not content with killing the old Archdeacon, now you want to accuse the one priest who's actually doing some good down here? You're obsessed."

I tried not to be offended. He was right. "You got any better ideas then?"

"Perhaps." He took a long slug of his drink. He looked sick, but that could have just been from the beer. "I'll talk to a few people, let you know. In return, I need you to talk to Perak, because he sure as shit isn't listening to anyone else."

I frowned over my own drink. "I can try. What about?"

"About the generator – I told you he'd pinned all his hopes

on it, that with that going he had enough leverage to tell the Storad and Mishans to bugger off. Even now it's destroyed, he's *still* pinning his hopes on it, on being able to fix it. On you. Can you get him to admit he has to *try* to negotiate? Or at least talk to them? Because I think we're screwed otherwise. No, I know we are."

It should have struck me sooner, but it became clear as air when Dench started pleading their case. A point of view I hadn't considered, having been too busy being up to my knees in dead bodies, pain labs and willing women. Who benefited from the generator going? The Storad and the Mishans and any cardinal on their side – or maybe just not on Perak's side. With no power, if we were forced to capitulate, well, any cardinal that was chummy with them was going to find himself in a very nice position. Maybe even new Archdeacon. That's a powerful incentive.

It was a pretty persuasive argument too, as long as you were one of the few prepared to believe that Outside actually existed and that people could live there. Scripture said that Mahala was the Goddess's whole world. Scripture said. Unfortunately logic said we had to be trading with someone, though if you've got enough brainwashing it can replace logic. It was one of those unacknowledged dichotomies – some people firmly believed in both the scripture and Outside, in the same way you could believe in rainy days and sunshine; they both occur but not at the same time. This is because people are so screwy in the head and seem built for deluding themselves. I sometimes wondered if I was the only sane one, or if I'd already gone batshit and this was my madness.

A cynical shrug from Dench, a swig of the hooch. "Maybe they just want to use the pass without paying through the nose for us being middlemen. Or maybe they'll wait for more mages to be born. The Storad in particular always play a long game."

I thought back to the only Storad I'd ever seen, a granite-faced man in the Death Matches. They were a hard race, it was said. Hard like the stones they mined, and we were soft, too soft, after years of living off trade and now with no food in our bellies. Mahala might fall if they breathed hard on it.

It was a theory anyway, one I didn't want to share just yet, in case I was wrong. Dench would undoubtedly sneer at my obsession with the turncoat nature of the Ministry.

Maybe these murders weren't as connected as I thought – at least Dwarf's murder. Could be someone just using the previous murders to cover up that they wanted the generator gone.

Because if even the staunch Dench felt this way, there were bound to be others who not only thought it, but did something about it.

"Well?" asked Dench. "Will you talk to him?"

"I'll try," I lied, and changed the subject. "You'd know if anyone came in from Outside, wouldn't you? Except the ambassadors, of course."

"Ah, Rojan, not just a fucked-up face, eh? Not that I know

of, but there are ways and ways. Means to communicate. You know that."

Why was it I always got the impression he wasn't telling me everything, but only enough to get me worried, to get me to do something? Experience, because he never gave away more than he had to. He'd given me more than he probably should have, though.

"So what are you doing about it?" I asked.

"Me? Not a lot. I don't have time. I've got riots to keep down, and an Inquisition I didn't want that I have to oversee, I've got people dying like flies and no more space in the Slump for the bodies. I've got an archdeacon who's pissed off all the wrong people at the worst possible time, when he needs them behind him. If they get behind him now, it'll be to knife him in the back. He's a bit like his brother in that regard." The sardonic look warped his moustache to new glory.

"It's up to us, then, that's what you're telling me. That I can't expect any help from you?"

"I just did help you. More than I technically should. Rojan, you're good at finding people, better than I'll ever be. We need them caught, whoever it is. Need *someone* in the dock, someone we can say, 'Look, we caught the bastard' about to all the Downsiders. Whoever it is. If the Downsiders calm down, then the Upsiders will calm down, and we'll be back to something approaching normality. I hope. Then perhaps we can get on with surviving, on concentrating on how we're going to get through this and what we're going to have to give the Storad and Mishans in return for them not killing us. I'll help you as much as I can, but I've got more shit going on than I can handle and my first duty is to keep your brother alive. Someone's already tried for him once."

He dropped that titbit in as though it was a bit of fluff, nothing of consequence but I thought it might have been the whole point of this conversation. To tell me things were worse than I'd thought, that I'd better get my arse in gear. As if the day hadn't been bad enough.

"What? When? Why didn't you tell me, why didn't he tell me?"

"Yesterday, and probably because you're his brother and he doesn't want to worry you. Well, I *do* want to worry you. We've got our hands fuller than we can cope with. Talk to Perak if you can, because if you don't ... shit, I don't know how, but things will get worse. And try to stay alive yourself. No telling who this killer might go for next. Like I said, I've got a couple of men quietly keeping an eye on Lise, so even if it is Guinto – not that I'm saying I believe you, because I think you're full of shit – even if it is him, he won't get her and neither will anyone else, like whoever it really is. I'll set some guards about the lab, too, and another to watch your office. I'll tell that one to help if you ask, and he'll be one of my best, so keep an eye out for him. That's all I can spare, but if it's pain-mages they're after, well, you've been advertising."

He left me there, staring at what was nominally alcohol,

wondering whether I dared drink it. And who was going to be left alive come tomorrow. Right then, the way things were, maybe none of us.

Dench had been pretty cagey, as usual, but he *had* given me an idea whether he'd meant to or not. Something to dig into. Who knew, maybe it would help.

Because the thought of the Storad and Mishans, that they would be the ones to benefit from the generator going, had taken hold of my head. That and the thought of a cardinal with enough desire to see himself Archdeacon by saving the city when Perak couldn't, or wouldn't, do what the cardinal thought necessary – negotiate, capitulate, call it what you will. Dench said no Outsiders except the ambassadors, and I believed him. Those ambassadors would have no contacts, and certainly wouldn't be allowed out in the city. Even if they were instrumental in the why, I didn't think they were the ones actually killing these kids, or Dwarf.

So who did have the freedom to roam anywhere they liked in a city that looked up to them, or at least obeyed everything that they ordered? Who had the powerful desire to come out on top? I could think of one or two people, and, given the way my mind works, anyone in the Ministry topped the list. Factions within factions against factions. Maybe I'd been wrong instead – maybe the murders had nothing to do with Guinto after all. I thought back to that first sermon of his I'd seen, to all the Ministry men sucking up to Perak at the back of the temple. The ones that looked at his face with nodding heads, and at his back with daggers for eyes. I'd seen one of them Under since, too. And what was a cardinal doing Under? Only one way to find out, currently, but it meant I had to take my bollocks in my hands in case they got injured along the way.

Someone had managed to scrub most of the scorch marks off the walls of Erlat's house, but that didn't help much because someone else had scrawled a lot of anatomically incorrect drawings on the clean patch.

Inside was still the oasis of calm it always had been but Kersan, normally so serene, was noticeably keyed up. He kept glancing over his shoulder though there was nothing new to see there, just the same arty nudes and velvet drapes. When I asked to see Erlat, he positively flinched.

"Kersan, it's important. Really."

"I'll ask," he said eventually and slipped through the door.

I fidgeted my way around the room, not really looking at the pictures, wondering if perhaps I'd gone just slightly mad. A cardinal murdering boys. Dench was right, I was obsessed with it being someone in the Ministry. But what if I *was* right?

Kersan came back and silently led me down red-draped corridors to Erlat's room. She stood in the centre of it, the centre of her world, and arched an eyebrow at me like I was a cockroach in her bed. All polished stone today, all gleaming jade. That's not what made me stop dead before I was two steps into the room. No, that would be the gun she had in her hand. It wasn't pointing at me, but still she was pissed off at me and she had a gun – never a good combination. My only – small – consolation was she wasn't an ex. After my plentiful experience of them, if any had a gun in the same room as me, I'd make a jump for it out of the window and any long drop be damned.

Erlat smiled slowly at my obvious reluctance before she shook her head and put the gun down on the table, allowing me to breathe again.

"What is it, Rojan?" A smooth, cool question, no teasing. It made my shoulders itch.

She sat on the lounger, curled her feet under and motioned me to the chair opposite. Having put me off balance, again, she seemed content to wait while I sat and gathered my jangled thoughts. It seemed best just to come out with it.

"You have a cardinal as a client?"

Her mouth twitched and a frown marred her smooth forehead. Her voice was cold as winter. "So? Are you making my business your business now? Think you have the right?"

"No! No, I just want to know how often he comes here, that's all. What's a cardinal doing Under?" Especially one who'd sneered at all the temple-goers, like we were beneath his contempt.

"If you'd ever taken me up on my offer, you'd know." She stood in one elegant movement and glided towards me, all professional persona now, none of the other Erlat anywhere. Smooth and sleek and, actually, pretty fucking tempting. I stared at the table instead of giving in. I couldn't, not with her. The blush was creeping up my neck, hot and uncomfortable.

"Erlat, how often?"

She stopped at my tone and cocked her head, but her voice was still sleek with ice. "All right, I'll play. Cardinal Manoto. Once or twice a week, since we set up. Maybe a dozen times or so, all told. Why do you care?"

A dozen or so times. Thirteen murders.

I stood up with a jerk, startling Erlat. "Is he due again? An appointment?"

"What the hell does that have to do with you? Jealous?"

"Stop it!" I grabbed her by one shoulder, worried and angry both. "Stop trying all that seduction on me, and stop all this. I don't know what the fuck I've done to piss you off, but I wish I hadn't. All right? I'm not asking because your business is mine, or because I'm poking my nose in. I'm asking because someone's killing people, because Dwarf is dead and Lise almost was too and I don't know who's next. Now tell me, is he due again?"

She pulled away from my grip, and I couldn't tell now if she was pissed off or what. All I could tell was that I'd probably just fucked over a good thing, same as I always did. She wouldn't look at me as she sat down again, kept one shoulder my way.

When she finally spoke, her voice sounded blurred, but at least she'd stopped with her act. "He comes when he feels like it, no appointment. Could be next week. Could be tonight."

Chapter Thirteen

Dendal was waiting for me when I got back to the office, dog-tired, with the rank taste of rat hooch on my tongue and Erlat's door slam in my face, the sound of something solid hitting the back of the door as I left ringing in my ears. I hoped whatever it was he wanted, Dendal would be quick about it.

Then I looked a bit harder. Dendal kept hopping from foot to foot and he had a piece of paper in his hand that was crumpled from the way he clutched it. It wasn't going to be good news.

"Go on." My voice sounded weary and petulant even to me. Everyone seemed to be dumping responsibility on me from a great height. Why should Dendal be different?

He didn't say anything, but held out the paper. It didn't say much. Just one sentence. *Our son is dead.*

I sank down to the sofa. Another murder. It had been too much to hope I could sleep first.

"I'll go to the mortuary first thing." Oh goody, something to look forward to.

"No, no." Dendal did another little hop. "Their son isn't dead. They only wish he was."

I watched him closely – something bothering him, something close. Something I was missing. I needed about a week's sleep, but it didn't look as though I'd be getting it any time soon, so I said, "Start at the beginning."

"It's Pasha's parents," he blurted out, and that was all I needed to know. Which didn't stop Dendal blathering on. "I, well, the *tone*, you know?"

I did know. Dendal's speciality, his Major, is communication. He takes and sends messages in his head. Not like Pasha, he can't read a mind as such. Instead, he acts like a conduit for messages. And being such a gentle soul, he was pretty good at picking up tone, or emotional backlog or call it what you will. If he said they knew Pasha wasn't dead but hoped he was, then they did. It was the last thing Pasha needed right now. It would be like ripping up his dreams while jumping up and down on his heart.

"We don't have to give him this. Not now, not yet.' Maybe in a year's time, if we were all still alive, when he'd got some sort of life back and he'd unfucked his head a bit. "We've all got other things to worry about." Like, was Erlat going to be safe if Manoto came back? At least she had a gun, which gave me a small bit of comfort. She was pissed enough to use it on me, though, which wasn't. Goddess's tits,

191

I even managed to fuck it up when I *wasn't* sleeping with them.

Dendal hopped again, back and forth, till my eyes went all screwy. "I promised, Rojan. I can't not send on a message. It's what I do."

"Seriously, now is not the time. The generator is all but dead with fuck all hope of fixing it, we're hip deep in dead mages, Pasha's already strung out by—" Discretion became the better part of valour as I decided not to tell him what Guinto had said to Pasha, about the Inquisition and how Pasha was feeling about being a mage. "Now isn't the time, believe me."

"Don't say fuck, it's not nice. We have to tell him."

I fought the urge to tear some hair out. Living around Dendal, it's a wonder I'm not bald. "What you mean is, you want *me* to tell him."

He beamed at me in that vague way that always meant I ended up doing what he wanted. It's really difficult to argue with a man who's only half here. "Yes, that's right."

"Dendal—"

"You have to. I . . . I don't know why, exactly. But you have to, and you have to go *now*. Please."

"I'm not going to hear the end of it if I don't, am I?"

Too late – he'd wandered back to his pile of papers and was humming a happy fairy song, smug in the knowledge that I'd do what he asked. What really fucking grated was that he was right.

I owed Pasha, more than I wanted to, and I couldn't keep this from him. I stared down at the paper. So *bald*, so fucking cold. Pasha had said to me once how proud they'd been when the Ministry had recruited him. Not so proud now, when it was fast becoming common rumour what pain-mages in the 'Pit had been up to. He'd been from somewhere up high, I knew that. Heights or Clouds. For people like that . . . I knew he'd spent a lot of time looking for them, spending hours with Dendal trying to remember his real name. Jake had done, too, but with less luck. She'd been small when they'd taken her. Not so Pasha: he'd been old enough to remember bits and pieces. Heights or Clouds. Respectable, wealthy. Keenly aware of appearances, particularly now. Everyone else had rejected him, spat on him, hated him. Downsiders, Upsiders, Ministry, priests, and now even his own parents. All he had was Jake, and that relationship seemed fraught with some difficulty I only barely comprehended. He had her, and me.

Poor fucker, all he had was me to believe in him and I believe in shit, in doing the job and taking the cash, in not messing with Ministry, getting the girl into bed and screw the rest. And making sure Pasha didn't get too fucked up. Not if I could help it. I folded the paper into squares and slid it into an inside pocket.

I have never walked so slowly anywhere in my life.

It's always weird going back to where you used to live and seeing the changes, the way the place has moved on without

193

you. I didn't really want to get to the rooms, or think about what I was going to say to Pasha when I got there, so instead I looked around and noticed the change.

It had never been a nice area – the lower rent had meant I could save some cash. Now it wasn't just not nice, it was downright fuckawful. Most of the shops were boarded up, having nothing to sell. Some had been burnt out during the riots, or ransacked by the Inquisition, others had graffiti scrawled over them. Not nice graffiti either, no funny jokes, no "I was here" or "Bebbi loves Janna" or even crude anatomical diagrams that made you wonder if the people who'd drawn them were at all in proportion. There was a lot of "Downsiders fuck off", "Pain-mage perverts", "Little Whores must die so the Goddess can save us", that kind of thing.

How had I not noticed that before? Because now I came to think of it, similar sentiments were scribbled all over. I'd shrugged it off because it wasn't really relevant to me – even the pain-mage ones didn't sting because I hadn't been the sort of pain-mage they'd had in the 'Pit and never would be. But Pasha couldn't shrug it off, even if he'd never joined those pain-mages, or not willingly. A Downsider, a pain-mage, a Little Whore – everything that was despised, he was. Now I had to twist that knife all the way round.

I stood outside the door a long time, unable to bring myself to knock. In the end, I didn't have to; Pasha opened the door. Must have known I was there, heard me in his head perhaps.

I hoped like crazy he hadn't heard any more than that, but he greeted me with a puzzled grin.

He looked better, as though the time at home with Jake had done him good. More relaxed than I'd ever seen him. Jake, too, when he beckoned me in. He sat next to her on a makeshift sofa and the way she took his hand, the way she looked at him, it was obvious to me that the "obstacles" Guinto had hinted at were overcome, or at least smaller. It hurt to watch, but at the same time she was happy, happier than I could ever have made her. I have never regretted that. Saving him, pulling him out of his black so that she could be happy, so they both could be for once in their crappy fucked-up lives. If I'm wrong and there is a Goddess up there somewhere, if she ever asks what I ever did to earn those Brownie points to heaven, I'll offer her that and be satisfied. And if she isn't satisfied, too, well, she can go screw herself.

It made doing this even worse.

"I went to the lab, but you'd already gone," Pasha said. "That Bulahan, he's a real piece of work, isn't he? Kept trying to screw more out of me, until Jake stopped him."

"He's temporary, I hope. But I – we – need him. Unless you suddenly know how to fix everything?" I couldn't stop the bitterness in my voice. Why send me, Dendal? Why couldn't you have told him yourself? Why has the message come now, not next week, or never?

My tone made them both frown and Pasha sat forward. I hoped, oh I hoped he couldn't see in me.

"What?" Suspicious now, an edge of fear to the question. Not without cause.

Best just to come out with it. "Dendal had a message for you." And because I couldn't bear the sudden hope in his eyes, I said it straight out. Like ripping a bandage off quick so it'll hurt less. Bollocks of course, but helpful to think so. "Your parents consider their son dead. Even if they know he isn't."

Odd, how differently people react to things. Jake shrank back, her face tight, back to her ice-queen façade. Furious on his behalf, I could tell that, her hands going to the only reassurance she had, where she'd usually wear her swords. Brought up in violence, it was always her first, gut reaction to any threat. But Pasha sat there like a man in a dream, his face slowly collapsing in on itself as he realised what I'd said. No anger, though if it'd been me I'd have shouted the place down probably. No anger but a terrible, hopeless sadness that seemed to radiate from him, to crush him.

"Pasha, I'm sorry, I—"

He stood up, slowly, dreamy still. "It's all right. Really." I didn't hear his feet on the bare boards as he drifted into the bedroom and shut the door behind him on silent hinges.

Leaving me alone with Jake. But that was all right, because she was angry enough for four people and I wouldn't have risked it. Not when she had those swords within reach, hung on the wall. Still, it was a guilty little pleasure to be near her without him.

As soon as Pasha shut the door she leapt up and began to pace like a tiger, kicking the sofa in frustration. Even now, all fired up and snarling, she was glorious. Graceful, furious, haunting, with a broken soul, but glorious. When she stopped pacing in front of me, I was hard put not to reach out and touch her. That's all, a touch of her hand.

"Why would they?" she asked, her voice on the cusp of anger and hurt for Pasha. "Why would they do that? He's their son, they should – I mean they're his *parents* ... "

I thought she knew the answer well enough, but was so angry she couldn't say anything else.

"It was all supposed to be different up here. Better. We were going to have a new life only we can't, and they've screwed us and screwed us. Screwed everybody. Turned the Goddess into, into, I don't know what and *we're* the heretics. And everyone hates us, all those smug Upsiders, the Ministry. Rounding us up, taking us away. Even his own parents ... Well, I hate the fuckers back, twice as hard."

There wasn't a lot I could say to that, because I agreed. I was about to reply anyway when her head came up. A muffled sound from the bedroom, a tickle of words in my head that I couldn't quite grasp. I got up, a sudden drop in my belly of something wrong. Then the words weren't a tickle any more but a shout, a scream of swearing, of warning.

Jake grabbed her swords and still beat me to the door, but I barged it open, left it hanging from shattered hinges and stared into the room, dimly lit from a single rend-nut lamp.

197

I don't know what I expected – Pasha twisting his fingers, falling into the black perhaps as he had once before, wanting to escape into pain-filled bliss. I know I didn't expect the spray of blood on one wall, the sight of a black-clad back as it dived out of the window, or Pasha slumped on the floor clutching an arm.

Jake got to him as I raced to the window, but it was darker outside than Namrat's heart and I couldn't see anything. No running figure on the walkway below, no movement on the mound of rubbish in a gap opposite. Nothing and no one. I turned a leery eye on the window. Too narrow for Fat Cardinal to get through, and I couldn't see him climbing up either. My head felt like a pendulum, swinging from one suspect to another and back again.

I turned to where Jake was frantically wrapping a ripped sheet round Pasha's arm. His skin was pale as curdled milk, but he looked up at me with his monkey grin and his voice was all false bravado. "Shame we're not at the lab. Got a good bit of juice."

"What the fuck happened?"

"I'm not sure." He rubbed at a temple and winced, and I wondered what he was hearing with all that juice running through him. Half the building probably had their thoughts in his head right now – Pasha's own peculiar curse, and the reason why his black is silent as snowfall.

"I shut the door and leant against it. I didn't hear them coming, not a footstep or a thought – no juice, and without it

I can only hear someone real close. I didn't even have my eyes open. I felt a kind of breeze, and when I looked this big knife was coming for me. For my throat. I managed to get an arm up, and when the knife went in I got enough to call out. Then you started on the door and they shot out of the window."

I crouched down beside Jake and tried not to see the panic in her eyes. A big knife, going for his throat.

Don't say it, he thought at me. *Not in front of Jake.*

I kept my voice as steady as I could. "Jake, could you fetch the box? I'll have a go at stitching this if you like."

She threw me a suspicious look, but went to find the box.

"This is getting fucking serious," I said.

Pasha raised an eyebrow. "You think?"

"Ha ha. You get anything from them?"

"Only after they cut me, and once they were outside they sort of got lost in the general noise. Mostly they were thinking 'Shit, it wasn't supposed to be him! I need to get out!' when you barged the door. Two things I got. One, they were running to the temple. I don't know which one. Sanctuary, that's what they were thinking. A temple has to give sanctuary. Two—"

He broke off when Jake came back with the box. She rummaged around and held up the ampoule of painkiller. Pasha shook his head – it'd hurt like fuck, stitching him, but we were going to need all the juice we could get, because he thought the last at me.

Two, your name was next on the list. Your real name.

Chapter Fourteen

The cut to Pasha's arm wasn't as bad as the blood had suggested, so it didn't take too long to get him stitched. I was even getting pretty good at it, what with all the practice I'd had stitching Jake up after her Matches. The argument after took longer, but I won in the end for once. My name next or not, if whoever was doing all this was getting this close to us, I wasn't leaving Dendal on his own, especially given the would-be killer's thought "It wasn't supposed to be him". Who else was supposed to be there? Who else had a reason to go and see Pasha right then? Dendal, with his message from up high. Fair enough, Lastri was enough to frighten the most crazed serial killer – she scared the living crap out of me – but it was the middle of the night and she wasn't at the office. And the office was where anyone would go to find me, mister-next-on-the-list. They'd find Dendal, too, and another mage might be a temptation too far.

That was the reason I gave, anyway, and I meant it. I didn't voice the thought that that message had just been too nicely timed. Someone knew about Pasha trying to find his parents, about Dendal and how insistent he got about delivering his messages. Maybe a ruse to get Dendal and Pasha together and kill two mages with one big knife, which I'd thwarted by being there and being big enough to knock the door down before they got the chance to finish off Pasha. Goddess knows what they'd had planned to keep Jake out of the way.

Anyway, added bonus to me checking on Dendal was that I didn't want to stay at Pasha and Jake's place. I couldn't, not with her so close. Because I would have caved in, and Pasha didn't deserve that. Pasha didn't deserve any of what happened, then or later. Besides, he'd be safe enough because there was as much chance of Jake leaving him alone as me becoming Archdeacon, and she was a mean fighter, all the meaner when it was Pasha at stake, and she'd got Pasha to call to Dog, too. Between the two of them, they could probably take on a whole battalion of elephants armed with guns.

So I was pretty jittery as I made my way back to the office. I kept my good hand on the pulse pistol in my pocket, just in case, and jumped at every moving shadow, every noise. Which meant I was jumping a lot because, if there's one thing Mahala does well, it's shadows. The moon was up there, somewhere. Every now and again, a faint silver shaft would appear, reflected a hundred times before it reached this low, growing weaker each time. A few windows had flickering lights in them, but the quiet light just seemed to make the shadows worse. For the first time, I was truly afraid in my own city.

The office was dark when I got there, and that was odd. Odder still was that when I sidled my way in with my pulse pistol out and ready, Dendal wasn't there. Dendal was *always* there, scritch-scratching away with his pen, surrounded by his candles. Not now, though. His corner was empty, his candles unlit. It really creeped me out, especially given my earlier thoughts regarding ruses and big knives. If there was one thing in this crappy city I could rely on, it was Dendal being there, in body if not in mind. I tried not to imagine the possibilities and failed, badly.

So I was feeling like throwing up as I edged into the room. Tripping over any dead body would be bad enough, but Dendal's? That would be like tripping over a dead puppy.

No dead body and no one trying to kill me by the time I got to the candles, so I took my life in my hands, lit a few and took one over to my desk. He'd left a note in his spidery hand. *At Lastri's, all sick – bacon was off. Took boy with me. Back in the morning.*

I tried to restrain the smile, then realised no one was watching and let it loose. The only thing better than me eating bacon was using it in the escalating war between me and Lastri. I felt a twinge of guilt and told myself not to be so soppy – only last week Lastri had "accidentally" laced my tea with laxative. A shame that Dendal and Allit had got sick too, but better than the alternatives that had been playing across my mind.

I flopped down on the sofa and put my feet up on Griswald. If anyone – whoever the hell it was, and I had less idea now than I did when I started – was after Dendal they'd look here first, so he should be safe enough, the boy too. Not to mention I happened to know Lastri's place was situated between the rooms of two very well-built guards, heavy, gnarled men who were surprisingly protective of her. Dendal was safer than I was. Especially given that my name was next on the list.

By the time I'd done my best with all the locks, rearranging the one on the main door so that even Dendal with his key wouldn't be able to get in, the clock showed after three in the morning and I was pretty sure I'd think straighter after some sleep. I needed to think straight if I was going to untangle the mess we were in. I was asleep as I thought it. Sadly, not the black and dreamless kind.

A sound, close and furtive, dragged me back awake and thankfully out of the dream. I lay there, a sweaty mess with dream-visions dancing in my head, of Jake and blood and a boy with his throat cut, of Pasha driven to his knees by all the voices he could hear in his head, each of them lit by the Glow we couldn't provide.

All the candles were out again except the one I'd left on my desk. It didn't show me much, except that I wasn't alone. Something, someone, moved in the darkness beyond. I had a bad feeling that they had a big knife with them, and groped for the pulse pistol in the pocket of my jacket where I'd slung it over the back of the sofa. I hoped I'd have a chance to use it.

A dim shape moved out of the shadows and I swung the pistol. Luckily I didn't fire it off willy-nilly, because an ethereal face appeared in the gloom, dark hair fluttering round her face and she smelled of angels.

I sat up and stuffed the pulse pistol back where it had come from. "Abeya, you scared the—" I restrained myself from saying something very rude indeed. She was a priest's daughter after all. "What are you doing here? How did you get in?"

Her mouth twitched in a hesitant smile. "I came to see you."

"That's—" I didn't get a chance to say anything else before she kissed me. I was impressed; normally I have to do a bit of chasing at least. Maybe this new face was good for something after all. Then I realised I'd just woken up. I didn't – couldn't – keep up my disguise when I was asleep. And then I stopped thinking with my brain entirely as she pressed into me, all soft and willing, with tongue and hands and . . . Other parts of me started thinking, if you can call it that, very rapidly.

Was it fair? No. No, it wasn't fair to her, or to me much either, but I was lonely and in love with someone who I couldn't have. Abeya was there, lonely, too, I suspected, and warm and kissing me as though there was no tomorrow. In my defence, I'd have made every go of it, I'd have tried, though

I suspected my Kiss of Death tendencies would have screwed it around the two-week mark as usual. So I protested, but not much, and we . . . had a nice time. Twice. Still, it wasn't fair of me.

Then again, it wasn't very fair of her to try to kill me afterwards.

Chapter Fifteen

There are moments in a man's life when he's particularly vulnerable. That has to be the worst of them. Naked, as I was, and in that little fluffy, contented world that inhabits your brain after such happy activity. I was warm and she was soft against me with her head on my shoulder, smelling like angels and if all wasn't right with the world, it was a damn sight better than usual and with a great view, too. Those are about the only brief moments in my life I don't hate everything, am not angry at anything or afraid of anything, and I savour them. A few brief moments of belonging with the world, *in* it rather than being outside and hating it.

Which made the big fucking knife one hell of a shock, not to mention it shattered all my nicely thought-out theories about who was killing mages.

One minute warm and fluffy with an angel on my shoulder and the next, said angel is an avenging harpy with a knife heading for my throat. In instinctive self-defence I fell off the sofa next to the desk, which decided now was a good time to end our truce and shoot out a drawer straight into the side of my face. Handy, as it happened, because it gave me a jolt of juice. I only had to try to decide what to do with it.

Rearranging is my Major but I was pretty new at it, and it usually took a bit of time. Still, a sodding great knife going for your throat at speed concentrates the mind wonderfully. I managed to grab her wrist and slow the knife down, enough so that maybe I could do something about the sharpness of the blade. It was only when I caught her that I saw what the dim light and my own lusty shallowness had made me miss before: the brand burnt there in the tender skin under the thumb. Why she was killing pain-mages was clear now. It didn't explain why she'd jumped me first, though, and it didn't stop the knife.

I pulled in the pain from the smack to my face, let it flow through, welcomed the flutter of the black, the song of it. It wouldn't take much, soften the metal, dull the edge. I rather overdid it – the knife hit me in the side of the throat and bent like a rotten banana.

Lastri always said I'd get my comeuppance for my womanising ways, that one day I'd push some poor woman too far, over the edge. Sickening to think she was right.

When Abeya saw the knife was doing no good, she threw it across the room with a snarl, grabbed my throat with both hands and squeezed. I tried to ignore the burn of my lungs, my brain's increasingly frantic calls for air. Instead I shut my eyes and fell backwards into the black, let it well through me, not too much now, not too long, however tempting, or I'd never come out, and then blew it all out again. At least I managed to control it, well partly, this time. Dendal's interminable sermons on control and mastery seemed to be paying off.

When I struggled back up again, not without a longing backward glance at the calling black I'd skimmed, opened my eyes and started rasping in lungfuls of crappy but oh-so-sweet air, Abeya was slumped at the bottom of the wall.

"Lastri always said any woman would be nuts to end up with me, but I never thought I'd get a real loony." My voice was croaky and it hurt to speak, but I had to say something. "You could have just killed me rather than taking me to bed first. I wouldn't have minded."

"I didn't know you were a mage at first. I only knew Father didn't approve and that was enough. I *liked* you. You didn't care that I was Downside, didn't spit on me for it. You liked me anyway, I thought. Then I found out what you are, all of you, you, Pasha, Dendal and ..." Weird how her face changed, from angelic and innocent to psychotic. Those brands – what must it be like to think you like someone and then realise they're exactly what you hate, exactly the sort of man who made your life a tortuous misery? How would that break a mind that was fragile to start with?

Her face kept flickering between the two extremes, angelic to hatred and back. I don't think even she knew which was her. "You weren't supposed to be still alive, but as you were, I took the opportunity."

Nice, and then what she'd just said popped something into my brain – not supposed to be *still* alive. The bacon, the damned bacon.

Not off, poisoned. Only it had been shared among three rather than one, so maybe the dose was weaker. I hoped that Dendal hadn't pigged it all.

Abeya got up into a crouch, like a tiger waiting to spring. Her face twisted into a rage so deep it seemed bottomless, and I didn't blame her. Be nice if she took it out on whoever had given her the brands instead of me, though.

"You look different." Her head cocked to one side and her lip curled. "You look like *him*."

It didn't take a genius to realise she'd spotted how like my father I looked. She couldn't take everything out on him; as I've said, he was dead, but it seemed maybe I was the next best thing, me and any other pain-mage available. She was on me again before I could get to my feet, clubbing me over the head with something, shouting formless words of hate, sobbing as she did it.

She'd lost whatever reason she'd had, clearly, because she was only making it easier for me to cast a spell. Even under that provocation, I couldn't bring myself to hurt her. I'm such a gent.

209

I got her off me, making her swear as she hit the floor, and legged it to the door on to the street, rearranging the lock as I went, then slamming the door behind me. It didn't take long to ensure the lock would no longer work, a moment's rearrangement of the tumblers. She thudded into the door and banged at it from the other side, her voice a thin screech of hatred so vitriolic I took a step back, just in case she could break the door down.

Someone sniggered behind me, and that's when I realised I was out on the street, stark bollock naked. Not only that, I still had Rojan's face on, and if I didn't change it quick smart, I'd have no face at all. That wasn't too much of a problem; I could do the face from memory. Nakedness was another matter entirely. As was the problem of a murderous Abeya in the office. At least I was still alive. Always a plus.

I gave rearranging myself some clothes a go, but with nothing to work with it was tricky. I even tried just making it look as though I was covered up, but no dice. Still starkers.

The sniggerer turned out to be the Special that Dench had arranged, Tabil. He tried to hide the snigger behind a hand and a bitten lip, but the laughter kept snorting out of his nose. "Did your date not go very well then?" he asked in between giggles.

I could hear Abeya through the door, faint but unmistakeable. "Bastard, fucking bastard."

Not the first time I'd been in this situation, or similar.

Normally it was the husband on the other side of the door, though.

I glared at Tabil, but that only reduced him to a smirk. "How did you know I had a date? *I* didn't know until she turned up."

"I didn't see her go in, but when I checked on you, you seemed to be enjoying yourself. Super-int – er, Dench said I was to ignore all your antics with the ladies. He said whoever it was wouldn't last long and anyway, we didn't have much choice."

"I seemed to be enjoying myself? Were you watching?"

That wiped the smirk off. "Only the kissing part. Once I realised it was, you know, I stood over the walkway." He pointed to the dark doorway of an abandoned apothecary.

Abeya stopped thumping on the door, and I was glad. It was giving me a headache, between that and Tabil.

All right, now that explained it – if she'd known he was keeping an eye on the place, she'd have lulled everyone into thinking just a date and then ... and then bye-bye Rojan, hello death. By bacon or by knife. Loony she might be, but she wasn't stupid. And she'd seemed so angelic, so *normal*. Shows what I know.

"Look, Tabil, I need your lot down here straight away. I'm pretty sure we've got a killer trapped in there."

Only, by the time he'd lent me his coat and we'd peered in through the window, we hadn't. There were no other exits but somehow she'd escaped.

211

Twice in one night, the killer – Abeya, I corrected myself, angelic, beautiful, soft, warm, psychotic Abeya-of-the-bacon – had got away from me. Twice she'd not quite managed to finish the job. I wondered if she'd try a third, to make the evening worthwhile. If so . . .

The note lay on my desk, but not where I'd left it. She'd spiked it on the nail I use for old receipts. She'd also left something else behind in her hurry. No exits, I'd thought, though in reality there were no exits me and Dendal knew about or used. She'd found one, though.

A neat little doorway behind a behemoth of a wardrobe we'd not bothered trying to shift when we moved in. If we had, we'd have noticed that the wardrobe moved on rusty rails, and seen the hidden doorway. I thought back to the hidden door in Guinto's temple. Maybe they all had one, because this doorway led to a room behind the altar in the neighbouring temple. Or maybe it was just a handy bolthole for the drug-dealing ex-owners of the office. Abeya was, of course, long gone when we checked.

I thought about it as quickly as my knackered mind would let me. First, I sent Tabil off to Lastri's to make sure Dendal was safe, telling him to get some more Specials down to Guinto's temple quick smart, especially given that Lise was there, too. I was taking no chances. Tabil bitched about it, told me how much Dench would create, but I told him he'd fucked up once and not to make the same mistake twice, so he went, moaning all the way.

On my part, I scoured the office for something, some trace of Abeya that I could use. It took a while, because candlelight isn't good for searching, but in the end I had it. Or, rather, them. Two dark hairs on the sofa, too long to be mine.

Two hairs to tell me where she was, whenever I liked.

Chapter Sixteen

Before I did anything else, I put some clothes on. Naked in public isn't only embarrassing, it's sodding cold as well, especially that close to winter. An extra layer between me and the world made me feel better, too, gave me something to hide behind.

I glared at the desk, daring it to try something but it behaved for once. I laid the two hairs across the blotter that was covered in doodled arty nudes, or, as Lastri called them, the perverted recesses of my disgusting mind encapsulated in ink.

Two hairs. Not much but enough, I hoped. I'd worked with less before, but it was going to hurt. I knew it was stupid, even as I clenched my bad hand into a fist. I was in no fit state for anything, but I had to know where she was, or at least that she was far enough away that she posed no threat for now.

I didn't get much – Up, she was going Up. Fast, too,

constantly moving so I couldn't get a good fix. Not unless I pushed harder, so I did and knew it for the mistake it was almost instantly. The song started, running through my brain like the sweetest drug ever. I was on my own, no one here to get me out if I should fall, but it sounded so good . . . If I fell, then no one would know it was Abeya we were looking for, killing mages, only Tabil, and I couldn't trust him. She'd come back to try for Pasha again, for Dendal. I used the little discipline I'd managed to hoard over the years and pulled out at the last possible moment. Back in the here, I was kneeling on the floor with my face scrunched into Griswald's fur. I stayed there a while until I had the strength to stand up, and turned over what little I'd learnt. Up, going Up. A snatch of conversation heard underneath the song. Abeya's angelic voice twisted into something new – "Your poison didn't work. If you'd told me what was in the bacon, I could have—"

Not much to go on but she was Up, out of the way for now, and getting further. That complaint, too – the bacon had been poisoned, but maybe Abeya hadn't known it, not then at least. Maybe not known I was a mage then either, though she had her proof now. So who *had* known about the poison? Who'd given her the bacon? *Don't ask me where from*, she'd said, and I'd known it was from the Ministry, that they were the only people who were likely to have access to it.

I needed more to go on, needed to know who she was talking to, but I'd had enough of pain for the day. Black was at the edge of my vision even now waiting for me to try and it wasn't even dawn yet. Plenty of time to go mad later.

After staring at the hairs for a while I decided that cowardice was the better part of valour or at least the better part of not going batshit, folded them into an envelope and shoved it in my pocket. Given the choice of the pain-free or the painfull method, sense dictates not dislocating anything you don't have to. Besides, trying any more magic while I was in that state was asking for trouble, no matter how tempting it would be to give up and fall in. Most of all, Abeya was going Up, taking her killing knife away from Pasha and Dendal and, just as importantly, me. I had time. A bit at least. Room to breathe, to work out what the fuck was going on before I followed her. Forewarned is forearmed, or something. Though I'd rather have a gun.

First I checked on Dendal, Lastri and Allit. The three of them were throwing up at regular intervals and the way their eyeballs had turned bright green was enough to show me that, yes, the bacon had been poisoned. Tincture of rendnut, works a treat on rats. If I'd eaten all the bacon – and I *would* have eaten it all if I'd been left to my own devices, because the existence of bacon is the one thing that may persuade me there is a Goddess – I'd be dead. Which would at least have spared me the green-eyed glare that Lastri managed, in between retching up green froth. A glare that said she knew I'd done it on purpose and there would be retribution, oh yes. I made a mental note not to eat or drink

216

anything she might possibly have touched. For about the next decade or so.

I was safe enough for now, though, because she could barely move. I called in her burly neighbours, impressed upon them the importance of not letting anyone in, *especially* if they were female and angelic looking, and left.

My next port of call was Guinto – maybe Abeya had gone to him for help, or for absolution. Abeya was further up than his temple, but who knows if she'd stopped by to say hello to Dad on the way? Given magic was a bad plan just then, with him was the logical first place to ask for information. I was kind of looking forward to it, in a sadistic way. Mister Holier-Than-Thou had been harbouring a murderer, and I was pretty sure he knew it, too, encouraged it, maybe even directed it. Someone certainly had. For all his sermons on tolerance, he certainly hated pain-mages enough, and I had a burning urge to let him know I hated him back.

Maybe I should have waited for Pasha or gone to get him, but I didn't want to face him right then, or subject him to another one of Guinto's guilt trips when he had enough to be dealing with, so I went on my own. Dawn was breaking somewhere above me, probably. It was hard to tell down there, except the darkness lightened enough that I could see my hand in front of my face and the night people – muggers, beggars, street whores, drug dealers and anyone unlucky enough not to have even a hovel to call their own – began to find a dark place to hole up for the day. There might be a curfew, but the sorts of people who lurked on the walkways round here at night didn't care about that. They didn't care about anything much, poor bastards, not any more. The Inquisition might even come as a relief.

The Glow tube at the end of the street was on its way out, the Glow fading as it bled out its last, lighting up no more than a couple of feet around it. Making everything else seem darker, and the night people only ragged shadows. I gripped the pulse pistol harder, my finger hovering near the trigger. It's always been rough down here, always been a place for those who can take care of themselves, but lately the squeeze on Under, the hate and fear and hunger, had made them bolder. The guards barely bothered any more, or, if they did show up, came mob-handed.

I jittered my way to Guinto's temple, always feeling that eyes were watching me, that someone was stalking me. Abeya perhaps – maybe she hadn't gone as far as I'd thought, or she was even now on her way back down. Maybe I was being incredibly stupid, out on my own in a dark city with a killer loose, one who'd already tried to kill me once. Maybe so, but sitting in my office waiting for her to come back would have been just as stupid. I told myself that, and very nearly believed it.

By the time I was on the right level and at the end of the right street, my good hand was numb from gripping the pulse pistol so tight. My bad hand was just numb. In places anyway. The other bits were a big, angry throb. At least I'd have juice handy, if I needed it. I was hoping I might get an excuse to zap Guinto. It probably wouldn't help, but I'd feel better. The black tittered at the thought and I squashed it – no matter how tempting, Guinto wasn't worth losing my sanity over.

The temple shone with light, a brightness that lit the dark and made it look welcoming. I didn't trust it. Let's face it, I don't trust anything that's Ministry. Ever. Years of hard experience have led me to that, and it hasn't sent me far wrong before. I stood in the doorway a few moments, squinting against the light of a thousand candles, and wondering where Guinto had got them. How he could afford them.

When my eyes adjusted, I went in. A few hardy parishioners had braved the curfew and the Inquisition to come and pray. Their low murmurs of supplication as they chanted at the feet of statues or murals twisted my stomach. Fools, poor deluded fools. I felt sorry for them, too – perhaps this charade was all they had, all that stood between them and giving up. It didn't stop me thinking they were idiots, though.

Guinto wasn't in the main temple. Not surprising given the early hour, so I made my way past the statues towards the door at the rear. Something made me glance up at the mural of the Goddess. Not the nice, flowery, kittens and sunshine one – I stuck my tongue out at her, and felt both better for it and pretty stupid – the Downside version.

Blood and death and sacrifice and a tiger that looked as though it could jump out of the picture and eat you. I didn't like, or believe in, this version of her any better than the bland

219

one, but I suppose you could say I respected it. A bit anyway. It didn't hide the true, bloody nature of life behind sparkly sunbeams. It didn't pretend. I liked that about it, about her when you saw her depicted that way. She was still imaginary but at least she wasn't lying about what anyone could expect out of life, or death.

I was about to pass by when I saw it. Not surprising I'd missed it before; I hadn't been paying all that much attention, and it was tucked away behind Namrat and his big, shiny, *hungry* teeth which kind of drew the eye in a weirdly fascinating way.

The group of men and boys was small, as though at a great distance behind the Goddess. They looked like a later addition, too – the painter had less skill than whoever had done Namrat, that was for sure. I could feel those tiger eyes watching me, almost feel his hot breath down the back of my neck. This group was done in a much plainer style, but I could still recognise them. Still recognise me. Not the disguised me either, the real me. I peered closer. Whoever it was hadn't done me justice – I was way better looking than that.

When my vanity calmed down a little, I recognised some of the others. Azama, the previous Archdeacon, architect of wholesale torture by pain-mages, my father, and very, very dead. Taban was there, too. At least one of the boys I'd seen in the mortuary. Dwarf, looking even uglier than he had in life. Pasha, with his monkey face and angry, dark eyes,

Dendal's monkish air. I touched a finger to the mural. The paint was wet on Pasha, Dendal and on me.

"I see you enjoy the mural, even if you don't believe." Guinto's voice, all smooth and oily behind me, made me jump so I smudged mine, Dendal's and Pasha's faces. Made me feel a bit better, because this looked very much like a list to me and we were the only three on it still alive, and that was more by luck than judgement.

I straightened up. "Not enjoy, exactly. Where's Abeya?"

That put a crack in his voice. "In her quarters, as she's been all night. Please, leave her alone. She's been through quite enough without having to deal with someone like you."

I cranked up a smile. "And which particular bit of me is it that she shouldn't be dealing with? The bit that thinks all priests should be drowned in their own self-righteousness, or the bit that makes her sneak out of her quarters, seduce me and then make a fucking good go of murdering me? That part of me isn't too keen to deal with her, to be honest."

Although, even then, other parts would. No, it's not logical. It's probably pathological like Lastri says. Knowing that, or that it had been sheer loneliness on my part and some twisted urge on hers, didn't change it.

Guinto was good – I couldn't tell if he was surprised, appalled, or guilty as hell and covering it up. I wished I'd brought Pasha with me. Not that he'd read the mind of a priest, but it would be nice to have someone on my side.

Guinto slid a glance over his parishioners. One or two looked at us furtively – I hadn't made any effort to be quiet – but he smiled in his unctuous priest way, made a sign of blessing in the air and they bent their heads again.

"Maybe you should come through," he said at last. His voice was still smooth and oily, but there was an undercurrent of something. Guilt possibly. Priests are always guilty of something and I had every inclination to believe he was, too. He was Ministry, that was enough for me.

He led me through to his office, as spartan and neat as it had been before. "Please, sit down," he said, though he didn't sit himself. "Your sister is showing signs of waking."

I shut my eyes against the relief, against the release of the darker thoughts that I'd kept at the back of my mind. "Good. Thank you." That thank you hurt worse than my throbbing hand. "Abeya?"

"Allow me a moment." A smile, as oily as his voice. "I promise not to try to abscond."

Another door hidden in the mouldings and cracks in the plaster at the rear of his office. They were everywhere, and I'd never noticed. Kind of the point, I supposed. Guinto left the door open and I could see into the rooms he shared with his adoptive family, through another door he opened into what I recognised as Abeya's room. When he came out again, he looked thoughtful and scared and angry.

"What did you do to her?" His indignation was almost pitch-perfect.

"Nothing. It's more what she did to me. Have you seen the new additions to the mural?"

"I – no." He sat down behind his desk and ran a hand over the smooth wood, as though comforting himself. "Where is she?"

"That's what I came to ask you. I thought she'd come back to you."

His twitched his lips in a sardonic smile. "She's not stupid, you know. If she really did try to murder you—"

"And Pasha. Was possibly planning to murder Dendal, too. And I've got good reason to believe she murdered those boys. Taban. All people on their way here or on their way back from here, except Pasha, Dendal and me, and Pasha's one of your more faithful parishioners. All mages."

"She – oh." He rubbed a hand over weary eyes. "Yes, I see. Why would she come back here if you knew it was her?"

I shrugged, offhand. It had been a long shot but she'd been pretty irrational. Well, most murderers are, wouldn't you say? "Maybe she thought you'd save her."

"Save her? Yes . . . yes I suppose she might. I would, too. If I knew where she was I wouldn't tell you. Even if she hadn't – after you left, we argued."

"What about?" Like I couldn't guess, but I wanted to hear him say it.

Guinto sat up straight and smoothed his robes. "I told her about you, Pasha and Dendal being pain-mages. She didn't know – I'd taken pains to keep her away from your office, that sign. You're ... " His voice dropped to a shocked whisper. "Unnatural, sinful. *Unholy*. You should pray to the Goddess to help you resist, to stop you in your madness, to atone for everything. You'll destroy us, all of us."

That pricked my conscience, small though it may be. I had already destroyed us once. "No, Father. We're trying to save Mahala."

"Save us with magic." He might as well have spat in my face, the tone of his words was that vitriolic. "Kill us, destroy us. Make the Goddess turn from us."

Like she'd ever looked at us, if she even existed. "And thus ends the theology lesson for today, thank you. Where is she?"

"I don't know!" But he had a clue, I could see it in the sudden shift of his eyes as he thought of it. She wasn't here, but he thought he knew where she might be.

"All right, you don't know," I lied. "Did you know what she was doing, that she was the one murdering boys? Pain-mages specifically? Did you put her up to it?"

His mouth flapped open as though he was speechless with shock. "No!" he managed at last. "I swear on the Goddess herself, I didn't make her, I didn't know, *if* it's true. Why would I help you to find the killer if I knew it was her? I'm still not sure I believe you, that it *was* her. You don't like me, I'm aware of that, and you know how I feel about pain-mages. But that – no. All life, everything created by the Goddess, is sacred to me. Even your life, unholy and sinful as it is. I do not wish death on you, I wish that you see the way

224

clearly and renounce your magic, that you be cured of what ails you."

Do you know, I even half believed he might be telling the truth, at least the truth as he saw it. He was so earnest in it, so *sure*. If it was a lie, he was good at it. Still. "But if the Goddess exists, then she gave me this unholy magic. Why would she do that if I'm not to use it? I've seen priests before who thought they were the Goddess's weapon." I smiled brightly. "They usually go completely mad. Or get murdered when it turns out faith isn't much of a weapon, physically. It's a great emotional cosh, though."

His answering smile was withering, full of disgusted pity so I wanted to tear into him with words that would shake him to his core. "One day you will see, and you will be blessed. In the meantime my daughter is missing and your sister awakes. I can take you to Lise, and then I must try to find Abeya before you have her arrested. Do you have any evidence?"

Nothing concrete, except my testimony and who would believe me? Not many people and none of the ones that mattered – the Inquisition – that was the trouble. Not that I was going to admit that. "An eye-witness, and some other evidence."

The smile became more genuine as he realised I was probably bluffing. Must have been losing my lying touch. When he got up, he seemed relaxed again, in control. I didn't see how I could get anything else out of him, so I let him take me to Lise.

He left me alone with her, which I appreciated. She was still pale under her dusky skin, still shadowed around the eyes, but those eyes flickered when I spoke and when I took her hand she squeezed it. It seemed very small and fragile in mine, and I dreaded having to tell her what had happened to Dwarf.

"Hey, Lise, you've been lollygagging too long, time to get up."

She squeezed my hand again and tried to say something but the breath of words wasn't enough to hear.

I kissed the back of her hand. "You're going to be okay, you hear? And I'm going to catch whoever did this." I was pretty sure by now it was Abeya, because I was sure as shit it wasn't looters or rioters, and as sure it was connected somehow. Destroy the generator, the people who knew how it worked, destroy the mages that would ultimately power it. Destroy the city, or at least make it weak enough to walk right in. Maybe Abeya only wanted a part of that – destroy the mages for all the torture they'd put her through – but I was fairly sure by then someone else was behind her, twisting an already fragile mind to breaking.

"If I ask you a question, can you nod or shake your head? Or squeeze my hand once for yes and twice for no. Can you do that?"

A squeeze on my hand, another flutter of those eyes. How can someone worm their way into your heart so quickly? Lise had, with her smarts, with her devious nature and her way with mechanicals and electricals that had me floored

226

in admiration. A sister I'd not known I'd had until a few weeks ago but she was everything to me now, pretty much all I had that I wanted and was mine. All this trying to work out who was killing people, who was running rampant with a knife and a grudge, it was for her, to find out who'd done this to her. I'm not saying I didn't care for those poor boys, or Taban but . . . it was there, in the back of my head all the same. I loved her in a way I haven't loved any woman since Ma died – platonically. I think it was that, the strangeness of it, that made it so much more real. She was an anchor for me in a life that had been utterly rudderless and pointless before.

"Good. All right. Who did this, was it a woman?"

A squeeze that made me smile, thinking I knew – and then another, telling me I was wrong. Or at least wrong about who'd killed Dwarf, who'd destroyed the generator, screwed the pain lab, screwed Mahala.

Maybe not Abeya then. Maybe . . . Guinto?

"Someone you recognised?" I asked. I knew she went to temple. It wouldn't be a stretch for her to come here; her rooms weren't far, and she spent all her time there or at the lab, as far as I knew. Hadn't Guinto said he'd met her?

Again, a single squeeze that raised my hopes, and another that dashed them. Maybe I was totally wrong. I never like to think I'm totally wrong. Who does?

One of the women who were acting as nurses came over, an older lady with grey hair and kind eyes that crinkled at the edges as though she smiled a lot, though she wasn't smiling now. I didn't even think about getting in her knickers, which shows you the sort of lady she was. She reminded me of Ma in a weird kind of way.

"She needs to rest now," she said, and the schoolmarmish tone of her voice made me nod before I even thought of disobeying. Instead, I kissed Lise on the forehead, promised her I'd be back soon and that she'd be better and left. At the least, who I now knew was murdering people wasn't here ready to attack her again.

It was a wrench going back out into Mahala, into the shifting dark of moving shadows that could hide anything, everything. I kept one hand on the handrail of the walkway, the drop beneath more of a threat to me at the moment than the people I couldn't see on the street

I kept feeling that I'd missed something, something important. When I got to the stairwell at the end of the street, Tabil was waiting for me in a darker shadow trying to look efficient. All I could think of were his sniggers, though, and whether everyone was safe.

"Reporting for duty," he said immediately, with a salute so sharp I could have cut a throat with it.

"Good. I need another one of your lot to watch over my sister."

Not Abeya, not who'd killed Dwarf and tried for Lise anyway, possibly not Guinto. Cardinal Manoto? It seemed unlikely that he could overpower Dwarf when he was defending his beloved gadgets. But whoever, they were still out there. The attack was on the machinery. Not on the Ministry installation, on the machinery. On what gave us power. Dwarf was dead and the only, best person who knew how it all worked – Ferret-face excepted – was Lise. I had a suspicion it was whoever had got into Abeya's fractured head somehow, though no real clue who that was except they had access to bacon and therefore it was someone with money, or power, or both. But that didn't mean I could neglect Abeya and her murders. "I need another two, on Guinto."

Tabil raised a sceptical eyebrow in the gloom. "On Guinto? Are you sure?"

The eyebrow wasn't the only sceptical thing about him; his voice dripped with it. A man after my own heart. Maybe he had a point, though – Guinto was popular, well liked, listened to, even by those who'd rather be rampaging all over the city and setting it alight. Putting Specials on him, given the mood of the city, would be like putting a gun to Mahala's head and pulling the trigger.

"Well, you don't have to advertise who they are. Be discreet. You can do that, can't you?"

A smirk, all cocky. "We prefer using the uniform for putting the fear of the Goddess into people."

I suddenly realised how aggravating I can be, because this guy was just like me and annoying the crap out of me.

"Can you do this or not? Dench said you were going to help."

He muttered something under his breath. I only caught a part of it, something about how I must have something on Dench or why would he help a worthless shit like me? Right then and there, after the day I'd had and the sun was hardly up yet, after the days that had come before, the days I knew were about to come that would be even worse, it was enough. Enough to have me grab at his throat so quick that the rookie didn't have a chance to duck away. Enough to make me say screw it and bunch my bad hand into a fist, to groan out some pain. To hear the song in my head, calling, always calling, pulling me in and down. I was stretched so far I was pretty sure he heard it when I snapped.

His eyes goggled over a gasping mouth as I squeezed, letting all the anger, frustration and pain well up into my fingers, and my voice. Such a simple thing it would be, to rearrange him. I could see how to do it in my head, see how I'd make him look. I shoved him up against a crumbling wall and my face into his.

"You're helping me because you want the power back on, don't you? Or do you want to sit in the dark and wait to starve, maybe wait till the Storad or the Mishans, fuck, maybe both, come marching in as though they own the place and there'll be nothing we can do about it? Dench has got other problems, but this one is mine and you will fucking well help me or I will make your face look like a duck's arse. Permanently. I could do far, far worse, if I wanted. And I'm hanging on by a thread here, and you are tempting me. So.

Very. Badly. So you do what I ask like Dench said, and you'll still have a dick to swing come tomorrow."

It was all I could do not to just have at it right there and then. Change his face, shrink his dick. A couple of other really nasty little things that occurred. The black was telling me to do it, do it, more pain, more magic, fall in, do it. *You need me, Rojan. You know you want me. Do it, and you can be free.* And I wanted to, oh, I did. To be free of everything, fear and pain and darkness, of the deathly weariness that ached my bones.

"Enough." The voice stopped me, commanding, smooth, expecting to be obeyed. I can't tell you how much I hated Guinto's voice. My vision cleared a little, though, and I watched him watching me with a curl of contempt on his lips. That was what made me let go – that contempt, from some-one like him, a Ministry man, maybe a man who'd aided a murderer.

Tabil fell back against the wall, taking great, heaving breaths. I pointedly ignored Guinto and leant in, keeping my voice low. "I know what he says. We're unholy, right? And you the Goddess's man. I can be much more unholy than that. Remember who you swore to serve. Her, not *them*. Do I get the men, or not?"

He rubbed at his throat, at the vivid red mark I'd left there, and nodded. "Subtle, as you say. But Dench will have some-thing to say about this."

I smiled at him, and savoured the flinch. "Yeah. Probably to you. Now do what you were ordered to do and help me."

By the time he'd scurried off, Guinto had gone, but Jake stood in his place. Come to temple perhaps for morning prayers. She watched me carefully, as though I was someone she'd never seen before. One hand rested lightly on a sword and her head tilted to one side, as though she was considering me. As though maybe I wasn't the person she'd thought. I turned away from that thought, that look and the vast anger that underpinned it. Maybe I wasn't who I thought either, even who I was under all my pretences and cynicism, but I couldn't take it, that look. Not the cool pity of it, not the sorrow that I wasn't the man she'd thought me, the rage that life Upside wasn't what she'd thought, what she'd hoped all those years for. The lady doesn't like it when you're not good and noble.

Instead I stalked off into the darkness of the stairwell, up and up, away from the fetid smell of home and into the corrupt air towards Trade and Over, wondering what the fuck I thought I was doing. Cocking it all up good and proper seemed the most likely answer. I fingered the envelope in my pocket, with Abeya's hairs in it. She hadn't attacked Lise, but she had tried for both Pasha and me, maybe Dendal, too, with that note. Or someone had – Abeya wouldn't have had any way to get to Pasha's parents, or to fool Dendal.

Maybe she'd got wherever she was going now, stopped her headlong run so I could get a fix. I had to find her, work out what was going on and she was the key, the link. Guinto wasn't going to help, so it looked as though screwing my hand up some more was in my immediate future.

I swear, the decision was nothing to do with the little voice that kept calling, that was a constant companion now, even when not using my magic.

Oh, Rojan, come on in. It's warm in here and no one relying on you. No one will die because you fucked up. It'll just be you and me. You and me. No fear, Rojan. Just blackness, sweet bliss. The freedom you always knew should be yours. Come on, you know you want to.

Not that, I swear it on Namrat's deathly bollocks.

Chapter Seventeen

I was cold and sweating by the time I reached the pain lab. It seemed the best place for the job. Familiar, lonely, with no one to disturb me. I'd forgotten about Ferret-face. He tried to talk to me, tell me something about the apparatus in the pain lab but I didn't really hear him. There had to be something here. Something I'd missed earlier.

Instead of listening to Ferrety, I wandered around Dwarf's desk, and Lise's. So odd to think of him not there any more. Just another cold body on a slab. I cast an eye over the odds and sods on his desk but it made as much sense to me as prayers and temples. That is, not a fuck of a lot. Cogs and wires and springs. His favourite pair of needle-nosed pliers that had always looked so doll-like in the big sausage fingers that were deceptively delicate. Despite Lise's desk facing his, he had a picture of her on his desk, nicely done in oils. She grinned up at me and I thought that I'd only ever seen her happy when discussing alchemy and electrics with Dwarf.

Her desk wasn't much different. More wires, fewer cogs. A slew of diagrams that looked like a bad case of noodles. Pictures on her desk, too – one of Perak with his daughter looking like a fairy princess. One of Dwarf that took pride of place, and I began to wonder how far their friendship and intellectual camaraderie had gone. How much she wasn't really mine, how nothing, no one, was, the black was right about that. How devastated she'd be when I had to tell her he was dead.

A picture of me too with my old face on, looking much younger, before me and Perak had fallen out all those years ago perhaps. I wondered where she'd got it, even as I thought that no one had ever kept a picture of me on their desk before. Why would they? The old Rojan was a bastard. Well, so was the new one, but in different ways, and now I was a Rojan with family, with people I cared about. I'd kept people away before, because I was afraid. Now I'd let them in, all of them, Dwarf and Lise and Perak, Pasha and Jake and Erlat, and the fear almost paralysed me, made me wonder why I'd done it. *So you can be a part of this city, part of the people who live here. So you can be a person, not an automaton. So you can serve the Goddess.* Dendal's voice in my memory, from a time just after I'd destroyed the Glow and guilt was weighing me down like a stone. But it was hard, and I was afraid for all of them so that my hands shook. So that the black looked ever more tempting. *No fear here, Rojan. Come on, fall in. No fear, just sweet bliss . . .*

I stared at those pictures for a long time, working up the courage. I had to do this, find out where Abeya was, who was working her like a puppet, so we could get back to pumping out magic before she killed all the mages. I had to be strong, for everyone. I didn't feel strong enough even for me.

Ferret-face made a strangled noise behind me as I made a fist, overstretched my poor fucked hand and something snapped in there. More pain than I'd expected, more juice. Too much for my ragged, overworked brain to handle. I had a brief glimpse of Abeya, somewhere where there was sun. Her face shining in light as she talked to someone I didn't know, deathly pale skin and hair so dark it was like it shut off the sun. Then the black swamped me, laughing as it took me, as it soothed away all my fears and thoughts and left me only with cool comfort and my own blinding light. No fear, no responsibility, no ever-present horror of fucking things up worse than I already had.

The voice penetrated after who knew how long. Insistent, inside my head. *Rojan, come on, get the fuck out of there.* Soft, but sounding harsh as a gunshot in my black. I willed it to go away, to leave me alone, but it kept on. *Come on, you aren't too far in, you can get out if you try now.* Trouble was, I didn't want to. I only recognised Pasha's voice when he said the one thing that might have brought me out. *Jake's here, waiting for you. We're all waiting for you. Don't fall in, don't be that person. Don't leave.*

Oh, he knew how to get to me all right, the little shit. I opened my eyes on a groan of pain from my hand that seemed to throb all through me. I was lying on my side on a bench in the lab. I'd been sick on the floor and my head ached something fierce. Didn't matter, though, because I opened my eyes to her, to Jake watching me with eyes blue like the sky. A consolation, but not much. Enough to stop me falling backwards into the black again as my hand throbbed and almost had me screaming when I moved.

Pasha moved up behind her, and the consolation faded except that he looked as worried as her. "Goddess, you almost gave me a stroke. If we hadn't turned up when we did – what did you think you were doing?"

Despite the lecture, he helped me to sit up. The room swirled nauseatingly. It hadn't been like before, when I'd gone right into the black. Before it had been a bright and glorious light inside, velvet blackness around me, power running through me and lightning for bones. This time it had been relief, pure and simple, and taking that away made me want to be sick all over again.

I tried to speak, to explain, but nothing came out. A hand on mine, comforting. Jake. "Didn't you see while you were in there?" she asked Pasha.

He gave me a dirty look at the way she held my hand and said, "I don't like to look too hard in his head. Never know what I'll find."

"Try living in it," I said. "It's not pretty." I tried to snap it out but I couldn't seem to get any force in the words. "I was trying to find who attacked you. And attacked me, too."

That sobered him. "They got you, too? How—"

"Because I should have stayed sworn off women. Because I'm a dick, or at least I think with it. Abeya. It was Abeya. I managed to get away, but then so did she."

"You have got to be—" Pasha sat down hard on the bench next to me, frowning as Jake squeezed my hand and let go. I resisted the urge to grab it back. Barely. "Why?"

I shut my eyes and tried to ignore the way whatever I'd snapped in my hand grated when I moved. Tried to ignore the juice thrilling through me, waiting to be used, wanting it.

"She's branded, like you. Same brand even. She found out we were mages and, well, there you are. I'm surprised no one else has tried it, if you think about it. All that time in the 'Pit, all that torture from the mages. Surprised all the Little Whores haven't ganged up on us and killed us all long before now. I think maybe Guinto added to it, all his talk of mages being unholy. Maybe he even put her up to it. He's a Ministry man, so he's guilty of *some*thing. Someone certainly is."

Pasha shot off the bench so hard that I opened my eyes again to see mousy little Pasha in mid-lion-roar. "So, he's a Ministry man. He's a good man, too! A good priest. Sometimes good men do bad things, and bad men do good. Don't you ever look at someone and *not* think what they're guilty of?"

238

"Not often, no. And I'm mostly right. Fuck's sake Pasha, you're defending a Ministry man, after all they did to you? All those scars they gave you and those mages were supposed to be pious men, too. After all the shit the priests have given you, Upsiders have, even Guinto has, because you're a mage, and you're defending him?"

I'd pissed him off bad by now, but I couldn't seem to help the words as they fell out of my mouth.

His eyes were dark with anger as he leant in and jabbed at me in time with his words. "Your trouble is you don't believe in anything except saving your own skin."

All my stupid rage drained away as I looked at him. He wanted so much to be the good guy, and he was, without knowing it. Better than I'll ever be, and still he thought it wasn't enough.

"And your trouble," I said softly, and, yes, I was acutely aware of the irony, "is that you only believe in other things, not yourself. You let Guinto persuade you that's as it should be. I don't need to read your mind to know you're thinking of doing what he said, stopping the magic, stopping being you so you can be some . . . some fakery of what they want you to be. He's given you some false promise of how it'll make everything better, for you and Jake, for your soul, for having your parents acknowledge you, for everyone. Well, it won't, and you'll still be a mage. All the prayer and belief in the world won't stop that."

For a moment, I thought he was going to hit me. I almost

hoped he would, that he would be as much of a bastard as me so I wouldn't have to think of him as the good guy any more. Instead he stood back, wiped a hand across his mouth as though my words tasted bad to him and turned on his heel. He stopped at the doorway, and turned to leave his parting shot. "I almost wish I'd let the black take you properly, let you drown in it. I almost wish I couldn't have brought you back, though you weren't far in. But we're even now. You saved me from it, and now I've saved you. I don't owe you anything, not any more."

The door shut quietly behind him and I let my head fall into my good hand. Oh, Rojan, so very good at pissing people off, even people you like, people you want to stick around. Kiss of Death. Obviously that extended to friendships as well as more romantic liaisons.

"Rojan." Oddly, I'd all but forgotten Jake. When I looked up, she was frowning at me but there was no anger there, at least not for me – there was a whole world of anger for other things, but not for me. No, I got a pity I couldn't stand. "Guinto's a good man, he is."

"So why's he tormenting Pasha like this? Why's he covering for a girl he knows is murdering people?"

"Why did you do that, risk falling into the black? Why push so hard?"

"Because . . . because I have to, because otherwise I'll hate myself even more than I already do. Because it's right, and I'm fed up with always being wrong."

"Did you ever think that's why Guinto is doing it? Why Pasha listens? Because he thinks it's right? You can't save everyone, Rojan. I know you think you should, but you can't. And you can't save Pasha from the Goddess, from what he needs, if he doesn't want to be saved. Or me. But you can do this. I know you can. Just don't lose yourself in the process."

I stared at her in horror, that she'd seen through me so easily, seen past all my act as she had once before. She believed in me, and that was the worst part. She believed in me and that gave me no choice.

Chapter Eighteen

Even I wasn't stupid enough to try magic again, despite the fact I had enough juice sloshing around to launch myself to the moon. Abeya was somewhere with sun. Up, that meant, somewhere above Trade almost certainly. Once Jake had gone I stared at Lise's picture on Dwarf's desk for a long while, then dumped what juice I had in a Glow tube where at least it might help when Ferret-face found it, and started.

Up, that was where I needed to go, but Up was dangerous for someone like me, someone from Under. I needed someone who knew how it worked up there, someone who could open doors and make people look the other way. Well, there's no point having a brother who's Archdeacon without using it, right? Besides, Perak had been conspicuous by his absence, and after Lise and Dwarf and what happened to them, after what Abeya had tried with me and Pasha, I was a tad jittery. Sure, Dench was looking after Perak, but I hadn't seen or heard much from him either, apart from nebulous comments about how someone had already tried for Perak's life once. If I hadn't been ready to go Up, the remembrance of that dropped into a conversation spurred me on.

First things first. I eyed the door with trepidation before I knocked. Lastri answered, green-eyed still and looking fit to split. At least she had the energy for a bit of hate, which meant she'd probably stopped throwing up. Shame.

I gave her a cheery grin and a wave to piss her off a bit more, and asked for Dendal. She let me in but I made sure to keep my back to the wall, just in case. Especially after I noticed all the knives in the kitchen. No point in tempting her.

Dendal and the boy seemed better, too – no more green froth at the mouth. They sat in the main room amid Lastri's spartan belongings and Dendal actually seemed pretty with it as he led Allit through a basic spell. He kept calling the kid Rojan, but that was normal for Dendal.

A little clay pot sat on the table between them. Allit pinched himself, squinted in concentration and the pot lifted off the table. Maybe only half an inch, and it wobbled like a lush's gut, but it was a start. Then Allit caught sight of me and the pot dropped, cracking on a corner of the table.

Lastri muttered something dire but at least Allit was pleased to see me. Dendal gave me a vague wave, and said "Grimbol, how are you?"

Who the hell was Grimbol? I shook that off – it didn't matter.

"Did you see? I made it move," Allit said, his voice a mix of fear and pride.

"I saw. Has Dendal helped you figure out what your Major is yet?"

A dejected shake of the head.

"Not to worry – I only figured mine out six weeks ago." And hadn't that been a day? Hopefully Allit would work his out without quite so much broken glass or blood. "Dendal, I need you to send a message for me."

Dendal's eyes came back from wherever they'd been, all attentiveness when communication was in the offing. "Of course. Who to?"

"Perak. I need an in, someone to help me Upside." I needed to warn him, too. If Abeya was Upside, then who knew who her next target was? I was sure she had a next target, too – you don't get that murderous and then turn it off like a tap. She wasn't going to stop, I was sure of it.

What I wasn't sure of was the why, or the next who, but Perak was already in danger of assassination so it wasn't a great leap to think it might be him. Because I was sure, sure as I could be, that Abeya wasn't doing this on her own. She'd known my real name, Pasha had said. And my real face, if it was her who had painted the murder list on the Goddess's mural. Someone had fed her that information, someone had given her the poisoned bacon. Someone was goading her, feeding her lies, twisting her hate for their own ends, I was positive. Who, was the question, but I had my suspicions.

Someone who wanted Perak's pet project to fail, who wanted Perak out of the Archdeacon's position. So, pretty much everyone in Top of the World, from what I could gather.

Dendal's head bobbed up and down as though it was on strings, his poisoned green eyes alight, making him look like a demented corpse. "Of course, of course."

The crack of his fingers made me wince in sympathy and Allit jumped out of his seat, but he soon settled. Odd how anything can become normal, if you see it enough.

I'm not sure how Dendal does it, the communication. As I said before, it's not like Pasha does it, he doesn't read minds. It's not like I find people either, because he doesn't know where they are, exactly, except what part of his mental map they occupy. This map, trust me on this, has no relation to anything that actually exists. From what he says, it's a map of how everyone is connected – so I am surrounded by a bevy of lovely women, which I can cope with. Who are all pissed at me, which isn't so good. But also I'm connected to Pasha, who's connected to Jake who's connected to Dog who's connected to . . . you get the idea. An interlinking web of people printed on the back of Dendal's eyelids.

Dendal described the actual communication once as sort of knocking on the door of someone's head. I knew from experience that it sounded like a pinging in the back of your eyes. You ignore it or you look to it, and that looking is Dendal's invitation, like a door-to-door salesman asked to wait in the hall because the home-owner doesn't want them making the place look untidy. Only Dendal isn't selling rend-nut oil lamps, or spurious ways to rid your home of synth, or cures for the tox that don't, can't, work. Sometimes, if the two communicators know each other well, he even acts as a conduit, a pipeline of thought and speech between them, which is seriously unnerving the first time. That conduit was what I was hoping for, because Perak's absence, when he'd been so involved up till now ...

Minutes ticked by, punctuated by mutters from Lastri about overtaxing Dendal and various things involving pokers, a fire and a judicious shove. Allit squirmed in his seat, and I squirmed with him. It shouldn't take that long – I'd seen Dendal get a fix in under a minute, and it usually took five, at most. After ten, and when sweat had popped out on Dendal's forehead like transparent worms, I reached out and pulled one hand from the other, stopped the twist of his fingers and the subtle little cracks of bone against bone.

Dendal swallowed hard and nodded, his eyes coming back from the faraway and to the here and now. Well, sort of. Enough that he remembered my name.

"I'm sorry, Rojan. It's – I can't find him."

Dendal never couldn't find them, ever. Except when ...

"Maybe he's not dead," Dendal carried on quickly, and my heart started again with a painful twist. "I just can't find him. It's like there's a dead space, sorry, where he should be."

"How could that happen?" Dendal could get anywhere, to anyone. I'd seen him do it before, through everything a really good Ministry security could do, past another mage even, once. Nothing could stop him if he didn't want to be stopped, except if the person he was trying to send to was dead. Until now.

Dendal wrung his hands, but at least he wasn't dislocating them now. "I don't know. I only know he's not there, he's not *any*where. No connections. No links. Nothing."

This was worse than bad, this was catastrophic. Perak should be connected to more than any man in Mahala. Cardinals, priests, rectors, advisers, guards, just about everyone knew him. Even if they'd never seen him; he was connected to all of them via Ministry, or should be. My stomach turned cold. "Dench, what about him? Can you find him?"

Dendal ducked away from my face and shook his head. Ashamed, almost. "I thought I had him, a tickle in my head, but it disappeared as soon as I saw it. I'm sorry."

I think I stared at him for a while. I'm not sure, because disjointed thoughts kept running through my head, such as, if Perak was dead, was Amarie all right? Was she safe? I'd done so much to keep her that way, I couldn't bear it if – Perak, was he dead, or not? And Dench, one of the few people I could call friend. Dwarf, Lise, Pasha, now Perak and Dench. Whoever it was behind all this, they seemed to have an abiding dislike for anyone connected with me.

I'd known when I came here that I was going to have to go Up. Mine and Pasha's and every damn pain-mages' life depended on it, maybe Perak's life, too.

I was going Up in the world, whether I liked it or not. I tried to look posh, but it didn't come easy.

I took the Spine, a once jostling road full of Glow carriages and people who ran from Boundary and twirled its spiral way right on up to Top of the World. I could perhaps have rearranged myself there, but I came over all sensible and didn't. Mainly because the black was giggling at the back of my mind, just waiting for me to do that so it could pounce. Later I'd let it, but not then.

The curfew had been lifted, at least partially – it had to be, or people were going to start starving in their own homes, and some probably already had. Even so, there wasn't much traffic. A few handcarts, some people trying to shop for food without much luck. The shops were drab and drear without their Glow lights flashing, advertising everything from herbs to Glow carriages to intricate little machines for anything you could imagine. Most of the shops were shut in any case. Nobody had much to sell except their services, or, in some cases, themselves.

I hunched into my long jacket against the seeping cold and kept my head down. Nobody gave me a second glance and I reached the underside of Heights without comment or trouble. Here was the line between the haves and the have-nots, visible as a grubby tide mark against the city. On this level, by Trade and Buzz, all was grime and filth and faces that barely saw the sun except second- or third-hand as the levels above stole it all. Those faces were hard and gaunt, like the lives that shaped them. Pinched in, closed off, at least when out on the streets when it paid not to look too friendly. Looking friendly was an invitation for a knife in the back and a careful mugging.

Less than twenty steps upwards, across the line from dirty and depressing into shiny and hopeful, and there she was. The sun, pale and watery in a winter sky, but worth stopping to look at because I saw her so rarely. As always I took a few minutes to savour it, real sunshine on my face. It probably wouldn't take long before some guard noticed me and tried to bounce me back Under, so I made the most of it.

Uncanny, people thought, how the guards always knew who belonged up here and who didn't. But there was no magic involved – Under the faces are pinched and wary. Over, the faces are sleek and bright-eyed. It's easy to spot when you look closely. Over, the faces know a real hope, and Under it's a desperate grasp that, perhaps, there might be some. If we're very good and lucky and pray hard enough, we might find a shred of hope somewhere, anywhere, for once in our lives. A different kind of faith, and answered about as often as prayers. It's hard not to let that show on your face.

I found a gap between towering buildings that even here dominated everything. The walkways were firmer up this far, more intricately decorated with little brass icons of the Goddess, but with a drop underneath to scare Namrat himself. I tried not to think of that, without much success, and looked out over Trade where they'd never build, not over the factories anyway, not unless they wanted to be shaken to bits.

For once no clouds marred the view, not a one. The sky was hard and clear, but the distant mountains were indistinct, perhaps shrouded in mist. If that's what they were – no one went Outside. Or if they did, no one ever heard from them again. Either it was so nice they never came back, or, more likely, they didn't make it out. Ministry had always been very firm about not going Out. They meant it subtly, of course, but dead is still dead.

The mountains, the pass that Mahala dominated, our not-so-friendly neighbours, they were rumours, things far off and unimportant to anyone Under, whose main concern was living to the end of the day. They said those things were real, but they say a lot of things. Most of which are a load of old bollocks to keep us in line, keep us hoping, wanting. But I was sure Outside was real – Pasha claimed to have been there once. Logically, it had to exist, but Ministry didn't like people thinking logically. It upset them. Opposite of faith, see? In a funny way, this was my own faith, that there was more to the world than Mahala. That maybe in other places it wasn't so shit. I had to believe that, or go batshit.

I didn't take long to look. It didn't pay to stay in the same place for long because of the guards, but of course I had a new way to deal with that. A small rearrangement. Make my face sleek and well fed, make my skin darken even further so it looked as though it saw the sun on a regular basis. I couldn't do much about the eyes, though, so I kept my head down and carried on up.

While I walked, I thought on what I'd seen, where it would fit. Abeya with sun on her face. That could be anywhere Heights and above, depending on the area. I tried to conjure the image again – Abeya, sun on her face, talking to a man I didn't know, who looked odd somehow, though I'd not seen enough of him to know why he seemed odd. Pale skin like milk, hair dark as Namrat's heart; I'd seen someone like that before but couldn't think where.

There had been . . . there had been grass. I knew that, I'd seen it once when I'd sneaked into an Over park. Not for long. I'd been thrown out for being from Under in approximately ten seconds. But ten seconds was long enough to catch a memory of grass, and I was sure Abeya and the man had been somewhere like that, which narrowed it down. A few parks. I'd heard that in Clouds, on the big estates that sprawled like weird, concrete mushrooms over the rest of the city, sucking up all the sun for the good and righteous, people had gardens. I wasn't *entirely* sure what a garden was, or what it was for, though Ma had shown me a picture once. Grass and flowers and shit like that. Not plants for eating or anything useful, it had seemed to me.

I came to a point where a big side road split from the Spine, and realised I was lost. I'd never been up this high before, and I didn't know what was where. Close above was Clouds – vast platforms perched on the tops of the higher buildings of

Heights. The shadows cut sharply into the sunlight, leaving whole areas of Heights and below – the ones with lower rents, naturally – in almost perpetual shade. At least their light was only second-hand, first-hand at dawn and sunset when light sliced across the city like a cleansing knife, which seemed luxury to me.

From here I could just make out where the Spine twisted through the concrete clouds and on, up to the rarest heights of the pinnacle that was Top of the World. Home of the highest of the Ministry, placed where they could look down on us mere grubby-souled mortals.

I looked back down and knew that for the mistake it was instantly. Down was a long, long way. I held on to a friendly wall. Me and heights don't mix. We are not friends. We ignore each other when possible. It's not the height that worries me exactly, it's the splat at the bottom. The thought of going higher brought me out in a sweat, but higher was where I needed to be. What I also needed was someone who knew their way around.

Or Pasha perhaps, with his knack of rummaging in people's brains. Which was handy, because, when I looked down, he was glaring back up at me. I held on to the wall, tried not to think about all the space underneath and waited for him to catch up.

He got to where I was and the glare dissolved into gawping. He was a Downsider, or had been for most of his life. The sky was a distant memory for him if he'd ever seen it other than a few glimpses since the 'Pit had gone, and the time he said he'd been Outside. I let him stare for a good while, watched him turn his face up to the sun with a tentative smile, before he shaded his eyes and stared at the grey smudge of the mountains.

"I wish I was there," he said at last, and I remembered his talk of being Outside, of having seen it. I'd scoffed at it at the time but now I wasn't so sure.

I was still pretty peeved about our row earlier – Pasha always made me look at myself hard and I never like what I see when I do that – but I needed him and he knew it. For more than just the ability to rummage in heads, and maybe he knew that, too. I hoped not. Anyway, I kept my voice level, and my peeves to myself.

Besides, I really wanted to know. "What's it like out there?"

He let out a little gusting breath that seemed to ache and turned away reluctantly as though turning away from the Goddess's smile. "Not shit."

He moved on, up, and I followed. Neither of us spoke about where we were going – I reckon we both knew the likely outcome and it wasn't kittens and sunbeams. We didn't speak about our words earlier either. We both knew we were never going to agree on a lot of things. But he was here and I was grateful not to be alone.

"I was hoping you could be a little more eloquent," I said and was rewarded with a hint of a smile.

"The sun is free there." The smile grew bitter. "People are

free there. No one cares what colour your skin is, what your accent is, what . . . what brands you have or if you use magic. No one cares about that."

The wistful way he said it, the way he left the important part unsaid – and here they do care – gummed up the words in my mouth. What to say to that? "I don't care either. And your problem is you care too much."

His gaze slid sideways to me, and there, mousy little Pasha with his monkey grin was back. "Your problem, too. Only difference is I don't pretend otherwise by behaving like a prick."

Ouch. That shot hit home. Luckily, he didn't dwell on it.

"So, where do we need to get to?"

I stopped and looked up, and up again. "Up there, I reckon. That's where Abeya is."

We both stared at Top of the World for a moment. A tall, impossibly slender spire that arched out over the city. All the better to see our sins.

Perak would be negotiating with Ministry, with Storad and Mishans, or should be, only . . . only if he was, why couldn't Dendal find him? He should be, was, I hoped, trying to make everything right somehow, though I was rapidly coming to the conclusion that in Ministry no one man could do everything, could wield all the power, even if he was Archdeacon.

But both our neighbours were waiting for us to make a wrong move, waiting for us to fail utterly.

"Think you can get us in?" Pasha asked.

"You mind having your face rearranged a bit?"

"No. You use my juice, though. No falling in. I couldn't swear I'd be able to get you out again." He grinned his monkey grin again, but it had a hard edge to it. "Or that I'd want to. I've seen how you look at Jake."

And seen inside my head, too, at least once. Because it was Pasha, because I liked the little sod and not *just* because he'd know if I was lying, I told the truth. "I look, it's true. Hell, I'd have to be dead not to. But that's all."

I could have said more, like if she was with anyone else I'd have given it a damn good try, but I couldn't bring myself to do that to Pasha, to strip him of the one thing that was his, truly. But if I'd have let that slip, well, I have this reputation as a hard-hearted bastard to keep up.

He nodded, as though he guessed what I hadn't said. "You aren't quite the prick you make yourself out to be, are you?"

"Yeah, well, don't tell anyone."

"Your secret's safe with me."

"Good. Why did you follow me, anyway? You could have stayed down there, fed the tubes like we should be doing right now. Could have stayed with Jake, and stayed safe because up there – it's Ministry at its greatest power. Perak's trying but ... " And at that point I wondered what the fuck I was doing trying this. Don't mess with Ministry, it's bad for your health. Rule two. I had magic to be making, Glow to produce, a sister lying in what was almost a hospital bed. Lies to tell to women. I didn't need this shit. "Dendal can't find Perak, can't contact him."

Pasha didn't look at me when he answered. He seemed entranced by the spire of Top of the World, as though wondering how something so slender could support the palace that was visible on the platform at the top. "I came because I need to show you it isn't Guinto, that there are some priests who are good, that there's some part of Ministry that is capable of that. I have to believe that or go mad. Because – well, because even if you are a prick, you're my friend, too. You helped us before, more than you needed to. You could have walked away like all the others. But you didn't, and that tells me a lot more than all your talk."

I suppose I couldn't expect much else from a man who reads minds, but I glossed that bit and said, "How did you get Jake to stay behind? I thought she'd be here, swords at the ready to watch your back. She's been angry enough for about ten people."

The low laugh made shivers run up my spine, made me wonder if I really knew Pasha at all. "I came because I can't find her. She's – you're right, she's angry, angry like you've never seen. At you, at me, at everyone probably. At life. You remember what Guinto said to me, about obstacles? We're trying, we're both trying but ... I can't ... She's really trying, Erlat's helping her, it's working, but I hate that *I* can't help, and she hates that I hate and ... we're all at crossed purposes, crossed *feelings*. Sometimes you can't put those into words, even in your own head. The thing ... with my parents. That just topped it off for her, that and the thought you planted in her head about it being someone Ministry. They gave us enough grief to last a lifetime Downside, and she hoped it would be different Upside. But it isn't, wasn't, and she can't bear that. I think she's going to do something all crazy and heroic, possibly with swords. The Goddess, *our* Goddess anyway, says it's that you fought that matters, and so that's what matters to her. She's going to show you, and me, and everyone. Up there. Got something to prove, I think. And I've got something to prove, too." He wouldn't look at me as he said it, and I got the feeling that if he did, he wouldn't be able to say it.

He strode ahead on up the Spine, singing one of the Downsider songs that, from what I could tell, was probably called "Bastards from Hell". For the first time I began to wonder whether the little git had outmanoeuvred me, whether he had some agenda I didn't know about, and whether it was him or Jake who had the death wish this time.

Chapter Nineteen

We hid in the doorway of a grocery shop just on the border of Trade and Heights. The window held an expanse of bare, expensive-looking shelves punctuated by two wrinkled apples and a lonely pomegranate, all for sale at roughly a month's income for anyone from Under. The shop owner looked briefly hopeful until he spotted the blue-white undertone of Pasha's skin and tried to shoo us off, but I shut the door in his face and ignored him.

It didn't take long to rearrange our faces, to the dismay of the grocer watching through the window as he stood protectively over his stupid apples. Screw him, mages were legal now and he could get bent. Luckily he didn't seem the sort to create a commotion, just watched aghast, mouthing some obscenity about Downsiders that, thankfully, I could only lip-read, not hear. We turned our backs to him, and got all the quiet and privacy we wanted, or, rather, I did. Pasha was tight-lipped against what he could surely hear in his head.

I used Pasha's juice even though the throb of my hand would have been enough for a hundred such spells – I could probably have rearranged things so I was a woman and he was an elephant. My black didn't like it, but I told it to piss off and it went back to chuckling, biding its time. It would have me in the end, and it knew it.

I took away the blue-white undercurrent of Pasha's skin that marked him as a Downsider, made him look a bit more imposing. Made him seem more the lion he was than the monkey that he looked like. I couldn't resist making him look more of an ugly lion, though. He took a look in the window for a mirror and waved at the open-mouthed grocer with a savage grin.

"Prick" was all he said, and turned back to me. "What about you?"

I'd been thinking on it as I'd walked. I – we – needed to get into Top of the World, where all the biggest and most influential Ministry lived and worked. No ordinary guards on the door, I thought we could be certain of that. Specials for sure. Maybe, and the thought made me shudder, maybe even Inquisitors. I needed to look like someone who belonged there. Someone whose presence wouldn't be questioned.

So I grew a moustache, careworn and drooping. Dench wasn't a good look, if I'm honest, but needs must when there's a killer on the loose with a thirst for your throat. I really hoped we didn't bump into Dench – he'd probably find new and interesting ways to kill me.

"Pretty good" was Pasha's verdict when I'd finished. "I wouldn't be able to tell the difference."

With a cheery wave to the by now rather sick-looking grocer, and hoping he didn't run screaming to the guards, we tried to hurry towards Clouds, progress slow because there were more people about here. The curfew hadn't been enforced, not in Clouds where many lesser Ministry kept their homes, all bright and shiny towers on their platforms. The curfew had been for us scummy types from Under.

I felt sick as we pushed past shoppers on the Spine, through the upper levels of Heights and on towards Clouds. Sick not only because they all looked smug and well fed, didn't have that ground-down look to them. More because of the shops, and what was in them. Down in No-Hope, the shops had fuck all. Some grey reconstituted mush if you were lucky and had plenty of money spare, which, with Trade shut down, no one did. No jobs, no money, no food, no nothing, except hunger and rats. Always there's rats.

The thought of starvation obviously wasn't crossing any-one's mind much up here, and, despite what it was costing me and Pasha and the others in pain, there was no shortage of Glow either. Someone had been siphoning it off from the factories where we sent it, and that really made me want to hurl. Factories, what they produced to trade, were what kept everyone Under alive and someone was stealing that. I shouldn't have been surprised – I suppose I wasn't – but I was still pissed off. Thing is, I always *want* to be surprised and the blow when everything is just as crap as I expect can really sucker-punch the air from your lungs.

The shops in the upper reaches of Heights weren't full, but they weren't empty like the grocer on the border had been, like all the shops in No-Hope and what they were selling was a damned sight better than mush. Fresh vegetables and fruits, some of which I'd never even seen before. Proper bread, rice that didn't have weevils in it. No bacon, sadly. I'd have fallen to my knees and promised eternal faith in the Goddess if there had been. Well, maybe. All right, probably not, but I'd have been very pleased.

So, little meat, and what there was, was stringy, full of grey gristle and barely enough to feed a very picky cat. But that was only to be expected – the synth disaster had killed off a lot of the animals, and, while there had been some, I suspected that what meat there was turned up secretly and for a select few. What had been brought up from the 'Pit was probably long gone, into the fat bellies above.

I stole a couple of green fruity things neither of us knew the name of and we headed on up with sticky hands, growling stomachs demanding more and sugar tingling on our tongues. The crowds thinned as we went higher, the shops stopped as Heights petered out, and then we were all but alone as we went ever higher. Once above the platforms of Clouds, which stood below with towers straining to reach us, they looked less impressive when you could now clearly see what was above *them*.

Top of the World hovered over us, a vast spire that seemed made of light and ice. The Spine spiralled up to the underbelly of the most powerful place in the city. Glow lights lit the deep shadow it cast, set at good intervals. More lights here than perhaps in the whole of No-Hope. I was tempted to smash them one at a time as we passed but Pasha persuaded me that if I wanted anyone to believe I was Dench, being a vandal wasn't going to help. Which was sensible, logical, but didn't stop me wanting to one little bit.

Instead, I hung on to my anger, pushed it down, formed it into a hard ball of hate. If Perak was alive – please, whoever might be listening, he was alive – if he was, why was he letting this happen? Especially when he'd seemed so concerned about people Under starving. I knew the answer – Archdeacon he may have been, but all-powerful he wasn't. Ministry was faction against faction, and most of them hated Perak and his liberal ideas. He'd said as much, and Dench had hinted at it, too. Made me wonder why they'd promoted Perak, but that was pretty obvious.

Perak had always been a pushover, that was the trouble. Easy to talk around, not much iron in his spine. He was quite happy wandering through life, inventing things and doing what he was told. Only now he'd hardened up, started standing up to them, and they didn't like that. He wasn't the daydreamer I'd left behind all those years ago. Not at all. They'd signed up for a warm body to do as he was told, sign what they told him to sign, be the pious face of the "new" Ministry after the old one had made such a hash of things.

What they'd got was someone too stubborn for that. He was probably doing more to piss off more Ministry men than a hundred people like me. It was enough to warm the cockles of my heart. It was also enough to make me fear for his life, and I had no way to know if it was too late for that. Rule two, remember? That goes double if you're in the Ministry and you mess with them, and now he'd disappeared. After Dendal couldn't contact him, I'd tried, too, tried to track him but with no more luck before I had to stop. The black had almost got me again, and I could still hear its chuckle, feel the pull. I really needed to sleep before I tried any more spells. Sleep for a long time, but that wasn't going to happen anytime soon.

By the time we reached the end of the Spine, where it led through an imposing arched gate into Top of the World, it wasn't just the shadow that was making things dark. The sun touched the tops of the mountains and Pasha stopped to watch it for a heartbeat.

"Are you sure about this?" he asked.

"No. You?"

"No."

"But we're going to do it anyway, right?"

"What happens if we don't?"

"She carries on murdering mages. Us probably, if she can. No mages, no power. No power, no trade, no food, no heat. Everyone dies. The Storad and Mishans just walk in." It helped to say it out loud. Gave me a bit of resolve.

"We could go straight to Dench."

"We need to get in first. I tried to find him, same time I looked for Perak but no luck, so we don't know where he is. Maybe, for Dench, I'd need a prop – I don't know him *that* well. Besides, no reason to say he'll believe me, or be able to help. Might not even want to. He sounded pissed off at Perak himself last time I saw him. Who knows what power plays are going on up here? Could be anything, and Dench's loyalty isn't to us, it's to the Goddess and the city."

Pasha's look was speculative, but he nodded in the end. "All right. Do you have any sort of plan?"

"Not really. Try to find Perak firstly, but looking like this will help."

No one was above an Inquisition, not even the Archdeacon. That was what my insides were telling me had happened to Perak, and the scary part. Well, that and the fact that they used divination – via goat's entrails, would you believe? – to decide if you were guilty in the eyes of the Goddess, and, if you were, it was a long drop off Top of the World into the Slump. All it would take would be the goat to have had a dodgy breakfast, or a bribe to the entrail reader, and you were dead quicker than spit. Even the Ministry had never been overly fond of the Inquisition as a rule. A desperate measure, because like I say, anyone is fair game. Unless you knew who to bribe. Who would *take* a bribe, because the Inquisitors were promoted Specials, and word was none had ever taken anything in return for lenience or turning a blind eye. Which made setting an Inquisition a desperate move by someone who was sure he'd not get nabbed himself. And here I was, disguised as the man in charge of those Specials.

All of which made my bowels rather watery as we approached the gate. Maybe looking like Dench hadn't been such a good move, but I didn't know any other face that would get us in well enough. I could have pretended to be Perak, but, firstly, the Archdeacon isn't going to wander along the Spine with no guards and, secondly, if Dench was to be believed, there was a good possibility people were trying to kill him. Or maybe already had, but I tried not to think of that.

It started off all right. The two Specials on the gate – the Specials we could see anyway – snapped off a couple of salutes and we were in. They gave Pasha a once over, but I growled out he was with me in the best imitation of Dench I could manage and they let him go with only a cursory pat down for weapons and a few questions.

I tried not to gawp as we entered the rarest of atmospheres. Mahala is built to make you look up, and up again. Top of the World more so. It wasn't just another area of Mahala, it was another world. A nice one.

A broad plaza stretched in front of us, so, so *clean*. That was what struck me first. No filth, no grubbiness. No taste of hopelessness in the air that seemed fresh and cold off the mountains that were clear from here and very real, black against the setting sun.

Space was the next thing I noticed – nothing crammed in, no buildings jostling for position like starving men round a plate of bacon. Here there was room to breathe, and air worth breathing. I found myself standing to my full height, stretching out my shoulders, expanding into the space. This was a place where people could *be*.

As the light waned, lamps came on. Glow lamps but like nothing I'd seen before. Gilded cages hung along every eave, outlined every doorway, and inside them birds flapped and twittered. Not real birds, but animated Glow tubes. Overhead, other Glows flitted about in the shape of moths, only moths like I have never seen, all colours pulsing through the Glow like rainbows. They flew around the spires, swooping down to the plaza a hand's span in front of me and then off again. The light they gave off was subtle but together they brought out a, pardon the pun, glow in the buildings, changed them from finely wrought to staggering in their beauty, all ethereal shadows and etched light. I'd never seen anything quite so glorious, never even imagined that anywhere in Mahala was quite like this.

So, space, no filth, the bird-lamps and fluttering moths, those were all wonders, but the floor of the plaza was something I'd never seen except in a faded picture. Never expected to see either. A mosaic of dressed stone, all mellow gold in the light of the fluttering birds, and, in between the slabs, bright grass and scented flowers. Flowers!

The pattern seemed haphazard, a random jumbling of green and gold and the colours of the flowers fading against the coming night, blue here, orange and black together there. A garden, I supposed. Quite pretty in its way but I still couldn't work out what it was for.

One side of the plaza was free of buildings, letting us get a clear view of sky, of peaks swathed in scarves of misty cloud, of the city below us like an oily black smudge.

The other three sides of the plaza were lined with impossibly thin spires topping gilded buildings that looked as fragile as spun sugar. No need for girders, for squatness to support the weight of countless houses above. No need for everything to be crammed together, because this was where Mahala stopped. And it stopped in heart-wrenching beauty so that I almost believed this city was a good and great place. Almost.

When I stopped staring, I noticed Pasha looking at his feet. "Grass. I haven't seen grass in years."

It felt weird under my boots, soft and yielding in a way I'd never known when I'd only ever walked on steel and concrete and soft under your boots meant you'd stepped in something it was best not to contemplate. I nudged him on – we were attracting a few stares.

As "Dench", I didn't have the luxury of looking too

awestruck, but Pasha made up for it. We approached an official-looking building that still managed to appear graceful and awe-inspiring in the way they'd managed to get the thing to stay up – I couldn't get my head around buildings that had no other buildings on top, no buildings leaning on them either side, propping them up, buildings that didn't need to worry about weight or space. I was about to ask Pasha to start rummaging in heads and find out where we needed to go, when it all burst out of him.

"It's all supposed to be like this. Not just here, all of it." He kept his voice down, but there was no disguising the wistful anger in his voice.

"I keep telling you about the Ministry—"

"It's not the Goddess that's the problem, Rojan. It's people, men, abusing what they have in her name. It's not Ministry, but the rotten few."

"You always knew that, and that Ministry are the rotten all. Now where should we—"

"It's different *seeing* it, though. There are good people here, too, even here. I can feel them. I'm going to prove it to you."

Oh great, just what we needed. Pasha on a faith kick. "Now listen—"

"No. Over there, that's the place."

I wished he'd let me finish a sentence, but at least he was thinking of why we were here. I looked at where he'd pointed.

There are temples and then there are *temples*. I used to love them as a child, all hushed reverence, the colours of the stained glass puddling on the floor, the scent of the incense, the murmurs of prayers. Haunting places they were, even for me, until Ministry stripped them, made them bland and soulless like their prayers, like the poor deluded faithful. Stripped for us scum, at least, because this was a temple to end all temples and in the old style, too.

Not *a* temple, *the* temple. The Home of the Goddess, even I knew that. Where her spirit was supposed to be strongest, where she'd fought Namrat for us, where she'd made her useless sacrifice of a hand to stop Death from stalking us. Ridiculous of course – if that had ever happened, and it hadn't, it had been a long, long time ago, before Top of the World even existed, back when we were just a castle in a handy pass with a sneaky bastard warlord ruling us. It couldn't have been here, not in *this* temple, but that didn't stop a little chill shuddering my shoulders, almost as though I was being watched and the watcher was keen on the contents of my soul. A quick buff and polish probably wasn't going to help there, so all I could do was put on a brazen front and sneer at the feeling in my head.

An arch pointed up, and up, towards the spire that reached higher than any other, the fragility of it enhanced by the translucent stone that caught the last of the sun. The Glow moths gathered here in huge numbers, flickering around and through the intricate fretwork making the stone seem to ripple, alive.

Through the open arch, the coloured windows painted patterns on the runner that led the eye down the aisle to the altar, all gold and ivory and bedecked with Glow birds in their cages and a few errant moths that flickered around the faithfuls' heads. A figure bent before the altar, limned in Glow. I recognised the robes. Perak, his hooded head bent in prayer. Something loosened inside my chest. A few cardinals knelt nearby. I recognised the spare woman with the hatchet face, and I couldn't miss the fat one. Manoto . . . who I was here to find. Perhaps.

I didn't want to be awestruck as I entered – I didn't want to give anyone the satisfaction of seeing me like that in a temple even if I wasn't wearing my own face – but it was hard not to be. The ceiling vaulted high above us, and that had been made bland with whitewash, but somehow the temple still retained a sense of the wonder it must have been in its glory days. More Glow birds and moths lit the whitewash in flickering lights and shadows. The depiction of the Goddess was the Ministry one, too, the bland one. No flowers this time, but still, sparkly sunbeams and the Goddess looking benevolent and rather stupid as she patted Namrat's fluffy head.

The effect was spoilt by the two large and very ugly guards, from what I could see of them at least. One either side of the aisle, blocking our way forward. Blocking anyone from getting too close to Perak – even the cardinals were kept at a distance.

I could make out more of the guards further in and it wouldn't have been a problem, not with this face, except they weren't Specials. They weren't even Inquisitors. Their uniforms were a mystery to me, nothing like anything I'd seen before. Not understated like the threat of a Special, not forbidding like an Inquisitor. Like a priest's robes, only shot through with pliable metal plating so that when they moved, the skirt swirled and clanked. They didn't wear gloves as such, but the gauntlets would have been enough to give Namrat pause, all bits of leather and nasty-looking spikes that gleamed in the flickering light of the Glow moths that settled on the guards' shoulders. The close-fitting helmets were similar to the Inquisitors', only they had a visor in place like a snarling tiger that almost hid the ugly mug underneath. Over their chests was some sort of plate affair, moulded musculature so that it looked like the guards could lift weights with their nipples. Maybe they did. They were certainly scaring the crap out of me.

Dench's face up here should have been a free pass – from what he'd said, he was in charge of looking after Perak, and that should have been enough. That and who isn't scared of Specials? Something told me that I had misjudged things. Maybe it was the glare from the guard on the left. More likely, it was the way the one on the right shot out a spiked fist and grabbed me by the throat. He growled, making me think irresistibly of tigers and Namrat, while his friend did the talking. Maybe Growler hadn't learnt to talk yet.

"If you piss off, nice and quiet," Talker said, "we won't spread your guts all over the carpet. No one gets close to the Archdeacon. Not even you."

What the hell? Dench should have been protecting Perak, and there Perak was at the altar. I'd thought the worst could possibly be that Dench would already be here, not that he wasn't welcome. Why not? I flicked a glance at Pasha. Sometimes he could persuade people ... but no. His lips were pinched, and *I can't hear them, I can't get in* sounded in my head. *I can see Perak, but I can't hear him either.*

Talker glared at Pasha for a moment then turned back to me. "You wouldn't be bringing a pain-mage in here, would you? That would be very unhealthy."

I tried to say, "Gosh, no, wouldn't dream of it." What squeaked out past the hand on my throat was, "Will be for you when your arse gets blown up."

See now, this is what I hate about being responsible and shit. Or one of the things. It makes me cranky and then something escapes from my mouth that shouldn't and then, well, and then people often try to kill me.

Luckily – although in retrospect it wasn't all that lucky – the gunshot distracted him. The sound echoed around the space like a lost soul and someone screamed at the end of it. A swift elbow into Growler's groin and I was free, gasping for breath and desperately trying to see where the shot had gone. Perak had been praying right by the altar, but I couldn't see him now. Instead, guards milled in confusion, some with guns out. They didn't look happy. Or most of them didn't. I caught a sly look between Manoto and a Special who was lurking at the back of the temple, but I ignored it for now.

By the altar a knot of these new guards shielded me from seeing anything much, but the blood on the carpet was unmistakeable. I couldn't help myself – as big brother I was always going to be responsible for Perak however much I hated it. That didn't matter. What mattered was whether he was still alive. I twisted away from Talker and Growler and ran. First Dwarf and Lise, the attempt on Pasha, and now Perak. If I didn't know better, I'd say someone up there didn't like me. Someone down here certainly seemed determined to kill everyone I cared about, or try to.

So when someone blindsided me with the butt of a gun, making pain burst in bright lights behind my eyes and magic seethe in my bones, I let the black take me, let my anger and fear suck it in and blow it out again before I had a chance even to think what I was doing. No control, not this time, not now. All I knew was that someone had tried to kill my sister, had killed one friend and tried for another, and now my brother, and I was pissed as hell.

When the dust cleared and my brain came back to the here and now, I sat on what was left of the carpet. There wasn't much of it and what there was, was mostly now not much more than coloured string. Talker and Growler were flat on their backs next to me, along with the guard who'd whacked me. All three were covered in a thin film of dust and scattered

Glow moths that were still and dark. All three guards had their hands over their ears and their mouths open. I wondered why they weren't screaming, before I realised they might be, but I seemed to be deaf. No noise, no voices, not even the sound of my own ragged breath, only a soft silence that creeped the skin on my back.

I'd never been so glad to hear a voice in my head. *"Goddess's tits, Rojan. Did you just blow up the Home of the Goddess?"*

"I think so" was all I managed to think back. *"Oops?"*

A whey-faced Pasha got me on to my feet and sounds started to creep back in again, faint to start with. My breathing was the first thing, followed by Pasha's as he surveyed the damage. Then little moans filtered through from the guards on the floor, and then, much worse, the ominous click of a gun right behind me, quickly followed by something familiar – the jab of a syringe. My father's best work in conjunction with the good Dr Whelar, developing a jab that deadens any pain and thus renders a pain-mage utterly useless. The next sound was a gasp from Pasha as a guard grabbed him, and he too got the syringe.

About half a heartbeat after the jab, everything was numb – feet, hands, tongue, arse, everything. I had my work cut out not falling over, never mind anything else. Hands turned me round, so I was face to face with Fat Cardinal. And without my magic, that meant *my* face.

The face that shattered a thousand Glow tubes, destroyed the tortured source, plunged thousands into darkness and

274

starvation and left the whole city teetering on the brink of col-
lapse and the Ministry in an embarrassing position, to put it
mildly. A face many people would like to see in tiny pieces.
The face that had been identified as dead by the face I had
been wearing until a few moments ago, Dench.

The face that was, if Fat Guy's look was anything to go by,
about to get broken in half.

Chapter Twenty

I'm not going into detail about the embarrassment that followed, the legs like wet noodles, the tongue that kept lolling out of my mouth like it wanted to escape, the march – well, pathetic wobble held up by two guards – across the dust-strewn plaza in front of hundreds of staring people. Most were still dazed from the explosion, and so was I, dazed and not quite right in the head.

The plaza kept swimming in and out of focus, but there were definitely bits of temple scattered across the stone. A gargoyle's face leered drunkenly from in among the flowers, or what was left of them. The blooms appeared to have been lopped off neatly at the neck, scattering petals that blew around the space like orange and black snow. A dead Glow bird lay in a smashed cage, nothing now but dull bits of glass.

Feeling began to come back, just a bit, and I didn't welcome it. I felt like I was in two places at once, here at Top of the World, in splendour that turned my stomach when I thought of the starvation below us and, at the same time, all was black around me, and I was light, and the voice was singing in my head, too sweetly, too much to resist. Only the grip of Pasha's hand on my arm, a solid pressure, brought me back to me.

Other than that, let's just say me and Pasha ended up in what Fat Cardinal probably thought of as a hellish and forbidding room but was in fact far plusher than any place I've ever lived. It had carpet and nice thick velvet curtains to keep out the chill. I've never had a carpet, and the only cheapjack curtains I ever managed to nail up were destroyed in the Paint Incident.

The room also had a Dench, which was stupid because he should have been protecting Perak. Why wasn't he? He didn't look too happy to see us – his moustache went from drooping and careworn to standing to attention as he shouted, "What the fuck are you doing here?"

He pinned me with a glare. I tried an ingratiating grin, but, as all my nerves were numb, I suspected it didn't turn out too well.

"That blast, that was you, wasn't it? Well?"

I tried to get an excuse out, tell him that Perak had been shot, but all that came out were mangled noises so in the end I just nodded.

"I should have fucking well known it. Holy shit, man, are you trying to make a habit out of blowing up archdeacons?

Even—" He pulled up short and glanced at the guard at the door, primed with more nasty jabs for when this one wore off. I hated that guard already. "Even Perak?"

Again, all I could manage were a few strangled grunts. Pasha tried, too, with pretty much the same result. In the end, I finally spat out an approximation of "Shot", that only someone off their tits on Rapture or very, very determined and used to dealing with drunks, might have understood.

I don't think Dench was on drugs, but he seemed to get it.

"Who was shot? You're not bleeding and neither's Pasha. Perak?"

Another nod sent Dench to a chair in the corner to think and stroke his moustache, looking us over all the while. By the time he hunkered down next to us and talked in low murmurs the guard couldn't hear, I could move my tongue to form words, even if I couldn't feel it.

"You were supposed to leave looking after Perak to me, not come dancing in here like you owned the place. You're an embarrassment up here, especially with your own face on. Most of them get by pretending the pain-mages all got destroyed, that the Glow they're getting is some genius replacement Dwarf or the alchemists dreamed up. The rest only want to see you thrown off the top of Home of the Goddess and splat in the Slump. You were *supposed* to be trying to find out who's killing all those Downsiders and stopping any more riots, helping to calm things down. Not making things worse. Remember?"

"Not Downsiders." Well, that's what I meant to say, but I had a heck of a good slur going on. "Mages. Definitely. I *told* you. I know who's doing it, too." Had he forgotten? Maybe he'd had worse things to deal with.

Dench went very still, staring at me like I'd gone batshit. Maybe I had, it was hard to tell any more. He was still staring when more guards came and dragged me and Pasha off on wobbly legs. "To see the cardinal," one said when Dench asked.

I really didn't like the way that unflappable Dench flinched at that.

Chapter Twenty-one

It wasn't far to Fat Cardinal's rooms. In fact, it was suspiciously close. Through a door, Dench trailing behind like a bad smell, along a corridor and then a cavernous interior echoed around us, all done in polished bronze and marble. Cold, austere, bland and somehow chilling to the soul as well as the skin. Pillars arched over us, moulding into the spire that topped every building here, it seemed, and skylights between them let in the dusk. No Glow lights, no birds or moths lit the place, for which I was glad, though I could see the fittings for the cages. Instead, proper wax candles in stark-lined candelabra lit the room in bronze flickers.

I somehow didn't feel right disturbing the silence, so I waited till Dench led us through to a room that was almost opulent in its faux-frugal simplicity. A plain desk at one end, but made of a wood I'd never seen before that shone like gold. Plain curtains, but thick and heavy and purple. Simple icons on the wall, religious images of saints and martyrs, but they were old, very old, and all picked out in gold leaf. A bare chair, made of the same wood as the desk. It seemed overlarge. I was starting to have a very bad feeling about this.

I turned to face Dench, thinking of trying to mumble out a question, and stared straight down the barrel of my pulse pistol. A quick pat down, and, yes, all that was left in my pocket was the vial and syringe Lise had given me, what seemed like an age ago, the lollipops I used to keep Dog sweet and the envelope with Abeya's hairs in.

"I always said you'd make a really crap Special, Rojan. If it helps, I'm sorry, you were supposed to stay Under. I have my orders."

With a sideways glance at the guards to make sure they didn't see, he dropped an eyelid in an elaborate wink.

Which didn't comfort me much, because then he fired, and the arcing pulse slammed into my forehead like a fucking great hammer. I didn't even have time to curse Dwarf for making the damn thing more efficient so even someone with Dench's little magic could knock out a rhino.

It all went blurry after that. A lot blurrier.

When my brain finally started sending urgent messages to my body again, along the lines of "get up you stupid sod before someone uses a proper gun on you", someone was sitting in the chair under the window. The candles didn't really help much lighting the room and his face was half in shadow, but

I could tell who it was. Fat Cardinal – Manoto. One of Perak's cardinals who'd come to the temple Under to see Guinto, who'd been Under a dozen times when Ministry men have long had a history of being allergic to Under. And here was me investigating a dozen murders. Who'd looked daggers at Perak's back, and murder at me. Who I'd last seen exiting Erlat's house, leaving her looking shaken. There was no mistaking that prissy pursing of the lips or the way the flesh folded around his ring of office. Fat when so many starved. It made me want to puke.

I pushed myself up off the carpet and tried for sitting. I managed on the second attempt, and found Pasha doing the same next to me. He didn't say anything but the look he shot Dench, standing next to us with my pulse pistol in one hand and a bullet gun in the other, was of pure hatred.

Dench kept his face carefully blank and I began to wonder what was behind that mask, and who he was taking his orders from. And if he was following them or just pretending to.

"Before we start," Fat Guy said from the comfort of his chair, "I'd like to point out that Dench is under instruction to shoot you in the back of the head at the first hint of you using your magic. With the bullet gun, that is." He shrugged in an oddly delicate manner. "I understand you've been tracking mages. Where there's one there's more, and more's the pity. Well, soon enough we'll be rid of you, whatever Perak says, no matter how he hides. No use for you now. Not now the Storad come to us with coal."

Resisting the urge to use the returning throb of my poor fucked hand, to use the juice I was just begging to use, may be the hardest thing I'd ever done. Instead, I said, "Coal? So?" and it came out quite well.

Manoto shook his head sadly, as though over a child that doesn't understand a basic lesson. "A new power. One where we wouldn't be beholden to the unholy. And yet Perak *still* refuses to negotiate. Even now, with mages dying and a generator in pieces. Still relies on you and your kind. Well, there's some of us who won't."

"We're keeping you in Glow, for now at least." I eyed the way his jowls wobbled. "And without Glow, you're going on one hell of a diet."

I didn't like the way he smiled at that, or Dench's awkward shuffle behind me. Had they bought Dench? *How* had they? Specials swore to the Goddess, not to man or Ministry. Utterly unbribable, except perhaps by her. Was he the cardinal's man? He'd been pretty pissed off at the way things were going, but this? I couldn't believe it of him. Not Dench, staunch and caring under that moustache.

I thought back to the wink, and found a flicker of hope that someone up here was on our side, even if he couldn't say so. Someone other than Perak. And where *was* Perak? Was he safe? Was he dead?

"You remember Doctor Whelar?" Manoto said.

Oh, I remembered him all right. He stepped out of the gloom in the corner, and seemed as I recalled – dishevelled, harassed, a bit smug but a good doctor nonetheless. Too fucking good. The concoction he'd invented, the one that numbed everything including my magic, had almost done for me once before. To his credit, and the only reason I hadn't left him to his fate like my father, was that he was a doctor first and a Ministry pawn second. I suddenly wished I hadn't been quite so lenient, especially when I saw the syringe in his hand and had to wonder whether he'd been testing things on dead people at the mortuary rather than the dead pigs he used to use.

"Hello, Doctor. How are your bollocks?"

I couldn't help the grin as he instinctively curled over as though to protect them. The memory of my sharp elbow was still strong, it seemed.

Fat Guy's sharp tone cut through that. "You're supposed to be dead. You and this other *thing*. That would have been the end of Perak's stubborn refusals, and we could start making this city work again. Why did you come here? What did you think you'd achieve? Wasn't the death of one archdeacon, the near destruction of our entire city, enough for you? You want to destroy the process of rebuilding, regrouping, avoiding allout war? What is it that you want, Rojan?"

So, he had recognised me. From where I'm not sure – maybe Dench had told him, and that didn't bode well. At all.

Call me cynical, call me stupid, call me whatever you want, but here, this was my chance, this was – what I never got to say, because Pasha was on his wobbly feet, lip curling, eyes hot with hate.

"I know you," he said. "I remember you, from a long time ago. When you told my parents I had a higher calling, that I'd serve the Ministry and they were so fucking *proud*. They didn't know what you were taking me to. Didn't know I was a mage. Neither did I, at first, but I found out. And when I wouldn't do what the mages told me, wouldn't torture people for Glow ... " His words dried up in a clamp of his lips, a scrunch of his monkey face.

Fat Guy didn't move for a moment, but I thought I saw a flicker of something there, of shame perhaps. Ridiculous, to think a Ministry man could have any shame left after all they'd done, and still did. Yet his voice held some sort of compassion to it when he spoke. Fake, it must be. Yet it seemed real to me.

"I didn't know. None of us did, not then. Mages! Scripture is quite clear on them. Later ... later we found out what the Archdeacon was doing, but he persuaded us. We had no other choice, or so he said, and we believed him. We wanted to. Wanted to ignore it, or maybe that was his magic, using his voice the way he did. He said it was the unholy killing the unwanted, the unfaithful, or converting them, for the survival of the faithful. The Archdeacon said so, and we ... we believed him. His voice, no one could resist when he used the voice, and that's when we knew he was a mage, too."

He turned a speculative eye on me, the twitch of his lip disdainful. "When Rojan destroyed all that, when he killed the old Archdeacon and Perak came into power, then it was pick a side or die, and those on Perak's side, those who'd keep the mages as useful pets – we didn't want that, them. Not any more, but it was only days before the Storad and Mishans realised we were all but helpless. We had to be strong, or appear to be, or we would be lost. All of it, every part of the city would die. We did what we had to do, always. And he wouldn't even *try* to negotiate, because he had his mages, he had his stupid generator that wouldn't work. That was why I had Perak shot. So I could bargain with the Storad, Mahala could live, even if the life was different. For the Goddess. Always for the Goddess."

For themselves more like. I'd long since given up the notion that any Ministry man did anything other than for his own comfort or wealth, and I wanted not to think of Perak, of whether he was alive or dead, so I let my mouth flap. "Does that include murdering boys who you think are becoming pain-mages?"

The confusion seemed real enough. "No. No, of course not. Dench?"

It didn't help that Dench side-stepped the question. "You're not as cynical as you seem, Rojan, I know that, and I knew you'd take it to heart. I had to keep you searching. Otherwise you'd be under my feet worrying about Perak, poking that nose about up here."

"And what would I have found?"

Fat Guy smiled, a patronising smirk that made me want to smack it off his face. "Dench knows you well enough, Rojan.

Well enough to know you'd have found things that would hurt your cynical soul, and that you'd interfere with."

Again, Dench's face was carefully blank when I looked. Far too carefully. In the thorn bed of my heart, a little flower of hope. Always played very close to his chest, Dench. A cynic as much as I was, and as hopeful. He'd helped me and Pasha before, against all expectation. He wasn't a Ministry man, not really. He was the Goddess's man. A small hope but, hey, I'm from Under. We take any damned hope we can get.

He watched me watching him, and his moustache twitched a fraction. There was more to this than it seemed, that twitch said and my nerves settled, just a bit. Not enough to forgive him pulsing me, but a bit.

"Politics," the cardinal said. A word that brings a nasty taste to my mouth. "I want you to understand. We want what's best for the city, truly we do. Perak and a few of his sycophants still think mages can save Mahala, can be relied upon, aren't unholy. The rest . . . the rest mostly are thinking of their own skins by allying with the strongest faction – the one that wants all Downsiders dead, and mages, too. The one that thinks they should ally with the Storad and use their idea for steam-driven machines, using Storad coal. But Perak insists, oh he insists that he has the answer, that we need only to wait. In the meantime, I've had Doctor Whelar make a few modifications to his little invention. Numbs the local area – the brain. Pain receptors still work, even if thought doesn't. While the brain is out, we can make and take as much pain from the mage as we want. Falling into the black won't be a problem – Whelar's concoction is like . . . an artificial black. You'll never know. Pain-free. A perfect, if temporary, solution."

I let my smile ratchet up a notch as Manoto fidgeted. "So, you wouldn't be interested in knowing that the murderer is almost certainly up here somewhere, then? That maybe she's got other people in mind to kill, other people she blames for what happened to her Downside? That I think that perhaps the Storad put her up to it, or at least helped her?" Because all this talk of them and their coal, I'd remembered where I'd seen Abeya and who with – and where I'd seen a guy like that before. In a Death Match against Jake, a Storad with jet hair and pale skin and a look as hard as mountains.

Manoto's mouth fell open, but neither he nor Dench had a chance to say anything. Pasha had fallen back behind me and maybe Dench had been concentrating too hard on pointing the gun at the back of my head.

"Guinto," Pasha said in a moan. "Guinto, Inquisition arrested him, he's here and . . . and, oh Goddess, and he's going to confess to the Inquisitors."

All eyes turned to him, where he stood in a corner twisting his fingers. "Only he didn't, he didn't. And this man, this cardinal" – Manoto flinched – "he knows more. Not what he says. I see in his head. All twisted in, Rojan. Knots on knots. But Ministry is rotten. All of it, you were right. Only Guinto . . . and Jake. Jake's here, too, and oh shit is she pissed."

That last, and he looked right at me. I knew what he was doing, making me do this because of her. If she was up here, she was as good as dead, and, let's face it, so were we. The gun cocked behind me, but I ignored it. Instead I let myself wallow in the throb of my hand, in the juice that had been building, slowly, all this time.

"Rojan, don't make me." Dench, giving me a chance. It didn't matter, because he'd shoot me if he had to, if he thought it was his duty. "I did what I had to, not what I wanted to. And I will again, if I have to, if it means this city lives."

I wanted to go, right there and then. My hand clenched into a fist without me telling it to and the sweet throb of pain filled me, made lights run in my eyes and lightning in my heart. I could feel Jake, somehow, through Pasha in my head. I knew where she was, I could find her with my eyes shut. I let the knowledge of where she was seep into me and squeezed my hand some more, let the black talk me into just doing it.

Right up until Whelar jabbed me with his syringe and my brain went bye-byes.

Chapter Twenty-two

Seriously, if I ever find the bastard who invented the syringe, I will not be held responsible for my actions. I may, however, stab the fucker in the eye with one.

I woke when I landed with a jolt of half-numbed pain as my bad hand hit a stone floor. I tried not to scream because Jake's boots were in front of me. Tried not to throw up, too, but didn't manage that. I lay there, panting, the taste of stale bile filling my mouth and the vague imitation of pain filling my head, making it twist, wondering what the fuck I was doing. I couldn't be sure any more because it was all too much, and I wanted to rest, somewhere quiet. In the black. I wanted to forget everything else, wanted it very badly indeed.

A flicker of movement in front of me resolved into Jake, who seemed torn between worry and spitting-blood-angry if the way she clenched her jaw was anything to go by. I fought to stop the shudders and only partially succeeded. She held out a hesitant hand, let it waver by my shoulder. Hated to touch, be touched, she always had, though she managed with Pasha now. And with me, because the hand fell soft on my shoulder and she helped me to sitting before she turned away to Pasha as he struggled upright. The warmth of that hand stayed long after it had gone.

Two Inquisitors in front of me got me on my feet pretty damn quick, had me clenching my fist to squeeze out some juice in a panic, almost forgetting I was still half numb and wouldn't have enough juice to squish a rat. But they weren't paying any attention to me, or to Pasha. They were, in fact, only statues. Very lifelike ones, sure, but no people inside the uniform, just stone.

I let my heart settle a bit before I tried saying anything. Mainly because whatever I wanted to say was going to be full of swearwords. Instead I took a look around. Square room, bare floor, whitewashed walls, two candles that guttered in the breeze from the open windows. No easy escape out of those windows either, even though they were big enough to fit through and had no bars. Outside it was a fuck of a long way down to a big splat, and I backed away hurriedly so I couldn't see the drop. One door, slamming behind us.

Guinto sat hunched in the corner, though I almost didn't recognise him at first. He seemed like a ghost of himself, pale and drawn, his lips trembling but determined as he glared at me.

Pasha and Jake argued quietly behind me, and I caught snatches.

"They came, and I couldn't stop them, not me and Dog on our own. Guinto said . . . he said it would be all right, that we should come with them. Besides—"

Pasha's voice, hot and angry but a worried angry. "This is the last place you want to be. I can see – they knew. They *all* knew, and they let it go on anyway. You can't kill all of them."

"Why not? And you can't protect me from everything. I can look after myself, remember? I wasn't leaving you up here, without even trying to help."

A pregnant pause, but I didn't turn because I was pretty sure what I saw would only burn a hole in my gut, especially when I could still feel her hand on my shoulder. Envy is such an ugly thing but I couldn't stop it, couldn't talk my way out of my feelings or even smother them with other women, though I'd tried pretty hard.

So it came out a lot sharper than I'd intended. "What the fuck is this place? I mean, are we likely to get Inquisitioned? Don't know about you, but I don't want that goat's entrails on my conscience."

I risked turning and got the full force of Jake in my face.

"You have to help me stop Guinto," she said. "He wants to confess to all those murders, but I know he didn't do them, and so do you."

"Jake, I – that's not really at the forefront of my mind at the moment. He can do what he likes, but there's Abeya up here somewhere on the loose, Perak getting shot at and I don't know whether he's alive or dead. Oh, and Dench is seriously pissed with us, me, and he's working for a cardinal now, too. A cardinal who thinks that he can zap our brains and suck our magic out and it's a perfect solution, at least until he manages to kill Perak, ally with the Storad and be rid of us for good. One priest having a fit of idealism doesn't figure high on my list of priorities right now."

Her mouth set in a determined line. Too stubborn by half, she was. Too sure that what she was doing was right. I admired that about her, even when it was being a pain in the butt.

"It should," was all she said before Pasha took over, his voice tight with, what? Anger, fatalism, exasperation? I couldn't be sure, but whatever it was it clipped his words into little bombs.

"You don't get it, you never got it. If he confesses, Under might as well die. It *will* die, in flames. Everyone knows it wasn't him, couldn't have been. And Downsiders would kill for him. He was the only one treated us as humans, as people. Only he accepted us, made us welcome. You Upsiders think you hate Ministry. Well, we had more cause, a lot more."

"Us Upsiders? You were born here."

"And my parents are too ashamed of that, of what I am, what I've become. A Downsider, like all the rest. I lived there too long, suffered there too long, to be anything else now and we hate with a vengeance your Upside Goddess doesn't know.

Our Goddess knows violence and pain, death and sacrifice. She knows it because so did we, the mages taught us that well. Too many Downsiders know it can't be Guinto. He was preaching when one boy died, and I've got half a dozen men say they saw another leave the temple, leave Guinto and he died on his way home. Guinto didn't leave, and those men will swear to the Goddess on that. He believes in us when no one else will, when all else they get is spat in the face. If Ministry take his confession, all Under will be in flames. I'll set the first taper myself."

I snatched a look at Guinto in the corner, pale but calm, his eyes steady. Waiting to do his duty. Sometimes I think I'll never understand people.

"You'd light Under for a man who hates you, loathes what you are, what we do?"

"And he's right to," Pasha said. "I hate what I am, too, I always have, but I can deny it, control it. Not use it, at least once we're set. But it's not just me, Rojan. It's all of us Downsiders. Left to fucking die, because of where we come from, what we sound like. A reminder of what was once done to us in the name of the Goddess. Except to him, and maybe you and Perak. You help us, and perhaps Under has a chance to survive."

I stared at Guinto again, and he looked back with serene eyes that were somehow touched with madness. Not a frothing at the mouth kind, not a laying about with any weapon to hand kind, but the quiet, determined kind of madness of a man who's deluded himself into thinking he's doing the right thing. For the Goddess. I wanted to pick him up and give him a damn good shake, maybe slap some sense into him, but it wouldn't do any good. He was putting everyone's lives on the line, directly or otherwise, but he was doing it for the Goddess, so that was all right then.

He might be useful, though.

"You knew she was doing it, didn't you?" I asked him.

His gaze flicked between me and Pasha, hunted, but he said nothing.

"It's all right. Pasha here feels constrained not to read the thoughts of a priest. Even you. You can lie if you want. The Goddess doesn't look kindly on that, though, and Inquisitors have some nasty ways of making sure people are telling the truth, so I've heard."

He avoided Pasha's look with a sideways hunch of his shoulders. "I suspected something, but not that. Abeya was – she'd suffered very much, and it affected her in odd ways. I wanted to help her. I *did* help her, she was getting better. Only she became odd, distant. Then the boys started turning up dead, and she was her old self again. It made me wonder, but I pushed that thought away. Not my poor, dear Abeya. So sweet a child under it all. Until the day you came to the temple."

"The boy at the end of the street?"

He nodded miserably, and I was surprised to see tears dripping from his chin.

"I knew then. After you left, I found her with blood on her dress and she was so *happy*. I tried to get her to pray with me, but she wouldn't. She used the blood to make the devotional, said the Goddess was guiding her. Told me they were all mages, and hadn't I always said they were unholy? She was doing the Goddess's work."

"And you believed that?"

His eyes grew haunted as he looked up at me. "Yes. No. I – I thought I could help her still, could stop her. She was clearly in some sort of mania, and who could blame her? Who could blame her for her hate after all she's suffered? I thought I could confine her to her rooms, until her mind became more balanced. Then *he* came."

"Who?"

"Cardinal Manoto." Guinto gave a thin smile at what was probably a snarl on my face. "Yes. He didn't say much, only a few words, but he came with some present for her – that bacon – and it all changed. She changed." The way he looked at me, pleading as though he wanted me to tell him it wasn't true, none of it, that Ministry wasn't corrupt, made me want to shake him again.

"So what changed? She was already murdering people."

"Everything. After I threw you out, she kept asking about you and Pasha, about what you did, where you worked. Kept needling and needling for answers. I told her nothing, until I found you in her rooms. I had to warn her, or she would have . . . I told her what you were. I thought it would help her to know what you were doing, the pain lab, the Glow, that you were helping the city, us, even if I don't approve of the methods. So I told her."

He told her. And how the fuck did he know what we were doing? We'd taken pains to keep ourselves and what we did under wraps – too many people wouldn't like it. For wouldn't like it, read probably kill us. It was bad enough that Dendal had insisted on that damned sign to advertise we were mages, but to Downsiders the news we were producing Glow, well ... Only Guinto wasn't high up enough in the Ministry to be in on that secret. Perak had told me he'd kept it down to maybe five or six people, all the highest rankers. So how did Guinto know what to tell her other than that we were mages? Only then I caught Pasha's eye and I knew.

Pasha and Jake at the temple, telling all their souls to their priest. Because they believed he was a good man. So they'd told him what we were doing at the lab, Pasha had confessed he was using his magic to make Glow. Guinto had given him a nice guilt trip about it, and then spilled it all to Abeya to "help" her.

"And then she tried to kill both me and Pasha, tried to lure Dendal in too, I think." Maybe she hadn't known the bacon was poisoned, but afterwards it didn't matter – what had mattered was that we were mages and we were making Glow.

"I didn't think she'd go that far! She liked you, I thought. Too much. I thought if she knew why you were doing it, that the only pain you inflicted was on yourselves, that she might take pity on you. As I did. I can't condone your magic, but at least you're using it for the right reasons, and so I don't hate, I pity. I hoped I might get you to see the light, in time. I had hopes for you both, Pasha especially. But you, I hoped to bring you to the Goddess, you see?"

"Shame it didn't work out that way, isn't it?" I couldn't keep the venom out of my voice, but Guinto hung his head like a penitent child. "And this is your way of making up for it, right? You're going to confess to all those murders?"

"I am to blame. I suspected . . . and I did nothing except make everything worse. I am guilty."

I said a very rude word indeed and, unable to watch his guilt-stricken face, went to stare at the statues. The implacable faces of the helmets, the thought of the inevitability of Inquisition, didn't help one little bit. Worse, when I was pretty sure if I used my magic again any time soon I wouldn't be coming back. That was looking more and more tempting. Maybe if I went totally batshit, I could take out Top of the World, like those long-ago mages had made the Slump out of a perfectly respectable area. Now *that* was tempting.

It wasn't what worried me most, though – that was, why had Dench left us here, not numb? Or not as numb as we could have been? I didn't have all my feeling back, not a lot of juice, but I had some and he had to know it. He was up to something, expecting me to do . . . *something*. What?

"So, where precisely are we? Are there Inquisitors out there?

Maybe we're just waiting for the goat? Have you actually confessed yet?"

"A holding cell, they said." Jake's voice was taut with dis-
approval, though I couldn't tell who for. "We told the guards
we had special information. Seems Cardinal Manoto had left
instructions that Guinto be let in."

"Oh, I bet he did."

"Dendal got this too, just before we left," she said and
handed over a slip of paper. I recognised Perak's neat, precise
handwriting, though it seemed dashed off.

*Ministers found out about pain lab, and that generator is
destroyed. All hell broken loose. At least one minister working
with Storad, possibly involved in murders, including Dwarf's.
No one to trust except personal guard. Even Dench . . . I can't be
sure about him. He thinks we should ally with Storad and
maybe he's right, but is he involved? Hope not, but must be
sure. Pasha's parents – the message from them was a lure to get
you and Pasha together to murder you. His mother confessed.
Only hope you are all still alive to get this.*

*Am lying low, using decoy, three attempts on life already.
Please, send Rojan. No one else to trust.*

I shut my eyes for a second, wanting this to be a sign he was
still alive, but Jake had received it before we'd even got to the
temple by the sounds of it. All I could say for sure was he *had*
been alive.

Things were starting to make a bit of sense, though. Kind of. But I still didn't know where Abeya was, what she was doing up here, and how she fitted into everything except as a puppet of some kind. But who was pulling the strings? Manoto, or the Storad? Both? Someone else? Were they pulling Dench's strings, too?

Pasha came and stood next to me, staring up at the Inquisitors with the same sort of dread that was churning my gut.

"I'm sorry. I didn't—"

It was my turn not to let him finish. "Forget it. Tell me later. Now we have to figure out what to do. Abeya's still out there, Fat Boy's up to something and there's still a Dench to see if he's picked a side, or he's still with the Goddess. Guinto can wait."

"But if—"

"*Later*. We need to get out of this cell, all of us. I can't manage that, not now. Probably not ever." Though it was tempting to try, even if I knew I couldn't rearrange more than me and another, even at my best. Dench knew it, too, and that I was far from at my best. The black was flapping at the edge of my vision, always calling. I wanted it like I wanted air to breathe. But not yet. Not now. Now I had things to do. Dench wanted me to do something, but what? *Why?*

"Sod Guinto, we've got other things to do. After we get out."

"How are we going to do that?"

I really wished he hadn't asked. Not as much as I wished I didn't know the answer.

The drop from the window was nauseatingly long, and I held on to the sill like grim death and tried to ignore the dizziness and the scream that seemed to build behind my eyes. In the gloom of a moon-ridden night, I could just make out the Slump below. I found a chip of stone and dropped it. As a measure of the drop it didn't help, because I couldn't hear when it finally hit something. I tore my gaze away, almost hypnotised, and instead tried to concentrate on what was around us at our level.

The Home of the Goddess, or what I'd left of it, wasn't far away, but it might as well have been miles. We seemed to be near the top of a spire, and *everything* was a long way away. Mostly down. I am not a big fan of down in large doses. Still, when the Goddess has your balls in a vice, you have to take what you can get. I shut my eyes and took a deep breath. It did nothing for my vertigo, but at least my voice didn't come out squeaky with terror.

"That way."

Chapter Twenty-three

It wasn't as bad as I'd feared. It was much, much worse. Even though I doubted the Inquisition ever expected anyone to try to escape – after all, where would you escape *to*, except straight into the arms of Specials, guards and Ministry men? – there was a reason the holding cell was there, and that reason was, it was suicidal trying to climb down. The sides of the spire were almost sheer, the stone was slick marble and not even a handy gargoyle to hang on to. And there was that long, long drop to consider, though I was trying my very best not to.

I suggested an easier way, of course, one that didn't involve me and heights, but Pasha gave me a mental slap.

"You're too close. I don't need to be in your head to know that. You're on the edge of a drop worse than that. Don't fall in."

So I lied and said, sure, no magic and the black rubbed its hands in my head. Pasha and Jake probably never noticed how

I rearranged their hands, the soles of their boots, with the little juice I had. Made them that bit sticky, all the better to grip the stone with. They might need it later, too, because I'd asked them to try to find Perak, help him any way they could. Being Archdeacon had to count for something, surely.

Pasha was as nimble as a monkey, naturally, and Jake didn't fare too badly either. They had a few hairy moments getting around an overhang, but before long they were safely down to the lower levels of the building where the roof didn't slope so sharply and someone had thought that fretwork and knobbly bits of stone looked good. From there, it was only a matter of leaping a nice chasm with death at the bottom, and they were out. I didn't watch.

Guinto, despite our every effort, refused point-blank to leave. I couldn't work out if he was irretrievably stupid or irredeemably pious. He was a pain in the buttocks, though. Whatever I said, all he would reply was, "I'm guilty, and I must atone to the Goddess for my sins."

"That's all very well, but if Pasha's right, you'll end up killing Under. Killing the city perhaps. Not a nice epitaph, is it? I should know."

What he probably meant to be a crafty look crept over his face. In fact, it made him look like a kid who's just figured out that, actually, there is such a thing as lying. Sad, really.

"If I'm still here," he said, "they might not look so hard for you three. I'm the guilty one, the one they can parade and say they caught the killer."

"Oh, yes, thank you very much, add another death to my conscience," I snapped. "All very well for you, to choose the end you get. What about everyone else? Hmm? All your parishioners, all those Downsiders you gave hope to, who'll burn the place down if you do this? Don't you care?"

A faded sort of smile. "When you destroyed the Glow, when you destroyed everything this city was built on, condemned a city to starve, did you pause to wonder? Did you care about them then? Or did you do what you thought was right?"

I hate it when people throw things back in your face. I tried, I swear I did. I cajoled and wheedled and threatened but all he would say was, "Abeya is my daughter. I have to do this, for her."

I tried swearing a blue streak at him but he wouldn't reply, only smiled at me with that beatific smile that I knew, *knew*, would haunt me. He was doing it because he was good and noble, and saving a Goddess-denying wretch like me. Maybe converting me in the process, though good luck to him on that point.

"I still won't believe in her, you know that?"

"Oh, you will in the end. They always do. You go, and may the Goddess bless your steps."

I kept my response shut down behind locked lips, because if I'd let it out they'd have heard me down in No-Hope.

Why we'd been allowed to come to, wake up enough that I could use the juice flowing through me, I had no idea, but

304

I thought I detected Dench's hand in the proceedings. But for what reason, I was only guessing. How far in that cardinal's pocket was he, or was he playing the long game, pretending to follow when really he was planning to arrest? Was he helping, or setting me up?

Whatever, there was no point being too obvious. Instead, and it wasn't a much better prospect, I stood by the window and looked out. No way, no way in the *world*, was I climbing down there, not with a long entrenched terror of heights and a buggered hand. But feeling was coming back. Pain was lurking. Juice was waiting.

I clenched my fist with a moan, and laid my head against the cool stone of the wall. The stone ran with blackness, a river, a tide of it swarming towards me. Not yet, I couldn't succumb yet. Later, I promised myself. Later I would, and everything would go away. Now, I had things to do. Without Pasha and Jake to worry about. With any luck, he'd get her out and safe, keep them both safe and Perak, too, I hoped. Because I thought that this was going to end only one way, and it was the least I could do for both of them, for believing in me when I was about to betray that belief. Because I had the funniest feeling I'd worked a few things out, and it didn't look good. If everything went tits up, and on previous experience I fully expected it to, at least they'd be out of it, maybe could keep Lise safe for me, too.

Because this was all just that bit too close together. The cardinal guiding Abeya, getting Dench in his pocket, having

Perak shot. Whelar had given him a great way to keep us under control. Manoto had destroyed mages and the lab so that either Perak had to negotiate with the Storad or he could step in and say, "I have a deal already", perhaps.

Whatever, it was all tied up together in knots, I was sure of it, and if I pulled one thread maybe it'd all come tumbling down. *He* would come tumbling down, and wouldn't that make a great splash?

Then perhaps we could get on and get the damn power on, save the city without having my brain zapped. Much. As an added bonus, maybe I could stymie the whole damned Ministry, bring the smug bastards to their knees, a thought which made me smile and ignore the laughter in the back of my head.

With my good hand, I rummaged in a pocket and found the envelope containing Abeya's hairs nestling next to the little vial Lise had given me. And was that a clue to what Dench wanted me to do? Why hadn't they confiscated it? What *did* he want me to do? Or had they just thought it was one of Whelar's syringes? They looked the same, and I suppose no one would think I'd willingly inject myself with one of his jabs.

I pushed that away – my brain would just go round in circles, with no answers. I needed to do something, that was for sure. It didn't take much – Abeya was close, very close. Twenty yards south-west, fifty down. Not far. Fat Boy was keeping her close, for who knows what reason. Maybe she'd been the one to fire the shot at Perak. Didn't matter. All that mattered was she was close and I could find her, get out of here and stop Manoto and Abeya and the Storad they were plotting with. Perhaps. If they really were.

Two things followed me in and through as I melted from one place to another – a thought from Pasha, quite a rude one asking what the fuck I thought I was doing, and, worse, a murmured prayer from Guinto for the Goddess to watch over me, because I was a good man really, even if I didn't know it. Shows what he knew, right?

Chapter Twenty-four

I probably should have looked a bit before I jumped in with both hoofing great feet, but my mind wasn't really thinking very clearly at that point. Mostly I wanted to get away from Guinto and his prayers. I found Abeya all right. Unfortunately I found someone else too: a big, mean Storad and he was pissed as hell when I landed on top of him.

Abeya screamed, and I may have done as well because the Storad's first action was to grab my poor hand and twist it up behind my back so hard that white spots ran in front of my eyes and it was all I could do not to let all that juice out in one glorious rush that probably would have killed me, them, and anyone else in a hundred yards' radius. Tempting, but I didn't want to die then. I'm not all that keen on dying now.

Then a familiar and terrifying sensation – a syringe jabbing into me. I tried to struggle, tried to rip it out before whoever held it pressed the plunger, but I was too damned slow. All I could do was hope like crazy it wasn't the new stuff the cardinal had tried on us that knocked out your brain but left your body nicely capable of producing pain, and power. Gibbering wreck isn't a good look for me.

It wasn't that much of a relief when numbness flowed out from the needle mark. I was still screwed seven ways from hell. No magic, and simple things like walking and talking were off the agenda for a while. My hand didn't hurt, though. There's always a bright side if you look hard enough. I don't usually bother, because, as in this case, even the bright side is a bunch of shit. No painful hand, no ready juice.

It was quite a relief when the Storad took his substantial bulk off my back, though, and him being there with Abeya answered a lot of the "why?" questions in my head.

Power, it was all about power. It always was.

I took a look around. I was lying on grass, soft and fragrant, but seemed to be in a room still. The whitewashed walls were circular and the grass was dotted with comfy-looking chairs and loungers. Instead of a ceiling, glass stretched across the top of the walls. Somewhere for enjoying the sun. I kind of wished that this was happening in daylight so that I could see it.

A door opened and shut behind me, an extra pair of feet shuffled in the grass. The cardinal, bound to be. Come to check up on the Storad he was negotiating with, plotting with. Come to see if Abeya was ready to kill someone else to help his cause, perhaps, or thank her for shooting Perak.

The bottom really fell out of my world when Dench said, "I knew he'd end up here, after her. Can't keep it in his trousers for more than two minutes together. Well, about time. Rojan, you really are an arse about fucking with my day. You know that?"

Even if I could have spoken around the lump of meat my numb tongue had become, I'd have been speechless. Instead I lay there like a slab of stone and stared uselessly at him as he strode over to me and hunkered down. He looked almost sorrowful, and his moustache drooped as if in sympathy with me.

"You were supposed to stay Under, idiot." He smiled when I twitched at that. "I tried to help you, I really did. But now you're here . . . it's too late. For both of us. I only wanted to help Mahala, for the Goddess. I wanted Perak to negotiate, I wanted us to start using coal and the city to *live*. Coal that no one need hurt for, die for. Negotiations, that's all I thought it was. Clearing up that last mess you made for me. Now here we are with another mess. Can't even blame you for it, either."

"Generous. For a murderer," I managed to mangle out.

Dench grabbed the front of my allover. "I murdered no one. *No one.* Certainly not Dwarf. Even the Inquisition . . . Manoto ordered it, and my men, well, they have their own prejudices, and their orders. I'm more forgiving of heresy than they are. But to start with, before all that, it was just negotiations, I thought. A little deal when Perak was being too damned blind about you and that fucking generator. A little shuffle of goods and services, and the city would live. Thousands of people would live who might otherwise die. Worth a few shady deals, right? By the time I found out, about the Storad and Manoto using Abeya to kill those boys, about the Storad killing Dwarf and Manoto's plans for the Inquisition ... it was too late. By then I was already involved, whether I wanted to be or not. So now it's just a matter of when, not if, we sign with the Storad, and making sure as few people as possible die in the meantime. I swore a holy oath to the Goddess, to protect Mahala to the best of my ability. So I took a little sin on my soul, for the good of the city. Now, well, now we don't need you, or your Glow. Because the Glow can't sustain us, not with so few mages and that generator was never going to work. So now our negotiations with this gentleman here can proceed apace. Think of it, Rojan. No more pain, for anyone, not to power the city."

He pulled something out of his pocket, black and rough looking. Nothing special.

"Coal, remember? Coal to drive steam-powered factories, carriages, lights, heat. War engines that rumble towards our gates even now. But Perak wouldn't hear of negotiating – you were going to persuade him for me, but you didn't, did you? If you had ... If we stall much longer, the Storad and Mishans, well, they're sitting pretty outside the city. War, Rojan. But Manoto, he's reached an agreement with our nice Storad ambassador here. With no Glow, and Perak out of the way, we can have peace. A few lives are worth that, don't you think? Manoto thinks it's all we can do, if we want to live, and I agree with him. Be good for once in your life, and stay out of trouble until it's done. Don't make me do something we'll both regret. Because I will if I have to."

He stood up and shook his head sorrowfully over me, like I was a child who'd deeply disappointed him. The Storad said something in a language that sounded like two rocks being banged together. It startled Dench, but he stared down at me and said a few words back. I didn't like the feeling that they were discussing my fate, but there wasn't much I could do about it.

"Abeya, you stay and make sure he stays numb. Same for Pasha when the guards bring him, and yes, Rojan, of course I knew you'd escape. I planned for it, hoping you'd lead me to Perak. Abeya, sadly, shot the wrong man."

My relief and confusion must have shown, though I couldn't get a word out.

"She shot a decoy, I think. Perak's around somewhere, hiding, planning something and I hoped you knew where he was, that you'd take me to him. Sadly, it appears not. If it helps, I'm glad that it wasn't him. If he wasn't so stubborn, he might make a good Archdeacon. Maybe if he's seen the light, he still can be. Maybe with you here and in the shit, he'll let himself be drawn out. Abeya, no killing any of them." But his eyes added "yet" to that. Keeping me alive, in case his plans didn't work out perhaps, in case he needed a mage or two. But if his plans went well ... I didn't rate my chances, to be honest. I'd make a nice handy scapegoat.

The Storad ground out a few words to Abeya, and then he and Dench departed. Leaving me alone with a serial mage killer. Just when I thought my day couldn't get any worse.

I contemplated getting up, doing something, anything, but my legs were like dishrags and I had enough trouble lying there without dribbling. The only part of me that wasn't numb was my brain, so I tried to use that. It became quite difficult when Abeya slunk over and sat next to me. Partly because it seemed she'd finally snapped in two. Part innocent seductress, part raging killer. She kept wavering between the two halves so I wasn't sure which was her any more.

Mainly the trouble I was having was because she'd decided to take her dress off, and naked women have always been a big distraction. Especially when they do that with their hands, even if I couldn't feel it. My head knew what was going on, and there was a kind of warm pressure that was enough to stop almost any coherent thought.

She leant over me, close enough that her hair fell over my cheeks. The face of an angel, I thought again, and then wondered why I hadn't twigged before. As you can imagine, I've never believed angels are all sweet and kind, so why would I think that of her because of how she looked? She'd suckered me in by my own weakness for a pretty face. Her eyes seemed to pull part of me out of myself and drink me into her, and her soft voice was hypnotic as her free hand stroked my cheek.

"He wants to keep you as a pet, the Storad does." The luscious curve of her smile was enough to make grown men

313

weep. I would have done, but I kept reminding myself that she was a killer. It didn't stop all those very distracting thoughts. "Keep you numb like this, a trophy of how it was him who finally bested Mahala. Bested the mages. Keep you like this for ever."

Her fingers trailed across my cheek and on to my lips. I couldn't feel it, but I could imagine it, remember when she'd done that before, and wished I couldn't. My brain's never been good at doing what it's told, especially when naked women are involved.

"Shame really." She came in even closer, and all I could see was her, the smile that could curse a man to never wanting another. She kissed me, slowly, and sat back with a sigh. "Such a shame that I'm not going to be allowed to kill you."

Who knows what she might have done then – I'm never sure whether I regret not finding out or not – if the door hadn't opened and two Inquisitors shoved a limp Pasha through before they slammed the door behind them? Pasha fell in a heap, but he was awake because his eyes flickered and he tried to say something. All that came out was a garbled sort of grunt. Amazing how we take our tongue for granted really. Poor Pasha couldn't even fall back on mind talk, because no juice, no rummaging in heads.

I wanted to ask, find out if Jake was safe, if they'd found Perak, but I had no way.

Pasha's eyes almost fell out of his head at the sight of Abeya sitting next to him in her naked glory. She seemed proud of her brands now, flaunting them at Pasha as though to show him why she'd done what she had. Why she hated mages like us, why she wanted to kill us, had been such an easy pawn for Fat Boy and the Storad to turn to their own ends.

Pasha fumbled about and Abeya shot back when he finally managed to free a sleeve, roll it up and show her – an identical brand. Proof that not every mage was a torturer, that at least one had been a victim.

"Bastard," Abeya hissed, and cracked off a slap at Pasha that knocked his head a whole half-turn. "*Fake* bastard. You never had to take it, I bet. Those are fake brands." She slapped him again, and again, her angelic face twisted into something more demonic as she let out her rage and hate. I could hardly blame her either – mages had taken her and, over who knew how much time and lovingly applied pain, turned her into this.

I tried to say something, some words that would make her see, but it came out a garbled mess, though slightly more coherent than I'd dreaded. Still, she wasn't having any of it. She leapt from crouching over Pasha and on to me, her arm swinging and swinging, hard enough that I was briefly glad I was numb. Finally, after what seemed an age, and when some small feeling started to come back, making her slaps and punches start to sting, she stopped. She seemed breathless but calmer, purged for a time, perhaps. If that had helped her, in any way, then a few bruises and what was starting to feel like a new shiner were the least I could offer.

"Fake," she whispered.

"Not fake." My voice wasn't quite right, but the words were at least recognisable and I needed, please any deity that might exist, to keep her on this, on hating me, mages, everything, make all her delusions worse, throw her already unbalanced mind even further out of whack. Or perhaps persuade her that we were the good guys, honest, but I didn't think I had a hope in hell of that. But anything so she didn't remember the syringe glinting on the table, didn't remember to use it. I felt like a real shit doing it, but I didn't seem to have much choice. The only thing that made me feel any better was that it wasn't a lie.

"Not every mage helped Azama. Pasha was as much his victim as you. And I killed him. For you, Abeya, and all the people like you."

The truth, sort of, though I buffed up my reasons to look a bit shinier. I'd killed him because I couldn't bear the thought that my own father had twisted his mind that far to think torture was the good thing to do. Because I was afraid I might be too like him. Because it was the only way to make Jake happy, and I'd wanted to give her that – peace from the demons in her head, and the largest was Azama.

"No." She spat the words with a vigorous shake of her head. "Dench killed him. He told me. He killed Azama, for the Goddess. For *me*. His Specials, they came and took us away. He took me to Guinto."

"Not Dench. He helped you after. But he didn't kill Azama." She launched into a kind of frenzy at that, as though I'd

316

destroyed any last sane part of her. She wasn't thinking with her head if she ever had been because she was, quite clearly, batshit crazy. She was thinking with her heart, with her scarred soul, and just then I think I loved her a little bit. Broken, inside and out, like Jake. But unlike the object of my innermost desires, Abeya had stayed broken, couldn't quite bring herself to try to heal but had festered her hate into madness. Maybe she didn't want to get better, maybe she just couldn't. Maybe she would never be anything else, but I couldn't help her because I had to help everyone else, all those people relying on me, shadows at my back, on my wished-I-could-be-feckless heart.

At least she seemed to have forgotten about the syringe, about keeping us numb. The slaps and punches started to hurt now, but I held still. Let her power up my juice. Until she grabbed up a knife and came for me with it, a scream on her lips and quite possibly a long and messy murder in her heart. I didn't try the same trick as before – she may have been batshit, but crazy isn't the same as stupid, or Dendal would be a drooling idiot. I still didn't have much juice. Not much, not really enough, and I needed to keep it, so I played my strongest card and lied through my conniving, womanising teeth.

She was fast, but movement was easier and she was as unstable as black powder and flame mixed together. I caught her off guard, good hand on a wrist thin and fragile, the other pulling her into me so I could kiss her. She struggled for a moment, but not for long. Like I said before, I can talk almost any woman into bed, the exception being the one I want to most. What can I say? It's a gift.

I put everything I had into that kiss – the wish that things were different, a hope that Abeya could be saved, at least from being used as some killer pawn in Manoto's game, maybe even from her own broken mind. A hope that maybe I could be saved from loving an impossibility, that Abeya would be the one to save me from that. That we could save each other. For those few moments, I really meant that kiss. I always do, that's half my problem.

Then she pulled away, stared at me for long, long moments and I wondered, perhaps, if it could happen. I let go of the arm that held the knife, and that was my mistake. Women and how I love them: always and to the end of the world my downfall. She smiled like fallen angels and went for me.

It probably would have ended messily one way or another and I'd have regretted a lot more than I already do, but Pasha put a stop to it by lurching to his feet and whacking her round the back of the head with a vase. Even crumpling to the floor, she was graceful as angels. I wished, very hard, that I had anything that could help her, save her, and as usual came up wanting.

"You're a real piece of work, you know that?" Pasha mumbled past his numb tongue.

Feeling was definitely starting to come back, though we still sounded like a pair of drunks. "*I'm* not the one who just hit a lady."

"You are such a fuck. I've got no idea why that makes me like you."

"Because I'm a god with women and you wish you were like me? Don't just stand there, help me up."

He snorted derision and held out a hand. We were both still as wobbly as day-old kittens, but at least we could stand up. In my case, if I leant against the table.

"How much feeling have you got back?" I asked, though I was pretty sure I knew the answer because I could only feel bits of me.

"Not enough to do much. Something small perhaps. You?"

"Same. Got a bit of juice, maybe enough to change my face to something less kill-worthy. That's about it. Jake – where is she? You can talk to her, got enough for that? Can she help us out of this, because I don't think I'm up to a couple of Inquisitors outside the door and who knows what the fuck else before we get to that stupid, backstabbing bastard Dench."

"She's still looking for Perak. Bastards got me, but they'll get more than they bargained for with her. And backstabbing?"

Then followed an expletive-ridden account of what that stupid backstabbing bastard had done and was planning to do. I may have said "fuck" and "bastard" and "Namrat's bitch" more than strictly required.

Pasha's face wrinkled into a monkey frown. "But Dench – I thought he was your friend. He helped us, before, helped all the Little Whores."

"You may have noticed I'm not good on the friend part. He helped before because Azama needed stopping, because Dench had been made a party to that without him knowing. He's doing this because Manoto thinks we have no choice but to ally with the Storad, and Dench agrees.'

"But Lise, the generator . . . " His voice trailed off as he thought about it. "Dench doesn't think it will work. None of them do. A false hope."

"It'll work, if anyone can make it work it's Lise. But they don't believe it will, so Manoto, or the Storad, made sure of it by using Abeya to kill more mages – I think they found out it was her to start with, then played on it. Finding the boys, telling her where and when. I don't think Dench knew about that to start with. So, then the lab, because without the generator we're screwed. And, of course, when it becomes clear that Perak hasn't got anything to back up his claims that he can get the power on, then out he goes as Archdeacon, and in comes Manoto who already has a deal with the Storad. But right now, what we need to do is get the fuck out of this place."

"Good point. What have we got?"

Not a whole hell of a lot. I patted down my jacket, in case any handy door-opening explosives had appeared in the pockets. All I found was Abeya's hairs, the lollipops for Dog and the vial and syringe Lise had given me. I was definitely going off syringes.

"What's that?" Pasha looked like he was feeling the same way.

320

"Something Lise wanted me to try, but if it's all the same to you we'll leave it as a last resort."

"Coward." Pasha's grin was evil. "What's a little jab between friends?"

I looked at the vial and shuddered at the sight of the needle. But we were running out of options, and magic. If Lise made it, it was probably all right. By which I mean I expected it wouldn't kill me. Probably.

"Any *other* bright ideas?"

Pasha's evil grin deepened. "You know, I think I might."

Chapter Twenty-five

It seemed to me that Pasha took a perverse amount of delight in it. He had ways of using his thought magic that I'd never dreamed of, and some of them were deliciously evil. I don't suppose he'd ever have used them, being the good guy that he was, but being told you're unholy by all the people you respect, well, if you hear it often enough, and you're contrary enough, perhaps you want to prove them right. Pasha had a hard little grin on his face, one that didn't bode well for anyone getting in his way. Sometimes I wish I had his talent so that I could know what people were thinking, but I was pretty sure being a good boy for the Goddess wasn't on his mind. Maybe something a bit more visceral, like the Downside version of the Goddess. Blood and vengeance, perhaps. I had the feeling that mousy little Pasha had just turned lion again.

He didn't have any more feeling than I did, but it had to be worth a try. The sick crack of him dislocating his fingers was followed by fruitless minutes searching for anyone outside. If there was anyone, he couldn't hear them. Which made it a shock when the key ground in the lock and the door flew open.

Sadly, it didn't open on to freedom but on to the pissed-off face of Dench. Well, part of his face – the rest was covered with an Inquisitor's helm which didn't really go with the moustache. Behind him, another two Inquisitors loomed in the doorway.

Dench smiled and in the absence of seeing anything of his eyes, my own seemed glued to the moustache.

"Think I'm that stupid, that I'd leave you with her any longer than I had to? Oh, Rojan. I thought you knew me better. Only for long enough to fetch these gents here, plenty of time before Whelar's little concoction wore off enough for you to do anything useful."

He was right, which didn't make it any easier to hear. We were still half numb and too slow to avoid the Inquisitors as they grabbed us, one each. Dench snatched Lise's syringe out of my hand.

"I'll take that, thanks."

And without magic, without enough juice to zap a rat, that was all it took. Two beefy Inquisitors and a syringe. Made me feel pretty pathetic. Dench took a savage pleasure in shoving the needle into my neck, and I could feel enough for it to hurt in a vague, dreamy kind of way which seemed to disappoint him before he did the same to Pasha.

"That should be enough to keep you where I want you, for long enough." Dench jerked his head at the Inquisitors and they shoved us through the door. "And you're going to do what I want, Rojan. Just what I want, because if you don't, poor Lise's recovery could very well become a relapse."

Odd, how regretful he sounded, but that wasn't what filled my mind.

Fire spread out from the needle mark in my neck, ran through me in heartbeats, made that heart speed like a Rapture addict sprinting for his life from Namrat come to take him. What had Lise done to Whelar's concoction? I didn't care, because it wasn't numbness that Dench had injected us with, wasn't dead legs that made me stagger. It was feeling, not just feeling but *feeling*. Every nerve ending blazed with it, my fingertips fizzed with life, my skin felt like it was on fire. Sadly, every little ache also became magnified, so that I had to bite down on a scream when my bad hand brushed my leg.

But the best, and the worst, was the juice. I didn't just have some, I was overflowing with it. It should have dripped down my cheeks, out of my nose. I was surprised when I blinked and lightning *didn't* shoot down the corridor and blast the crap out of a fresco of some happy horseshit that involved things looking sparkly and nice.

With the juice, came the black. And, oh, it was loud now. It had power. It knew me better than I know myself, and it used it. *Dip in, Rojan. Just a bit. You could have more magic than you ever thought possible. Forget blowing up temples, you could blow up the whole of Ministry. Take the whole fucking lot down, once and for all. You and me, Rojan, we could fire Top of the World, let the light Under. We could scare the crap out of the Storad and Mishans, enough to make sure we had no war. We could make it so it was kittens and sunbeams for everyone. Come on, come in, just a while, just a moment. Be everything, be everyone, leave all your fears at the door. Come in, you know you want to.*

I staggered again, barely able to hold myself up. Dench smiled at that and must have thought I was numb as fuck, and I almost wished I was. Pasha glanced my way from the grip of an Inquisitor and I could see it in his eyes, too. He didn't need to say a damned word, not out loud or in my head. Say nothing, do nothing. Yet.

I tried to still the black, tried to shut up the small voice in me that said *Yes, yes, let's blow it all the fuck up, right now, and start again, properly this time.* The black is all your hopes come true and all your fears soothed away, and that is very, very tempting and I wanted it. When I shut my eyes I could see the spires of Top of the World in rubble, could see the vast estates of Clouds melt away and sunlight, real, first-hand sunlight, lay a cleansing hand on Under, scour it of corruption and take the Shitty out of No-Hope.

I was on the verge of doing it and to fuck with the consequences when Pasha fell into me, accidentally-on-purpose almost certainly. It wasn't much, but it was enough to distract me from temptation. Just as well, really.

The Inquisitors shoved us down a short corridor that

ended in a mean little door. Dench didn't send us through, not yet.

"We *have* to ally with the Storad. There's nothing else for it. They're at our gates with machines Dwarf would have been proud of, and we're screwed. I'm sorry, Rojan, I really am, but I'm doing what I can for Mahala, for the Goddess. And to do that, to pacify the Storad, keep them sweet with the ministers, I need someone else to take the blame for the murders – what I wanted you to do in the first place, find a scapegoat. Nice bit of providence, Guinto coming to confess like that. The Goddess provides, eh? I know you're a contrary bastard, so don't forget that Lise is under my protection. And Pasha should remember that I'll have Jake in my hands within the hour. Goddess's tits, she left a bloody trail, but it won't be long. Not long. So you two play like good little boys, confirm Guinto's guilt and you won't end the day in the Slump. It's the best I could do for you both. It'll be easy. Just testify that a priest is a bad man and you save the city. It's a lie – but a lie that will help people live, and most certainly help the people you love to live."

And then he shoved us through the door into my idea of hell.

Chapter Twenty-six

The Inquisition, the real part of it where they judged you guilty or innocent, was even worse than I imagined. This was the true Top of the World, a circular platform right at the top of the palace. It was ringed, for the most part, by pillars made of some weird stone that seemed to glow in the moonlight, and with ministers, cardinals, priests and good men come to see what Dench had for them. There was no light but that of the moon, and all I could see of them were dark, swishing robes and glittering eyes.

We stumbled forwards ahead of the Inquisitors and the juice made lights run in front of my eyes and laughter run through my brain.

Guinto was already there, standing in the centre of the circle in his white robes like a sacrificial lamb. Strange, how peaceful he seemed, his hands clasped in front of him, his gaze steady, as though he was only going to deliver another sermon.

I, on the other hand, was trying not to scream like a girl at the thought of what was on the far side of the circle. Namely a gap that made the wind whistle through it like ghosts, and beyond that a very long drop into the Slump. My nerves were not helped by the fact that what I could see past the edge from here was nothing but dark sky, hard stars and the secret light of the moon.

We were prodded to the centre of the circle next to Guinto and I thought I could make out a few very dim, very distant lights down there. I started to wish I had someone I could pray to, then told myself not to be so fucking stupid.

It seemed we'd missed Guinto's confession. A murmur ran around the circle as ministers tutted, cardinals censured. Dench strode to the centre in front of Guinto and I'd never realised how tall he was, how imposing. He towered over the priest, and his faint shadow with its helmet towered further, and it seemed to me it was no accident that shadow looked like Namrat creeping the walls.

At a nod from Dench, Cardinal Manoto scurried forwards at a wobble. I'd been sure for a while that it was Manoto behind everything. Then sure he'd somehow lured Dench, chief of the unbribable, unturnable Specials to his cause by way of some Goddess-invoked duty, before Dench had made me think again. But with that nod and scurry, I had my final proof I'd been wrong. I knew who was dealing with the Storad, who had Fat Boy in his pocket rather than the other way around. And who, as head of the Specials and therefore head of the Inquisition, was safe enough to order the Inquisitors out, who knew he would never be called on to justify himself here in this circle. Who could rig the entrail reading because it was him that did that reading. The goat stood at the side of the circle now, chained to a pillar, chewing with equanimity and staring at me with liquid eyes. I dare say it looked a damn sight calmer than I did.

Manoto turned to face the crowd and, after a sideways glance that begged permission from Dench and an inclination of the head that gave it, launched into his speech.

"Your Graces, Excellencies and most Revered colleagues, we have heard from Father Guinto of his sins, that he has readily confessed, may it bring him swift mercy from the Goddess. Now I ask you to witness the Inquisition of heretics, and worse, of pain-mages who would bring about the downfall of Mahala, of the Ministry. Of everything we know. Men who have tried once before to destroy us, by destroying both the Glow and the previous Archdeacon."

All eyes turned on me and Pasha. I stood as straight as I could, given the circumstances, and tried not to think how much of the whole fucking Ministry I could take out with one well-aimed blast of magic. Right then, with all those eyes on us, greedy, bored, malevolent eyes, with only one or two showing any hint of mercy, I'd have shot the whole fucking palace sky-high. Everyone Under, well they'd be screwed, but probably no more than they were already and they'd not have that yoke on them, tying them to what they thought they knew.

No Ministry stealing their sun, the food from their mouths, the joy from their souls.

I snuck a look at Pasha. Like the goat, he seemed a damn sight calmer than I was, though that wasn't hard. Where I'd been flicking my gaze over everyone, trying to find a friendly face – Perak, surely Perak would be here if Dench was right and he was still alive – Pasha's look was fixed on a woman at the back of the ring. She couldn't hold his dark, angry gaze for long and turned away, her mouth curved down as though she was ashamed.

"Inquisitor?" Manoto inclined his head and Dench stepped forward. Under the rim of his helm, his moustache bristled and twisted with his lips – not quite a smile, or if it was it was full of regret. Which was nice enough, but not as nice as stopping this fucking charade. The thought of the big drop only feet away from me was making me very nervous indeed and I didn't have a clue what to do, or even if there was anything I *could* do other than make things go boom, which, while incredibly tempting, wasn't going to do anything to help. I had at least to *try* to be rational. I had no friend in Dench, no brother around to help me. All I had was my wits. Which meant we were probably dead.

"This," Dench said, landing a hand on my shoulder. "This is Archdeacon Azama's son and murderer. This is Rojan Dizon, destroyer of the Glow, opponent of the Ministry, spreader of false rumours, a pain-mage and a disbeliever."

Funny, really. Barely a murmur at the murderer part –

330

I was pretty sure my father had had an enemy or ten, or at least a lot of people who no longer wanted to be reminded they had been his supporters while he was alive. Destroyer of the Glow brought a disgruntled shuffle and a few voices. Disbeliever, though – it was like Dench had dropped in the fact he was the Goddess, or maybe had accused them all of goat buggery or something, because the ring of the good and great seemed to explode.

A pair of hands grabbed me from behind and tried to drag me to the open space on the far side of the ring. Only shoving my weight back and all but falling on whoever it was stopped my forward slide to oblivion, but that wasn't much better because I was surrounded by a sea of angry faces, not shouting, nothing so crass, but so quietly *intent* that I pretty near pissed myself. That long drop was mine, one way or another, I knew it in my bones. I also knew that, if I fell, I'd be too piss-scared and short of time to do anything about it, like rearrange myself somewhere else.

Dench managed to get some order, eventually, and I was still in one piece but mutinous murmurs ran round the crowd like rats in pipes. It wouldn't take much to set them off again – if there's one thing the Ministry really doesn't like it's someone who refuses to believe their claptrap.

But Dench didn't create order for my benefit. He hadn't finished. His hand landed on Pasha's shoulder and yet still Pasha didn't move, didn't tear his gaze away from the back of the crowd.

331

"This is Pasha, pain-mage, adherent of the Downside Goddess, maker of the blood and ash devotional, and heretic." The woman that Pasha was staring at looked sick at that. Both hands flew to her mouth like startled birds and trembled there. "Both these men have used their magic to start up a pain factory, against everything the Goddess stands for, a crime of high treason against the Ministry, the people of Mahala and the Goddess."

At Dench's signal, Manoto stepped forward again. He stood in front of the pair of us, wobbling with anticipation, or fear perhaps. He kept darting little glances to Dench and back again.

"The evidence we have against you is quite damning. If you confess, your deaths will be quick. A mercy from the Goddess. If you deny the charges and are found guilty, then there is no mercy."

"What if we're found innocent?" I asked.

"Is that likely? Beside the point. Once brought to the Inquisitorial Circle, no one has ever been found innocent. Pasha, how do you plead?"

Pasha didn't seem to have heard him, never looked his way but just kept on staring at the woman. But something must have got through, because he said, "I deny nothing. I can't deny what and who I am, not any more. I am a Downside man, I worship according to our ways, and I am a pain-mage. I am not ashamed of that, or of anything I've done. Not any more." He broke his stare at last to look to Guinto. "Sorry, Father."

"Rojan? Maybe if you can corroborate what Guinto has told us, the Inquisition will look more kindly upon you."

I'm a lot of things, as perhaps you've guessed about me by now. Liar, philanderer, cynic, bastard. I'm pretty proud of that list, too. When I went to sleep at night, at least I could tell myself I wasn't a fucking sheep, bleating out what I was told to believe, doing what Ministry said was the good and right thing. I can work that out for myself, mostly, though I've been known to fuck it up on occasion. But this – this was hard. I could do what I've always dreamed of, really stick it to a priest, good and proper, tell everyone that, yes, it was Guinto who had goaded Abeya into murder, yes, I was an unbeliever, a pain-mage and, fucking right, I was using pain to make Glow.

Or I could look at Dench, my friend, a good and true man who believed and who did what he did for that belief, I could look him right in the eye and drop him so far in the shit, he'd hit bedrock.

Either way, Mahala was in trouble – if Guinto went over that drop, Under would burn. No doubt about it. He was who they looked to now, the face of the Ministry they relied on, the ear that listened when Top of the World was deaf. I looked him over and he spared me a glance – no disgust there, not now. Just a serene knowledge he was doing the right thing, and maybe that he thought I would, too.

If I fingered Dench and his pet cardinal, if I scuppered their plans with the Storad, it'd be worse. It was a good plan, and would save us, though we'd be beholden to the bastards and the part of me that belongs to this city, to the ancient legacy of being a sneaky bastard who takes shit from no one, balked at that. But people would live, Under would have food again. No one would starve. He was a good man who'd done a bad thing for a good reason. A better man than I'll ever be.

Sometimes I feel that my life is blighted by the tyranny of good men.

Whatever I did, people were going to die. I was going to be responsible for a whole lot of shit. Again. So I did the only thing I could do.

I lied.

Chapter Twenty-seven

If I've learnt anything, it's this: Rojan, keep your stupid fucking mouth shut. I may even make it a new rule number one.

Because when I dropped that lie into the cold space at Top of the World, I once again managed to screw the city, and everyone in it. Go me. All I can say is that it seemed like a good idea at the time. I'd rather see possible war than an innocent man Inquisitioned, even if he *is* a priest.

"Dench killed those boys. With his own hands. He's working for the Storad." It felt like a betrayal, until I remembered that Downside family taken by the Inquisition, and all the others like them. Remembered that Dench could have stopped that. Then it felt pretty good.

All hell broke loose. Fat Cardinal wobbled so hard I thought he might actually fall over. Pasha stared at me like I'd gone completely mad. Everyone else just went crazy.

"You *fucker*."

A smack across the chops from an Inquisitor's gauntlet isn't pleasant at the best of times but with Lise's concoction blasting through me like a furnace it felt like the top of my head had come off. I landed flat on my back with a scream, sliding inexorably towards the gap, and the drop. Dench's lip curled in contempt, but I thought I read something else there, too.

I scrabbled at the smooth stone, trying to grab something, anything, to stop my slide but there was nothing. Even if there had been, Dench strode towards me and it seemed no one was able, or wanted, to stop him. There was a lot of shouting, a lot of angry men, but no one wanted to get in his way. That Inquisitor's uniform was really doing its work.

I started to slow and began to hope I'd stop in time, but a kick from Dench set me going again. It was slicker than soap, that stone, and my fear of the drop stymied any thought of using my magic with anything approaching delicacy.

"Can't leave well enough alone, can you?" Dench growled. "Couldn't just stay Under, out of trouble, out of my fucking plans. Couldn't do as you were told for once in your life. I was going to save the city. I still am, once I'm done with you – I am *the* Inquisitor and I don't need any entrails to know you're a fucking unbeliever. I'm going to drop you in the Slump. Do you think they'll care?"

Another kick, and my legs dropped over the edge. I could have sworn I felt every inch of the drop below me and that paralysed my brain as surely as any concoction of Whelar's.

Behind Dench, Inquisitors flooded the circle and all of a sudden everyone stopped shouting. Obedience is ingrained into us somehow and, faced with those uniforms, everyone's subconscious took over and shut them up. One or two tried, to my surprise, tried to protest, tried to fight back against the inevitable. They ended up crumpled heaps on the floor.

Which wasn't much help to me. The weight of my legs dragged me further over, and the wind caught at the hem of my coat, whipped it round and snapped it out like a banner. I was torn between pissing myself and throwing up, neither of which was a helpful response, true, but the only responses I'm capable of when dangling half a mile above what would soon be my final resting place. I hoped the rats choked on me, and that was the only rational thought I was capable of because the rest of my brain had shorted out in terror.

I lost sight of what was going on in the circle – nothing good was all I could figure in the swirl of people – when my head dropped below the stone. My good hand scrabbled about, hoping perhaps to grab at Dench's foot when it came for another kick. I'd have grabbed anything at that point.

I did a stupid thing – I looked down. I couldn't *not* look.

Space stretched out below me, a dizzying, vomit-inducing void with the faintest of lights, tiny pinpricks to show me where I'd splat. Beyond was the darkness of mountains, and a smaller spread of pinpricks – a camp, a siege parked right on the craggy flanks of the mountains, the only space to be had. Right underneath me was the huge bulk of Trade, great blocky warehouses next to the mess that was the Slump, no lights, no inhabitants, just waiting to swallow me up. The rest of Under was just as dark, just as far away. Should have stayed there, Rojan, should have stayed where you knew, with the people that are yours. Should have remembered not to care.

Hindsight is such a wonderful thing. My bad hand lost what little grip it had. All that was left between me and oblivion were a couple of fingers gripping slick stone and a brain that refused to work for horror. Even the black had shut up.

But I had whatever Lise's little concoction had given me, and I had pain. Oh yes. I slapped at the stone with my fucked hand and if I screamed it wasn't a bad sound, it was the sound of magic running through me till I thought I might burst.

Dench's helmeted face loomed over me, and the moustache wasn't drooping now. I had time, perhaps, for one spell before I dropped and terror blanked my mind completely. Time to save myself, or to kick back against that tyranny.

"I'm sorry, Rojan. Really. But the city needs this. I'm doing this so people will live."

He sounded like he meant it.

"Yeah, me too," I said and let the magic take me. And him.

If I'd thought about it straight, I'd have done something more useful, like get myself off that damned edge. But the drop would be worth it for the look on his face as he started to fade. Just before he disappeared completely, I caught a faint, "Oh you *bastard*."

Then he was gone. Rearranged. I think I was quite merciful, really. I could have done all sorts of nasty things, but he was a good man still, better than me. So I sent him Outside. From this high up I could see it, clear as clear. I could see the lights from the mass of humanity camped on our doorstep that, I hoped, were the Storad, waiting. They were welcome to him.

The effort had been too much, though. The black had only been waiting, biding its time until I did something as stupid as cast a spell while I was so shagged. It leapt on me with tiger's fangs. The world whipped away, ceased to be important. Footsteps headed for me, but it didn't matter, because that song was in my head, the sweet pull of it too much.

Just as I was expecting a crunching boot to come down on my fingers, the sound came. A sound I've always associated with Jake – the unmistakeable swish of swords sliding out of scabbards. Everything went quiet above me, so quiet I could hear the squeak of my fingers as they slipped ever further along the stone. Even that didn't matter.

A voice slipped into the quiet, not loud, not forceful, but determined, measured and oh so sure of itself. "I think that's enough."

Perak, head-in-the-clouds, dreamer Perak, sounding like he owned the world and all should obey. Good, he could sort out the mess, because I was busy.

Welcome home, Rojan. You're going to love it in here.

My fragile grip finally gave way, and I didn't even care.

339

Chapter Twenty-eight

I gave myself up to falling, to just dropping back into the void and the welcome arms of the black. Endless bliss, endless comfort. At least until I hit the Slump. That was fine. Everything was fine, because I had the black to wrap me in warm words.

The fingers that gripped my bad hand were strong. The jolt snapped my eyes open and almost ripped my arm from its socket as a bonus. Even then, my eyes saw only black and my light in there, blazing and brilliant. No fear. There was no fear here, no one relying on me, no one trying to kill me.

Stay this time, Rojan. Stay in here where it's safe.

"Yes." I think I said it aloud.

"No." The voice penetrated, slid through the black like a knife in the guts. The voice of reason, of hope for the hopeless. "No, you're staying."

I tried to ignore it, tried to concentrate on the black and

what it was promising me, but the voice wouldn't let me. I opened my eyes and the black was still there but I could see a shape, a man above me.

"You're staying," he said again. "We need you to stay."

It was that "need" that did it, cleared my head so that the black screamed in frustration. Lise, Lise still needed me, especially with Dwarf gone. Little Allit, who needed someone in the here and now to teach him how to use his magic and not blow his own legs off while he was doing it. Pasha and Perak, too, perhaps. They needed my magic, if nothing else. Everyone did. The magnitude of that almost crushed the breath from me, but it gave me enough to tell the black to fuck right off. It went, but not without a parting shot.

You'll come back, you know you will. You know you want to. Only I can give you what you want.

"Yes," I said again, because it was right. But not now. Not yet.

"Good," said the voice, and my vision cleared.

Guinto stared down at me, and my first reaction was to yank my hand away. Not a clever reaction, but, still, saved by a *priest*. I'd almost rather have dropped.

Almost.

Neither of us spoke as he helped me back on to the platform, or as I lay there gasping like an asthmatic pig. It took a while before my head cleared and my legs didn't keep jerking like they were sure there was still that drop beneath me. Guinto helped me up, and I remembered my manners. "Thanks. Though I'm not sure why you did that."

His smile was as beatific as ever and still made my stomach turn, and so did his words. "Because the Goddess sent you to me. How could I let her gift die?"

He turned away before my stunned brain could think of a suitably waspish reply. Beset on all sides by the tyranny of good men. And that was a revelation, too – thinking of a Ministry man, a priest, as a good man. But there, Pasha had said it. Good men do bad things and bad men do good. I kind of wondered where that left me. Deep in the shit probably.

The circle of people had thinned now, and no Inquisitors to deaden the mood. Enough guards to populate a whorehouse or six, some of the uniforms we'd seen in the Home of the Goddess with their wrought metal nipples, but no Inquisitors, or Specials.

A man strode towards me with a confident step, a smile splitting his face. It was only when he engulfed me in a hug and the waft of incensed robes I realised it was Perak. What the hell had happened to him?

"I knew I could rely on you," he said. "When the temple exploded – who else would do that?"

There was nothing left of the Perak I'd thought I'd known, the soft-hearted, head-in-the-clouds little brother whose sole purpose in life seemed to be to drop me in the proverbial. Well, he had, but everything else . . . "What happened?"

He didn't seem to catch my meaning. "Jake – I mean, I

know you told me about her, about the Death Matches and the swords, but my Goddess, she's something else. You got my note? I had to stay out of sight, because I knew someone was trying to kill me, I just wasn't sure who, or why. My personal guard helped me. Hid me from everything and everyone, I don't know how. One acted as my decoy, so that people would think I was still around while I tried to get support. But I didn't know what to do, there wasn't much I *could* do, Inquisitors at every turn. They – they almost had me. Then she came, and, well, there's some Inquisitors who won't be walking very well for a while. Or fathering children ever perhaps." A frown creased his forehead as he remembered. "She – actually she gave me a damn good talking to. I've never seen anyone quite so *passionate* in their belief. Certainly not any of the cardinals it's my misfortune to have inherited. And she believes in you, too, Rojan. She knew you wouldn't let an innocent man be found guilty. She believes in you utterly."

Now that was a thought to warm the deepest recesses of my anatomy, especially the more mobile parts. "But the Storad? The Mishans?"

Perak's genial face hardened at that, into something I'd never seen on him before: grim determination. It looked like he was really taking all this archdeaconry seriously.

"Do you think I'd have allowed it, the destruction of all our mages? Of *you*? I was just a figurehead, am still, perhaps, but I could stop it. I'd have browbeaten every last cardinal into accepting it, you. But I don't think I need to any more."

He glanced behind him, and there was where I saw the change. Cardinals and priests and all the holy fuckers were looking at me, at Pasha, with a new gaze. Not distaste, not horror, not hate. Appreciation, maybe only of what we could do for them rather than us as people, but it was a start perhaps. Felt pretty weird, but I was sure I could get used to it.

The woman whom Pasha had stared at all through proceedings tried to approach him now, but he turned a cold shoulder on her and had eyes only for Jake.

The woman stopped, hesitant, hand outstretched as though she wanted to touch him but didn't dare, and her eyes . . . her eyes were the same as Pasha's I saw now, the same blackness to them, the same shape of sorrow at the corners.

But Pasha didn't see. Jake took his face in her hands and there, they were talking in their heads again, that invisible string that bound them together. I don't know what she said, but I could guess – I love you as you are, everything you are. I believe in you. It was in the soft look of her eyes, the tender, hesitant movement of a lip as she leant in to kiss him, a soft kiss that grew between them so I had to turn away. Pasha, who'd had nothing except everyone's hatred and Jake, and had everything I wanted.

I turned away sharply before I got an ulcer. "The Storad?"

Perak said nothing but walked over to the gap that looked down on all of Mahala. He crooked a finger at me and, not wanting to look like a big girl's blouse in front of my little brother, I sidled over. I kept one hand on the end pillar, though.

The sky was lightening in the north in a haze of yellow that slid over everything and I realised I'd never really seen a dawn, not properly. We stood there for a while, watching as the light grew, as the city began to look like buildings again rather than humped black shadows below us. A flash of emerald green as the light hit some Clouds estate, and it took me a moment to realise the green was grass under the sun. I wondered what a real garden looked like, and what sun on the flowers would feel like.

Finally, the sun cleared the horizon and I closed my eyes, let it warm the back of my lids. Here at Top of the World, sunlight was free.

"Rojan, what do you see?"

This was going to be one of those talks that ended up with someone trying to convince me the Goddess was real – I'm familiar enough to recognise the start of that talk, but I hadn't expected it of Perak.

"Please, Rojan."

I reluctantly opened my eyes and looked down, and then gripped the pillar hard enough that I yelped as a bone grated in my bad hand. What *did* I see? Across and slightly down from us sat the vast estates of Clouds, open to the sun, bright and cheerful like nothing could touch them. Under lay Heights, a little shabbier, a little shadier. Below Heights, where Trade raised its bulky, ugly head, it was like a line was drawn. Light and dark, bad and good. Below was all twisted shadows, noisome mist that snuck out over the Slump directly underneath us. Under didn't look real, not from up here. From down there, up here looked mythical.

Perak pointed to somewhere, a dark mark on the far side of the city where buildings stopped and mountains began. Outside. Out of this shithole, out of this place where I was sure there would always be two sides, always corruption and ease versus blind hope and poverty. It was far away but I thought I could see a hint of movement.

"What's that?" I thought I knew – after all that's where Dench was, I hoped – but I wasn't sure.

Perak said nothing but handed me a long brass contraption and indicated I put it to my eye. A telescope; I'd heard of them but Under had no need of them, not when you were crowded in like fish in a barrel. Up here, though, maybe if I looked I could see for ever.

When I looked, it wasn't for ever I saw. Inside, guards mooched about with weapons bristling. No other people – the gates further in put a stop to wandering around, or out. I guessed that maybe this was some sort of trading position, outside the city proper but inside the actual walls. A buffer so that Ministry could maintain the position of "Outside doesn't exist so don't get any funny ideas about leaving". Crates stood lonely and abandoned with nothing to put in them. Massive cranes towered over everything, their Glow tubes dark, their moving parts still, looking like dead animals. The gates themselves, the ones that led to mythical Outside, were firmly shut, and solid-seeming enough that they looked as though they'd never been opened, nor ever would be.

Outside was a seething mass. The Storad probably. A lot of them, and in among them was some monstrous carriage, five times the size of any I'd seen on the streets of Mahala, covered in thick plates of metal. Smoke belched from a little chimney on the top and it rumbled very slowly towards the gate. On the top, a long tube swivelled round looking like the barrel of a gun only much, much bigger.

"Coal," Perak said. "Steam. In there, they were all afraid that we'd lose our edge. Our superiority that came from the Glow. With that, with the Storad making their own machines now, using coal and steam, we were always going to lose that edge. That thing's been sitting there for over a week now, and there are others. Sometimes they practise firing, and one of those can take a chunk out of a mountain. Dench, and he wasn't alone, thought negotiation was our only hope. If the Storad weren't the people they are, I'd agree. But even as they tried to start negotiating, the boys started turning up dead. Playing two games at once. I knew they were connected. And I knew that, even if we negotiated, the Storad would walk in afterwards, that we'd be their slaves. I won't have that. With no mages, we'd have no protection against those, or whatever other things they've come up with, and my ears tell me they've come up with a lot. Really, I think Dench was a misguided idealist. He wanted the city to survive, and this was the only way he could see. He wasn't a bad man, mostly. What did you do to him?"

I shrugged. "I sent him where he wanted to be, I think. Down there, with them. Perak, you . . . you aren't how I remember."

"We're neither of us the boys we used to be, Rojan. You think I'm dreaming, but I'm not. I'm thinking. There's a difference."

I stared down at the Slump, at the last resting place of so many people. If I'd been a religious man, I might even have said a prayer for Dench, except for that family that got Inquisitioned, and for Dwarf – I couldn't know if he'd had a hand in that, but I had a feeling that maybe, maybe he had, or at least knew about it and had said nothing. "Not a bad man, but some of the things he did . . . "

"None of us can do good all the time, the Goddess teaches us that, and that is why there is forgiveness. When I look at this city, I see the temples, I see the Slump and Trade and Under. I see . . . A city built on two things. On the Goddess, and magic. I am one, and you are the other. I see very clearly, and I'll make the rest see, too. This city cannot survive without both. Maybe a third thing – pure bloody-minded and inventive stubbornness, which we have by the shovel-load. Whatever we did, whatever *you* did, the Storad were ready, waiting. They were just trying to make it easier for themselves, give themselves a lever for negotiations. Now we're past the point of no return." He looked at me, and there was none of the dreamer there, but all of the drop-you-in-the-shit. "We need mages now more than ever, we need Glow like we've never needed it before, to stay alive. The city is relying on you."

I rubbed my good hand over one eye, and wondered if at least I'd get some sleep first. Whether, if I didn't, one spell and I'd be batshit crazy. I was pretty close right then anyway. Which was probably why I laughed and, once started, couldn't stop until I had no breath left.

"Perak, if you're relying on me, do you realise how fucked that makes us? I've screwed this city twice now. You want for the third time to be the charm?"

He took me by the arms and shook me until the snickers and hiccups subsided. "No, Rojan. Why do you say that? You've saved this city from itself twice now, though you don't seem to think so. Third time pays for all."

That sobered me like a slap to the face. If I needed to pay for what I'd done, I probably didn't have enough bollocks for everyone to jump up and down on. I'd like to say quite clearly that those weren't tears. It wasn't the thought that everything might get even worse, that I'd lost one friend and now everyone was on the line, again, because of what I'd done. Because I'd had a fit of conscience and couldn't see an innocent, if not particularly likeable, man die for something he didn't do. That people had already died because of me, and would keep on doing that until I put everything right, if I could, if it was even possible.

They weren't tears, oh no. It was windy up there, that was all. Still, I was grateful when Perak held on to me until the wind stopped.

Chapter Twenty-nine

The pain lab looked different without Dwarf in it. Felt different, too. I tried not to think about him, about how I'd failed him and how I was setting myself up to fail everyone else. It was carry on or curl up and die, and fuck that.

Instead I watched Lise in the half-dark of a couple of rend-nut lamps as she scurried about the generator. Like me, I think she was trying not to think too hard about who should have been here and wasn't while another boom-shudder reminded us all of what I would rather forget: the Storad were at the gates. Not for long – if they kept their barrage up much longer there wouldn't be any gates left.

They hadn't started straight away, which was luck on our part. Well, luck and Perak becoming a real hard-arse negotiator, which had surprised everyone. He'd managed to stall for ten days or so by telling the Storad powers that be that he was listening to their negotiator and was confident an accommodation could be reached, while I'd found him a really first-class forger – Dendal, who else? – for fake communications from their man inside the city. Their man who was actually in a rather nice cell. Surprisingly, given Dench had to be whispering the Goddess knew what in their ears, we'd managed to pull it off for that long, but of course they'd twigged eventually.

Another ten days of escalating threats before Perak told them to go stick their head in a pig. And all the while we'd been busy ransacking every damned thing we could find in Top of the World to trade with the Mishans for food, weapons, whatever we needed. A few cardinals had screamed about it and the news-sheets were full of vitriol and bile, along with a fair bit of scaremongering filtered through from the more upset clergy, but it was funny how they shut the fuck up in the face of the new leader of Perak's personal guard – Jake with her swords out will do that to a person. An archdeacon who has suddenly turned out to have fangs helped, too. I wasn't the only one seeing Perak in a new light.

And all that time, Lise and Ferret-face had been working flat out. Even Perak had rolled up his sleeves to help in the lab. The generator was just the start of it – once it was running, Lise had some plans for a weapon or two that would make the Storad piss kittens and sunbeams and possibly crap flowers. She's a girl after my own heart. She'd also, with Jake's help, made sure that all Whelar's research had disappeared, along with his concoctions. Hopefully I need never fear

another syringe, except that Lise had kept just the one concoction, the one that made magic bloom at the slightest hint
of pain. Might come in handy.

Another boom-shudder that I felt more through my feet
than heard. I concentrated on the generator. It wasn't hard, the
damn thing took up half the room. Thick twists of metal
cables snaked away from it, linking it up to the old Glow network, or what Dwarf had managed to convert before he died –
something about power differentials or some such. Incomprehensible knobs and dials covered the generator, and Perak
smacked my hand when I went to touch one.

Finally, after a double boom-shudder that made plaster drift
on to Pasha's head, Lise pronounced it ready.

She'd cobbled together some sort of linkage to one of the
chairs in the pain room and I sat down and let her plug me in.
She didn't say anything but looked me in the eye and let me
have the ghost of a smile so that I squeezed her hand.

Perak, his head obscured by the guts of the generator and
screwdriver in hand, said, "Try it. Not too much. Just a little
to start her off."

I nodded and shut my eyes. It was still there, the black,
calling at me, laughing at the edges of my brain. It knew it
would have me one day, so maybe it decided to bide its time
because it faded away, lurking. Watching, waiting.

I concentrated on Lise's hand in my good one while I
closed the bad hand into a fist. Gently, not too much, I
ground out a bit of pain. I almost couldn't bear the silence

352

that followed, wondering if it was working, what I'd see if I opened my eyes.

"Try some more," Perak murmured and my hand closed further, became an aching throb in my head.

Come on in, Rojan, you know you want to. Yes, oh yes. I would, I promised it. *One day. One day, when I've paid for all, you can have me.* Until then, the black could piss off.

A little more, then more, then a little more. A gasp from behind me – Pasha. Then an "Oh, that's pretty!" from Dendal which might or might not have meant a damn thing.

"You can stop now," Lise whispered and I sagged back in the chair. I didn't open my eyes as everyone milled around. They seemed excited, so I took it things had gone well. Then Lise muttered, "Shit," under her breath, then louder, "Perak, that coupling down to Factory Six—"

"I see it." They left, spouting incomprehensible jargon.

"You made fairies, Rojan!" Dendal's papery voice, more excited than I've ever heard him. "Pasha, come on, let's go and play chase the fairies."

Pasha laughed and said, "Why not?" and then the room was silent except for the beat of my heart and the throb of my hand. I waited a while, then cracked open my eyes, unsure what I'd see.

Fairies. Oh, Dendal, you soft old bugger. Fairies indeed. I pushed myself up off the chair and caught hold of the arm to steady myself for a moment – all the time Lise had been working on the generator, me and Pasha had been flat out in the pain room and it had taken its toll. Not just on my body either, though I was feeling like a particularly frail eighty-year-old. My brain had taken to laughing at me in quiet moments.

Through the window, with its vista over Trade towards the burnt-out shell of the Sacred Goddess Hospital, fairies danced everywhere. Little golden bobs of light that seemed to twirl in my vision. Light. We'd made light for half the city, with as little power as I'd once needed for just a couple of Glow lamps. Not only light either – the boom-shudder of the Storad's infernal machines faded away as a more familiar thump started, built, began to shudder my bones. Trade was running, and not a couple of factories. All of it, the whole blocky, ugly mess of factories was running. Not for long – I hadn't given it enough. But it was starting, was running. Plaster floated down in a fine dust as the monster breathed again.

"We did it." I couldn't quite believe it – in my heart of hearts, where cynicism is written in large letters, I'd expected the generator to blow up, or catch fire or maybe fry me in my seat. I'd never expected it to work, not really.

"You did." Jake's voice was low, awestruck even. She stood in a shadow in the corner, looking out over the city like she'd never seen one before. She'd never seen Mahala like this, I knew that much. "I knew you would, knew you wouldn't give in to the easy lie."

She turned to face me and I struggled to find something to say that wouldn't make me sound like a gibbering idiot, because she was looking at me like that again, like she believed in me.

"I wish you'd told me, because I didn't have a clue," was all I managed to come up with.

It got me a low chuckle and a smile and that's about all I could have wished for. Oh all right, almost all, but I couldn't have that so I settled for what I could get.

She moved out of the shadow, hesitant, and somehow fragile for all her swords and the new breastplate – without nipples, I noted sadly. The broken ice queen, who was trying her best to mend herself. I knew then what it was that I loved about her. She'd taken everything life could throw at her, things that could and had sent people mad, and she was fighting back, every step of the way. Looking at her now, in the light of our new fairies, I was inescapably reminded of the Downside Goddess, that the fight was the thing. Jake was her and she was Jake. It was the closest I've ever come to having a religious experience. Though not that close, because wanting to drag your Goddess off to bed to show her just how much you admire her rarely features in those. I think – I don't have much experience in that area.

All of which meant that when her hand touched mine, a soft almost not there touch, when she reached up and kissed my cheek, it felt pretty much like being personally blessed by the Goddess and I stood like an idiot statue as she smiled like she believed in me and left me to myself.

*

The walk to Guinto's temple was like a walk into another world. Almost every other Glow tube was lit and I'd forgotten what Under looked like in the light. Pretty shit, naturally, and the light showed all the grubby little secrets of humanity, but it felt like home again.

The streets and walkways were thronged with people. Happy people this time, and I took comfort in that. We were about to get the crap kicked out of us in a war we probably had no hope of winning but for now we had light, we had Trade running, we had heat and even some food. Still no bacon, a fact I mourned, but it was food nonetheless.

I went down another cramped stairwell to the right level and a party was in full swing between the temple and the bar opposite. Altar boys loaded a table with food while the bar owner dragged out a barrel of Goddess-knows-what alcoholic beverage. Upsiders and Down mingled with smiles on their faces, glad-handing each other. The animosity would be back tomorrow I had no doubt – hating people not like you is too much fun for many people to give it up for long. But for now, for tonight, there was a truce. They needed this night, we all did. One night where they could pretend that everything was going to be all right because the lights were on, food was on the table, because they could feel the comforting rumble of the vast machines of Trade powering up and maybe there'd be work for them in the morning.

Guinto stood at the top of the temple steps, staring out over his domain with a smug look. I still didn't like him, was still suspicious. But I didn't want to slap him any more, which I took as a sign I was becoming more mature. Or something.

He caught my eye and his smile slipped, but he waited for me and offered his hand when I reached him. I didn't take it – I'm not that mature yet. That only brought a tiny snort of laughter and then he gestured for me to enter the temple.

We ended up in his room again, him behind his dark wood desk, me casually draped over a chair, going for nonchalance.

"A drink?" he asked. "I promise it's not made of rats."

"It would be churlish of me to refuse."

He poured out some liquid the colour of blood into two glasses and we sat and sipped for a while in silence. I don't think either of us knew quite where to start, so I took a deep breath and said, "How's Abeya?"

He took another slow sip, considering. "Better. I don't think she'll ever be cured."

I thought of Jake and how she hated to be touched, but was trying to get over it. How she was fighting back against everything her life had been. "I don't think it's a cure she needs, or that anyone who's been through that can be cured of it. They need to learn how to live with it, if that's possible."

"Maybe. Or maybe the Goddess will help her."

"Bet you ten she doesn't."

He set his glass down on the desk, prim and precise. "Why do you hate the Goddess so much?"

Ah, now that was a question. And an answer I wasn't going to get drawn into. I lied a bit. "It's not her that's the problem.

357

It's what people do in the name of her that bothers me. Do this, be that or get damned for eternity. If you let us brainwash you into behaving how we want, we promise you'll get biscuits and ice cream in the afterlife. It doesn't allow for people to be *people*. And that bothers me a lot."

"I noticed that." He was still smiling that unctuous little smile, but there was something maybe just a bit less oily about him. More real, perhaps. "You're still unholy."

"I've never denied that. And I'm proud of it."

He spread his hands in a gesture of giving up. "No, that's true. And sometimes . . . sometimes even unholy men can do good things. I wanted to thank you—"

"Please don't. A priest, liking me? I couldn't live with myself. I'd have to go and kick some children or something just to redress the balance."

Ah, now that smile was genuine, I was sure of it. Without any further words, we both stood and went to watch the party that was just getting going outside. Someone had started singing, one of the old songs, the ones Ministry banned years ago. A few wavering voices joined in, maybe fearful that even now they'd get it in the neck for knowing the words. Guinto pretended not to notice.

The altar boys leapt away from the barrel, looking guilty as hell. One of them still had a froth moustache on his top lip. Guinto pretended not to notice that either.

When I gave him a sideways look, he shrugged. "No-Hope-Shitty needs a night of hope. Just one night – it might be all any of them ever gets. I'm not so Ministry I can't see that."

He was right, too. In a place where hope was something that happened to other people, there was plenty of it about tonight. Irrational, yes, considering, but also needed, wanted. A hope that tomorrow might be better than today. A fool's hope perhaps. It was all we had.

"In life, it's always best to take the small consolations wherever you can." Mainly, in my case, because there weren't any bigger ones.

We both watched as the party progressed – Downsiders fired up their drums and the wailing, throbbing beat of anger in their music echoed across the walkway and far beyond, bringing in more and more party-goers. Some of the younger crowd began to dance, furtively at first. But when the guards at the end of the walkway took no notice and Guinto only smiled at them, their movements became more hurried, more frenzied.

Dendal appeared at the bottom of the steps looking happy and confused, with Allit in tow. Luckily he hadn't brought Lastri. I wasn't sure I could have coped with her just then, or I might have contemplated suicide-by-asking-her-to-dance. Erlat was with them, and that wouldn't be much better, though she didn't completely ignore me. I found myself wanting her to say something, anything. Even if it did make me blush in public.

"Pasha!" Dendal said to me. "Did you see the fairies? Aren't they pretty?"

"Yes, I did, and yes, they are." Looking at his wide-eyed wonder always helped dissolve a part of my cynical shell, and tonight was no different. It was impossible to be anywhere near him and not feel the hope, the wonder. I even smiled.

Dendal wandered off with Guinto in a deep heart-to-heart about something. The Goddess probably, or my innumerable shortcomings.

Allit looked up at me, and I tried not to see what was in that look.

"You did this?" he asked.

"Not just me. Lise and Perak made the generator that made it possible. And Dwarf."

"But you made the magic?"

"Yes."

He nodded, a determined shine to his eyes. "You're going to need mages, aren't you? I heard Pasha talking about the Storad. Is it true? If it is, why is everyone so happy?"

"Do you always ask this many questions? Yes, it's true. More than they put in the news-sheets."

"Do you think we'll win?"

"I don't know. No one does. So, tonight, we're celebrating the lights being back on and we'll worry about tomorrow, tomorrow."

Funny how I knew as soon as she was there. Pasha was coming along the walkway and Jake ran to join him. Whatever trouble she'd had with touching, that part of her that had been broken, Pasha must have worked pretty hard on it because about the only thing of theirs that didn't touch was the backs of their knees. They drew a few stares, and a raised eyebrow from Guinto, but it didn't matter. I didn't even mind, no incipient ulcer to bother me, no jealousy to burn at me. Well, not much. Because she was happy, happier than I could ever have made her, and I couldn't begrudge Pasha the one thing that was his.

"Don't you mind?" Erlat's voice, soft and silky, startled me. Surprised me how much I minded that she'd been so angry with me. How pleased I was she was speaking to me again.

She didn't look at me, only at Jake and Pasha and I watched her watching them. She seemed wistful, a touch of sadness in the cant of her eyes.

"No, no I don't think I do." It came, in a flash of understanding. "You were helping her, with the touch thing. That's why she was coming to you."

She still didn't look my way, but she smiled, the slow smile of a cat playing with a mouse. "Of course. She – we all deal with things differently. It was hard for her, that the first man she wanted to touch was a pain-mage, just like those that . . . turned us into what we are." She looked at me finally, a sly sideways smile. "And that the first man who *did* touch her was also a pain-mage. Easier if she learnt to touch from a woman, from someone who knew. Besides, I'm great at massages. Among other things. You really should try those. No charge."

And there I was, blushing again. Blushing because she was

flirting with me, and usually I'm on that like a starving man on bacon. So why was it that when *she* did it, it made my shoulders itch? Because of who she was, what she'd been? How she'd learnt those tricks? Because . . .

She must have watched these thoughts flick across my mind. I expect I looked pretty confused, which probably accounted for her laugh. "Did you work it out yet?"

And I hadn't, not till she asked. In my defence I'd had a lot of other shit to deal with, but there's something about Erlat that makes me see things differently, *think* differently. It remains to be seen if this is a good thing. But now she asked, had I worked out how I'd made her so angry, and my mind flicked over all that had happened, and latched on to one thing Pasha had said. *I want people to treat me like a person, not a thing.* And I had, and I did. Hadn't I thought that Abeya was angelic because of how she looked? And how did that turn out? Not so well.

Erlat made me blush when she teased me because, when I looked at her, I looked at *her*, not at how I could talk her into bed. And then I'd turned round and disregarded all she was and is, and treated her like a doll that needed big old strong me to protect her. Because it made *me* feel better.

"Erlat, I'm sorry." I couldn't think of a single other thing to say, nothing that wouldn't sound stupid, or make things worse.

I tried for shamefaced, and the effort made her laugh. A good sound, that loosened things inside me, just a little.

"Good." She wrinkled her nose in faux-disgust. "You could do with a bath. I promise not to take advantage of you. Much."

With that, she left me standing there like a gawping, red-faced idiot and went to make some other poor sap blush by using her best seductive slide of a walk, smiling her professional smile and getting him to dance with her. She disappeared into the party, into groups dancing, drinking, laughing. Feeling the hope, just for once.

I couldn't join in the party, though. It felt like I was staring at it through glass, so I only watched and stared at the lights, at Dendal's fairies. The thump of Trade was a comfort, the knowledge that the life of Mahala was pumping through its veins again. But I could still feel the boom-shudder of the Storad engines as they tried to take down the gates. This was a night of hope, but I had none for me.

So I watched and drank the hooch and wondered where the hell we'd be come tomorrow.

Acknowledgements

The usual suspects – my family for putting up with me being off in my own head so much. Absolute Write for invaluable advice on all aspects of writing, and for the friendships I've made there. The T-Party writers' group for camaraderie and curry and for telling me when my writing sucks. Bettie and Luke for much the same. Alex Field and my editors go without saying!

This feels like the worst kind of Oscar speech, doesn't it? I'd like to thank my parents for having me, and the dog for being fluffy and every book I've ever read and Microsoft for making Word and the postman for bringing me my contracts and . . . so I'll finish by saying I've probably missed out someone, so here, have an acknowledgement.

extras

www.orbitbooks.net

about the author

Francis Knight was born and lives in Sussex, UK. She has held a variety of jobs from being a groom in the Balearics, where she punched a policeman and got away with it, to an IT administrator. When not living in her own head, she enjoys SFF geekery, WWE geekery, teaching her children *Monty Python* quotes and boldly going and seeking out new civilisations.

Find out more about Francis Knight and other Orbit authors by registering for the free monthly newsletter at www.orbitbooks.net

if you enjoyed
BEFORE THE FALL

look out for

BITTER SEEDS

by

Ian Tregillis

PROLOGUE

Murder on the wind: crows and ravens wheeled beneath a heavy sky, like spots of ink splashed across a leaden canvas. They soared over leafless forests, crumbling villages, abandoned fields of barleycorn and wheat. The fields had gone to seed; village chimneys stood dormant and cold. There would be no waste here, no food free for the taking.

And so the ravens moved on.

For years they had watched armies surge across the continent with the ebb and flow of war, waltzing to the music of empire. They had dined on the detritus of warfare, feasted on the warriors themselves. But now the dance was over, the trenches empty, the bones picked clean.

And so the ravens moved on.

They rode a wind redolent of wet leaves and the promise of a cleansing frost. There had been a time when the winds had smelled of bitter almonds and other scents engineered for a different kind of cleansing. Like an illness, the taint of war extended far from the battlefields where those toxic winds had blown.

And so the ravens moved on.

Far below, a spot of motion and color became a beacon on the still and muted landscape. A strawberry roan strained at the harness of a hay wagon. Hay meant farmers; farmers meant food. The ravens spiraled down for a closer look at this wagon and its driver.

The driver tapped the mare with the tip of his whip. She snorted, exhaling great gouts of steam as the wagon wheels squelched through the butterscotch mud of a rutted farm track. The driver's breath steamed, too, in the late afternoon chill as he rubbed his hands together. He shivered. So did the children nestled in the hay behind him. Autumn had descended upon Europe with cold-hearted glee in this first full year after the Great War, threatening still leaner times ahead.

He craned his neck to glance at the children. It would do nobody any good if they succumbed to the cold before he delivered them to the orphanage.

Every bump in the road set the smallest child to coughing. The towheaded boy of five or six years had dull eyes and sunken cheeks that spoke of hunger in the belly, and a wheeze that spoke of dampness in the lungs. He shivered, hacking himself raw each time the wagon thumped over a root or stone. Tufts of hay fluttered down from where he had stuffed his threadbare woollen shirt and trousers for warmth.

The other two children clung to each other under a pile of hay, their bones distinct under hunger-taut skin. But the gypsy blood of some distant relation had infused the siblings with a hint of olive coloring that fended off the pallor that had claimed the sickly boy. The older of the pair, a gangly boy of six or seven, wrapped his arms around his sister, trying vainly to protect her from the chill. The sloe-eyed girl hardly noticed, her dark gaze never wavering from the coughing boy.

The driver turned his attention back to the road. He'd made this journey several times, and the orphans he ferried were much the same from one trip to the next. Quiet. Frightened. Sometimes they wept. But there was something different about the gypsy girl. He shivered again.

The road wove through a dark forest of oak and ash. Acorns crunched beneath the wagon wheels. Gnarled trees grasped at the sky. The boughs creaked in the wind, as though commenting upon the passage of the wagon in some ancient, inhuman language.

The driver nudged his mare into a sharp turn at a cross-roads. Soon the trees thinned out and the road skirted the edge of a wide clearing. A whitewashed three-story house and a cluster of smaller buildings on the far side of the clearing suggested the country estate of a wealthy family, or perhaps a prosperous farm untouched by war. Once upon a time, the scions of a moneyed clan had indeed taken their holidays here, but times had changed, and now this place was neither estate nor farm.

A sign suspended on two tall flagpoles arced over the crushed-gravel lane that veered for the house. In precise Gothic lettering painted upon rough-hewn birch wood, it declared that these were the grounds of the Children's Home for Human Enlightenment.

The sign neither mentioned hope nor counseled its abandonment. But in the driver's opinion, it should have.

Months had passed since the farm was given a new life, but the purpose of this place was unclear. Tales told of a flickering electric-blue glow in the windows at night, the pervasive whiff of ozone, muffled screams, and always – always – the loamy shit-smell of freshly turned soil. But the countless rumors did agree on one thing: Herr Doktor von Westarp paid well for healthy children.

And that was enough for the driver in these lean gray years that came tumbling from the Armistice. He had children of his own to feed at home, but the war had produced a bounty of parentless ragamuffins willing to trust anybody who promised a warm meal.

A field came into view behind the house. Row upon row

of earthen mounds dotted it, tiny piles of black dirt not much larger than a sack of grain. Off in the distance a tall man in overalls heaped soil upon a new mound. Influenza, it was claimed, had ravaged the foundling home.

Ravens lined the eaves of every building, watching the workman, with inky black eyes. A few settled on the ground nearby. They picked at a mound, tugging at something under the dirt, until the workman chased them off.

The wagon creaked to a halt not far from the house. The mare snorted. The driver climbed down. He lifted the children and set them on their feet as a short balding man emerged from the house. He wore a gentleman's tweeds under the long white coat of a tradesman, wire-rimmed spectacles, and a precisely groomed mustache.

'Herr Doktor,' said the driver.

'Ja,' said the well-dressed man. He pulled a cream-colored handkerchief from a coat pocket. It turned the color of rust as he wiped his hands clean. He nodded at the children. 'What have you brought me this time?'

'You're still paying, yes?'

The doctor said nothing. He pulled the girl's arms, testing her muscle tone and the resilience of her skin tissues. Unceremoniously and without warning he yanked up her dirt-crusted frock to cup his hand between her legs. Her brother he grabbed roughly by the jaw, pulling his mouth open to peer inside. The youngsters' heads received the closest scrutiny. The doctor traced every contour of their skulls, muttering to himself as he did so.

Finally he looked up at the driver, still prodding and pulling at the new arrivals. 'They look thin. Hungry.'

'Of course they're hungry. But they're healthy. That's what you want, isn't it?'

The adults haggled. The driver saw the girl step behind the doctor to give the towheaded boy a quick shove. He stumbled in the mud. The impact unleashed another volley of coughs and spasms. He rested on all fours, spittle trailing from his lips.

The doctor broke off in midsentence, his head snapping around to watch the boy. 'What is this? That boy is ill. Look! He's weak.'

'It's the weather,' the driver mumbled. 'Makes everyone cough.'

'I'll pay you for the other two, but not this one,' said the doctor. 'I'm not wasting my time on him.' He waved the workman over from the field. The tall man joined the adults and children with long loping strides.

'This one is too ill,' said the doctor. 'Take him.'

The workman put his hand on the sickly child's shoulder and led him away. They disappeared behind a shed.

Money changed hands. The driver checked his horse and wagon for the return trip, eager to be away, but he kept one eye on the girl.

'Come,' said the doctor, beckoning once to the siblings with a hooked finger. He turned for the house. The older boy followed. His sister stayed behind, her eyes fixed on where the workman and sick boy had disappeared.

Clang. A sharp noise rang out from behind the shed, like the blade of a shovel hitting something hard, followed by the softer bump-slump as of a grain sack dropping into soft earth. A storm of black wings slapped the air as a flock of ravens took for the sky.

The gypsy girl hurried to regain her brother. The corner of her mouth twisted up in a private little smile as she took his hand.

The driver thought about that smile all the way home.

Fewer mouths meant more food to go around.

23 October 1920
St. Pancras, London, England

The promise of a cleansing frost extended west, across the Channel, where the ravens of Albion felt it keenly. They knew, with the craftiness of their kind, that the easiest path to food was to steal it from others. So they circled over the city, content to leave the hard work to the scavengers below, animal and human alike.

A group of children moved through the shadows and

alleys with direction and purpose, led by a boy in a blue mackintosh. The ravens followed. From their high perches along the eaves of the surrounding houses, they watched the boy in blue lead his companions to the low brick wall around a winter garden. They watched the children shimmy over the wall. And they watched the gardener watching the children through the drapes of a second-story window.

His name was John Stephenson, and as a captain in the nascent Royal Flying Corps, he had spent the first several years of the Great War flying over enemy territory with a camera mounted beneath his Bristol F2A. That ended with a burst of Austrian anti-aircraft fire. He crashed in No-Man's Land. After a long, agonizing ride in a horse-drawn ambulance, he awoke in a Red Cross field hospital, mostly intact but minus his left arm.

He'd disregarded the injury and served the Crown by staying with the Corps. Analyzing photographs required eyes and brains, not arms. By war's end, he'd been coordinating the surveillance balloons and reconnaissance flights.

He'd spent years poring over blurry photographs with a jeweler's loupe, studying bird's-eye views of trenches, troop movements, and gun emplacements. But now he watched from above while a half dozen hooligans uprooted the winter rye. He would have flown downstairs and knocked their skulls together, but for the boy in the blue mackintosh. He couldn't have been more than ten years old, but there he was, excoriating the others to respect Stephenson's property even as they ransacked his garden.

Odd little duckling, that one.

This wasn't vandalism at work. It was hunger. But the rye was little more than a ground cover for keeping out winter-hardy weeds. And the beets and carrots hadn't been in the ground long. The scavenging turned ugly.

A girl rooting through the deepest corner of the garden discovered a tomato excluded from the autumn crop because it had fallen and bruised. She beamed at the shriveled half-white mass. The largest boy in the group, a little monster with beady pig-eyes, grabbed her arm with both hands.

'Give it,' he said, wrenching her skin as though wringing out a towel.

She cried out, but didn't let go of her treasure. The other children watched, transfixed in the midst of looting.

'Give it,' repeated the bully. The girl whimpered.

The boy in blue stepped forward. 'Sod off,' he said. 'Let her go.'

'Make me.'

The boy wasn't small, per se, but the bully was much larger. If they tussled, the outcome was inevitable.

The others watched with silent anticipation. The girl cried. Ravens called for blood.

'Fine.' The boy rummaged in the soil along the wall

behind a row of winter rye. Several moments passed. 'Here,' he said, regaining his feet. One hand he kept behind his back, but with the other he offered another tomato left over from the autumn crop. It was little more than a bag of mush inside a tough papery skin. Probably a worthy find by the standards of these children. 'You can have this one if you let her alone.'

The bully held out one hand, but didn't release the sniffling girl. A reddish wheal circled her forearm where he'd twisted the flesh. He wiggled his fingers. 'Give it.'

'All right,' said the smaller boy. Then he lobbed the food high overhead.

The bully pushed the girl away and craned his head back, intent on catching his prize.

The first stone caught him in the throat. The second thunked against his ear as he sprawled backwards. He was down and crying before the tomato splattered in the dirt.

The smaller boy had excellent aim. He'd ended the fight before it began.

Bloody hell.

Stephenson expected the thrower to jump the bully, to press the advantage. He'd seen it in the war, the way months of hard living could alloy hunger with fear and anger, making natural the most beastly behavior. But instead the boy turned his back on the bully to check on the girl. The matter, in his mind, was settled.

Not so for the bully. Lying in the dirt, face streaked with tears and snot, he watched the thrower with something shapeless and dark churning in his eyes.

Stephenson had seen this before, too. Rage looked the same in any soul, old or young. He left the window and ran downstairs before his garden became an exhibition hall. The bully had gained his feet when Stephenson opened the door.

One of the children yelled, 'Leg it!'

The children swarmed the low brick wall where they'd entered. Some needed a boost to get over it, including the girl. The boy who had felled the bully stayed behind, pushing the stragglers atop the wall.

Seeing this reinforced Stephenson's initial reaction. There was something special about this boy. He was shrewd, with a profound sense of honor, and a vicious fighter, too. With proper tutelage . . .

Stephenson called out. 'Wait! Not so fast.'

The boy turned. He watched Stephenson approach with an air of bored disinterest. He'd been caught and didn't pretend otherwise.

'What's your name, lad?'

The boy's gaze flickered between Stephenson's eyes and the empty sleeve pinned to his shoulder.

'I'm Stephenson. Captain, in point of fact.' The wind tossed Stephenson's sleeve, waving it like a flag.

The boy considered this. He stuck his chin out, saying, 'Raybould Marsh, sir.'

'You're quite a clever lad, aren't you, Master Marsh?'

'That's what my mum says, sir.'

Stephenson didn't bother to ask after the father. Another casualty of Britain's lost generation, he gauged.

'And why aren't you in school right now?'

Many children had abandoned school during the war, and after, to help support families bereft of fathers and older brothers. The boy wasn't working, yet he wasn't exactly a hooligan, either. And he had a home, by the sound of it, which was likely more than some of his cohorts had.

The boy shrugged. His body language said, Don't much care for school. His mouth said, 'What will you do to me?'

'Are you hungry? Getting enough to eat at home?'

The boy shook his head, then nodded.

'What's your mum do?'

'Seamstress.'

'She works hard, I gather.'

The boy nodded again.

'To address your question: Your friends have visited extensive damage upon my plantings, so I'm pressing you into service. Know anything about gardening?'

'No.'

'Might have known not to expect much from my winter garden if you had, eh?'

The boy said nothing.

'Very well, then. Starting tomorrow, you'll get a bob for each day spent replanting. Which you will take home to your hardworking mother.'

'Yes, sir.' The boy sounded glum, but his eyes gleamed.

'We'll have to do something about your attitude toward education, as well.'

'That's what my mum says, sir.'

Stephenson shooed away the ravens picking at the spilled food. They screeched to each other as they rode a cold wind, shadows upon a blackening sky.

23 October 1920
Bestwood-on-Trent, Nottinghamshire, England

Rooks, crows, jackdaws, and ravens scoured the island from south to north on their search for food. And, in the manner of their continental cousins, they were ever-present.

Except for one glade deep in the Midlands, at the heart of the ancestral holdings of the jarls of Æthelred. In some distant epoch, the skin of the world here had peeled back to reveal the great granite bones of the earth, from which spat forth a hot spring: water touched with fire and stone. No ravens had ventured there since before the Norsemen had arrived to cleave the island with their Danelaw.

Time passed. Generations of men came and went, lived and died around the spring. The jarls became earls, then dukes. The Norsemen became Normen, then Britons. They fought Saxons; they fought Saracens; they fought the Kaiser. But the land outlived them all with elemental constancy.

Throughout the centuries, blackbirds shunned the glade and its phantoms. But the great manor downstream of the spring evoked no such reservations. And so they perched on the spires of Bestwood, watching and listening.

'Hell and damnation! Where is that boy?'

Malcolm, the steward of Bestwood, hurried to catch up to the twelfth Duke of Aelred as he banged through the house. Servants fled the stomp of the duke's boots like starlings fleeing a falcon's cry.

The kitchen staff jumped to attention when the duke entered with his majordomo.

'Has William been here?'

Heads shook all around.

'Are you certain? My grandson hasn't been here?'

Mrs. Toomre, Bestwood's head cook, was a whip-thin woman with ashen hair. She stepped forward and curtsied.

'Yes, Your Grace.'

The duke's gaze made a slow tour of the kitchen. A heavy silence fell over the room while veins throbbed at the corners of his jaw, the high-water mark of his anger. He turned on his heels and marched out. Malcolm released the breath he'd been holding. He was determined to prevent madness from claiming another Beauclerk.

'Well? Off you go. Help His Grace.' Mrs. Toomre waved off the rest of her staff. 'Scoot.'

When the room had cleared and the others were out of earshot, she hoisted up the dumbwaiter. She worked slowly so that the pulleys didn't creak. When William's dome of coppery-red hair dawned over the transom, she leaned over and hefted him out with arms made strong by decades of manual labor. The boy was tall for an eight-year-old, taller even than his older brother.

'There you are. None the worse for wear, I hope.' She pulled a peppermint stick from a pocket in her apron. He snatched it. Malcolm bowed ever so slightly. 'Master William. Still enjoying our game, I trust?'

The boy nodded, smiling around his treat. He smelled like parsnips and old beef tallow from hiding in the dumb-waiter all afternoon.

Mrs. Toomre pulled the steward into a corner. 'We can't keep this up forever,' she whispered. She wrung her hands on her apron, adding, 'What if the duke caught us?'

'We needn't do so forever. Just until dark. His Grace will have to postpone then.'

'But what do we do tomorrow?'

'Tomorrow we prepare a poultice of hobnailed liver for His Grace's hangover, and begin again.'

Mrs. Toomre frowned. But just then the stomping resumed, and with renewed vigor. She pushed William toward Mr. Malcolm. 'Quick!'

He took the boy's hand and pulled him through the larder. Gravel crunched underfoot as they scooted out of the house through the deliverymen's door, headed for the stable, trailing white clouds of breath in the cool air. Malcolm had pressed most of the household staff into aiding the search for William, so the stable was empty. The duke kept his horses here as well as his motor car. The converted stable reeked of petrol and manure.

Mr. Malcolm opened a cabinet. 'In here, young master.'

William, giggling, stepped inside the cabinet as Mr. Malcolm held it open. He wrapped himself in the leather overcoat his grandfather wore when motoring.

'Quiet as a mouse,' the older man whispered, 'as the duke creeps around the house. Isn't that right?'

The child nodded, still giggling. Malcolm felt relieved to see him still enjoying the game. Hiding the boy would become much harder if he were frightened.

'Remember how we play this game?'

'Quiet and still, all the same,' said the boy.

'Good lad.' Malcolm tweaked William's nose with the pad of his thumb and shut the cabinet. A sliver of light shone on the boy's face. The cabinet doors didn't join together properly. 'I'll return to fetch you soon.'

The duke, William's grandfather, had gone on many long expeditions about the grounds with his own son over the years. Grouse hunting, he'd claimed, though he seldom took a gun. The only thing Mr. Malcolm knew for certain was that they'd spent much time in the glade upstream from the house. The same glade where the staff refused to venture, citing visions and noises. Years after the duke's heir — William's father — had produced two sons of his own, he'd taken to spending time in the glade alone. He returned to the manor at all hours, wild-eyed and unkempt, mumbling hoarsely of blood and prices unpaid. This lasted until he went to France and died fighting the Hun.

The duke's grandsons moved to Bestwood soon after. They were too young to remember their father very well, so the move was uneventful. Aubrey, the older son and heir apparent, received the grooming expected of a Peer of the Realm. The duke showed little interest in his younger grandson. And it had stayed that way for several years.

Until two days previously, when he had asked Malcolm to find hunting clothes that might fit William. Malcolm didn't know what happened in the glade, or what the duke did there. But he felt honor-bound to protect William from it.

Malcolm left William standing in the cabinet only to find

the duke standing in the far doorway, blocking his egress. His Grace had seen everything.

He glared at Malcolm. The majordomo resisted the urge to squirm under the force of that gaze. The silence stretched between them. The duke approached until the two men stood nearly nose to nose.

'Mr. Malcolm,' he said. 'Tell the staff to return to their duties. Then fetch a coat for the boy and retrieve the carpetbag from my study.' His breath, sour with juniper berries, brushed across Malcolm's face. It stung the eyes, made him squint.

Malcolm had no recourse but to do as he was told. The duke had flushed out his grandson by the time he returned bearing a thick dun-colored pullover for William and the duke's paisley carpetbag. Malcolm made brief eye contact with William before taking his leave of the duke.

'I'm sorry,' he mouthed.

William's grandfather took him by the hand. The ridges of the fine white scars arrayed across his palm tickled the soft skin on the back of William's hand.

'Come,' he said. 'It's time you saw the estate.'

'I've already seen the grounds, Papa.'

The old man cuffed the boy on the ear hard enough to make his eyes water. 'No, you haven't.'

They walked around the house, to the brook that gurgled

through the gardens. They followed it upstream, crashing through the occasional thicket. Eventually the crenellations and spires of Bestwood disappeared behind a row of hillocks crowned with proud stands of yew and English oak. They traced the brook to a cleft within a lichen-scarred boulder in a small clearing.

Though hemmed about by trees on every side, the glade was quiet and free of birdsong. The screeches and caws of the large black birds that crisscrossed the sky over the estate barely echoed in the distance. William hadn't paid the birds any heed, but now their absence felt strange.

Several bundles of kindling had been piled alongside the boulder. From within the carpetbag the duke produced a canister of matches and a folding pocketknife with a handle fashioned from a segment of deer antler. He built a fire and motioned William to his side.

'Show me your hand, boy.'

William did. His grandfather took it in a solid grip, pulled the boy's arm straight, and sliced William's palm with his pocketknife. William screamed and tried to pull away, but his grandfather didn't release him until the blood trickled down William's wrist to stain the cuff of his pullover. The old man nodded in satisfaction as the hot tickle pulsed along William's hand and dripped to the earth.

William scooted backwards, afraid of what his grandfather might do next. He wanted to go home, back to Mr. Malcolm and Mrs. Toomre, but he was lost and couldn't see through his tears.

His grandfather spoke again. But now he spoke a language that William couldn't understand, more wails and gurgles than words. Inhuman noises from a human vessel.

It lulled the boy into an uneasy stupor, like a fever dream. The fire's warmth dried the tears on his face. A shadow fell across the glade; the world tipped sideways.

And then the fire spoke.